THE GREAT MARTIAN WAR

TEXAS FRONT: SALIENT

by SCOTT WASHBURN and
JONATHAN CRESSWELL-JONES

ZMOK
BOOKS

The Great Martian War: Texas Front - Salient
Cover by Michael Nigro
This edition published in 2018

Zmok Books is an imprint of

Pike and Powder Publishing Group LLC

17 Paddock Drive
Lawrence, NJ 08648

1525 Hulse Rd, Unit 1
Point Pleasant, NJ 08742

Dramatis Personae

General Francisco 'Pancho' Villa,
    revolutionary military leader of the Northern Division *
Enrique de Gama Magana, former theology student, Martian prisonor and "priest"
Juan Mendez, rail engineer

Mexico South:
Emiliano Zapata, rebel leader based in Mexico City *
Manuel Palafox, secretary and adjutant-general to Zapata *
Colonel Felipe Angeles, artillery specialist *
Rear-Admiral Charles Favereau,
    commanding French 4th Light Cruiser Division, Veracruz *
General Charles E. M. Mangin, commanding French 12th Division, Veracruz *

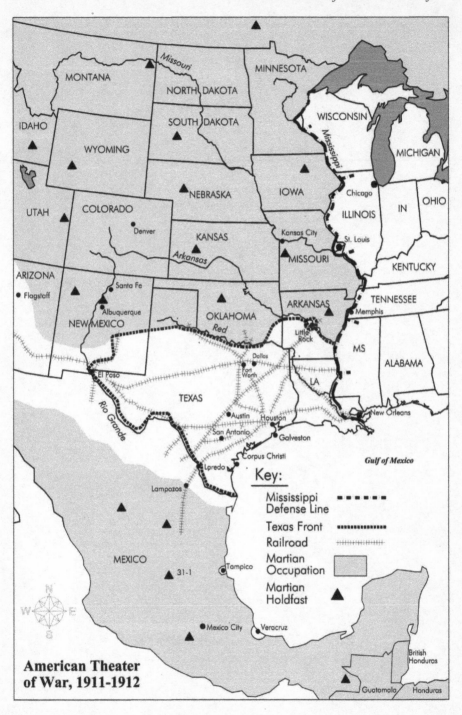

American Theater
of War, 1911-1912

Prologue

March, 1910, South of Albuquerque, New Mexico Territory

Lieutenant Willard Lang stood on the roof plating of *Davy's Sow*, the twenty-eight ton Mark II tank that he commanded, and peered north through binoculars. The predawn sky shaded from indigo to blue; the air was crisp and cool, with spring's promise of warmth to come. A light breeze kept the coal smoke of the *Sow's* firebox from troubling him and carried the dry scent of sagebrush from the top of the low ridgeline the tank faced.

Lang was vividly aware of his situation; he expected to die shortly.

The binoculars' view trembled along with his hands. His eyes were gritty with fatigue; no survivor from the 304th Tank Battalion had slept within the past day and a half. Not since the night battle at Albuquerque, when the Martian tripods, more than eighty strong, had punched through the lines of the 33rd Division in a concentration that Lang hadn't known was possible. Most of the battalion had been wiped out in half an hour of nightmare, with heat rays slashing out of a darkness lit only by gun flashes and burning tanks. The few tanks still mobile had scattered, most heading southeast; the *Sow* had trundled through the outskirts of the town, ignored once by a fast-striding tripod, often passed by running men and horses, with plenty of light to steer by from the burning buildings. It was then that they'd joined up with *The Judge*, a Mark I under Second Lieutenant Baker, and finally gotten word from a dispatch rider to rally with other elements of the 33rd at a depot located along the rail line to the south.

Hours later, before they'd made it there, another rider showed up – from General Funston, he said, 'Fearless Freddie' himself, the author of all this misery – and directed Lang to form a rearguard on the low ridge a mile northeast of the crude depot buildings where a few hundred men milled about. There was a train loading there. There were wounded; a few artillery pieces, most without their munition limbers; and of course Funston to oversee it all. Too much for two tanks to protect, but he had his orders, and Lang had never much liked running anyway, even if they could have made another five miles without breaking down. He was afraid but determined. The *Sow* wouldn't come cheap.

The two tanks were backed below the ridge; Lang's driver, Eddie Painewick, had done so expertly despite his misgivings about the loose dry dirt along the slope. Now Lang watched and waited. The day continued to brighten. The sun warmed his back, sharpened the horizon – and glinted off the three tripods that rose into view a mile to the northeast.

Lang swallowed in a dry throat and waved to Baker two hundred yards along the slope. The answering wave was as jerky as his own, but Baker had seemed steady enough and knew what to do. Lang stepped to the roof hatch, gripped the raised edges, and lowered himself into the tank, ignoring the ladder, to drop onto the decking with a clang of boots on iron.

The interior was dim and stank of coal smoke, oil, and five exhausted men. The breech of a four-inch gun, mounted forward, took up much of the space; the firebox glowed to the rear. Three faces looked at him bleakly; Eddie was tucked forward in his driver's seat. All were even younger than Lang's twenty-two years, and Albuqerque had been their first battle.

"Yeah," said Lang, "they're here. Three of 'em in the northeast. Eddie! When I give the word, advance us just up to the ridgeline."

"Will do, Loot." The driver had named the tank for its clumsiness after his first trials – 'as drunk as *Davy's Sow*!' – but Lang knew he would perform the movement perfectly.

"Carson, take whichever one is on the right. *The Judge* will be shooting from the left." The gunner nodded; his loader, Billings, already cradled a shell to follow the one loaded in the four-inch. Eight more were racked at his feet; they'd fired most of their ammunition during the night battle, but that would be enough one way or the other... "Make it count," he added softly. Carson patted the gun's sights without speaking.

"Jed, bank the firebox, would you? I don't want the smoke to give us away."

"Yes, sir. There's plenty of steam up for – for what we'll need."

"Won't be long now." Lang clambered back out into the morning light, crouched, and cautiously raised the binoculars – there. Even without standing he could see them now, closing fast with that alien, undulating gait. He waited long minutes, tensely calculating time and range. They'd pass maybe four hundred yards ahead – if they didn't change direction.

Oh, Dad, I should have stayed on our farm. But they'd be there some time anyway, burning you and Ma and Jill right along with me.

They were close enough. He dropped back into the *Sow's* iron belly, swung the roof hatch shut, grabbed a handhold, and reached forward and down to clap Eddie on the shoulder. "Move her up!"

Painewick wrenched his levers; *Davy's Sow* let out a hissing grunt of steam, jerked, and began to clamber up the slope with rhythmic chuffs and clanks and the syncopated clang of treads. The compartment lurched around them; Lang hung on, peering out the view slits cut into the raised hatch coaming. The ground ahead slowly sank from view, then abruptly reappeared as the tank lurched over the ridgeline, halting in a gush of steam that vanished to reveal the tripods looming over the sagebrush.

"Target tripod, four hundred yards, straight ahead!" yelled Lang by rote, but Carson was already cranking the handwheels to traverse his gun the few degrees necessary; he squinted through his sights for an eternity, making fine adjustments, then pulled the firing lever. The four-inch slammed deafeningly, its breech recoiling; the shell casing clanged onto the deck. Outside, the third tripod was beginning to turn toward them when the shell exploded on its central cylinder. It seemed to stagger but kept turning, a black streak showing on its casing. Far downrange, a spurt of soil indicated that the *Judge* had missed. Its target was already loping to the left.

The gun breech rumbled into battery. "Loaded!" cried Billings. After a moment, Carson fired again. Lang was looking directly into the red eye of the tripod, his guts clenched for the searing flash that would blind and char him, when the second shell hit dead at the joint of globe and cylinder. The explosion was muted as though some of it went inside – and yes! The legs buckled and the tripod spiraled down to crash into the dirt.

The one adjoining it fired its heat ray. The world dissolved in a buzz-saw shriek that drove Lang to his knees, hands over his eyes, despite his determination. Molten iron speckled his back, burning holes in his crew jacket, as the hatch cupola began to melt. Iron plates groaned, expanding and buckling, and Lang opened his eyes. The crew needed him, they had only seconds now.

"Loaded!" Billings' voice was an octave higher.

"I'm out of traverse!" cried Carson.

Lang reached forward and slapped Eddie's left shoulder. "Neutral left!"

Eddie cranked both levers in opposition, twisting with his whole body. The Sow's treads hammered into motion, right forward, left backward. The tank pivoted left, lurching in the loose soil. The interior was a furnace, hotter every second. White-hot iron trickled from seams on the forward slope, spattering the deck. The sudden concussion of the four-inch splashed more droplets free; Billings yelled as some struck him.

Lang risked a glance; two tripods up, one with a hit showing. He turned to Carson. "Did–"

Carson screamed and doubled over in his seat, a hand covering his eyes. The Sow shrieked along with him as two heat rays converged on the forward and right sides. Everyone staggered; the right tread had jammed.

"Eddie, *halt!*" shouted Lang, but fresh welds were already popping in the tread links, the soil was giving way beneath the tank's weight as the left tread churned it, and the Sow's right flank was exposed to the double attack focused onto it. The thinner sheet iron erupted in a curtain of red-hot destruction and a heat ray flickered through it, incinerating Billings and Jed in an instant and lighting the rear interior in flames.

The Sow tilted left, sliding uncontrolled back down the slope. Eddie shouted "I can't–" and two armor plates collapsed inward, disintegrating in a splash of red-hot metal. Carson gave a queer grunt; Lang grabbed his shoulder, but the twenty-pound chunk of plate had already melted halfway into his belly, and his eyes were going blank with shock. The ripsaw sound of the heat rays cut off as the Sow disappeared from their line of fire; then the tank crunched into hard soil at the base of the slope and halted, gouting clouds of steam like its dying breath.

"Loot, I can't move her!"

Lang hacked a cough and looked around the interior of his command. Daylight through the melted holes showed three corpses; the gunsights were wrecked. On the off chance it would help the *Judge*, he moved Carson's limp hand from the firing lever and blasted out the last round into the sky. Choking on fumes, he undogged the left side hatch that mercifully hadn't fused shut, shouldered it open, then grabbed Eddie's jacket and hauled him bodily out of his seat. "We're bailing!"

"Carson–"

"He's dead! Move!" He shoved Eddie through the opening and climbed out after

11

him. "Go! There!" He pointed to a dense clump of brush forty yards away, upslope. They scrambled down from the burning, crippled tank and punched boots into the dry soil in a ragged sprint. Lang glanced over his shoulder; still two tripods, both firing again, and the *Judge* exploded in a rising ball of flame-shot smoke and debris. *Never knew Baker's first name*. He ran a few more gasping steps, dropped, and squirmed into the brush beside Eddie, looking out through the knotted branches that suddenly didn't seem like much concealment at all... but the tripods were stepping down the ridgeline now, and it was too late to try for anything better.

Flames gushed from the *Sow's* open hatch. "Loot," said Eddie in a tight voice, "there's still ammo in there."

"Don't you move, Eddie. Don't you goddamned move." Lang pinned his driver with an arm. Growing up on a hardscrabble farm had shaped him compact but very strong, and Eddie subsided. "Look, they'd burn you down in five steps." The tripods had halted, seeming to peer down at the burning tank.

"What are the bastards waiting for?" hissed Eddie.

"I think they know she's crippled. But they're not shooting. Do you – do you think they're short on ammo too? For that heat ray?"

"How would I –" said Eddie, and the *Sow* exploded in a punching concussion that jolted the ground and sent fragments howling. Eddie twitched and yelped. "Dammit! Loot..."

"Hold still! I see it. It's not bad." A shard stuck out of the driver's left leg. Metal plates and pieces fell into the dirt around them, but nothing further struck either man. "Once they move off, we'll see to that."

But the tripods didn't move off yet. Instead they recrossed the ridgeline and huddled around the spot where Lang figured the downed tripod must be. One sank out of sight for a while, then rose up again with a canister latched onto its back.

"Did they just rescue the critter out of that thing?" wondered Lang; his driver didn't answer, just clutched his leg white-faced. It didn't matter; Lang knew that he was just trying to focus his own mind on something other than what had happened to his crew. There wouldn't be enough left of them to bury, and somehow that troubled him more than their deaths...

Then one tripod moved off northward, and the other swung away to the west. There was something significant about that, but right now, Lang was more concerned with tearing the sleeve off his shirt and bandaging Eddie's wound, which had soaked the pant leg with blood. He carefully did not pull out the fragment; that was a surgeon's task. If a tripod came back...well, then it came back. He pulled Eddie upright, slung the man's arm across his shoulders to take as much weight as possible, and they started to walk south.

The twin funeral pyres behind them marked the last stand of the 304th.

They limped southward together for nearly an hour. Lang was staggering with exhaustion by the time they reached the depot, but he still refused to allow Eddie to put weight on the bad leg. The wounded were marshaled under the shade of the depot buildings, suggesting that delays were expected. He dropped his driver off to the care of an orderly. Men rushed about, most with some seeming purpose. An improvised crane was hoisting an artillery piece onto a flatcar where others lay stacked like cordwood. No tanks to be seen. If there were any other survivors, they'd broken down on the way and been abandoned.

He thought dully that he ought to report in to someone, but asking for the 304th's officers just drew blank stares. Finally an older sergeant said, "Son, there's no one left from that outfit that I know of. If you've something to report, best find General Funston's staff."

Lang followed the direction down the rail line to a knot of officers arguing with one another. As he came up, a colonel was saying, "I've told you, there's not enough space in these cars for anything more than the wounded. Barely for them!"

"I won't leave the ammunition after we brought it this far. It's irreplaceable." The major who spoke adjusted the bandage over his eye with obvious discomfort.

"Neither are my men! If –"

"Gentlemen," rasped a voice behind them. The two figures parted to reveal a man shorter than Lang, haggard, wearing a goatee and general's stars. "We'll carry every wounded man and whatever ammunition we can cram into the corners."

"Sir, we can only load the cars so much. They have limits."

"We'll proceed slowly; they can carry a little more. No axle's going to break at a marching pace." He looked at Lang. "Who are you?"

"Lieutenant Willard Lang, sir. Late of the 304th. My tank was part –"

"Of the rearguard, yes. Report."

"We engaged three tripods, General. Knocked one out, and I think we hit another. Both our tanks were destroyed."

"Both? You had only two?"

"Yes, sir."

"I was told 'elements of the 304th' were available," grumbled Funston. "Didn't think it was two tanks! You did well with that little, Lieutenant. But there's still two more out there? What are they doing?"

"That's just it, sir. One seemed to pick up the... pilot... creature, from the downed tripod. I think it went back north with it. The other, it went west."

"But it was coming south initially?"

"Yes, sir."

"Then it's on its way here," said Funston grimly. "We've got to get moving. Finish loading the wounded immediately; you can triage on board the cars. This train has to be moving at the soonest it can!"

The officers scattered. Funston was turning away when Lang asked, "General? Is there anyone from the 304th I can join with?"

Funston regarded him silently for a moment. "No. I don't think there is anyone else, Lieutenant. Walk with me a while. Tell me more about what you saw them doing."

They began walking down the row of train cars. Lang kept his voice flat as he spoke to the man who had flung his crew away so casually that he hadn't even known how many tanks he'd sent. "Well, sir, I did see the second tripod pick up something. I'm just assuming it was holding the first one's pilot. I'm pretty sure the *Judge* – the other tank – hit the third one. But that's what's odd; you'd think they would send the one already damaged back, and instead that's the one that pressed on. I also think–"

A man ran down the rail line toward them. "General! We've spotted one of 'em, to the west!"

13

"Dammit!" Funston broke into a run; Lang did likewise. A few moments brought them to one of the freight cars; Funston, already panting, leaped up onto the steps, then began to clamber up the side ladder. Lang stayed close behind, so when Funston's grasp slipped and the general skidded down a rung, Lang spared a hand to brace him; it took little effort. Was he just a uniform full of bluster, then?

Funston staggered up onto the car's sloped roof, stooped, and gasped for a moment. He spared a wry glance up at Lang. "Malaria, in Cuba. Shot through both lungs – in the Philippines. Not much at – obstacle courses any more." He straightened, lifting his binoculars. Lang echoed him.

Two miles to the west, a lone tripod stalked along. Lang held his breath, straining to see. There it was; the scorch mark of the *Judge's* hit. *You hurt them, Baker. Rest easy.* He turned back to Funston.

"We've got two working guns," said Funston tightly without lowering his own glasses. He swayed on his feet; Lang instinctively braced him, thinking of the limping Eddie, of Carson...

"Two more to throw away, General?" He'd lifted milk cans that weighed more. A terrible rage was boiling up inside him.

Funston grunted and snapped his head around as Lang's grip tightened. Something glinted deep in his eyes. "So that's it. You presumptuous sprat! D'you think no one else lost a crew? Most of my colonels are dead. Most of my damned *army* is gone. They beat me and I know it! We salvage what we can and fight on. Now either throw me off this roof, or get to work. We're short on everything, time included."

On everything. Suddenly it made sense. Lang opened his hands. "General, you need to know this. All the tripods were only firing as much as necessary, not waving the beams around like I've seen. And it's the damaged one that's still coming on. I think... they're running out of something as well. I don't know what, but just maybe that's why it's not run over here and finished us. It's the only one that can keep advancing, but it doesn't want to risk another hit. So perhaps– "

"We can bluff it," said Funston. "Perhaps." He turned to the two staff officers who had appeared at the top of the ladder and were staring at the tableau before them. "Lieutenant Willard Lang. You will go with these officers and follow their instructions."

I've just assaulted the general commanding Second Army. Court-martial. Leavenworth. Lang slumped and stepped forward.

"They will explain to you the duties of an officer on my staff."

He gaped. "General?"

"You can use your eyes and think. You can command a tank. That'll do until someone better comes along. Oh, and Lang... if you ever lay a hand on me again, I'll hang you."

"Understood, sir." He followed this pint-sized fire-eater down the ladder, with one last glance at the tripod that still kept its distance. On the ground, the two officers waited.

"Major Otto Prendergast," said the one with the eye bandage. He was as drawn as the others, but the visible eye twinkled. "You've made an impression, young Willard. He's never threatened to hang me. I'm quite jealous."

Willard shook his head, bemused. "So he was kidding, then?"

The twinkle vanished. "No. Do not make that mistake. General Funston is a very serious man."

They loaded the wounded. They loaded the ammunition. And by three o'clock, they loaded two working 4.7-inch field guns onto the only clear space on a flatcar, discarding the carriage wheels. The barrels poked threateningly over the side, but the Lord only knew what would happen if they fired. *Probably land somewhere in Arizona,* thought Lang.

Funston's command post was set up in the front end of a boxcar; holes chopped in the wooden sides gave a view to both sides and ahead overseeing the gun crews manning the pieces, which had been braced in position with baulks of timber as best they could be. At five o'clock the train hooted and grunted into motion, the clunk of the rail joints sounding much more slowly than Lang was accustomed to, as the train paced the marching soldiers beside it, trudging along the eastern side in the dubious shelter of wooden rail cars. Just as the lone tripod paced them all in turn.

And at five-thirty, it began to close in, slanting gradually toward them.

"What range d'you make it?" shouted Prendergast forward.

"Twenty-four hundred yards, sir!"

Funston nodded to Prendergast, who replied, "Commence tracking your target!" The gun barrels hunted around, then steadied.

"That's the one card we can turn over," muttered Prendergast to Lang. "The rest stay down. But will they call it?"

"Twenty-two hundred yards, sir!"

The taller of the two staff officers – Walters – shifted nervously. "General, they'll open up somewhere under two thousand yards. We should shoot first."

"Those guns will jump like mules. Probably kill the gunners. We'll wait a bit."

Lang cleared his throat. "Uh, we fired at four hundred, sir, and hit twice. But these guns are bigger – and look bigger. For whatever that's worth."

"Two thousand yards, sir!"

"If I could get my hands on that thing over there," snarled Funston, "I'd cut it up to see what makes it tick. Is it just watching – gloating? Frog-marching us all south for a while?" He glared out through the splintered wood with incandescent hatred.

Lang could understand that. He wished he was looking through a piece's sights himself. And if the recoil killed him when he fired? A hit would be worth that; worth anything.

"Eighteen hundred yards, sir!"

Prendergast's eye was expressionless. Walter's faced worked. "Sir, the cars are tinderboxes! If we went at full speed–"

"We'd leave nearly a thousand men to that thing's mercies. If we run, it will know it can burn them with impunity. No, sir. We'll stare it down together, or burn together, but I *will not run.*" Funston leaned out the forward gap and shouted, "Clear away all crews but the gunners! Stand by to fire on my order!"

He flicked a glance to Prendergast. "It has to be on *my* order, Otto."

"The gun layers are staying put as well," said Prendergast without looking away from ahead.

"They're *what?* Why, I'll –" Funston grimaced. "We'll settle it when this is over. They know their work."

"Sixteen hundred yards, sir!"

Funston looked at Lang. "Do you think–" The long-range rasp of a heat ray cut him off. Two cars ahead, flame sprang up from wood and paintwork; the firing cut off.

"Test shot," rasped Lang. Prendergast nodded. Men clambered out on the car roofs, hurling water buckets; brave men, and it was working, but it would be like pissing on a blowtorch at closer range.

"Fourteen hundred yards, sir!"

"That shambling son of a bitch," said Funston softly. "It just has to know." He leaned out forward. "Fire when ready!"

For a few moments, there was only the chuntering of the train; then both guns went off within a second of each other, a stunning twin concussion. Through the driving smoke, Lang saw dirt spout upward just short of the tripod, and just to the left beyond it.

He looked forward; the guns were still aboard, but several of the timber baulks had disintegrated under the recoil, sending splinters in a vicious pattern. Two men picked their way through the wreckage; two more lay bloodied and still. If the surviving crews could load, they might get one more round off from each gun...

"Sir, look! It's turning away!"

Funston did not look away from the flatcar.

"It's *running*! We did it!"

"They did it," muttered Funston. He scrubbed at his face. "Alright! Get those guns repositioned in case it comes back. Lang, can you handle a 4.7?"

"Yes, sir."

Funston looked him full in the face. "Willing to man one?"

"I am, sir."

"Good. Get down there and sort things out."

Carson. Billings. Young Jed Gillray.

He'd nearly thrown away his career for them, but there were better ways to honor them. And to get payment for them. Because the *Sow* would never come cheap.

Chapter One

April, 1911, Austin, Texas

Emmet O. Smith ducked through the side doorway of the adjutant-general's offices. He doffed his Stetson hat left-handed by habit; as usual when in town, he wore a jacket and trousers to blend in, but even a job interview couldn't part him from the hat and his well-worn boots. His right hand held a leather pouch of letters at his side. Two clerks looked up from their counter with bovine incuriosity; he settled on the nearer. "Afternoon. I'm Smith, here about my Ranger application."

The clerk brightened. "You're Australian Billy? Well, now, I always– "

"No. Emmet Oswald Smith."

"Oh. Well, let's see, here." The clerk shuffled out the papers. "Lot of applications right now, you know. Texas is stepping up to the plate."

Emmet said nothing, waiting to see if this was a bid for a bribe. That wouldn't go well. He'd gotten pretty good in the past at declining such offers without riling anyone, but this was more important than, say, a rancher asking him to wink at a wrong cattle brand.

"Hang on... Jerry, wasn't there a notice on him?" said the other clerk.

A look of enlightenment crossed the man's face, and he grabbed another paper off his desk. "Damn right there is! Says here the A-G wants to see him soon as he gets here. Mister, could you please wait in the side office? He'll be right down."

Emmet took the untouched papers back, followed the clerk into the office, and commenced cooling his heels. Within half an hour – lightning-fast by Austin standards – a moustache barged into the room, with a lean, pinch-faced man behind it. "You picked a fine time to get here!" he snapped.

"How's that, sir?" Emmet recognized the spanking new adjutant-general easily enough: Henry Hutchings, late forties, brigadier-general in the Texas National Guard, and in practical terms, the man who would be his boss. Emmet rose and offered a hand; Hutchings shook it.

"His Excellency is upstairs, and I made the mistake of mentioning why I was called away. Now he wants to see you too... Let's see your application." He snatched it from Emmet's hand and hummed over it. "Seems to be in order. You've been around some. Not too old for this work, are you?"

"I'm thirty-four. I figure I can keep up with the young'uns."

"Former Ranger 1903-1905 in A Company under John Hughes... that's good... worked as detective for the Northern Railroad Company 1906-7, brand inspector West

Texas 1908, then joined the Thiel Detective Agency in El Paso 1909-10. Speaks fluent Spanish. Border man, huh?"

"I grew up in El Paso," agreed Emmet.

"That's a hot spot these days. Well, Smith, if the governor asked for you, that pretty much makes you a Ranger. I'll fill out your certificate and sign it. Just remember who you answer to, alright? I'll decide where you go and what you do, based on what he asks to have done. Probably put you at the Kenedy camp – Company B under Captain Sanders."

Emmet knew what a 'Ranger camp' generally meant – a rented house stinking with hard-traveled men, and a crabby landlady slamming a plate of beans on a table – but he hadn't joined for luxury even in '03. "Will do, sir."

"You'll still need to provide your own horse and saddle, but we have arrangements now with all major railroads for passes. You'll know people at the Northern line, anyway... You can pick up a scout belt at the arsenal in the cellar. Try not to wear it in town; it draws attention. Now, I have standardized what was a terrible arrangement prior. You'll draw a Winchester chambered for .30-06, so we can share shells with the army."

"Oh, good, sir. I'd not want to face a Martian tripod with only a sidearm."

"We'll also issue you a better sense of humor. As for sidearms... I don't see one?"

Emmet shrugged. "Never felt the need to be heeled in Austin. I have a Navy Colt .38."

"We do not issue that caliber. You'll need to buy your own shells." Hutchings seemed pleased by that; a penny saved. "Some of the men are carrying automatics now. Much lighter."

"A Colt's no bad weight if you need to bend it over a fellow's head. It can avoid an argument."

Hutchings smirked. "Indeed." He produced a pocket watch and glanced at it. "Right, let's go attend upon His Excellency."

They snaked through stairs and hallways; the building had hundreds of rooms. Hutchings opened the door to a well-appointed one and ushered Smith in: carpeting, a teak desk a mile wide, and two men in thick-upholstered chairs. The governor rose, smiling. "Well, hello! I'm Oscar Colquitt." He looked up at Emmet unselfconsciously as he shook his hand; a strong grip for such a small man. He turned and gestured. "This is my good friend Francisco Chapa, one of my personal staff. Excuse the glamorous suit; he's just been on a troop review in the National Guard."

Chapa was thick-set and olive-skinned; his colonel's uniform dripped gold lace. He nodded to Emmet without getting up. "I would not try to impress you with a costume, Mr. Smith. I'm really just a newspaperman – the *El Impartial de Texas*."

"I've read that. Do you write for it?"

"I own it."

"And he says positively splendid things about me," put in Colquitt. "He's very persuasive, especially around election time. Carries about half of Spanish-speaking South Texas. Have a seat, Mr. Smith, Henry." When they'd settled, Colquitt continued. "The reason I flagged your name, Smith, is that you worked for the Thiel Agency recently. I'm keenly interested in one of your clients."

"Which one would that be, sir?"

"The Provisional President of Mexico. Francisco Madero."

"Ah." Smith shifted in his chair. "Well, I can't discuss any business that–"

"No, no. Of course not. I mean, what sort of a man is he?"

Chapa snorted. "A little man."

Colquitt shot him a wry glance. "Careful there."

"I mean, a weak man. Not a military man at all. That is –"

"You're not getting any further out of that puddle, man," muttered Colquitt, who'd never worn a uniform, gaudy or otherwise. "Come on, Smith."

"Well. Madero's family was in Nuevo Leon, very well off. When President Diaz finally offered to hold presidential elections back in 1909, Madero ran as a candidate. Looked like he might win. The Martians sure messed *that* up. Once they came boiling out of central Mexico and smashed the federal army, Diaz called off all elections. But losing to the Martians made him look too weak to keep a lid on things. Now they've got two revolutions going at once, one in the north, one in the south. Madero, he was living in San Antonio until March this year, but he's crossed into Mexico now. He's pretty much in charge in the north – Chihuahua and Coahuila states especially. The federals mostly gave up when the Martians cut them off from their bases."

"A pity they all did not drop their quarrels and unite against the Martians," said Chapa.

"Y'know," said Emmet thoughtfully, "if anyone would, it'd be Madero. He doesn't much care for killing. More of a builder, if you follow. But those 'quarrels' run deep, Mr. Chapa. Why, you've written about them yourself."

"Endlessly," said Colquitt. "Can Madero be trusted?"

"I'd say so, yes. There are revolutionaries everywhere you look in Mexico – hell, in San Antonio – but he believes in what he's doing."

"And he believes in spiritualism too," put in Chapa. He rapped his fist under the table next to him. "Ooooh! The spirits are here. They are troubled."

"I can't speak to that," said Emmet. "But if it's my opinion you want, it's a good one."

"Well, thank you." Colquitt rubbed his chin. "The Mexican situation does keep me up some nights. With the Martians having split the country in half, President Diaz has no power in the northern states, and if all order fails, there's nothing between those Martians to the south and *us* except a rabble. I can't have General Funston looking over his shoulder to the south when he needs to protect us to the north! Until their revolution is resolved, our southern flank is hanging in thin air. Francisco here keeps clamoring for General Reyes to step in, but I like to get a wide picture... At any rate, looks like we'll have to work with Madero to get much of anything done about the border situation."

"For now," said Chapa.

"Yes. For now. There could be another leader in six months. But the neutrality clause still holds in Texas, Francisco, y'hear?"

"It was my impression," said Emmet mildly, "that that would be federal law, and federal jurisdiction."

"Of course it is. But honestly, Smith, it's like being between two fires! Washington wants strict neutrality – well, fine. We've got Martians to fight already; I'm not invading Mexico with the Guard, and no would-be revolutionary is either! But every mayor along the border wants order as well and wires *me* to somehow provide it. We've got twenty thousand Mexican refugees here that the Martians and the revolution drove north, we've got cattle rustlers crossing the Rio Grande every minute, bandits crossing north to raid Texas, filibusterers crossing south to plunder Chihuahua..."

"And a billion dollars of U.S. investment in the northern states of Mexico," added Chapa. "Becoming more nervous by the day."

Emmet tried to grasp a billion but gave up. "And so you're expanding the Rangers? What's the budget this year?"

Hutchings said, "One hundred and two thousand, four hundred and seven dollars. And twenty-five cents."

"But that's for the Guard as well, you know," said Colquitt. "It disappeared in a handful of months. We are paying the men in state scrip for now. Washington, bless them, has voted us a plethora of funds – after both General Funston and I spent months begging them for military aid beyond resuscitating his Second Army. They cannot spare what we really need – artillery, shells, tanks, concrete for fortifications, the things that would actually enable my citizens to prevail against Martian tripods – but at least they have thrown us some money, as to an indigent in the gutter." Colquitt's voice was genuinely bitter despite his speechifying. "So I will do what I can; yes, I will expand the Rangers. There are bad times ahead. I want men who can shoot, and will shoot – when necessary."

"But not shoot too much," said Chapa. "There are other newspapers. Stories of Anglo lawmen killing Hispanic citizens are not helpful."

"The Rangers *must* be fair," said Colquitt with intensity. "And seen to be so. Every Texan is looking to me for protection and order, and the military is a clumsy tool for this work. I ran for governor on a platform that would keep the Rangers honest in their dealings with our citizens–"

Emmet smiled inwardly. To his recollection, that campaign promise had been to keep the Rangers away from citizens. But politics was a flexible line of work.

"– but they must be effective too."

"Are you a shooting man, Smith?" asked Hutchings.

Emmet regarded the adjutant-general evenly. "From time to time. Once, I went to arrest a Mexican who'd been spotted near El Paso; Hernandez, his name was. Cattle rustler and bandit sort. Bad reputation, so when I found him at a general store in Eagle Pass, I didn't give him any slack – just drew on him and told him he was under arrest. That's when I got stabbed."

"So now you'll shoot first?" inquired Chapa.

"I didn't say *Hernandez* stabbed me. Storekeeper behind me did – in the neck with a letter opener. No warning, no reason that I could tell. He wore *spectacles*," said Emmet in wonderment. "Hernandez came along peaceably. Maybe the storekeeper had something he didn't want me to find and mistook what was going on, but I never knew what."

"He didn't say?"

"I shot him. I was a mite surprised."

"I can imagine," said Colquitt. "Well, that is the stamp of man I am looking for. And you're satisfied with him, Henry?"

"Better than most we get," admitted Hutchings. "Too many men trying to dodge being called up into the Guard to fight Martians; they'd rather bust up a saloon fight."

Emmet cocked his head. "If that's meant as a question as to why I wasn't in the

Guard myself–"

"Of course not."

"That storekeeper had his revenge. Wound got infected, and I spent four months recovering. They passed me over."

"Enough of that, Henry. Have you got a posting for him?"

"Yes. At–"

"Scratch it out," said Colquitt cheerfully. "I have been thinking. Between the Bureau of Investigation, the Justice Department, and State, and who knows else, there's about half a herd of federal agents roaming over Texas nowadays. If they can have them, why can't I have them? Didn't you give the other Smith, the Australian, his own company so he could go anywhere?"

"Yes, Excellency, but we can't just keep adding companies of one man. There are already eight companies as of this month. The administrative efficiency, well..." Hutchings looked positively pale.

"Of course. Then we'll create a new *category*. A special category. Not assigned to any company or fixed camp. We'll call them 'Special Rangers'. How do you like the sound of that, Smith?"

"Pretty well, Governor." Emmet mentally tipped his hat to that phantom landlady. "Then–" There was a tap at the door; Colquitt turned. A page thrust his head in and said, "General Funston to see you, Governor."

"Well timed. Send him in." Colquitt jumped to his feet. "Gentlemen, if you will excuse me? Welcome to the Rangers, Smith."

"Thank you, Governor." Emmet rose, nodded to Chapa, and made for the door. Two men waited outside beside the page, both of them smaller than Colquitt. Emmet was beginning to feel far too noticeable in this company. General Funston looked worn but determined. The young, dark-haired captain beside him was gripping a large leather satchel as though it were a weapon; he had the tight-wound look of a guard dog on a leash. Emmet clapped his hat onto his head, tipped it to them, and followed Hutchings down the hallway.

April, 1911, Austin, Texas

Lang spared a glance for the blonde, lanky fellow in civvies sauntering behind the adjutant-general, then turned back to the governor's office entrance. By habit, he preceded General Funston into the room, looking into corners. He'd realized long ago that he was doing this, but the general didn't seem to mind; besides, it made Lang feel better.

"General, welcome," said Colquitt. "Hello, Captain Lang. Can I get you fellows anything?"

"No, thank you."

"No, sir."

"You're easy to please. Now. Can I go before the Senate and honestly tell them that Second Army is ready and able to defend Texas?"

Lang glanced at Funston. He knew what the general was thinking; he'd grown into that ability by necessity.

The task of reconstituting Second Army from the beaten remnants that had

21

limped into Texas in spring 1910 had taken more than a year's work. Lang had learned on the job; as a line tank commander, he'd thought staffers had it easy, and he'd been wrong. The job was Herculean. Coordinating half a dozen railroads to move troops to permanent camps where they could be fed, housed, and reorganized back into coherent fighting units. Transferring in replacements of skilled officers from other divisions or back east – and knowing how to spot the sad-sacks that his opposite number in that division wanted to get rid of.

And drawing up final casualty lists so the dead could be acknowledged at last, with far too many listed as missing – sometimes a heat ray left nothing to find. Everyone knew now what Martians did to – did *with* – human prisoners. The family of every missing man dreaded that, and they might never hear otherwise. That had been the worst. A few times he'd changed a 'missing' status to 'dead' if the battle had been far enough from any Martian base to make capture unlikely. It seemed a small mercy.

At least they'd filled out the numbers, and Lang thought the temper of the troops was good. He'd recognized his own fury at defeat in many of the men he'd met; the desire to hit back. But he knew what Funston would say.

"Ready?" mused Funston. "Yes. Absolutely. Able? No."

Colquitt digested that for a moment. "But you are at full strength. I've read the reports."

"There is no difficulty with manpower," said Funston. "We're turning fit men away at recruiting stations. I could have rebuilt the 33rd Division from the New Mexico refugees alone... No, Governor, it is the lack of heavy weapons that concerns me. Second Army has been given very little in the way of artillery, and only seven battalions of tanks to spread among fourteen divisions; thus most of those can only be classed as infantry divisions. In practical terms, they have little fighting power against Martian tripods. And I doubt that any more artillery or tanks will be forthcoming. It is clear from my communications with the Chief of Staff and the War Department that they classify Texas as a salient which they will not commit major forces to defend."

"I did not think I would live to see the day that Americans would be abandoned by their representatives, by their soldiers."

Funston sighed. "I too am infuriated. But I can see the necessity as well. With the influx of refugees from the west, Texas has perhaps four million people, and little industry useful to war. The states east of the Missisippi, with ten times the population and nearly all our heavy industries, must be protected. Politically, Washington can say they have rebuilt Second Army into a powerful force and it is ready to defend Texas. Militarily, that is not possible."

Colquitt walked to his desk, shoulders set tensely. He swept the mass of papers and files aside. "Show me."

Lang laid out maps on the cleared space: Texas, northern Mexico, Arkansas, New Mexico. Funston pointed in a wide sweep. "We have a very long line indeed to defend. It stretches from the Mississippi along the Red River, all the way to the Rockies in the middle of New Mexico, a distance of nine hundred miles. Then south along the Rockies to El Paso, and then along the Rio Grande to the Gulf of Mexico. Almost two *thousand* miles altogether and an impossible distance for any sort of defense we can hope to build. As we saw at Albuquerque, the Martians are able to concentrate tremendous force against a small part of our defenses. Even with earthworks, a division such as, say, the 24th can only hope to hold five or six miles of ground against such an attack. A continuous front is indefensible. There is the possibility of placing defensive forces only to protect key points within the state, such as cities and major rail lines..."

Colquitt shook his head vigorously. "Then I would be doing to West and North Texas exactly what Washington has done to us. That could only be a last resort. There *must* be something better! Now, if we cannot defend... Can we attack?"

Funston frowned. "I... Second Army is not supposed to undertake offensive operations."

"I can tell you, sir, that I will use the Guard, the militia, and the Rangers as *offensively* as I possibly can. Texas will not sit idle... and perhaps Mexico will not either. But I know you are a part of a United States organization and not a Texan one, and I can appreciate your position."

"My instructions from the Chief of Staff are quite clear, Governor."

"Yes. The question is, will you conform to them?"

Funston hesitated – rare for him – and looked at Colquitt intently; then his face shifted in the way Lang knew meant he'd made up his mind.

"Washington is timid and defensive-minded, I believe. If we leave these devils alone, they will simply attack when and where they choose. If I have your support, sir, then I too will strike at them wherever I can and be damned to my instructions."

"General, you have yourself a deal." Colquitt thrust out a hand; Funston shook it. "Now. We know all too well what our limitations presently are. But I can offer something of an alternative to the limit on your own military strength."

"That would be welcome news."

"I have been exchanging letters with the French Ambassador Jusserand for some time now. While his primary work is in Washington," – *and yours is not in the least*, thought Lang – "Senators Bailey and Hudspeth, along with Ed Lasater – he owns half a million acres of ranching – have been arranging to supply beef cattle to feed the French corps at Veracruz for over two years now. That has generated a certain amount of goodwill... and opened the door to other agreements. Cotton's at a peak price with the disruptions to the Indian trade, and while we can't ship all that much through minor ports... well, suffice to say that the French government has just proposed to advance us loans for the purchase of military equipment from them."

Funston gazed at him intently. "Now, that could be very useful. What sort of–"
Colquitt lifted a hand. "I am turning *that* entirely over to you, General. My job is to make sure we are not hornswoggled into handing over half the state; yours is to choose your weapons. Hopefully within the next year they can commence shipments."

"Good. However, in the short term, we're still severely short of material. My subordinate here has been working on a plan."

Colquitt turned. Lang cleared his throat. "We have been considering a more mobile unit that might outmaneuver the Martians rather than slug it out with them." *Orange flames gushing from a hatch—*

"Cavalry, you mean?"

"Er, no, sir. A tripod can run down a horse eventually. We've had reports. No, we are in the age of fighting machines, and we are going to have to adapt. An automobile is faster than a tripod, and suitably modified, can be driven where no roads exist – if the terrain allows, of course. While it couldn't withstand a heat ray much closer than a mile, it could use hills or gullies to stay out of reach of the beam."

"Interesting," said Colquitt. "Do you have any?"

Lang glanced at the general. "Well, no, sir. Other divisions back east have been equipped with armored cars, but we've been told to make do with horse cavalry. Still, I don't think an armored car would do well without a road to drive on. Too heavy. Something would break soon enough. In fact, nothing the army currently has would work. But... well, there are more than twenty thousand private automobiles in Texas. Could you get us, say, forty of the fastest?"

Colquitt grinned. "Senator Hudspeth has a Peerless tourer that he says will tear up a road and leave it wrapped in a bow. I'll beard him on the floor of the House about it... *Your patriotic contribution, sir!* Yes, I think I can do that."

"They'd need to be modified, of course. There's shops in Dallas that do custom work..."

"Yes, yes. But what weapons can they possibly carry? No artillery, surely."

"There are some reports from back east of a Dr. Goddard and his work on military rockets," said Funston. "They are being coy, but there is obvious potential. Such weapons have no recoil but can hit very hard indeed. They could give this type of unit some real teeth."

"But I don't suppose Washington will be sending you any of the new toys either," muttered Colquitt. "Not for a long time yet, anyway."

"I have to assume not. But, Governor, such rockets do not need to withstand the shock of gunfire. They can be manufactured without the forges or steel lathes that artillery components would need. In essence, they are simple metal tubes."

"Tubes," said Colquitt. He banged a palm on the desk. "Pipes! We make, Texas makes, how many miles of pipeline a year now? It's here somewhere..." He reached for a file, then thought better of it. "No matter. This is something we can make for ourselves, and we *will*. Start organizing this long-range scouting group, General. I'll get you this Dr. Goddard."

"Sir, he is working on a top-priority project for the entire War Department!"

"General, you're a good man, but you're not from around here. You have no idea how persuasive a Texan can be." Colquitt straightened from the desk, walked between the two others, and clapped a hand on each of their shoulders.

"I think we will get on famously, gentlemen."

Chapter Two

June, 1911, Holdfast 31-1, Zacatecas, Central Mexico

"It's better to be the right hand of the Devil than to stand in his way!"

The voice of Ronald Gorman echoed harshly through the large underground chamber as he addressed the men before him. This place had the touch of the Masters about it; sloped, glassy walls, dim reddish lighting, and incomprehensible machinery in places. It smelt of blood and death. The Devil would be comfortable here.

Three of his trusted followers stood to one side, two holding ropes tied around the necks of scrawny dun-brown calves that fidgeted constantly. The other eight humans nearby looked as vacant and frightened as the animals. Still, there was hope for them. Gorman had picked them himself, but it was always unpredictable when humans first met Masters.

It was often unpredictable when the two met at *any* time. Gorman knew all this could go badly. A man played his chances.

The man standing apart from the others stared into infinity, as he usually did. de Gama's rags were his priestly robes. Gorman had tried to change them – the stink was terrible – but de Gama would shriek and claw at him every time; so he let his companion choose his garb. Gorman himself had a fine coat gleaned from a once-haughty *hacendado* who had not survived a week in this place. In Tennessee, he'd worn bespoke seersucker suits.

"You are all alive because of me," Gorman continued. "And my good friend Enrique de Gama, there. It was he who first heard the mind of a Master. He is brilliant, you know, and a scholar, and would have been a priest one day in the old world; but here, his destiny was to feed far greater minds in their work. Yet he did not give up! He scribbled his little markings on the wall of the cell we shared – shapes and lines and numbers – and when a Master noticed, just as he was being taken for food, it reached to him," Gorman splayed his fingers before his face, " and caressed him, and somehow it understood that here was another mind, that could learn – that could be useful to it. He says that it ground its mind upon his like a millstone on a kernel of corn... but that stone felt the kernel. A miracle."

The men looked at de Gama. He shivered and turned away, mumbling.

"And it spared him, and told the others, and they knew. He told me, and I guessed the great secret: the Masters must feed, but it does not have to be upon *us*. It was hard, very hard, to find a way to tell them that we also eat lesser creatures, that we owned ranches, slaughterhouses. And that these creatures were still here after all the humans had fled. But Enrique had found a way. At last, they understood, and being wise, used their last few humans to bring them lesser creatures instead." He gestured to the calves. "A far greater supply. Others had to be told, commanded, and organized to do the work. And all this I did! They know that I serve them, and they reward me."

"They don't reward *him*," muttered one. de Gama giggled.

"Yes, poor fellow. They have touched his mind many times, and each time, it drives him a little more mad. But it's a beautiful madness. He sees angels where you see monsters..."

"What is all this to do with us?" sneered a blocky, bearded man.

Gorman clapped his hands. "I like you! A man who gets to the point! Do you know what it is you all have in common?" They looked about blankly. "All of you, in the old world, were nothing. Nothing! Bandits, thieves, convicts, outcasts. Like me! And who ruled you? The great and powerful ones. *Cientificos*, governors, *haciendados*... and someday, when they could no longer use you, the *rurale* policeman who pointed to a ditch and said, *Run, so I may shoot you*." The familiar rage boiled up. "Or the high and mighty ambassador who ignored *me*, left me to rot in a Torreon jail... Now we are all nothing before the rule of the Masters, and in the end, we will all die. But you can choose how you live! To eat steak, not corn. Drink fine wine. And to be powerful! To have a pretty girl for the night, not a hag in a farmyard. To be the boot that kicks, not the face that bleeds. To –"

Three metallic raps sounded behind Gorman, then a steady clicking. The men's eyes shifted past him and widened.

"It's time to feed them," said Gorman. He steeled himself, as he always had to, and turned.

A Master approached in its mechanical, many-limbed chair, steel claws clicking on the floor. Lifted higher than a man, it was still smaller, a shapeless sack of skin draped between tentacles. The huge black eyes were opaque pits.

Gorman suppressed his shudder and bowed before the creature. There were times he envied de Gama his madness.

He knew this one. It seemed larger than the others, more heavily limbed, and it moved more quickly and easily than they did. It thrived where they struggled. This made sense to Gorman; after all, he had survived the first period of captivity by being bigger and stronger than most others – certainly stronger than those he'd pushed to the front of the cell when the Masters came for their food. It was simply a law of nature, even for creatures that might seem to be outside nature entirely.

It walked its chair down the row of men, turning it smoothly to study them. Three were trembling. It rotated back to Gorman and gave a single sharp grunt. *Yes*.

Yes. But – yes to feed them, or yes to spare them? Hesitation could bring punishment. Mistakes could bring death. He waved to de Gama and walked quickly to join him. "My friend... please ask it..."

"No," whimpered the priest.

"Please, Enrique. I need to be sure. Just for a moment, an idea. Do they wish food of these men, or work?" He caught de Gama's thin arm and shuffled him forward. "Easy. Just for a moment."

"I... oh, the light!" de Gama's face turned upward to the Master as to a beacon. Gorman released him gently. He staggered forward a few more steps and stood before the chair. The Master reached out with the fine tendrils surrounding its mouth; they sought out de Gama's close-shaved skull, settled upon him, squirmed on his scalp. He gasped, then howled, an echoing sound that filled the chamber and set the calves to bucking. Then it released him. He turned, face empty and working.

"What does it want?" hissed Gorman.

"Work," said de Gama. He coughed and swallowed hard. "Much work. A world's worth of it. All of you are chosen, all are blessed. Rejoice! Rejoice!" He crumpled to the floor and lay shuddering.

Gorman knelt beside him and rubbed his shoulders. "It's all over, Enrique. You are a good friend. Thank you. Pedro! Send up the first calf."

Two of his trusties led the calf down the wide bay of the chamber to the metal frame adjoining a mass of machinery. They shoved it into the bars, then locked them in place. It blatted and kicked futilely.

The Master had returned to its duties – researches, amusements? Who knew? – beside the same assembly. It made motions over controls with its tendrils. Metal arms reached out from the machinery, then with a snakelike speed, impaled the calf. It thrashed, wailed, then fell limp. Fluids moved visibly under its skin. Feeding had begun.

With the calf silent, a rhythmic hooting could be heard; the sound of the Masters feeding.

"Such hymns they sing," said de Gama. He struggled up to his knees. Gorman rose and stepped back. This would be a show.

"What is it, Enrique?"

"It is communion! Blood of my blood, flesh of my flesh. This is my body, that I may pass to the angels' use! This is my blood, that I may nourish thy hearts!"

"Shut him up," said the tallest man in the row. His voice shook.

"Why?" beamed Gorman.

"This is blasphemy!" The man fumbled out a crucifix from his shirt.

"The sun feeds the corn. The son feeds the father! Blood of my blood! I am the Master and the Master is I! We are–"

"This is a sick heresy! I'll have none of you!" The man spun on his heel and walked away. He made four steps before the trusties seized him. "Let me go, curse you!"

"It's all right," said Gorman. He walked toward the group. de Gama had fallen silent. "He's a man of principle. Admirable! He chooses not to work for the Masters, and I respect that." He placed a hand on the man's shoulder approvingly, then drove his other fist into his belly, doubling him over.

"So he will feed them." He gestured with a thumb. The trusties hauled the gasping man to the frame and secured him. He managed a few shrieks before the mechanical arms closed in.

Gorman folded his arms. "Perhaps there are others who have principles?"

Heads shook, eyes slid away from his.

"Then we are agreed. Welcome to the service of the Masters! You two, help my dear friend de Gama. Bring the calf; we'll feast tonight. We have much work to do!" Behind him, the contented hoots rose again.

27

Chapter Three

SS Espagne
September, 1911, Port of Veracruz, Mexico

Lieutenant Henri Gamelin leaned on the upper deck rail, careful of the coal dust that coated it. Along with a throng of other passengers, he watched as smoke-belching tugs nudged the liner *SS Espagne* into her dock, completing the two-week voyage from Le Havre. Henri's own journey had been much longer; he had left Saigon, and command of a river gunboat along the Mekong Delta, two months ago. It seemed bizarre to transfer a naval lieutenant halfway around the world when there were Martians in the Far East to fight already; but Henri was philosophical, and he had enjoyed the trip aboard the *Espagne*.

He shifted back from the rail and caught sight of a familiar face further along. "Felipe!" He waved. "Felipe! Here!"

Colonel Felipe Angeles turned, smiled, and eased his way through the throng. "Henri! I thought you would be at the head of the gangway already." He spoke Spanish by their mutual agreement. His own French was flawless after five years living in France; Henri's Spanish needed polishing. They had met at a formal dinner aboard ship; Angeles' Mexican Army dress uniform sported a Chevalier de Legion d'Honneur medal, which caught Henri's attention. He was delighted to learn that Angeles, an artilleryman, had worked on the final details of the '75' artillery piece; that he considered himself of Indian rather than Spanish heritage; and that he had been effectively banished on a study mission with the French army for the crime of speaking his mind too often under the rule of President Diaz.

"My luggage is being brought up, still," explained Henri. "May as well sight-see."

"It is a magnificent port." Felipe looked over toward the ancient stones of Fort St. Juan de Uluan looming over the harbor. Henri wondered how long it would withstand Martian heat rays. But the French and British light and protected cruisers anchored awkwardly throughout the harbor, wherever their guns would bear, would surely see to the defenses.

There was more than the ancient fort to protect, of course. The entire port was busy with freighters. Some – United States flagged and others exiled from Central and South America – were bringing food for the hundreds of thousands of refugees who swelled the city and filled temporary camps on its outskirts. They might leave crammed with them as well. Others transported war material from France. After an agreement with the Mexican government in 1909, an entire French corps had landed at Veracruz

– now the de facto capital of Mexico, after Mexico City was overrun – and taken on the defense of the port and its relocated government. Once the Mexican federal army was re-manned and re-equipped, trained and provisioned, its dependence on the French force should lessen. At least that was the theory...

"Did you get your final assignment yet?"

Felipe nodded. "The cable just arrived. I will be training officers and crews in the 184th and 241st Artillery Battalions, just inland. We hope that in six months we will be able to fully operate with the new artillery pieces you have given us. I never did express my thanks for that, Henri. When the Martians defeated our army, the loss of life was bad enough, but the material... we barely salvaged anything. It is bad enough to have lost Mexico City. It would be horrible to see the Martians sweep over Veracruz state and have no way to stop them until they came under the guns of these ships."

"You speak as though you were there," said Henri.

Felipe smiled grimly. "I read enough in letters. And it must be bad if they are letting me come back! It has a whiff of desperation, no?"

"I shall take the next ship back out again. But... Felipe, a word of warning. I do not think France's help comes without a price. Do not waste any time getting ready... for anything." Henri glanced aside as the gangway rattled into place. "I hope to see you again."

"And I." Felipe shook his hand warmly then disappeared into the crowd of bustling passengers.

Henri had hardly expected to be hurled into fighting upon arrival. But Veracruz began to take on an air of unreality after a time. From disembarkation, to meeting a white-jacketed orderly on the dock, to the private car sent for him, and finally the busy downtown streets that only showed by the vast number of uniformed men that anything was amiss; it all seemed rather unwarlike. The hotel he was to stay in was a towering masonry castle of high whitewashed colonial archways; his room was luxuriously appointed. Henri appreciated it; he had slept on the metal deck of his gunboat on many sweltering nights.

However, no one seemed to know what to do with him.

He was *supposed* to be Rear-Admiral Favereau's liaison to the army corps deployed around Veracruz; at least, his orders said so. But next morning, the admiral's shore office sent him to the Mexican Army headquarters in the colonial district; and in the afternoon, they sent him to the office of General Charles Mangin, commanding the 12th Division of IV Corps.

Henri was arguing with a staff officer and two clerks simultaneously when the general thrust his head out of his doorway. "What is this infernal noise?"

Henri saluted. "Lieutenant Gamelin, sir. I am to be the naval liaison to your corps. But I have not been able to –"

"Whose idea was this?" Mangin was a stocky, scowling fellow. He rubbed a hand through a bristle of black hair.

"I was told in Saigon that the Office of Central–"

"They sent you from *Saigon*?" rasped Mangin. "Who are you supposed to be representing to me?"

"Admiral Favereau."

"I don't give a shit what Favereau does. If the Martian *monstres* drive us back close enough to the coast for his pretty ships to shell them, I will already be dead... Look, young fellow. Do you want a staff position or a fighting command?"

Henri swallowed. "A fighting command, sir."

"That's better. I can send you to Tampico, the oil terminal, north along the coast. The Navy is terrified of putting a foot ashore there, they want to please the British too much. Baron Cowdray wants the oil there for his king and his pocketbook. Do you care about that?"

"Not at all, sir."

"I suppose you're a republican like Favereau?" Henri nodded. "Well. It is forgivable in one so young. There are some gunboats stationed on the canal, and they have been bothering me for officers for them. I leave it to you."

"Thank you, General!"

"Oh, and wait." Mangin ducked into his office, then returned holding two tickets. "These are for some damned dinner affair. I have no time. You go; it will amuse me to have the Mexicans feed you instead of our commissary."

"I... very good, General."

Mangin huffed and returned to his office. Henri blinked down at the gilt-edged tickets: a state affair, tomorrow evening at the Imperial Hotel.

"I'll draw up your orders, Lieutenant," said one clerk. The others had already turned away in disgust. "Lucky bastard," muttered one.

Henri figured that he could find a girl easily enough – a fine dinner, and who knew what after? – but then a grin spread over his face.

"What are you smirking about?"

"Corporal," said Henri with some dignity, "please place a call for me to the 241st Mexican Artillery Battalion."

Evening found Henri at the Imperial Hotel. The main ballroom was magnificent: two stories tall, colonnaded arches on each side, and a table laid with gold and pearl settings that stretched nearly the length of the entire chamber. Chandeliers blazed with light; glittering uniforms, black coats, and evening gowns circulated. Feather boas seemed to be in vogue. Henri could see why Mangin would have none of it.

The maître d's eyebrows lifted to his hairline when he saw Henri in his lieutenant's uniform, but he admitted him and his companion and showed them their seats near the table's foot. The name card read *Gen. Mangin*; the maître d' whisked it away.

"Well, this is interesting," said Colonel Angeles. "I could catch up with so many people, if any of them would speak to me." But he was smiling as he studied the crowd. "I see General Huerta got his divisional sash at last. If anyone would be promoted after losing half the country, it would be him. He is a dangerous man, Henri." Henri glanced at the short figure with the strange, white-sheened eyes and did not disagree.

"You must recognize President Diaz." Henri nodded; he did, if only by the currents in the figures surrounding him – the rock in the river. Leonine, white-haired, erect... but some of those figures stooped close to shout in his ear. He must be growing deaf. "Next to him is Finance Minister Limantour. He may be the next president. Or one of the generals may be, if they can only win. But who knows? Diaz keeps us all guessing."

"I suppose you are not fond of him," said Henri.

31

Felipe shrugged. "Another ruler with his power might have had me quietly killed. He is not a bloodthirsty man, I will give him that... Those prosperous men in their frock coats are the *científicos*. You would say, industrialists? Cronies? But with money. Railroads, mines, oil. He, and they, changed Mexico so much. Progress is good, Henri, but so much of our country has been left behind by it. And now left to the Martians. This," he waved at the room, "is all beautiful, but does it not feel desperate as well?"

Felipe inclined his head toward the United States ambassador, surrounded by eager petitioners. "You saw all this before, in Vietnam, didn't you? The local... potentates... trying for the favor of the colonial power. It is all familiar."

Henri clapped Angeles on the shoulder. "No, my friend. It will be different now, I am sure."

Felipe smiled thinly. A bell rang in the lobby; the figures stirred and made for their places. Henri followed Felipe to theirs.

The meal brightened Henri's mood again; grilled meats, seafood, some with delicate flavors, a few mouth-searingly spiced. The champagne was excellent. To Henri's left, a Mexican Army colonel explained some of the dishes helpfully, and they fell to conversation.

"Does anyone know what goes on in the interior?"

"There is nothing in Mexico City but rubble and looters," said the colonel dejectedly. "General Huerta made a probing assault there six months ago, but he was driven back immediately. Brigadier-General Diaz, the President's nephew, was killed leading a charge – he still grieves. Tripods stalk the streets. Do you suppose they know what it does to us, to have lost that city?"

"I do not think they understand us that well... but who knows?" Henri drained his glass and held it up to a passing waiter.

"We should take it back," muttered the colonel. "A pack of peasant rebels claim to still be fighting there. And our army is not! If they *are* there, it is an insult."

"I think General Mangin is willing to fight alongside you," offered Henri. "You will not be alone the next time."

The colonel snorted. "From a looter to a butcher, then?"

Henri set his glass down carefully. "What is that supposed to mean?"

Angeles' hand settled on his shoulder. "Henri, you've had a lot to drink."

"I had not," said Henri. "Haven't not." He reverted to French in momentary frustration. "*Espagnol passé stupide...* No, I merely wish to hear this man's opinion."

"I meant no offense," said the colonel. "But everyone knows how General Mangin got his promotion to divisional command. When he was in Algiers, his native infantry brigade was deployed against two Martian tripods that had become unmovable – lamed. He attacked all day – again, again, again. They finally brought them down, using only rifles and machine guns, and destroyed them. Yes, a great victory. But he started with four regiments of infantry, and ended with one. Do you know what he said after? 'There were only two machines, but I could always bring up more men.' That was when they started to call him 'The Butcher'. He did not count the cost of sending the Algerians. Perhaps he will not count it when he sends us?"

"Colonel," said Felipe coldly, "this is no place to ask that sort of question."

"Of course, Colonel. As I said, I meant no offense. We are all grateful for French help." The colonel sketched a smile; Henri nodded in acceptance.

He managed to behave better for the remainder of the meal. There were speeches; they seemed to Henri like a glittering crust over a deeper reality.

When he rose and left the ballroom, he staggered a little, but felt fine physically. His *elan* would return; it always did. Better a challenge than this glamour. Perhaps General Mangin was right.

As he followed Angeles down the hotel's back stairs, a small man stepped out of the shadows. "Your pardon, sir. Are you a friend of General Mangin?"

"I do not think he has many friends," said Henri, then caught himself; he was still very drunk. "But I know him. Who are you, sir?"

"My name is Manual Palafox. Could I trouble you a moment? Here?" He gestured to one of the archways along the sidewalk.

Henri glanced at Felipe, who said, "I will wait. I do not wish to burden you."

Palafox bowed to him. "No, Colonel Angeles, your reputation is no burden here. But thank you." He ushered Henri aside.

"We had expected General Mangin tonight," he said. "Perhaps you could bring him a message?"

"We?"

The man's face was pocked with scars; it cracked into a smile. "Others were here tonight. Forgive me if I do not identify them... The message is from Mexico City. There is a man there that I serve, who still fights. In the streets, in the rubble, in the sewers. He and his people will never give up. But he is a rebel, and the government will never support him. They would be happy if the Martians killed him... But all humans must fight these devils. If someone from the general's service could come to Mexico City, I could show him, prove to him. The federal army is beaten. We are not, we shall *never* be. Give us weapons, and we can take Mexico City back – for all Mexicans." He glanced over Henri's shoulder. "I must go. Will you relay this message? I can contact you later."

"Yes. Tell me, who is this man?"

"His name is Emiliano Zapata." Palafox faded back into the shadows.

Chapter Four

September, 1911, Laredo, Texas

"Telegram for you, Ranger Smith," whispered the desk clerk of the Ross Hotel as Emmet walked through the lobby. He slid the paper across the counter without looking at Emmet, who obligingly sidled up to the counter with the utmost nonchalance. The clandestine style suited the Ross; Emmet was staying there to monitor the efforts of General Bernardo Reyes to organize his takeover of Mexico. Half the hotel guests seemed to be would-be revolutionaries, gunrunners, Mexican exiles, American supporters... and the federal and state agents both countries sent to watch all of them. Emmet slid a dollar back in return, trying not to laugh at the absurdity of his covertness when everyone knew what was going on here. The clerk was taking money from both sides. Business was good. The elderly Reyes seemed to Emmet to be going nowhere, but it was prudent to keep an eye on him.

The telegram read, '*2 RANGERS ARV TRAIN 3:35PM SHUT DOWN LA CRONICA*'.

Emmet twiddled the paper thoughtfully. Adjutant-General Hutchings was as thrifty with wired words as he was with anything else that cost money, but the gist was clear. *La Cronica*, a Laredo newspaper, was run by the Idar family and a thorn in Governor Colquitt's side. The thorn had become too painful.

He had a few hours to prepare. Emmet mulled a few ideas while he returned to his hotel room and retrieved his Ranger certificate of authority and his sidearm.

Shortly after, he walked a few blocks through the afternoon heat to an auto shop and arranged to hire a car. It proved to be a near-wreck 1909 model; there was little choice for civilians with so many requisitioned and no new production. He was becoming more familiar with the machines, but it still took a while to get it moving. It was a century of progress...

Emmet made it to the train station in time for the arrival of the 3:35 from Eagle Pass. Once the packed crowd of passengers had shoved their way off the platform, the two remaining men in long dusters and hats, carrying weekender grips, were obvious. They shook hands and introduced themselves as Stubbins and Hicks.

"First thing to do," said Emmet as they walked out of the station, "is take off those coats, roll 'em up, and stuff 'em in the car boot. You're in town now."

They grumbled but obeyed. "Why'd you get a car anyway?" asked Stubbins as he pulled his coat off. "I know Laredo, it's not more than five minutes walk from here."

"We need a getaway vehicle."

"Huh?"

"Just get in. I'll explain as we go." Emmet spun the crank, jumped back from the dangerous kick it gave, and climbed up into the driver's seat.

The explanations took longer than the drive, but both of the Rangers seemed to grasp what he wanted them to do. Emmet dropped them off a block from the *La Cronica* building, swung around and drove up in front of it, and deliberately retarded the ignition spark so that the engine backfired noisily. Heads tuned in the street; a curtain moved in the ground-floor office window. Emmet jumped down and swaggered his way to the front door. He hammered on it loudly.

A woman in her twenties opened it; black hair in a bun, black eyes, upright posture; black skirt and a faded blouse with sleeves rolled up above ink-stained hands. "What do you want?" she said.

"Texas Rangers, miss. My name's Emmet Smith. May I come in? This isn't for them out in the street." He doffed his hat.

She gave ground, allowed Emmet to walk into the office, and then closed the door. "I'm Jovita Idar. Let me see your certificate." He handed it over; she studied it carefully.

"I'm here on the personal authority of Governor Colquitt. I'll need to speak to all your staff. Can you gather them here?"

Her face clouded. "Are you arresting them?"

"No, miss. This is just a... friendly talk."

"I doubt that." But she left through the inner door, calling, "Eduardo! Come in here and bring the pressmen! It's the *rinche!*"

Idar returned followed by three men. The office grew crowded, but they all fit. Their flatly hostile expressions showed what they thought of the Spanish slang for the Rangers.

"Now, I'm not arresting anyone," said Emmet. "So don't worry about that. I'm just relaying a message from Governor Colquitt. He'd like to appeal to your patriotism, encourage you to support the war effort against the Martians, and basically, well, lay off him."

He was greeted with incredulous laughter. "You've been out in the sun too long," said Eduardo. "My father and my sister write what they want."

"I'm not saying to praise the governor. He makes mistakes like everyone else. Just be more... supportive."

"Should we support his putting Mexican refugees into camps like so many cattle, then?" said Jovita. "The rich have found comfortable places to stay. The poor are in tents – if they're lucky. Soon there will be disease outbreaks. Why are they not allowed to move freely?"

"Now that you mention it, I was in Brownsville two weeks ago, enforcing a smallpox quarantine on your fellow American citizens. You see, we don't want that spreading through cities – or camps. It sure doesn't care where you're from. The, uh, sanitary arrangements at the camps, they're actually pretty good. Better than most would know how to carry out on their own." He paced to the window, noted that the car was gone, and turned back. "The governor's main responsibility is to American citizens –

Texans – but he's not neglecting anyone else. We're all in this war against the Martians together."

"And it is this war that makes a free press even more vital!" snapped Jovita. "When frightened people turn to a strongman to save them, they can give up rights that it took centuries of progress to gain. They need to know the truth. Tyrants and dictators cannot bring progress, and we must have it! We must organize – not the powerful, but those without power. We must unite society so that it can advance. Why are the Martians so much more powerful than us? Not because each Martian is stronger than a human being. Because they are a more advanced society!"

"I never thought of cannibalism as advanced," said Emmet.

"It isn't cannibalism, it's anthropophagy." Emmet blinked at the term. "Eating of humans. Of course it looks evil from our perspective – and it is. Being advanced doesn't mean being good. But look how far they've come! All the kings and emperors in our history couldn't conceive of crossing an ocean for thousands of years, and these creatures can cross between planets! Just as North America was conquered by those who could organize themselves better, more efficiently – who could utilize knowledge gathered by many people – who had overthrown old ideas and beliefs. That is what made them so much stronger! We must do the same against *these* conquistadors or we are doomed!"

"Miss Idar, you have a fighting spirit," said Emmet sincerely.

"It would not surprise me if the Martian females fight alongside the males. Why not?" she asked as Emmet stared in shock. "They fight with machines, not muscles. I can run a press as well these men can! Twice as many fighters. Perhaps we must learn to do the same."

"I don't disagree at all. Eduardo, do you feel the same?"

"Of course," said her brother. "Jovita is the soul of this newspaper. She would bring the same spirit to anything."

"Well," said Emmet slowly, "she may need to, I'm afraid. *La Cronica* will have to cease publishing. For a few months, anyway. Now, wait," he held up a hand as they spoke over one another. "Wait! Like I said, no one is being arrested. And you're all free to move as you wish. But you can't undermine the governor at this juncture. I'm sorry."

"So you're going to close down our newspaper?" demanded Eduardo.

"I closed you down five minutes ago," said Smith gently.

They all stared at him for a moment; then Jovita's face drained of color. "The presses! You *rinche* swine–" She spun on her heel and shoved a pressman aside. "Stop them! They're wrecking the presses!"

"Now, that's not true," said Emmet as he followed the stampede into the main floor. And, indeed, the staff had pulled up short at the sight of the three intricate masses of sculptured iron, perfectly intact. "Why, that'd be vandalism. And plain mean. No, my confederates have, um, borrowed all your type. And the setting frames." And they'd spilled a few of the lead type pieces on the floor on their way out, he saw; but they'd done the job. "So you can print all you want, just not with any letters."

"That was a filthy trick," said Eduardo coldly. "But we will get more."

"I think you'll find not many willing to sell to you right now. As I said, it's just temporary. Sorry, folks, it's my job."

Jovita stalked up to Emmet. He braced for a slap, but she kept her fists at her sides. "I think you enjoy your job too much, to be such a trickster."

"You misunderstand. I've known pressmen – and Rangers. Tempers can get short in these things, and people can get hurt." Emmet donned his hat, tipped it. "I just wanted to avoid an argument."

He walked back through the office to the door as the angry voices rose again behind him.

Cycle 597,844.9, Holdfast 31.1, Zacatecas, Central Mexico

Ulla! Ulla! Ulla!

Taldarnilis jerked its tendrils away from the controls of the food processor. The general alarm of Holdfast 31.1 was the single loudest sound that could be heard in the entire complex. Taldarnilis mentally discarded all ongoing thought processes, tensed its flaccid body to full strength, and readied itself for action with a focused mind – but where was the threat?

It touched a single tendril to the control bar and received the neural impulse of: *All individuals join to primary neural link. All individuals join to primary neural link. All...*

Taldarnilis touched additional controls and switched to that frequency. Instantly it was assaulted with the background hum of one hundred and forty-four minds located throughout the fortified complex, the processing units, and the nearby fighting machines, all seeking to identify that same threat. Although Taldarnilis was only one-point-four cycles old, it easily filtered the familiar traffic. Here and there a questioning individual's thought rose momentarily over the background, but none reported contact – all waited to hear.

"There is a historic change to Group 31," spoke the mind of Natqarnas, the group's leader. "As the senior member of Guljarnai Clan, predominant clan in this group's company-of-three, I shall communicate it to all of you. After extensive scouting and sampling, our group has obtained few elemental resources in our immediate area, beyond the already-processed metals and hydrocarbons retrieved from the formerly populated prey-zone to the southeast. Therefore, we had requested the Conclave to supply an additional seven hundred and fifty-five units of element 92 in the forthcoming third wave of ballistic reinforcements scheduled to arrive in two tenthcycles.

"That request has been denied. Appeal to the Council has been denied. Negotiation attempts on the Homeworld by all three of our main clans have been denied."

Taldarnilis spared a moment's attention to bring up an aspect of the Race's stored memories that it had never needed before: the traditional process of power generation. The techniques that had sustained the Race through millennia of scarcity were well established. Heavy atoms were fissioned into fragments, and the released energy was gathered to perform work at the highest efficiency that had been devised. Elements 90 or 92 were preferred. As Taldarnilis continued to listen to the broadcast, it sidebarred data on Holdfast 31.1's supply of both. The amount shocked it. Group 31's supply of fissionables, brought from the Homeworld, had depleted to the point that little more than a cycle's steady use was left. It dug deeper. *Access quantity brought on initial launch.* Estimated four local cycles' consumption. *Access quantity brought with second wave reinforcement.* None.

Every energy requirement of Group 31's colony was supplied by the reactor at the holdfast's core – power to run the base, to charge the fighting and refining machines' power cells, to energize the defenses. Once that ran out, the base would die, and the members of the Race along with it – most being unable to move any significant distance without their powered mobility chairs. Although Taldarnilis itself could move better under gravity than the Homeworld-origin members, it calculated the odds of its personal survival without technical augmentation as negligible. But, surely, another and more successful group could offer help?

"Guljarnai Clan has been in contact with Group 30 on the southern continent. They have agreed to subsume Guljarnai into their own clan, in exchange for Group 31 dismantling and transferring its northern Holdfast 31.2 reactor, along with its heavy transport machines, seven hundred telequel south to a region near the isthmus fortifications recently constructed by the prey. There a clanless support base will be constructed, to be operated by Group 31 but available to all clans participating in the assault on the isthmus barrier at such time as that takes place. If the reactor has insufficient supply of fissionables to carry out that mission, more will be supplied by Group 30 to fulfill the needs of the assault.

"Attempts to negotiate subsuming of other Group 31 clans have been denied by both Groups 32 and 30. We will leave Vantarsilas of Tarqirtat Clan in command of Group 31."

Taldarnilis filed that information for later processing; it belonged to the Tarqirtat Clan. Perhaps it would gain influence... in a group rapidly losing status among others on this planet.

"Elder Dartalnat of the Tarqirtat Clan has recently become deceased due to an unexpected propellant leak in the Tarqirtat launching tube assembly." Taldarnilis almost released the control bar but controlled itself. *An assassination on the Homeworld? Did Dartalnat oppose this defection of a clan?* "The elder will not be replaced. Once the waterway has been conquered, and the support base is closed down, the remaining two clans participating in it, or at the primary holdfast 31.1, will be released to their own goals."

At that, Taldarnilis contracted its tentacles in reflexive shock. Without oversight from the Homeworld – and the representation that came with it – Group 31 would certainly receive no shipments of fissionables, nor any other aid. The logic was inevitable. Their most productive machines were to be taken from them, so even if they were to locate a supply, it would take too long to exploit it. The reactor would die. The group would die.

Taldarnilis would die.

With stored memories of hundred-thousand-cycle lifespans for contrast, it seemed even worse to perish so rapidly. It could barely keep from emitting a verbal distress call. On the neural link, minds buzzed in similar shock. Natqarnas overrode them. "The Council's decision is final. Clan leaders, form secondary links to begin planning for the dismantling and transfer. Natqarnas out."

The other minds faded from the link. Taldarnilis was left alone, slumped in its chair. Its mind churned frantically, emptily. Then there was a tingle from the link controls – a new connection.

"Taldarnilis?"

"Yes, Lantergis."

"Guljarnai Clan has acted in its own interest and not the group's."

"That is clear." Lantergis must be in shock as well. "Bring the other Threeborn into this link."

That would require some to communicate while simultaneously performing other tasks. Taldarnilis had found that the Threeborn generation of individuals were comfortable doing so, but not the previous generations which had budded on the Homeworld. Some of its cohort considered this to be due to the heavy sensory input of this world's chaotic environment, but Taldarnilis was doubtful. There was also the factor of spending so large a fraction of one's time in travel chairs, with constant access to neural links. Which was itself arguably an environmental factor...

Other minds blossomed on the link. They belonged to several varied clans, but had all budded on this world and referred to themselves – although never to an elder – as those of Planet Three. The combined signals were jarring, incoherent. Taldarnilis braced its mind and spoke over the tumult. "All Threeborn group members! We are presented with a problem. Our existence is at stake. Without further shipments, our energy supply will be finite and diminishing rapidly. Traditional methods of finding more supplies have failed. We must devise new ones."

The minds vibrated with stress and confusion. Taldarnilis summoned its own to a strength and pitch it had been unaware was possible. "All of you were bred upon this world! It is your destiny to survive here, and you will! Did not you, Raqtinoctil, sense the prey-creatures' minds and make possible the alternate food supply? Did not you, Arctilantar, devise the tracking system to allow these goodprey to carry out tasks outside the holdfast? Do not accept limitations in your thinking! Now, begin."

Chapter Five

September, 1911, El Paso, Texas

The locomotive's whistle blew three times. Captain Willard Lang shouldered his haversack and set off past the shouts and turmoil of soldiers preparing to board their train cars. He headed down along the length of the train which extended well past the simple platform. Two passenger cars were filling with men; next, four flatcars carried two steam tanks on each. Two more flatcars held four strange-looking contraptions: the lower chassis of a tank topped with a boxy metal compartment and an A-framed crane. These 'armored recovery vehicles' could pull a wrecked tank right out of a ditch, or lift a boiler out of one. Lang reflected that some men deprecated such vehicles because they couldn't fight. But having seen a tank battalion lose half its numbers to breakdowns, he knew such equipment was worth its weight in gold.

Lang's pace slowed as he reached the next flatcars. Loaded on these were automobiles: the fruit of Governor Colquitt's leverage, civilian coupes and tourers that had been stripped down, modified, fitted with solid tires, and painted a motley assortment of whatever each of a dozen garages in Dallas and Houston thought was 'light tan'. He spotted what was left of a Peerless tourer and suppressed a grin. *Thank you, Senator. We'll take good care of her.*

He stopped, studying the vehicles. Most of the cars had a fifty-caliber heavy machine gun mounted on a pintle. Some had two. The soldiers assigned to the Long Range Scouting Company had been given a free hand with the new cal-fifties, and they had taken full advantage. The big-barreled guns looked threatening, but Lang knew how badly they were outclassed by a Martian heat ray. The small sheet-metal gunshield on each mount almost seemed like a joke.

The last six flatcars were empty, waiting to be loaded with salvaged material. That was the ostensible mission of the LRSC and the elements of the 325th Tank Battalion attached to it: proceed toward Albuquerque along the Second Army's line of retreat, remove or extract as many tank cannons and artillery pieces as possible, and bring them back. The LRSC would scout out to a distance and provide warning of any approaching tripods; the regular tanks would provide security for the ARVs. At least that was the theory. None of this had ever been tried before.

As the last soldiers boarded, Lang unobtrusively checked his watch. *Two and a quarter hours?* That was too long. The cranes mounted on the ARVs could easily lift an automobile, so loading those hadn't taken long. The ARVs themselves lifted one another on, then the last one was very carefully driven up a ramp.

They might have to load up a *lot* faster next time. Maybe if they rebuilt the flatcars so the vehicles could drive *along* them...

Metallic clinks sounded from inside the Peerless. Lang hopped up on a step and banged on the car's sheet metal – the small amount that remained. "Eddie! Come on out."

Eddie Painewick wriggled out from under the dash. "Almost done here, Cap. Clutch is still a bit tight."

"We're about to move out."

"I can come up later. I want it just right."

"Well, don't fall off. That'd break my heart."

Eddie scratched his neck. "Uh, Cap – Captain Lang. Thanks for getting me out of the stockade. I really appreciate that. It was just a misunder– "

Lang lifted a palm. "I don't want to know. I didn't even look at the papers I signed. But when the general said I was going on this little vacation, I didn't want some random driver who mightn't know left from right, never mind how to read ground. What are the rules, Eddie?"

"Don't get drunk. Don't steal anything that isn't Martian. And drive like a sonofabitch."

"See? Easy." Lang hopped down and walked back to the passenger cars. Two other captains and Major Plainview were shaking hands in turn with a small man in a general's uniform. Lang smiled and joined them.

"All ready, Lang?" asked General Funston.

"Yes, sir."

"Remember, Plainview. This is a routine salvage operation. The fact that you happen to have other units sharing the same transportation should never be interpreted as a reason to attack the enemy if they are encountered. That's official."

"I understand entirely, General," said Plainview.

"Lang, I'll need to know everything about how these ideas are working out in practice. But I need a live staff officer more than I need a dead hero. Be careful." Funston nodded to him and walked off.

Lang climbed aboard the car and pushed past two men. "Was that General Funston?" asked one.

"Yes."

"And he came here to see us off? Personally? This ain't no salvage operation, is it?"

"Nope," said Lang. He moved forward, looking for a seat open on the wooden benches.

Major Plainview caught sight of him and waved him over, then motioned to the man seated beside him. "Captain Lang! I'd like you to meet Frederick Burnham. The governor sort of attached him to us. He's got some wonderful stories."

The man stood up to shake hands with Lang rather than salute; he wore a civilian bush jacket and not a uniform. He was about Lang's own size, maybe fifty, with pale blue eyes that had a distant look. "Pleased to meet you. Frederick Russell Burnham."

"Willard Lang. Are you..." he tried to find a courteous phrase for *what the hell are you doing here?*

"Ah. We haven't met before. I've become involved with the LRSC on and off as a sort of consultant. Things are awfully quiet right now in this war, so this seems like the best place to be in order to... contribute."

"That's admirable," said Lang. "Would you excuse us a moment? Major, I have a question about the flatcar loading." He propelled Plainview down the crowded aisle to a quieter spot.

"Major, why is there a civilian coming along on this? We don't have much space for supernumeraries."

"That's what I told General Funston about you," said Plainview dryly. "Burnham is a personal friend of President Roosevelt. And John Hays Hammond, who owns a lot of mining concerns in this part of the continent and is richer than God. Burnham's keen on this idea of 'motor scouting' and wanted to get in on it. And he didn't come empty-handed. How do you think we got twenty of the new heavy machine guns when every soldier in America is screaming for them? Burnham pulled some strings." Plainview smiled at Lang's expression. "Really, Lang, he's spent plenty of time in Arizona and northern Mexico. Learned to scout against Apaches. Fought in the Boer War for the British."

"That's all before the Martians – ancient history. Can he handle a cal fifty?"

"He demonstrated the first one for us."

"Huh." Lang considered. "I suppose he'll do. But... hang on. How did he and Roosevelt and Hammond all know about the LRSC in the first place?"

"That's what I'd like to know," said Plainview.

The train clattered north for most of that day, following the east bank of the Rio Grande. Each hour they traveled closer to Albuquerque – and to the Martians that had reportedly occupied the town. Major Plainview ordered a halt at dusk while they were still over a hundred miles away; the risk of running into a tripod in the dark was too high when they would be at a disadvantage. The men camped close by the rail cars, ate, slept, and nervously whiled away the time.

In the morning, Plainview sought out Lang, who was drinking coffee by the embers of a campfire. The air was cool enough now that the cup was welcome. Plainview waved away an offer. "Let's get one of the cars unloaded," he said. "I'm going to proceed along the roadway a couple miles ahead of the train and scout. Want to come along?"

"Yes, sir. I know just the vehicle."

Lang chased down Eddie and one of the ARV commanders. They managed to get the Peerless unloaded in half an hour; it was already stocked with fuel, ammunition, and water, and they tossed in their personal gear, mounted up, and drove out.

Despite the visible road to follow paralleling the railway, there were plenty of ruts, and by the time they'd gotten a mile ahead of the train, the car had bottomed out its suspension several times. At the next lurch and jolt, Plainview barked, "What the hell are you doing there, driver?"

"I don't get it, sir," said Eddie. "It wasn't like this back in El Paso. It's like there's six people in here. Big people."

"Well, the gun mount weighs a hundred pounds..." Lang turned and clambered carefully back along the open body then poked through the supplies. At the bottom, he glimpsed rows of wooden ammunition boxes. "Here it is. There's a thousand rounds back here! Three hundred, four hundred pounds?"

"That's too much weight. We'll have to lighten things later. Just go slower there, Painewick."

Eddie obliged and the car labored less; in a few more minutes, they slowed to the train's speed anyway and it began pacing them. They proceeded along the bank, beginning to see foothills to the northeast. By midmorning, Brushy and Timber Mountains loomed in the distance.

"There's not been much worth even looking at so far," said Plainview. While there was detritus left behind by any army on a retreat, there had only been a few abandoned trucks and cars.

"Well, any tank that didn't get loaded on a train car wouldn't have made it more than forty or fifty miles before it broke down. The pickings will get better soon, sir."

And indeed once they crossed a bridge over the Grande onto the west bank, more wrecks appeared. Wagons, trucks, even a boxcar that had been heaved off the tracks. Then the first tank sat desolately near the railway.

"Not worth setting up for one," muttered Plainview. He studied the map spread out on his legs. "But we'll have to stop soon. A lot of flat open ground past Elephant Butte, and I don't want the train visible from twenty miles off. These guns aren't effective beyond a few hundred yards. We must get something better, Captain!"

"There is work being done on that, sir."

"Wasn't there a remote-operated automobile in the works? Able to rush a tripod and destroy it using a bomb?"

Lang shook his head. "I saw the trials for that two weeks ago. It was a disaster. They could barely drive one of those things underneath a water tower they were pretending was a tripod – as though it would stand still – and twice the wires broke. Then the general insisted he wanted to see how powerful the explosion was. It did make a nice bang, but the look on their faces when they destroyed their prototype... It sort of made it all worthwhile. I think that file is closed."

"Don't you think the idea of steering a weapon to its target is useful?" asked Plainview. "We waste so many shells trying to hit those damned tripods."

"It would have to be something faster. Much faster." Lang glanced ahead. "Sir, look!"

They were coming into a positive acreage of abandoned material. Lang could see three tanks already, as well as artillery pieces and ammunition limbers. The nearest still had two equine skeletons harnessed to it. None of the wrecks showed scorching from Martian attacks, but they had a forlorn quality just the same. He pictured the ugly scene: foundering horses being shot, boxes heaved off carts and trucks, soldiers shoved out to march on foot – perhaps wounded. He remembered his crew, most of them killed in their tank. He remembered Funston's rage...

"Sir, how about there? Good cover in the arroyos and open roadways beyond."

"Yes. I think that'll do to start. Driver! Get us up on that ridgeline. I want a look well around." They veered off the roadway and accelerated up the mild slope, scrub bushes scraping under the chassis. Eddie halted them at the top; Plainview and Lang both stood up and scanned the horizon with binoculars, slowly, carefully.

"No sign of 'em, sir."

"Good. We'll set up here." Plainview retrieved a green flag from under the seat and waved it. Below, the train's brakes keened and brought it to a gradual halt. Eddie turned and drove back down the slope to where the work would begin.

Plainview did not waste a moment. In half an hour, the salvage train was boiling with activity. ARVs trundled along the roadway in both directions to seek out their prey; Lang, supervising the reluctant offloading of half the ammo load of his cars, saw one of the ARV crewmen emerge from a nearby wrecked tank, drop to the ground, and vomit. *I know what he found in there.* He had his own duties; the LRSC cars were to fan out and find good spotting and hiding positions several miles to the west, north, and east. Plainview felt there was lesser risk enough from the south to not spare vehicles to cover it; Lang concurred. They would have to reconcentrate fast if more than one tripod showed up. The eight line tanks – Mk IIs and IIIs – took up positions within a mile of the train; there weren't enough to push out further. LRSC cars began pulling out. "Whenever you like, Eddie."

"Oh, hell," said Eddie quietly.

Frederick Burnham walked up and waved cheerfully. "Mind if I come along?"

"Be my guest, Mr. Burnham." He vaulted aboard with easy grace despite the slung haversack he carried; the Peerless barely rocked. *Good line of work for little guys*, thought Lang. "Move her, Eddie. Due north about ten miles, then we'll see."

Freed from the plodding train, Eddie drove with verve, and the Peerless responded splendidly. Fortunately, Burnham was either taciturn or had an instinct for when to keep quiet. The drive took less than twenty minutes – less than planned.

"Hold up, Eddie!"

Half a mile ahead, the tracks ended; rather, the rails did. Empty ties marched northward from that point.

"Cap, that's not good."

"I know. Let's go have a look." They pulled up at the rail's end. Sure enough, Lang spotted the triangular imprints left by tripods.

Burnham hopped down and stooped to examine them, brushing dirt loose from the print's edge. "These aren't fresh. It's not like any vehicle track I know, of course, but at least a week old." He bent closer and sniffed. "No odor to it. What do you suppose a Martian tripod smells like, Captain?"

"Never gave it much thought," said Lang, nonplussed.

"Everything has a scent. That car does. Lubricants? Ozone? If the Martian occupant has a scent, the local birds or animals may react to it long before we could. I'm curious to find out."

"We'll oblige you if we can. If they've used up those rails, they'll be back for more."

They picked a spot within eyeshot of the tracks even at night, drove there, and set up camp beside the car; Burnham dug a ramped firepit that wouldn't show the flame at a distance. While two of them busied with routine tasks, the third was always on watch, even when food was ready. Burnham seemed to eat very little, and Lang hadn't seen the man drink anything yet. As dusk fell, with no hostile sign yet, Burnham sat cross-legged with his back to the fire – to preserve night-sight, he said – and recounted a few of the stories Major Plainview had been so impressed by.

"I was prospecting near the Yaqui River in northern Mexico when the first landings happened. Didn't hear about it for six months. In one of those cosmic coincidences, I'd found a remarkable boulder carved with symbols – they call it the Esperanza Stone.

Priceless artifact."

"If it isn't portable, I'm not interested in it," said Eddie from where he stood on the car's bonnet.

"Oh, not priceless for wealth, but for knowledge. Probably Mayan, but I had a notion it might have been left here by aliens! Can you imagine how foolish – yet vindicated – I felt when I learned they had really arrived here?" Burnham chuckled. "But then they began killing us, and what I felt hardly mattered any more... Mr. Lang, what affairs of yours were interrupted by their arrival?"

Living to a ripe old age, thought Lang; but he only said, "Legal studies. I had hoped to pass the bar by next year or so, get married, argue each case with my wife, and develop that muscular jaw."

"Ah. Lewis Carroll. Well, an Army commission never hurts for that sort of career. I trust you can return to it." Burnham glanced over diffidently. "I noticed that fellow in the dark gray suit loading some rather large cases onto the train at El Paso. I take it he doesn't work for your state government?"

"Nope. He's from Washington. Doesn't say much."

"I believe there's a department of the Bureau of Investigation that handles this sort of thing now. He'll want to obtain any piece of Martian equipment you fellows find."

Lang shrugged. "If they can figure out a better weapon from it, I've no objection."

They spent the better part of two days camped at that location. While the weather was still mild – chilly nights, warm days – Lang found it difficult to rest fully with the constant strain of keeping a lookout organized. Four men would be easier; but more crew weight meant less supplies. He missed being free to load anything onto a twenty-eight-ton vehicle that caught his fancy. On the second morning, a scout car drove up from the south to check in with them. Plainview was finding rich pickings for his buzzards, they said, and the train would be fully loaded soon. Lang noticed that Burnham followed the report with the same focused intent that the famous scout directed at his surroundings. He also noticed that Burnham listened far more than he spoke and had a knack of steering conversation to topics he chose. He wondered at the man's purpose... and then forgot completely about it midday on the second day, when Burnham shouted, "Two tripods in view, heading south!"

Lang grabbed the second pair of binoculars seconds before Eddie and scrambled onto the car bonnet. "Start her up," he said as he scanned the horizon to the north. "I see them, Burnham." The objects were mere nicks on the horizon. In minutes, they grew to the swaying tops of tripods, heading south – directly toward them – and a third appeared behind. "Don't think they'll see us yet, but we need to go." They dropped back into the Peerless and Eddie swung them in a spurt of dust. "Not too fast! Don't leave a plume, they'll spot that." They descended the low rise he'd parked on, putting it between them and the Martians, and headed south – first at an infuriatingly slow pace while their dust might still be sighted, then a faster one that brought them within sight of the salvage train in half an hour.

Lang fired a red flare and pandemonium broke loose. By the time they pulled up by the locomotive, running men and moving vehicles had brought the landscape alive with activity. Major Plainview jumped down from the locomotive cab; smoke was already curdling from the stack as it worked up steam. But that would take time... He ran up to the car's side. "How many?"

"Three sighted, sir. There might be more, but we came back immediately."

"That's fine. One we could try and fight off; three is already bad odds. We'll pull out. Train's near fully loaded with salvage anyway...What ground have you got to the north?"

Lang knew what that would mean, but he kept his voice steady. "Good ground, I think, sir. Arroyos to the west, and if it comes to that, we could risk going into the river floodplain to the east – there's a fair drop there to the bank. It might not even come to a fight. They've been pulling up the rails five miles north of here, so perhaps they'll just keep doing that and not push south today."

"I'd like that," said Plainview, "but we can't assume it. I'm going to leave two tanks deployed in cover until the last minute, and we'll load some of the rest skewed on the cars, so they might get a firing angle as we pull out. I've already sent two cars out to recall the other scouts. We'll load up all but three. Those will join you as soon as they can." He hesitated a moment. "Obviously there won't be time to load you four, or those two tanks, if this gets hectic. Play it by ear. If the tripods are in range of the train, try and draw them onto the tanks. I sure don't want to leave them, but we may run out of time. If we do, pick up the tank crews as best you can time it, and drive alongside the train as we leave. Clear?"

"Yes, Major. Come on, Eddie, let's go see." They swung out and proceeded back north, leaving the bustle behind. Soon, another pair of cars appeared, angling over from the west as they found routes that suited. Another came up from behind, overtaking steadily but leaving a tall dust plume. Lang cursed, but there was no way to warn them – and it was hard to be angry with someone rushing to get in a fight. "Pull up here," he ordered instead. The two cars arrived in a minute; the last braked in a skid of dust and soil. Eddie sniffed audibly at the rough technique.

"We'll go on together," shouted Lang. "Not so fast!"

The group had covered perhaps another mile, driving in close order but avoiding one another's dust, when they came over a rise and saw the oncoming tripods four miles off – all three of them, and closed up in a bunch. If they'd come to scavenge rails, they weren't looking for that any more.

"Damn it," said Burnham. "They saw *our* tracks! They knew those weren't there on their last visit!" He racked the bolt on the cal fifty, unasked.

Lang cursed his own curiosity. *Might make us the cat... First let's be a mouse.* He called out to the other cars. "Open out when I wave! We'll outrun them through the west arroyos and try to buy some time! But we'll have to sting them first, make sure they keep coming! Don't waste ammo, but if you think another car's in trouble, knock on that thing's tin can and get their attention!"

The other crews waved acknowledgment.

"Eddie, I'll give you routes, but if for whatever reason I can't, then don't get within a mile of one of those bastards."

"Got it, Cap."

"If a heat ray gets onto us, try and shield your eyes."

"Ah," said Burnham. "That reminds me." He tugged out a small metal strip with a fabric strap attached to its ends and passed it to Lang. "This may be useful. It's adapted

47

from goggles the Eskimos use against sun glare."

There was a narrow slot in the metal. "How –"

" Just look downward if a beam passes by. Here, Mr. Painewick, I brought several of them. And, Mr. Lang, you may wish to roll down your sleeves."

They each donned them, Eddie steering with his knees as he did so. When he finished, he looked at the others and snickered. "We look like damn fools."

"Better than blind ones. As long as you can drive." Lang cocked his head; the world was reduced to a narrow dark-edged slot, but he could see well enough, and the sky sure didn't interest him right now.

Two miles. The closing speed was remarkable, between the cars' dusty rumble and the purposeful stride of the tripods. Lang marked an arroyo two hundred yards ahead, swallowed in a dusty throat, stood up, and waved.

The vehicles drifted apart in their directions; two opened out to the east – did they figure they could navigate the floodplain? – and the third stayed fifty yards away from the Peerless. Just about a mile now. "Left, Eddie!"

They swerved left just as the first heat ray opened up. It missed, then swung back to track them. Lang's right side burned for a moment; he did not look around, but he watched the oncoming arroyo mouth. He smelled burning paint; the car's ride suddenly roughened a little. *Tires melting?* Then the noise and heat stopped. He risked a glance back; they'd opened the distance slightly. One tripod still pursued them; the other two were turning south again. "Try the fifty on them, Burnham!"

The gun hammered earsplittingly above his head. He looked again; it was hard to tell if any rounds were hitting, and they wouldn't do much at that range anyway, but it was getting the Martians' attention and that was what mattered. More fire arced in from the right as the other twin-barreled car joined in. *If it gets them mad enough to draw 'em after us—*

All three came after them. *Great.* Burnham was firing short bursts, with pauses to cool the barrel. He did know his stuff... They drove around the arroyo's first curve and the rising bank cut off the Martians.

"Hold up, Eddie!" They braked. The other car joined them in moments, the crew wild-eyed but unhurt. "Back up til you see 'em, stop, and hit them again," he shouted, "then go on to the next bend!"

The commander nodded; both cars reversed in a spray of dirt. Two tripods came into view. "Stop, Eddie!" Painewick braked and shifted, ready to accelerate forward. "Fire!"

Burnham opened up again. More than a mile was difficult shooting on a moving target, but he looked to be scoring hits from their stationary position. It would take a box's worth to chew through that Martian armor even point-blank, though. One second, two...

"Go!" yelled Lang an instant before the heat ray hit them again. Burnham grunted and dropped into the seats. They peeled around the bend, shaking off the beams in moments, and headed for the next one. Lang grabbed Burnham's shoulder, but he shook off the hand.

"I'm all right," he said. "Just a bad sunburn. Had worse in South Africa – but it took much longer there!"

At the next bend they repeated the maneuver: draw them on, pop out and shoot, duck away. They'd still escaped serious damage, although Burnham's face and neck were indeed turning an angry red as he dragged out a fresh box of ammo and attached it to the gun. Lang doubted it would work a third time, though. *If I were them, I'd be tired of this game already. I'd go for high ground and pot-shoot us. If they get within fifteen hundred yards, they can kill us in seconds.*

He lifted off the goggles, scanned the ground ahead, and matched it in his head with the map. "Go in there, Eddie!" He pointed. They drifted right across the arroyo floor and approached the new gap.

"They're close behind!" shouted Burnham and opened fire. Lang looked back; the two tripods had crested the ridge. He whipped around, remembering to pull on his goggles, as the Martians returned fire. Burnham continued with short bursts as they pulled away. If the scout cars had driven along the existing curve, they'd have been within that deadly mile's distance. One disabled car or incapacitated crew and that'd be it...

They dropped into a deeper gully and broke contact again. Rocks chunked under the tires and the ride grew rough. "Follow this around to the south," said Lang, his voice shuddering with the jolts, "and then climb up on the ridgeline!"

Burnham fell into the seat beside him. His clothes and hat smelled of burned cotton, but he grinned at Lang under the metal goggles, flaking burned skin from his cheeks. "Clever folk, the Eskimos. I hit the closer one several times... Don't think I hurt it much, though."

"We're not tooled up proper for that... Here, Eddie! Go right!" They climbed the slope in a low gear, tires slipping at times, and reached the top. The two tripods seemed to glare at them from two ridgelines away.

"Oh, *do* come out and play," crooned Burnham.

As if they'd heard him, the Martians started directly toward the two cars. Lang had a feel for the game now. The cat-and-mouse continued for a quarter hour, drawing the tripods further west and south, but eventually the Martians appeared to give up – and there was a limit as to how close Lang would drive to a potential ambush when he hadn't sight of them. He waved over the other car. "We'll drive straight to the train now. It's been nearly half an hour; they ought to be about ready to move out when we get there."

"I could do the same myself!" called back the commander. His gunner was laid out across the seats; he stood at the twin mount himself. They headed directly cross-country but stayed low beside the ridgelines, not on top where they might draw the Martians on that they'd spent so much risk to draw *off.*

No tripods appeared behind them, but they had to be out there, and probably coming on. Just before the cars reached the overlook of the train's position, Lang spotted one scout car parked below it. He directed Eddie to pull up beside the other vehicle, noting as they did that, half its paint was burned off. *Do we look like that?*

"There's one of 'em down there!" said Hobbs, the car's commander. Lang gestured to him and jumped down. They climbed up the slope and crouched the last few steps. The train was already gone.

"Where's Car Two-One?" asked Lang.

"Bill got stuck in the floodplain," said Hobbs. "That damn thing just walked up to them and roasted them. Nothing left. I kept trying to draw it off westward, but it wouldn't have it! So I went up here. The tanks crippled it, just like the major said, but it got both of them, and it's still 'live!'"

Lang lifted his binoculars. The train was already a mile south and picking up speed. He doubted the two mobile tripods behind him could catch it now... A fresh Mk II tank wreck directly below, and less than a mile north from it, a tripod sprawled on its shattered limbs close beside another wrecked tank, still firing its heat ray at the receding train. *We'll have to swing south and*—

Human figures moved on the near side of the wreck. "Survivors, Hobbs?"

"Yeah. I've been trying to figure a way to grab 'em, but it's awful close."

"Might do it with three," mused Lang. "Let's go back." They shifted back to the three cars; Lang studied them for a few moments. "Right. Two cars to cover, one to drive down there. Eddie and I will pick up the crew. Burnham, take our fifty and shift it to Two-Two, they've got an extra pintle. That'll give four guns. Spread out below the ridgeline, and when I drive over it, pop up and start hitting that bastard; then duck back if it starts hitting you... Eddie, go on up and have a good look. That's quite a slope – let me know if you can drive it."

While the crews unshipped the gun and lugged it to the other car, Painewick squirmed to the top and spent some time there. He came back grinning. "Cap, anyone ever rolled a Priceless Peerless before?"

"I have no idea."

"We might be the first. But I don't think so. I'll try it."

"Well, then. Ready, everyone?" They acknowledged, got in, and drove off, the two cars separating by a couple hundred yards and moving into their cover positions. Lang climbed in next to Eddie, leaving the rear seat open. He gripped the seat's flange tightly with one hand, the door break with the other, and looked over at his goggled driver. *We still look like fools.* "Whenever you're ready."

Painewick revved the motor, shifted, and clutched in smoothly. They trundled up the slope, gaining speed – a *lot* of speed. Lang yelped involuntarily as the Peerless pitched over the ridgeline, back wheels catching air as the front tires crunched into the slope. They drifted for a horrible moment, Eddie countersteering expertly, and angled down the slope, accelerating to what seemed like fifty miles per hour. Gunfire sounded from the ridgeline, blurry with overlap from four weapons; Lang did not look away from the wrecked tank. Heat washed over him, searingly strong; he flinched, then it cut off as the tripod shifted fire to the stinging hornets on the crest. Eddie dodged a boulder in neat sweeps and sped up further. In the midst of the hammering, wind-rushing ride, Lang realized he'd never traveled this fast in his entire life. The tank loomed ahead; Eddie barely slowed, aiming to skim past it. The crew shrank back from the oncoming machine. Lang couldn't blame them. Eddie still wasn't slowing much. A hundred feet, fifty—

The heat ray blasted them from the flank. Glass shattered in the left driving lamp, the sound lost in the ray's shriek. Lang flinched down, head behind his arms. The Peerless caught fire – and skidded into the lee of the wrecked tank, banging Lang hard into the dash. The heat ray raved above them for a moment longer, prickling Lang's scalp, then swung away as the covering fire opened up again.

"Get in!" yelled Lang, but the tankers were already scrambling aboard. He beat at the side panel with his sleeve – which was also in flames. *Oh, hell.* He tumbled out, rolled in the dirt, beat at his left leg until it went out. There were burns under the cloth; how bad he couldn't tell yet. He twisted upright. "Eddie!"

"I'm all right, Cap!" One of the tankers had thrown his jacket over Painewick and snuffed the clothing. "I looked down, just like Mr. Burnham said, and I had my arm over my face that last bit. Just braking, no shifting. Damned if them goggles didn't work!"

"Going to keep them, are you?" said Lang as he climbed into the now-crowded vehicle, favoring the burned leg.

"Oh, hell, no. I'll sell 'em. I can always make another pair. Maybe a lot of pairs..."

"Just goddamn *drive*. And keep that wreck directly behind us as long as you can. We'll all meet up two miles south and then catch up to that train." He twisted around, hissing at the blossoming pain; but he was alive. "Welcome aboard, gentlemen."

"Damn glad to see you," said the tank commander as they moved off, the left tires thumping rythmically-- chunks had melted out of them. In a few moments, they left the wreck's cover, and Eddie floored it. Everyone clung for dear life and flattened into the seats, but no fire stabbed after them. "We only had twenty rounds – no point in more, huh? – and shot all of them off while it was killing poor Tommy's beast. Figured we'd at least try to bail out, but then we had nowhere to go that it couldn't burn us before we got anywhere. I'm buying you both a steak dinner tomorrow and that's for sure!" He squinted at Lang.

"You boys kinda look like Martians yourselves!"

Cycle 597,844.9, Holdfast 31.1, Zacatecas, Central Mexico

The chime beside the door aperture pealed twice, giving permission to enter. Taldarnilis advanced its travel chair through the opening, skittered it in a formal bow, and addressed Vantarsilas while keeping its eyes lowered. "Greetings, Group Leader."

"Greetings. You may look up... Do you know that the chime is a different sound in this thick air than on the Homeworld?" said Vantarsilas. It stirred in its sling, motioning welcome.

"Interesting. I had no idea."

"It sounds somehow wrong to me, yet not to you. Perhaps there is no right or wrong sound at all. I have contemplated on this a great deal in the last tenthcycle, since our betrayal by the Guljarnai Clan. I understand that several of the Threeborn which you represent have been contemplating on this as well."

The group leader's den could have held five of the Race comfortably. Its curving walls were glazed in a continuous sweep of color ranging from orange down into infrared, with white overhead. Taldarnilis understood this to represent the Homeworld's surroundings. Those originating there often reported functioning more efficiently when placed in such an environment.

"I agree," said Taldarnilis, sensing the concept that Vantarsilas had delicately placed before it. "As with many practices or actions, the methods laid down in the Race's genes and established practices – while they are justly revered – sometimes cannot apply on this world. The practices of detecting and mining energetic elements such as 90 and 92, for example. The planetary structures, composition, and processes on this world – and in this region – are different enough that our mining efforts have not succeeded to date, and with so many of our heavy manufactory and transport units diverted south,

51

they have no possibility of success in the time remaining before our supply of element 92 runs out. Therefore, I have consulted with Raqtinoctil and Arctilantar, our most... original... of thinkers upon this." Taldarnilis brushed a tendril over the chair's control bar to reassure itself that its compatriots were in neural link. Braced by their support, it continued. "They drew analogies between the salt flows on slopes on the Homeworld and the way in which large quantities of water on this world can carry dissolved elements over great distances. The water also cuts deep channels; thus, flows from a large area may be concentrated into a single channel. And all channels eventually proceed to the far larger, heavily salted water bodies. So it should be possible for machines equipped with detection gear to seek out such watercourses and determine if any traces of energetic elements appear in them."

"But that would only determine one axis," said Vantarsilas. "Unless..."

"The watercourse may be followed until the signal grows stronger. Precisely, Group Leader. While this method samples less area than a regular grid search, it is much faster per machine. It also differentiates possible sites that are close to watercourses, which may be useful. Arctilantar has speculated that the sedimentary type of rock found near such watercourses should be much softer and more readily mined than the hard volcanic rock we have encountered previously in our region."

"Speculated," said Vantarsilas.

"Yes. It estimates eighty percent probability. But the process will have to be attempted at a potential mine site to determine fully if it will work."

Vantarsilas shifted in unease. "We no longer have enough strength to establish and defend a full holdfast in a new location. The fuel-refining machinery is too valuable to risk without such defenses – how far away from the holdfast would it need to be moved? Further than our previous mining attempts?"

"It might be many hundreds of telequel. But, Group Leader, the refining does not need to take place at the mine site. Due to the prevalence of element 12 in this world's atmosphere and rock, element 92 can be chemically linked to element 12 in the initial process of extraction, while separating it from other rock elements such as 14. It is a powerful reaction and requires little energy input with our catalyzing techniques. Once the 92-12 compound is extracted, it is compact enough to transport back to the Holdfast where it can be refined for use as fuel. Raqtinoctil has tested this process with other, more common elements, and it is working."

Vantarsilas digested this for a few moments. Taldarnilis tried to gauge whether it would be wise to present Raqtinoctil's *other* idea. It was so radical that it could very well shock Vantarsilas into refusing any new practices altogether. Part of it had originated with the goodprey. And it might not even be necessary if a mine site could be located nearby...

"Using water as a detection medium," muttered Vantarsilas. "Only on a mad world such as this one could it even be contemplated... Very well!" It shook itself in determination. "There is no time to waste. Have you determined how many machines remain to us that carry detection apparatus?"

Taldarnilis felt its own approval and excitement echoed on the link. "Four, Group Leader. With six armed machines to escort them, that would allow for two scouting groups. They would proceed to the coast and divide into a group moving north along it, and one moving south. The southern group would require caution in how far they travel due to the large prey concentration two hundred telequel to the south."

"And the northern group must halt at our border with Group 32."

"Of course," said Taldarnilis. "Although, if energetic elements *are* detected within that watercourse, it is arguably worth pursuing as the origin might still be within our territory. After all, Group 32 is heavily engaged with the prey along its eastern borders. Our activity in this region would only be helpful to them by providing a diversion."

"That is true," agreed Vantarsilas. "They must pursue all available possibilities. Our group's future is at stake. Impress this upon all members of the Race that you command."

"Command?"

"Yes. You will take one of the fighting machines, and lead the overall expedition. Upon division, you will then lead the northern exploration group. Does this please you, Taldarnilis?"

"It does, Group Leader." The mental traffic on the link was also blooming with approval, despite the fact that this would be Taldarnilis' first sally against the prey in one of the fighting machines. While aware of this, it was determined to uphold its peers' expectations.

The fortunes of Group 31 were about to be reversed.

October, 1911, Washington, D.C.

Captain Willard Lang stepped up to the marble-tiled landing and paused, waiting for General Funston to catch up. The skylight overhead flooded the stairwell with welcoming light. It was the first welcoming thing he'd encountered in the War and Navy Building; there were hundreds of doors in the enormous structure, and it seemed like every one had been slammed in his face over the past week here in Washington.

Funston leaned on the rail beside him. He puffed a few breaths and grimaced at Lang. "They're trying to kill me, you know. Every appointment is on a different floor."

"Goddamned staff officers. Can't trust any of them."

Funston's smile was momentary. "Lang, this may be our last chance to get any further support from Washington. It took six months to get this meeting. Leonard Wood's a decent man, but he's under a great deal of pressure from others closer to home than we are. So when we go in there, don't mention any of our own projects back in Texas – rockets, the LRSC, anything of the sort. I don't want him to jump to the idea that we're handling things fine on our own."

"Sir, are you asking me to–"

"I'm *telling* you to leave the talking to me and supply information when you're asked to. Alright?"

"Yes, sir."

"Come on, then." They proceeded down the hallway and turned in at Wood's outer office. They were quite early – Funston would leave nothing to chance for this – and Wood's aide, a close-faced major, had nothing to offer them except a pair of the oak chairs along one side of the room; chairs that Lang's rump had grown all too familiar with. They warmed them for a time, each mentally rehearsing what he should – or shouldn't – say. His leg began to ache, as it still tended to do when seated; the burns were only second-degree, but they healed slowly. Then Funston elbowed him in the ribs.

He looked over and saw the Chief of Staff framed in the outer doorway, frozen halfway through a step. For a moment, Wood looked as though he'd rather turn around and leave, but he managed a smile and continued on into the room. Lang rose along with the general.

"Good to see you, Freddy! How was your trip?"

"Not too bad, Leonard, not too bad. More than the usual delays on the trains, though. Good God, but there's a lot of military traffic on the roads! Mile after mile of tanks and guns. Why in hell can't some of that be sent my way?"

Wood grimaced; Lang carefully did not. The general's idea of subtlety... Wood looked exhausted, and the fresh scar on his forehead must be related to the surgery he'd had the previous year. The fact that no one could replace him despite that meant there was no one else to turn to. "Come into my office and we'll discuss it. I guess you've met my aide, Semancik, here?"

"Yes, and this is Captain Willard Lang, my aide. He's been with me since Albuquerque." Lang shook hands. All three proceeded into Wood's private office. Semancik poured coffee and then withdrew.

"So, General, what's your situation?" asked Wood.

"I brought a detailed report, but in plain words, my situation stinks. You've given me an absolutely impossible task, General!"

"I know I have, but you're the best I've got, Freddy."

"Don't try to butter me up, Leonard! I learned all about impossible situations when I was a volunteer with the Cuban insurrectionists in '97. But they had it easy compared to this!" Funston was growing flushed as he spoke; that was a bad sign. "I've got nine divisions of regulars and seven more of Texas Volunteers, and you expect me to defend a line two thousand miles long! You've got sixty divisions on the Mississippi to defend a line barely half that length!"

"And you know perfectly well why that is, General," said Wood.

"Because Texas doesn't matter to the stuffed shirts and millionaires back east!"

"I think it would be more fair to say that the east matters more, not that Texas doesn't matter at all."

"Fair?! Fair!" Funston's cup clattered onto the saucer; he gestured with a fist. "When the Martians punch through my lines like they were tissue paper—and they will!—what am I supposed to tell my men and the civilians I'm defending? 'Yes, I know it's not *fair*, but Washington won't let me defend you'!"

"Freddy, calm down. I don't have to tell you the score. If we lose the east, it's the whole shooting match. I have to protect the cities and the factories. There's no choice, damn it!"

Wood's voice had risen too. Lang guessed what Funston's reaction to such an immovable object would be. He jumped in. "We're well aware of the situation, sir. But unless you look at Texas as just a forlorn hope, we are going to need more equipment. Men we've got, but they can't fight Martians with nothing but rifles. If we can't be better supplied, perhaps we should acknowledge that – and pull everyone back across the Mississippi rather than risk sacrificing them all."

Both senior officers swung to look at him. Lang suddenly knew what a lightning rod felt like in a storm; but it was worth it if it de-escalated things. Funston clenched and opened his fists, taking the opportunity to curb his temper.

"We *are* sending you equipment," growled Wood.

"But not enough," countered Funston more calmly. "My regulars don't have half the artillery and tanks as your troops on the Mississippi, and the volunteers have got virtually nothing heavier than a machine gun. As Lang says, with all the refugees, we could field twice the number of volunteer organizations, but we don't even have rifles and machine guns for them!"

Wood nodded. He rubbed at his scar as he spoke. "All right, Freddy, all right. I've got two new regular divisions, just completing their organization. I was going to send them to First Army, but I'll give them to you, instead."

"That would be wonderful, Leonard. But it's still not enough."

Wood lifted his hand palm-outward. "I'll also divert some tanks and artillery your way. There are a dozen train loads heading out to California, but things are still so quiet out there, I'll send them to you instead."

"That's good. I'll tell you, I've been damn tempted to grab those trains passing west! Hard to see all that equipment and not get any of it."

"So far you've gotten twice as much as we've sent to the west coast. We can't totally ignore them, you know."

"They don't need as much with all those mountains protecting them. Most of my line is stark naked."

"I'm also going to give you another gift. You've probably heard that we're starting production of a small rocket launcher for use by the infantry…"

"I've heard. When can we get some?"

"I'll send you the first thousand that come out of the factories, the very first, Freddy. You have top priority." Lang managed to suppress a grin. That was more like it! The weapons were short-ranged, but packed a lot more punch than anything the infantry had so far. And if the rockets could be made bigger...

"That's good," said Funston grudgingly, "but what we really need is the ability to produce weapons right there in Texas. Can't anything be done?"

Lang and the general carefully did *not* glance at one another as he spoke. Wood shook his head. "Texas doesn't have the infrastructure for that sort of thing. We can't just pack up and send you a tank factory, Freddy. Well, we could, but it wouldn't do you any good because there are no steel mills or foundries there. Texas has cattle and cotton and not a whole lot else."

"They've got oil."

"Yes, some. And I know there's the potential for a whole lot more, but you can't build tanks out of oil. It would take years to create the sort of industrial base you'd need. No, we'll ship the tanks to you. It just makes sense."

Funston snorted and frowned. "Well, if that's the best you can do…"

"Right now, it is. But, let me tell you about our future plans. The president wants an offensive as soon as possible and…"

"I bet he does! Everyone does!"

"Yes. And we are drawing up plans for some very deliberate advances starting next spring. We will move along a few routes, heavily fortifying them as we go to protect our lines of communication. I'm going to urge that one of the routes start out along the Arkansas River. As we advance, we will take over the defense of that part of your line. Your forces can then be redeployed to reinforce other areas. That two-thousand-mile line of yours will shrink and shrink."

Funston considered that and then nodded. "That would help. But if the Martians hit us hard somewhere else, we will be in trouble."

"I know, I know. But we'll have to deal with that when it happens. Sorry, Freddy." Wood rose to his feet slowly, but with a clear air of finality. Funston and Lang stood and shook hands.

"Thank you for your time, General," said Funston.

"Good luck, Freddy."

Funston walked quickly out of the office, not even looking at Semancik. Lang pursued and caught up to him at the hallway's end.

"Not enough," growled Funston. He was gripping the landing rail hard enough to mottle his hands. *"Not enough."*

"Sir–"

"When they come, the line will not hold. We'll have to give ground, but how much..." He half-turned to Lang. "Well. There will be time enough to plan what we must do. You'd better make sure that we do receive what the general promised... before someone else gets hold of it. Get the details worked out with his aide."

"Yes, sir."

"I'm going for a walk around the block – which should be just about right, given the size of them around here – and then I'll join you there." Funston pushed off from the railing and began to descend the stairs.

Lang watched the small figure disappear down the flight for a moment, then made his way back to Semancik's office, where he unpacked his satchel and spent a useful hour going over shipment composition and times. Semancik worked efficiently and impersonally, feeding the raw material of war onto railways and rivers, directing it to where it would be consumed. It was easy to believe that he'd played a role in moving a million men to date. To a former platoon commander, the scale was daunting. *This truly is a war between worlds*, thought Lang. *And I thought Texas was big...*

He was just thanking Semancik for his help when Funston returned. The general looked better; the fresh air had agreed with him. He was clutching a newspaper that he'd picked up, and after thanking Semancik in his turn, he waved it at Lang as they walked out of the office. "The New York Philharmonic is in town and Stransky's conducting. He took over after poor Mahler died. Beethoven's Symphony Number 5 in C Minor... Smetana, *The Bartered Bride*, now there's something exotic. Do you follow classical music, Captain?"

"Not at all, sir."

"We've done all we can here. There's just the meeting tomorrow morning with Harry Ward. I'll attend the performance tonight." They left the War and Navy Building and paused outside on the sidewalk. "Care to try it?"

"How much are the tickets, sir?"

"Two dollars."

"That's a lot."

Funston shrugged. "The prostitutes here would charge you more than that. It's an expensive town. But what else are you going to spend it on?"

The concert venue was packed with well-heeled Washingtonians, although there were plenty of uniforms as well. Lang still felt ill at ease moving through the crowd;

many of those uniforms were tailored. But enough people who greeted Funston acknowledged him as well that it would have been boorish to keep aside.

One swell in an evening coat insisted on a handshake. "It's an honor to shake hands with a man wearing that." He nodded to the Distinguished Service Cross on Lang's dress uniform.

"Ah. Thanks." Prendergast had gotten him that; Funston seemed to regard the events of Lang's rearguard fight last year as ordinary. And compared to some of the things he'd pulled off, perhaps it was...

The orchestra began making odd noises and they sought their seats. Funston explained a few things while Lang tried to keep up; then the proper music began and he settled in to listen. He was pretty sure that some of the higher notes were escaping him; having a cal fifty fired over one's head could do that. But the deeper thrum of the big strings was strangely moving.

He glanced over at Funston, who was listening with his eyes closed. Some of the deep lines scored in his face had smoothed. If the musicians were accomplishing nothing else tonight, that would do... He looked back to the stage and did his best to emulate the general.

When the performance finished, Funston shook himself and rose. As they eased out of the rows, he asked, "What did you think?"

"I think," said Lang – to his own surprise – "that it's something else to fight for. Can't imagine Martians creating something that lovely, sir." And indeed the fancy instruments, the art of it all, seemed less of a luxury than when he'd arrived.

"Nor can I."

"Although if I have to listen to *The Stars and Stripes Forever* one more time... Do they always end with that?"

"Always. At least nowadays."

As the crowd began to filter out, a large man in a frock coat caught sight of Funston and approached. "Good evening. Do I have the honor of addressing General Funston?"

"That's me."

"Allow me to introduce myself. I am the Mexican Ambassador to the United States of America, Enrique Creel. Your reputation precedes you, General." Lang looked sharply at him, but he didn't seem sarcastic. There had been criticism after Albuquerque from people with no right to open their mouths about it...

Funston returned Creel's bow. "Are you here for the music, Ambassador?"

"Yes. The Philharmonic is remarkable. I have traveled to New York to patronize them a few times." Creel edged them all aside from the crowd's flow without visible effort. "General, may I speak to you as one music patron – as one man – to another?"

"Very well."

"I have heard of your tremendous energy in defending Texas – and I admire it. All men must fight these dreadful invaders. However, there may come a time when a military situation arises that you may judge requires you to move forces across the border into Mexico. And we both know there are certain men now residing in San Antonio and Laredo who might take action of their own. These are delicate matters. The... lines of communication between your governor's office, your military command, and my own office may need to be strengthened, so that we may work as one. Perhaps your aide," he nodded to Lang, "and my junior secretary might strike up a correspondence? I would not trouble you yourself, General; you must have many duties."

"So does he," said Funston neutrally, "but we'll consider it."

"Excellent! It will be a relief to me to know this. I have family in Chihuahua province, you know – the Terranzas. Their safety, and that of their many properties there – and their American counterparts; we work together as one – concern me at all times. And I may say that even President Diaz himself would welcome another protector, a military protector, into the fold of our prosperity."

"Well, thank you, Ambassador. That's interesting."

Creel beamed. "So I'd hoped. Good evening, gentlemen." He merged with the crowd.

Funston glanced at Lang. "I think that was the slickest bribe I've ever heard. Agreed?"

"Oh, yes. What happens when we don't take it?"

"That will be interesting. Although I suspect they will have their hands full in the south for some time." Funston smiled wistfully. "Willard, you do have a peculiar opportunity here. I *could* let you confer with these men – I trust you not to jeopardize any of our own war effort or shirk your duties – and it would be a remarkable connection for you if you do become a lawyer some day. Movers and shakers abound here in Washington. I don't see you as a career Army man, and that's fine. But you might do better than just practicing law in North Texas."

Lang shook his head. "No, thank you, sir. It's true, I don't wish to have your job..." *I couldn't sleep with your job. How do you?* "But I'll stick with mine, and with Texas. If that means that prosecuting claim jumpers is the peak of my career after – after the Army, well, I'll be happy to be alive and free."

"Good fellow. Still, the ambassador does have a point. If we confine our efforts to simply protecting what's within our own borders, whether state or national, and wait for the Martians to attack us..." Funston's face darkened. "Are you familiar with Napoleon's maxim on defensive war?"

"No, sir."

"The inevitable conclusion of a defensive war is surrender."

Their last task in Washington was to call on Harry Ward, the owner of the Ward Leonard Electric Company, one of the few contacts that Governor Colquitt had been able to make within the federal effort to exploit Martian technology. They located a hastily constructed set of buildings on the eastern outskirts of the city; the cab dropped them off in front of a clapboard office. Lang considered the horse-drawn vehicle clopping away down the dirt road and wondered at the task of prying out secrets from machines that had crossed from another planet. *Well, dammit, if they can learn to do something, we can.* Texas needed its own weapon industries – new ones, if the old ones couldn't be supported – and they'd have to accomplish in months what might normally take years...

They found Harry Ward inside by a drafting table; he brightened when they approached and tossed aside a metal triangle. "You must be General Funston!"

"Yes, and this is my aide, Lang."

"Pleased to meet you."

"I'm glad we could catch you here," said Funston.

"Sure do meet more people in Washington. I'm usually back at the main company offices in Bronxville, the town in New York that nobody's heard of. What can I do for you?"

"The governor was wondering if you'd had a chance to consider his offer to come work for us in Texas."

"Ah." Ward leaned back against the table and crossed his arms. "You see, I have been giving it some thought. Problem is, I can't leave my company right now. We've been called in to work for Edison's team on the coil hysteresis problem." At Lang's puzzlement, he added, "The way the Martian power cells store electricity. Normally, when you stop charging a coil, the charge persists for a while. But with the Martian coils, it depends on whether the lengths of wire that had been adjacent in the original winding are still together or not. If they're not, they behave differently – but that shouldn't happen. We don't know why it does yet."

"Mr. Ward, we really need your help."

"I appreciate that. Now, I did mention the idea to an old friend I've worked with in the past, Granville Woods. He's about my age –" Ward looked to be in his fifties – "but not in the best of health, frankly. He came out to work with Edison last year, sort of coming out of retirement, but he had a stroke. Pretty bad one. At least we got him to a hospital right away. If he'd been alone in that New York City apartment of his, I don't want to think... Anyway, he's made something of a recovery, but there's no place for him upstate any more since Edison replaced him. He's here in the Washington plant, pitching in where he can, and I'd truly like to see him in a dryer climate. I think it'd do him good – not to mention his doing some real work again. He's being overlooked."

"What work has he done before?" asked Lang.

"Electrical engineering, same as me. But Granville – well, he figured out how to push a telephone signal over a telegraph wire... from a moving train. No one thought that was possible until he did it. If you're trying for an angle on some Martian machinery, he ought to have a good chance to figure one."

Funston considered this. "Do you think he'd be willing to go?"

"I talked to him this morning. He'd be happy to take my place. In fact, he can leave today."

"Well, Mr. Ward, we're kind of getting used to making do. If you're vouching for him, that's fine. Why don't we go over to meet him and set up an arrangement? I'm sure we could find another ticket for him on our train back. There's room in our compartment. If he's ready to leave, no sense wasting time."

"Ah," said Ward. "Right. Ah, Granville won't be able to ride with you. He's colored."

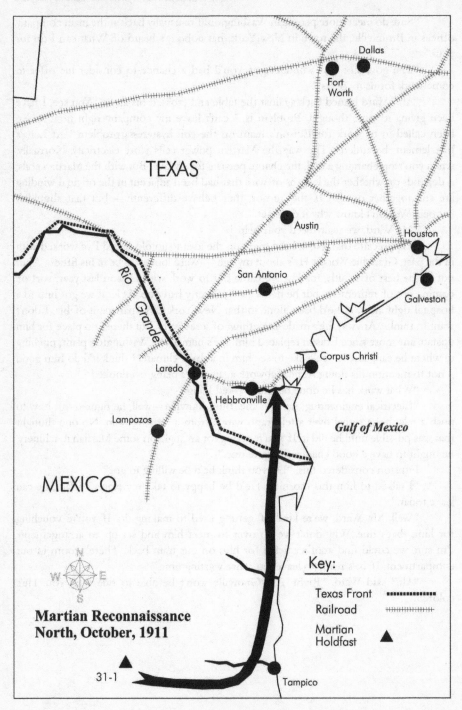

TEXAS

Dallas

Fort
Worth

Austin

Houston

San Antonio

Galveston

Rio Grande

Corpus Christi

Laredo

Hebbronville

Gulf of Mexico

Lampazos

MEXICO

Key:

Texas Front
Railroad
Martian
Holdfast

**Martian Reconnaissance
North, October, 1911**

31-1

Tampico

Chapter Six

October, 1911, Tampico, Mexico

Henri Gamelin could not sleep.

That was unusual for him. He'd shrugged off the disjointing transfer from naval liaison in Veracruz to this assignment of first lieutenant of the gunboat *Velocite* – an amusing name for a shallow-draft gun platform that could just manage eleven knots. But the warm tropical nights reminded him of his time on the Mekong River. Too often, as now, he found himself topside at the small hours; and, as now, thinking of a certain girl in Saigon he'd left behind three months ago. The argument had been ferocious – and pointless. Could a lieutenant marry? Of course not. It was only a thing for the moment. But there was always another side to any affair between citizens of the colonizing power and the possession. Perhaps it was only about possession to begin with...

The night was utterly black; the shore twenty yards away almost invisible, only a hint of the mass of trees adjoining the river. The soft slop of water and scent of vegetation were more definite. *Velocite* was moored five miles west of Tampico's town and port, part of the inland defensive lines that linked together several miles-wide lakes and lagoons surrounding the port – those, perhaps, the only impenetrable defense against Martian tripods. Soldiers of II Corps' 22nd Division manned the three miles of scrub and grassland to Henri's left. To the right and north of the river, the 12th was interspersed among the lagoons and swamplands. It was unhealthy country; disease might kill more men than any Martian attack if they stayed for years.

At Tampico port, a few old British warships cluttered the river mouth. *Velocite*, though, was the only French vessel at the moment, and she was attached to the 22nd division in a peculiar arrangement; a dangerous liaison as their 'riverine component'. As General Mangin had said, the French Navy must tread carefully in Tampico. President Diaz chose his allies carefully and often pitted them against one another, lest one grow too powerful; and while the French defended Veracruz alone, and manned Tampico's inland defenses, the British were permitted to protect their oil interests in Tampico itself.

Henri paced slowly past the lookout and murmured a greeting. *Velocite* herself never slept. Others might trust in the western mountains to protect them, but *Capitane de corvette* Auphan kept his ship vigilant. Both of the 100mm guns, bow and stern, were manned at all times. It meant grumbling from a small crew, but Henri and his fellow lieutenant, Charest, dealt with that. Three weeks of discipline and organization aboard a moored ship; he was accepted, but not challenged. Given long enough, as the British said, they might run aground on their own empty food tins...

A red flare soared upward in the northwest. For a moment, something taller than a building loomed in the red glow, like a ship's tripod mast that walked on land. Henri spun and rushed past the gaping lookout, threw open the bridge door and shouted. "Sound the general alarm!"

The alarm squalled through the gunboat, and *Velocite* woke to battle.

Cycle 597,844.9, Coastal Region, Mexico

"Commander! We have contacted the prey!"

Taldarnilis noted the report just as an illumination device spiked the night. Minor fortifications and projectile-throwers were visible a telequel ahead, well out of the prey's range of sight in darkness, but a hidden group of prey must have observed their passage even so.

The expedition had been timed for the minimum illumination of this world's enormous moon, which the prey were considered capable of seeing by. That had allowed them to probe stealthily as they approached the shoreline, avoiding the large bodies of water in their path and two defensive concentrations of prey, visible by enhanced starlight. The map was growing more complete as they worked southward, but now Taldarnilis faced an uncalculatable choice. Withdraw and probe again further south, hoping for a more open route but with the prey now alerted? Or follow the twisting riverbank? There was a smoothed track visible there which often linked the prey's habitation centers, implying a good route with no risk of a tripod bogging. But the prey's most dangerous war machines floated on water. A small one floated nearby; more, and larger, might be ahead.

We are not here to destroy — not yet. Taldarnilis activated all channels. "Follow the south river bank to the coast. Move at best speed. Conserve energy, fire only if attacked and do not stop."

Acknowledgments buzzed in return. Taldarnilis set its machine in rapid stride, closing on the river. Concussions sounded from the prey's lines, but it was a crossing target. The craft ahead posed greater threat; its weapon emplacements were turning. Taldarnilis targeted it and opened fire.

October, 1911, Tampico, Mexico

Henri's duty station was the aft 100mm gun. He jumped from the bridge ladder's last step, turned, and began to run aft. He'd gone three strides when a heat ray shrieked out of the night and lanced into the gunshield. White-hot metal lit the deck, throwing stark shadows as the beam sawed sideways. Behind him, the forward gun fired in a flat bang, jolting the deck. Henri ran on, throwing an arm across his face; then the ready-use ammunition in the mount exploded.

The world shut off for an unknown time, resolved slowly into a stench of smoke and flickering illumination. Henri became aware that he was crumpled in the lee of the port boat davits. Empty ropes dangled across him. His body would not obey him yet. Looking out over the side, head resting on the deck, he could see stuttering gun flashes that made no sound. A tripod loomed over them, strobed by them, striding east smoothly, rapidly. In moments, it was gone from sight. It had killed his ship without

62

breaking stride –

No! Henri pushed himself up from the deck, staggered to his feet. The aft gun mount was gone, the deck and hull torn asunder. Fires blazed in several spots, spreading, deadly. A wild-eyed crewman stumbled past; Henri grabbed his arm and jerked him to a stop. "Come on!" he shouted, his own voice tinny in his ears. "The number-two hose pump!"

He half-dragged the man to the pump station. The hoses seemed untorn; between the two men, they started the pump, wrestled the bulging hose aftward, and played the jet over the fires. The crewman – Joile, that was his name – seemed to gain composure as he worked; another joined them unasked.

Henri shouted in Joile's ear, "Keep this up as long as you see anything burning!" He clapped Joile on the shoulder, staggered forward to the bridge deck ladder, and clambered up.

All seemed strangely intact here. Captain Auphan nodded to him from where he bent over the voicepipes. Henri walked forward and looked over the foc's'le. The forward gun was wrecked, the half-melted barrel lying on the forepeak. Less damage to the hull from the explosion, but then, they'd fired off at least one shell... He remembered his duty and turned. "Damage report, Captain. Aft gun destroyed. Fires on aft deck, fire party is in action."

"It is the same forward," said Auphan. He looked haggard but calm. "The enemy has moved off east. I've ordered steam up, and the engine seems intact, but we are flooding both fore and aft. Lieutenant Charest and five men killed forward. Fires there nearly out. We are out of action, my friend."

"But not sunk. Permission to form a work party to repair the leaks?"

"Granted. Clearly they are moving toward Tampico as fast as they can. I do not know what we can do there, but we must go!"

Henri set off, mentally ordering tools and materials.

Cycle 597,844.9, Coastal Region, Mexico

Taldarnilis' fighting machine continued eastward at maximum speed beside the riverbank. The enhancement of its display panel also flattened the landscape somewhat, but it had learned to allow for that, and its stride was true to the ground's visible solid areas. They had broken contact and nothing could follow them! The other nine machines followed, although they had drawn apart as some struggled with the terrain.

Ahead, the skyglow of a prey habitation was drawing closer. Taldarnilis slowed its pace and opened a channel.

"Raqtinoctil, consolidate your group. Northern group, consolidate upon me." After a short time, the various machines drew together in two groups. "There will be many prey nearby when we reach the shoreline. Again, do not spend energy on attacks unless you are threatened. Raqtinoctil, when you return, I recommend you avoid this area by several telequel and find a new route back to the holdfast. I will do the same."

"Understood, Commander."

Taldarnilis disengaged and focused on steady movement. The river widened steadily as it curved from side to side. A habitation center appeared to the north side of it, speckled with lights. Floating machines in the river offered no threat as yet – but there, one large one mounted weapons. A tendril of light stabbed out from its upper area, brilliant in the enhanced view. Taldarnilis flicked its heat ray over it and silenced it. *Onward!* Concussions boomed out. A projectile rang stunningly on its machine's armor; it lurched and pressed on. Had it chosen correctly? More of the armed machines were visible now. Enough of this fire could cripple and destroy their machines... The river swung left, and ahead Taldarnilis saw a vast open body of water. *We have arrived!* The two groups approached the shoreline, projectiles exploding around them. They divided, Raqtinoctil's group moving off south, fading into the darkness. Taldarnilis and the other two armed machines strode north, firing quick bursts along the floating machines. Another light-tendril was quickly snuffed out. The wide river mouth slowed their progress for a time; another machine staggered as it was hit, but then they were on solid ground again and leaving the concentration behind. The floating machines had not stirred yet.

"We have won free," signaled Taldarnilis. "Proceed north one telequel, then machines Two, Five, and Six deploy detection apparatus. Let our work begin."

October, 1911, Tampico, Mexico

Dawn showed the port of Tampico buzzing with activity as *Velocite* drew up at dockside, low in the water, sluggish, but alive. Henri, exhausted from his night's labors, supervised their mooring. Beside them, the Apollo-class cruiser *HMS Brilliant* towered over the battered gunboat; minor damage was visible in her upperworks.

"She has been in a fight, but not our sort of fight," observed Captain Auphan when Henri reported back. "I feared those oil tanks downriver would be pyres by now. It's strange; the *monstres* ran through without doing any real amount of damage. Clearly they were on their way to something." His face darkened. "A pity they did not choose another route. Twelve dead, Henri. And she may never fight again."

"She could be repaired. New guns. Underwater storage for the ammunition, we lift up only one round at a time..."

"Later, later." Auphan studied him a moment. "Henri, I hate to ask it, but there is a message from shore demanding a liaison officer for the Navy. You are all we have in that regard. Could you..."

"Of course, Captain." Henri scrubbed at his eyes, braced himself erect, and saluted. "I'll go ashore at once. Where do I need to go?"

"The offices of the English Baron Cowdray, the Mexican Eagle Oil Company, in the building opposite the Imperial Hotel. That is—"

"Beside the plaza, one block east." Henri ghosted a smile. "I had my shore leave planned weeks ago, Captain."

"I am unsurprised." Auphan waved him on his way.

He took a moment to grab a fresh uniform jacket from his cabin and discard the scorched one of the night before; then a dockside scramble, a short walk, and a hailed cab brought him into the old city center. All looked bustling, peaceful, and prosperous here. Henri could not be angry about that. *Velocite* and others stood between this and the Martians, after all. But he missed Charest keenly.

The *Aguila Mexica* staff were in a turmoil of their own, but they showed him up at once five stories to a large, well-appointed corner office. Baron Cowdray rose to a considerable height behind his desk and stepped to its side to extend a hand. "Thank you for coming, my dear fellow. I am sorry to hear your vessel suffered serious losses. Is there anything my company may do to help? We have our own medical staff in country, you see."

"Thank you, but no, *Monsieur le Baron*. The Royal Navy has so kindly taken on our wounded aboard *Brilliant*. We received your communique – how may I help *you*?"

"Please, sit. I'll have something to eat brought up – a tea." They settled; the chair was so comfortable, Henri instantly feared he'd fall asleep. "Now. About our Navy. I have a considerable stake in this oil terminal – I came out to supervise it myself a month ago – and the Navy promised us protection in the form of these three cruisers. But they're terribly out of date – *Brilliant* is twenty years old! Worn out. She can scarcely make fifteen knots now, they tell me. The others are little better. We all saw how rapidly those damned machines ran through the port! They must certainly be miles along the coast by now. Even if *Brilliant* could somehow catch up and find them, they could outrun her. And if they were to turn back, return here, while these ships were away looking for them..."

Henri nodded. "You would be without defense."

"I appreciate the delicacy of relations among colonial powers in such matters. But if it were at all possible for the French Navy to assist us in the pursuit of these machines, I would be extremely grateful, and I may confide that His Majesty's Government would be as well."

Henri smiled. "You do not need to ask Admiral Favereau more than once to strike at Martians, *Monsieur le Baron*. If he can, I am sure he will. If you could direct me to a telegraph office?"

"We have one downstairs."

"Then I can send a priority signal." Henri paused to consider which ships might be spared. *Gueydon*, perhaps, or *Jeanne d'Arc*, the pride of the squadron...

"Splendid!" Cowdray's voice jolted Henri from encroaching sleep. "Perhaps someone will have sighted those devils by the time your ships arrive. We'll welcome them royally. Which reminds me – let's bring your tea along, shall we?"

Henri could not remember ever enjoying an English tea as much as that one.

The reply telegram ordered Henri to attend upon the vice-admiral aboard *Jeanne d'Arc* the following morning. This was no simple matter, as the three cruisers proceeding from Veracruz were not intending to put into port at Tampico; but after inquiring at several points around the harbor, Henri located a steam launch that was willing to take him outside the port in the morning. Any unsecured boat had long since been hired away or stolen by those trying to leave Mexico for safer ground.

At sunup, they had cleared the river mouth, and the launch was pitching with the long steady swoop of the Atlantic swells. "There'll be a storm in a day or so," predicted the boatman. He pointed to the eastern sky blazing with golds and reds. "High cloud there. But you'll be snug enough on one of those big ships."

The 4th Light Cruiser Division appeared in the south by ten o'clock. Henri watched their approach with admiration. *Jeanne d'Arc* led the way, the admiral's flagship, with her inward-sloping sides and tall observation towers giving her the appearance of a gray steel castle put into motion. Magnificent! Then the armored cruisers *Gueydon* and *Dupetit-Thouars*, more contemporary in their design. All three were fast and powerful ships, built to raid British commerce and sink their protecting warships in some future war which strategists had planned for but which, mercifully, had never come about. Now they pursued a common enemy instead. The secondary guns bristling from their sides were as large as *Velocite's* two main ones, and Henri doubted a Martian heat ray could pierce their thick armor.

He read the flag signals from *Jeanne d'Arc's* bridge wing and relayed the directions to the boatman, who swung them onto a parallel course as the big cruiser gradually slowed. The other two warships drew on ahead; the launch edged up cautiously to the looming steel hull, angling toward the boat platform. Crewmen hooked on, and Henri scrambled up the wet metal ladder to board the ship.

Other crew members directed him on his way. By the time he'd climbed several ladders and stairwells to reach the forward tower, *Jeanne d'Arc* was building speed again. Henri reported to the officer of the deck on the lower bridge, asked for the admiral, and was escorted up one deck further to the flying deck.

He found Vice-Admiral Charles Favereau at the forward rail and joined him. A light north breeze added to the ship's own twenty-one knot speed, whistling across the deck, cool and refreshing. The horizon was far broader from this height; shoreline to port, open sea to starboard, twin wakes of the other cruisers ahead and slowly closing.

"I fear we missed them in the night," said Favereau. "The ones who went south, that is. But others are looking for them now. We have a good chance to catch the ones traveling north, if they are still on the shoreline and have not found good going at all times." He smiled at Henri as to a private joke. "I was glad to get out of an office and onto the sea again. This is not the built-up puddle of the Mediterranean! Look at that jungle, those mountains beyond; we might be in the South Seas!"

"Do you suppose the Martians are there too, sir?"

Favereau scowled. "They are likely to be everywhere. Except Europe! Do you know, Gamelin, there are politicians at home who still feel there is no danger to France herself? 'Let the lesser races perish,' they say, 'they are not worth French lives. When the Martians rule those lands, we can trade with them instead.' The stupidity is mind-boggling, but any excuse will do for inaction, yes?

"Like General Mangin, I was promoted quickly because I was willing to serve here, outside of France and her immediate empire. I do not like Mangin's politics – monarchy is for the English! – but I am beginning to think there may come a time when he and I may agree on actions nonetheless. Perhaps now that you have seen action against the Martians, Mangin will be more disposed to hear you out?"

"It is possible, Admiral."

"Well, let us talk a while..."

By midday, Henri's belly was growling, and the admiral dismissed him to scrounge a meal along with his staff. But within the hour, Henri found himself topside again, staring forward, willing a sighting to take place...

When it did, it was not what he'd wanted. "Small craft, fine on the starboard bow!" called out a lookout from below. After a few moments, a crewman relayed his captain's report to the admiral, who spoke to his staff for a few moments and then gestured Henri to join him.

"It appears there are two refugee craft there. One has capsized and the other is standing by it, but this wind is pushing them south. I will not stop, of course. But we can drop off a steam launch to render assistance. Gamelin, I know you have reason to want to be in at the strike, but Captain LeBlanc has an opportunity here to weld his crew in action, and to detach one of them now, well..."

Henri nodded despite the pang he felt. "I understand. It is their ship, not mine. Who is the boat chief?"

"Suzerann. He is a good man. The launch is being readied now."

"Then I'll join them. Good hunting, sir." Henri saluted the admiral and left the open deck, making his way back through the ship's decks and ladders to the boat platform. By the time he reached it, the launch was already lowered into place a few feet above the water – a quick feat of seamanship, especially given the cruiser's tumblehome – and the crew of eight had readied it. Salt spray kicked high from the ship's bow wave. Henri boarded the launch, spoke briefly with the grizzled Suzerann, and *Jeanne d'Arc* slowed once again to a few knots to allow them to make the jolting descent into the water.

As the cruiser drew away from them, Henri sighted the two boats to the south and seaward. The launch proceeded toward them, puffing smoke and rolling heavily. The upright boat was a fishing dory rigged with a single pole mast; the capsized one looked to be some sort of barge or punt, hopeless in any seaway.

At close approach, there proved to be thirty people in total, most crammed onto the dory and some still clinging to the barge. Henri directed that those be recovered first; even here in the Gulf, the water was cool in October. He called out orders and reassurances in Spanish, but it was still a slow and clumsy affair to bring them inboard. He was lending a hand to pull in a man in soaked overalls when a distant rumble sounded from the north.

"Is the storm closer?" panted the man. "We should hurry! They have been bailing in the dory like madmen."

"No," said Henri. "That is gunfire." The sound twisted in him like a knife; but he made himself *not* look outboard. He had his task.

Cycle 597,844.9, Coastal Region, Mexico

Taldarnilis had not anticipated how *long* the sampling process would take.

Each watercourse they came to mean that the two detection-equipped machines must stop, prepare the equipment, and commence a tedious process of pacing from point to point, lowering almost to the water surface, taking in samples, and then analyzing them. The quantity required was large, and water was a shockingly heavy fluid, so each area must be studied, and approved or rejected, while they were in that place. It understood that the entire process had been improvised and that this planet often presented unexpected challenges to the simplest of tasks; but at times, it wished that Raqtinoctil had worked out a more polished way of doing things.

It was also routine for one or more machines to become mired in poor footing despite the modified digit-plates they had fitted to spread the weight over a larger surface. Raqtinoctil had developed a method for another machine to pull out the stuck one, but it was awkward and had no guarantee of success. Still, they had lost no machines so far...

"Negative report, Commander." That was the nineteenth of the day. Raqtinoctil's machine shifted, raised, and plodded toward the next point of analysis.

"Commander! Prey machines approaching from the south!"

Taldarnilis swiveled its machine. Three large floating craft had appeared, trailing dense black clouds of smoke.

"Why did you not detect them earlier?"

"I abase myself, Commander. I was assisting Valpurtis' machine."

Taldarnilis computed ranges and times. "We have enough time to complete the survey. Armed machines, move closer to the shoreline and draw the prey's attention. All will withdraw inland upon completion of the survey task."

Taldarnilis joined its fellows near the water's edge and studied the floating machines as they drew closer. The profiles did not match those that had been stationed in their exit watercourse; these had been sent from elsewhere. There had been no time to disrupt the prey's crude long-distance communication system, and clearly, they used it to dispatch these craft. Still, they had a good distance yet to cover before their projectile-throwers would be in range...

Smoke erupted at both ends of the nearest craft. After a moment, the others also blossomed. Were they firing wildly? The projectiles would need to arc so high that no aim should be feasible...

A rushing sound overhead ended in six shattering explosions along the shoreline that spouted dirt and debris taller than their own machines' height. None were close enough to be any threat. Did the prey think to panic them? Taldarnilis did not give an order to return the fire; the prey craft were still well out of effective range. It was an uncomfortable sensation to be under fire and not to return it, but it would be a short time only...

More explosions struck the shoreline. Three of them appeared to be closer. That seemed to be outside of random chance... "Raqtinoctil. Is it possible the prey can correct the flight of projectiles over time?"

"It may be so, Commander. Provided that there is observation–" Six fresh explosions erupted nearby, one close enough to buffet Taldarnilis. A metal piece rang off the armor.

"All machines, withdraw inland now!" Taldarnilis set its own machine in motion. A larger crash of concussions sounded over the water behind it; after a few steps, the explosions burst again – but now, more than twenty! The volume of fire was greater than anything Taldarnilis had known.

"Commander! My machine is disabled!"

Taldarnilis swiveled in its stride. Patingras' machine had fallen on its side, one leg clearly wrecked. Even as it watched, more explosions burst out on both the near and far sides of the crippled machine. The prey's fire had become continuous. The time required to retrieve Patingras from the machine–

Is too long. "All machines continue inland at best speed." Taldarnilis backed a few steps despite the greater risk of misfooting, unable to look away. While the explosions continued to pound at their general area, more converged toward Patingras. Inevitably, one struck close beside it. When the dirt particles cleared, the machine was a jumbled wreck and Patingras undoubtedly slain.

Taldarnilis turned inland and sped its pace, chiding itself bitterly even as a flurry of more detonations pursued it and the others up the watercourse's path. These larger floating craft were even more dangerous than it had known. And if they could appear so quickly...

Raqtinoctil's plan might be their only hope now.

Chapter Seven

December, 1911, Laredo, Texas

Emmet Smith winced as the Ford Model T drifted toward the right verge of the road. The driver, Ranger Hicks, peered downward as he stamped at the pedals controlling the planetary gearing.

"Hicks, look out!"

Hicks' head jerked up; he sawed at the wheel, veering left. Behind him, Ranger Tomlinson cursed from the back seat. Fortunately, there wasn't much traffic on the road leading east out of Laredo; the military vehicles were all to the north where the 3rd Texas Volunteer Division was encamped.

"You have to do one thing at a time, but always keep steering," said Emmet patiently. "You'll get it."

"I can thread a horse through a damn needle," said Hicks. "I hate these machines."

Privately, Emmet considered that Hicks' tension wasn't helping his driving. The mayor of Laredo had telephoned the governor's office with a panicky warning of a riot brewing at the Mexican refugee camps east of the city. There were plenty of soldiers within a day's march, and a rail line ran right beside the camp... but the governor was not in favor of sending companies of troops into possible conflict.

Instead, he preferred to send handfuls of Rangers. Emmet wasted no time on feeling flattered; he was thinking too hard.

They'd spent an hour in Laredo closing down every saloon and bar in the city; it was always a good first step to shut off at least part of the liquor supply in the area. Hicks seemed pleased to be working with him again, but Tomlinson, a newbie, was an unknown; still, he'd handled the saloon owners briskly enough. "The vital thing," Emmet had told him, "is to never let them see you rattled. Then you're sunk."

The Model T might be shaking them all to pieces, but it beat arriving sweaty and footsore. Once they–

"Hey, what's this?" crowed Tomlinson. Emmet twisted around; the Ranger was holding a newspaper clipping he'd pulled from Hicks' saddlebag. "The Gen-you-*wine* Martian Gold Electro-Wire Hair Net! Guaranteed–"

"Gimme that!" Hicks lunged at him. Emmet grabbed the wheel and steered as Hicks snatched ineffectively at the clipping.

"Guaranteed to reverse hair loss, in-*vig*-orate the scalp, excite the follicles – Why, Hicks, you need your follicles excited?"

"Leave him be," said Emmet. "Hicks, get back to the road, hey?" He turned over

71

the wheel. "You're not going bald. Not really. Besides, that thing's probably brass wire anyway. There's a mess of these snake-oil operators nowadays. If they really tried to grab some of that stuff off a Martian wreck, they'd likely get shot."

"Speaking of that..." said Tomlinson.

"Like I said. Bring the Winchesters, but sling 'em. Keep your palms out, take up a lot of room. Numbers don't mean anything, it's all about staying calm." He didn't like the edge behind Tomlinson's horsing, but the junior man usually followed what the rest did.

Ahead, a sea of dingy white tents appeared. A *lot* of tents. The rail line angled in from the north, passing them by where two large wooden shacks had been thrown up. Emmet pointed. "Over there, Hicks, head for that siding." Four rail cars were parked there; freighters, maybe? A food delivery?

It was difficult to tell, because there were nearly a thousand people standing in front of them.

"Jesus Christ," said Tomlinson in a small voice.

"Really? Well, that'd explain this here crowd." Emmet scanned the group as the car drew up to them, looking for weapons, expressions, postures, and leaders. Nothing spoke to threat – so far. No guns in sight, but the loose Mexican shirts and shawls could hide those. A townsman in a dark suit stood at one edge, talking to others but turning to look as they drove up. Beside him, a woman in a white dress.

"Well, well," said Emmet. "Hicks, stop here." He climbed out and slung his rifle, moving as slowly and deliberately as he would before a nervous horse. The others joined him, and they walked toward the crowd. The babble of voices faded as they approached. "Good morning," called out Emmet in Spanish. "I'm Ranger Smith, these are Rangers Tomlinson and Hicks. What's the trouble?"

He was looking at the townsman as he spoke, but he wasn't surprised when Jovita Idar replied instead of him. "They were promised doctors at this camp. It has been six months now and not one has come! There are sicknesses and injuries that are not being properly treated. Yesterday evening we sent a deputation to the clerks who run this place, and when they were refused, more people came. There was a train waiting, and all those clerks just climbed onto it and left!"

"I see," said Emmet. *And they went to the mayor, didn't want to admit they'd panicked and run, so a riot was born.* "Although you and that lady over there seem to be wearing uniforms – those caps. Are you nurses?"

"The *Cruz Blanca* is here, yes. Trying to do what is not being done by governments. Most are volunteers and not trained in medicine." People nearby murmured agreement; the crowd had spread slowly in two wings.

"We don't need any government at all," blurted the townsman. "The Martians have ended all that! People are free now."

"Have we met?" asked Emmet mildly.

The man drew himself up. "I am Antonio Targas. I and – and many others here, we follow the Flores Magon brothers. We put the government lackeys to flight!"

"If by that, you mean you chased away the people working to organize food for you, then yes. Do you have a way to get food for a thousand people, Señor Targas?"

"Yes! We march on the city, tomorrow."

"Laredo is a long walk from here. By the time you get there, the mayor will have troops brought in who will have no hesitation in shooting a bunch of *magonistas*. You don't want that. Here's what we'll do." Emmet pitched his voice to the crowd. "Good news, everyone! Señor Targas has agreed to travel to Laredo with us and look to getting some doctors for you!"

"I will not! Who knows what you'd do once we drive out of sight!"

"Well, if you're afraid, we'll just let these people choose someone else to represent them. I think I know who they will."

Targas glared at Emmet, his face working. He'd been outmaneuvered; if he refused, he'd seem weak.

"And who says you will not arrest him, or worse?" asked Jovita Idar. "I think he is right not to trust you."

"Why don't you come along too, then? This one is a nobody; yes, we could make him disappear if we were *that* sort. We're not... but just to make sure, half these people probably know you, and every one of them will see you leaving with us. I think you're pretty safe, Miss Idar. I know I wasn't very straight with you the last time we met, but I am now."

She considered it, studying him closely. "Very well."

"Better tell them to get ready for another food delivery tomorrow. We'll try to get things back to – well, back to something better than now. Anything you want to bring along?"

"These people came here with nothing. Why would I have brought baggage?" She turned and spoke rapidly to the man next to her. Others passed the word back; the crowd noise rose. Many individuals moved forward, clustering around Idar to pass messages, or perhaps just bid her farewell. Only a few in comparison were gathering to speak with Targas. It seemed she *was* well known here...

The harsh clack of a Winchester being cocked sounded behind him.

Emmet spun. Tomlinson was clutching the weapon in both hands – not pointing it yet, thank God, but it was a death grip. "Stay back!" he shouted in English. "All of you! *Vamos!*"

A corner of Emmet's mind realized he'd made a bad mistake – he'd assumed Tomlinson spoke Spanish. He walked slowly up to the man, stopped a pace away, and half-turned to him. "Now, Bill," he said calmly. "Bill. Look at me. We were just talking, that's all. It's all been settled, they're peaceable."

Tomlinson's eyes jerked around the crowd. "Too damn *many* of 'em–"

"It's never about numbers." Emmet placed his left hand gently on the Winchester. "You're a Ranger, Bill. Act like one. You're scaring the kids."

"Kids?"

"There, and there." Emmet lifted his left hand to point. "You think people bring their kids to a riot? Now, ease up."

"Okay. Okay." He slung the rifle.

"Now you're getting it," said Emmet. He eased his right hand off the holstered Colt. It would have been the best of a bad set of choices to bend it around Tomlinson's skull. Not a good way to welcome a new man...

"Come on, folks," he called out cheerfully. "We're going to Laredo."

Cycle 597,844.9, Holdfast 31.1, Central Mexico

"Greetings, Group Leader."

Vantarsilas returned Taldarnilis' obeisance. Its flaccid posture indicated receptiveness – or perhaps simply fatigue from gravity. Taldarnilis mentally shifted a few of the points it had prepared, gambling that this was indeed the case. Sometimes dealing with the group leader was like dealing with an alien mind entirely – more so than others of its generation.

It had discussed this with others of the Threeborn. It seemed that not only were their bodies different from those not bred on this world, their minds were as well. With far fewer links to other minds during the development of full sentience, they had obtained less information directly – although much of that information was irrelevant on a different world – but also absorbed fewer constraints on their thinking. For one, they seemed abler at operating the remote-controlled drones that Group 31 had begun producing. They were designed to root out individual prey from fortifications, but Arctilantar had already begun speculating about other uses. The contrast with tradition-bound practices inherited from the Homeworld was striking.

Of course, since Elder Dartalnat's death on the Homeworld, Vantarsilas as well had been granted more freedom of thought by being liberated from its imprinted obedience. The normal practice would have been to establish a new telepathic link and imprint Vantarsilas' obedience to a new clan elder. Interplanetary distance made that impossible. That left Vantarsilas without a direct superior within the Race. Its thinking might be affected by that. Taldarnilis' own mind raced as it settled into place.

"Have you reconstituted after the expedition?" asked Vantarsilas unexpectedly.

"Yes," said Taldarnilis without a pause. "The feeding arrangements are working at high efficiency. Goodprey are supplying quadrupeds to fill all our nutritional needs. I have heard some individuals remark that there is an aesthetic difference from nutrition supplied via the prey, but I have not been able to detect any."

"Both seem different to me from what was sourced from bipeds on the Homeworld. You would not have this comparison available... Perhaps there are other aesthetic variables to be found on this world."

"Perhaps so, Group Leader. Shall I summarize our results?"

"Yes."

"As we reported at the time, the attack from the prey's floating machines was a powerful one. They seem able to deploy stronger weapons more quickly by this method than by any other. While we were able to avoid further attacks by moving only at night along the shoreline, it adds considerable risk to any operational movement there. This may be a factor in our planning.

"While there were some findings of energetic residue in three minor watercourses along the way, they were not of a useful level. However, a strong residue was detected beyond the north side of the major watercourse that divides Group 32's territory from our own."

"How far beyond?"

"One hundred and twenty-four telequel."

Vantarsilas recoiled. "You traveled that far into another group's territory?"

"There were navigational difficulties which made the situation unclear. In any case, Group Leader, that part of Group 32's territory has been of no interest to them since our initial landing. Not only are there prey forces blocking access from them, they have been able to locate far richer deposits of energetic minerals in the north and central regions of their territory. Not a single fighting machine of Group 32 has set a digit near this region. It might be considered," Taldarnilis added carefully, "that our activity there, and 32's lack of it, constitute a legitimate basis for reassignment of the arbitrary territorial border."

"That would be a matter for the Conclave!"

"Of course – at some time. But in the meantime, we have done no harm to Group 32's efforts. There is really nothing to inform the Conclave about at all."

"An undisclosed border violation might invite punishment, Taldarnilis."

"Indeed. Perhaps they will withhold all our supply of energetic minerals?"

Vantarsilas hissed. "Your point is taken. Continue."

"We traced the signature inland thirty-five telequel until we were able to measure its rate of increase. Extrapolating from that, we determined it could be no more than one hundred and twenty telequel inland. As any further exploration would likely encounter prey, we withdrew at that point. But I have no doubt that we could locate the source in short order, Group Leader. Arctilantar's data is excellent."

"But what would we do once we had located it? Your proposed method requires transport of large quantities of material back to the holdfast. If the shoreline is too hazardous to traverse, can haulers be expected to travel inland through more difficult terrain?"

"No, Group Leader. The jungle and mountains we encountered on the return journey would be impassable by heavily loaded haulers."

"Then we are doomed," said Vantarsilas dully. "We must dismantle this holdfast in turn, and–"

"No."

The group leader looked sharply at Taldarnilis. "Your report–"

"Is incomplete, Group Leader. Raqtinoctil has made an... unusual proposal. Even if passable terrain could be found, the haulers would consume too much energy over the required distance to supply from the holdfast reactor, and our limited number of them would require too many trips. Raqtinoctil proposes instead that we exploit the transport technology of the prey itself."

"How is this possible?"

"Despite the primitive nature of the machinery involved, the process of moving weight on rolling metal discs supported by metal rods is surprisingly efficient. The prey have installed this system across long distances. Raqtinoctil has plotted the path from near the holdfast to many telequel northeast. We know that this system links all of their major habitation zones, and Homeworld telescopic observations of the group – of this general area – allowed Raqtinoctil to plot their locations and project routes further. Logically, the route we can access from the holdfast will continue to the region in which we can mine element 92. Goodprey will be used to obtain and compel skilled prey to operate the necessary machines, escorted by fighting machines.

"Once there, we must defend the mining operation. The areas it passes through are scarcely inhabited, and the prey in that region are hard-pressed by Group 32 to the north. With our transport needs met by repurposed prey machines, all machines of the Race will be freed for combat or exploitation, and the prey system may be used to transport spare energy cells without consuming any of their charge to do so. It will be as though the fighting machines fight within a quel of the holdfast."

"But you are speaking of conquering and defending a tremendously large zone. We are too weak to undertake a major assault on the prey – or withstand one they carry out!"

"We know that the prey require many tendays to shift large forces, and more still to prepare their strength. If they believe that they face a new holdfast, they may take half a cycle to be ready to assault it. But we will have completed our work and be gone well before then, with three cycles' worth of element 92."

Vantarsilas sat silent for some time. "There are too many variables," it said slowly. "I cannot estimate the chances of success. Even if we prevail, the Conclave will not look well upon us."

"Is it not better to perish gloriously for the Race, than to wither away like Group 39 in the frozen pole region? And if we succeed, we will have drawn off a good part of the prey's strength in a pointless preparation during a most active period of operations. Group 32 will surely acknowledge that we have aided them, not hindered them. Whatever may happen on the Homeworld, we shall have made our mark on this one."

"Very well," said Vantarsilas. "Undoubtedly you have planned in further detail. Show me."

Chapter Eight

December, 1911, Houston, Texas

"Fire in the hole!" shouted Major Palmer.

Captain Willard Lang ducked his head to the lip of the slit trench he stood in. The improvised fortifications and open landscape made this rocket test site, twenty miles north of Houston, seem like a mock battlefield. He'd been on battlefields, and some of those had *been* less dangerous than what was going on here...

A hundred yards away, a prototype four-inch caliber rocket thundered into life, blasting white smoke into a cloud that obscured the launch frame. It roared into the sky, arcing downrange... and drifted to the right... and drifted... and abruptly spun end-for-end and impacted into the ground in a powerful explosion. Which, since it carried no warhead, implied that plenty of the solid fuel hadn't yet burned up.

"Number seventeen," said Major Palmer calmly to the private scribbling notes beside him. "Ah, lateral instability at four-plus seconds, vertical instability at six, course intersected with ground at eight."

Palmer turned to his left, straightening upright. "Is that normal, Dr. Goddard?"

The man he addressed hadn't bothered to hunch down when the rocket fired. Although a civilian, in the week since his arrival, he'd proven as nonchalant around these erratic tubes of explosives as any artilleryman – maybe more so.

"Normal for this stage of development," he answered, making notes of his own. "Really, Major, you've done very well in such a short time here."

"Yeah," said Lang. "Now all we have to do is convince the Martians to start using 'em, and blow themselves off our planet... What do you think the trouble is, sir?"

"Hold the next test," said Goddard without answering. He climbed out of the trench with a thoughtful expression on his high-domed face and began walking toward number eighteen's test frame.

"Hold confirmed!" called out Palmer. "The, uh..." He looked after Goddard's striding figure. "The range is safed," he finished by rote. He began to fiddle with the handfuls of wires that terminated in the control trench, switching another pair onto the big switch that would deliver a firing jolt from the battery beside it.

Lang leaned back against the dirt wall. It was galling to have these rockets faring so badly in front of someone as accomplished as Goddard – and frustrating when Lang himself wanted so badly to have something better than a machine gun to hit the Martians with – but if the man from out east could figure something out they couldn't, it hardly mattered. Palmer had directed the effort so far by scaling up smaller rockets to something that would land a real punch. *'Land', well, that's the thing...* At least one thing they had in this part of Texas was plenty of room. The grandly named Houston Rocket Center was little but shacks so far; the rockets themselves were being built in Dallas.

He glanced to his right at the other man they'd retrieved from out East. Granville Woods slumped on his folding stool – his one request since, as he put it, "m'legs don't work so well now" – and scribbled in his own notebook. They'd brought a trunkful of those on the train from Washington, and Woods always seemed to have at least one on the go.

"Mr. Woods, are you sure you wouldn't like to set up with a better view?"

Woods looked up. "No, thank you," said in his careful, slurred voice. The left side of his face did not move when he spoke. "I can hear th' rocket's sound change when it tries to sheer. The vanes, y'see."

Lang nodded. Downrange, a series of clangs sounded. He looked over the trench lip and sure enough, Goddard was beating on a fin of the rocket with a hammer. *God help us...*

Goddard sprinted back and dropped into the trench. "Try the next one."

Palmer repeated his ritual warning and fired the rocket. It curved slowly to the left as it roared upward, rising on its trail of smoke; then the smoke cut off and the roar silenced a moment later, and after a few seconds sinking against the sky, the exhausted rocket plunged gracefully to earth at least a mile downrange.

"That's more like it!" exclaimed Palmer. "So, you added a fixed input to overprint the instability?"

They fell to talking gibberish, but after a few moments, Palmer gestured to Lang. He got out of the trench and waved to the vehicle park a half mile south. Shortly after, a truck pulled out and headed toward them. He dropped back in and nodded to Palmer.

"Now, Dr. Goddard, I've prepared something of a surprise for you," said Palmer with a distinct glint in his eye. "If you'll have a look to the south..."

The vehicle that rumbled up to the firing line was a half-ton Wichita truck adapted from their stock delivery vehicle. Welded atop it were metal launch rails that angled forward over the cab – eight of them, although only one had a four-inch rocket mounted to it. That seemed prudent to Lang until a *lot* more bugs got worked out.

"Well, that's interesting," said Goddard. The truck squealed to a halt and the two drivers jumped onto the hood, flipped a metal plate down over the windscreen, and then climbed back in behind it. "How quickly can you –"

The roar of an outgoing rocket cut him off. By some miracle, it actually flew fairly straight, landing almost as far away as the previous attempt.

"Impressive." Goddard grinned.

"We should be able to ripple-fire them," said Palmer. "We could unload a helluva lot of them if we can get them into position."

"The problem's accuracy," said Goddard. "With an artillery round, you can control the powder burn to the last grain, all inside the gun tube. But the solid motor casting burns unpredictably and the ballistics are impossible to control. That's part of the reason I'm looking into liquid fuels. They can be throttled, and if there's a second stage, it can be controlled precisely enough to place an object in orbit around the Earth – as the Martians have done. Or to intercept that object. We may need to destroy it one day if it turns out to be what some of us think it is."

Lang shook his head. "The Army's best photo-reconnaissance experts have spoken on that. Photographing the entire surface of the Earth would take decades! It must be for something else – maybe to do with their cylinders."

"Maybe," said Goddard neutrally. "Meantime, aiming a solid-fuel rocket horizontally is still a challenge."

Woods tugged at Lang's coat sleeve. "Excuse me. What about sheering vanes? Then it could be sheered t'hit a target."

Goddard blinked. "Well, yes, certainly. In theory. But I've spoken with Tesla on the subject – he's pioneered some interesting remote-controlled vehicles – and he's adamant that no radio can fit into a rocket like this, or survive the ride if it could. The Martians have some sort of super-compact radios, but we haven't been able to figure out anything about those as yet." He rubbed his chin. "Still, we're bound to get somewhere eventually. Mr. Woods, would you like to come back to Washington with me? I could use a control systems specialist on my team..."

Lang stared imploringly at Woods. *If I let Goddard poach our one inventor back east again, Funston will kill me...* But Woods was smiling and shaking his head. "Thank you, Dr. Goddard, that's ... a compliment. But I think I c'n make progress here."

"Very well. Major, if you'd have a look..."

Woods smiled at Lang and crooked a finger. Lang stooped close.

"Cap'n, is there any way you could get me a few miles of that Martian wire?"

Lang's train to Fort Sam Houston was delayed by hours – not uncommon now, with the incessant, mostly military traffic on the railroads – and he arrived very late in the day. General Funston was not in his office; his junior clerk still was; the corporal telephoned the general, spoke for a few moments, hung up, and fixed Lang with a baleful eye. "The general's compliments, and he requests you present yourself at his house."

The sun was setting as Lang walked across the neatly groundscaped Quadrangle. Shouted commands and tramping boots echoed; the sunset glinted redly on one of the water towers, looming over the troops in an eerie resemblance to a Martian tripod. *Good motivation*, thought Lang. Those new recruits weren't much younger than he was, but he felt a gulf separating him from them. It wasn't as though Lang came from a military heritage; his family had been farmers for two generations back. They'd wanted better for him, but when recruiters came calling in town in the years before the Martian invasion, promising adventure and patriotic service, Lang had always recalled the words of an old family friend: "There are other paths to adventure, lad, than over the bodies of your fellow men."

And maybe he'd have found one – the law classes had been going well – but after the invasion, everything changed. Educated men were snatched up and flung down again as lieutenants to face Martian machines within weeks of training. Lang had survived... where some hadn't. Now he was a staff officer, holding responsibility for thousands of men like these recruits. Strange, perhaps – but how could anything be, compared with Martians landing in America? And if the world had turned a different way, and those thousands of men had been pitted against thousands of other men under other flags, how many more bodies might Lang's own path have led over? *Best not to think too much on that.* Lang let his stride settle into the cadence of the troops and set his thoughts to the task at hand.

The commanding general's house was a two-story frame structure that anchored the row of officer's housing along the west side. The sentry saluted Lang; he returned the salute and knocked.

Funston opened the door. The general was in shirtsleeves. "Come in," he said. Within the parlor, his uniform jacket was slung on a chair. Papers filled a desk with a half-eaten meal as paperweight; but it was to the settee that Lang looked, touching his cap automatically, although he hadn't saluted the out-of-uniform general.

Mrs. Eda Funston nodded to him, placing her teacup onto a side table. "Hello, Willard. Please, sit down. I haven't seen you in a long time. Has Frederick been sending you to the corners of the earth?"

"Only to the corners of a trench today, Mrs. Funston. We were observing rocket trials. I hope I see you well?"

"Very well, thank you. Rockets? That sounds exciting."

Lang smiled. "I think Dr. Goddard found it so. We may actually be able to hit something with them one day... Sir, he'll have a proper report and recommendations to improve the production rockets by the end of this week," he said. "But I have an... odd request. From Granville Woods."

Mrs. Funston titled her head in inquiry. "Our Texan Edison," said Funston aside. "What is it? Why didn't he just add it to the report?"

"I think it's unofficial. He wants us to get him some of that Martian power cell wire. A few... miles, he said."

"Oh, wonderful," said Funston. "The Bureau's men in gray won't agree to *that*. Do you think he's on to something?"

"That notebook of his is like hieroglyphics to me. But right now, he's all we have."

"Yes. Well, officially, we'd have to ask for it, and we'd be refused. Of course, if some happened to fall off the back of a truck, that's different. Do whatever you need to, but don't get caught... You didn't hear that, Eda."

"Of course not, dear." Mrs. Funston dimpled when she smiled.

"What else... Oh, I had a request from Leonard Wood to find a fighting command for a Captain Patton. He's another tanker, so see what you can get for him."

"Yes, sir."

"Good. Good." Funston hesitated, oddly for him, and chafed one hand in the other. "Lang, I have something else I'd like you to take care of for me. For... us. Given the situation... the potential situation... I want you to arrange for Mrs. Funston to travel back east and set up in Philadelphia with my boys."

Eda Funston twisted to look at him. "Frederick! You never mentioned this."

"I have been thinking very hard about it. And it's a difficult decision, but..."

"It is my decision too."

"Not when it concerns your safety."

Lang felt the same sinking feeling he'd once had after answering back to a drill sergeant. He tried to meld with the furnishings.

"Am I in danger?"

Funston reached a hand out. "No, of course not. Not now. But, Eda, you haven't seen how *quickly* those things can advance. They can cross half of Texas in a day if they break through our defenses. We are a salient, and this base is in their path. If... I... I simply can't consider it. I want you back east, behind the real defenses."

Red spots had appeared on Mrs. Funston's cheeks; she sat very straight. "And if I go east, and the other officers' wives do not, what then? Or will you and I start a stampede of all of us? Then the enlisted families, will they go – or just watch the officers' families heading east, and wonder why? Frederick, you can do this if you choose to, but think of what others will feel. How much hope they might lose. The boys are children, our children, so yes, they should stay where they are – and so should I."

"The men are my responsibility. And – well, yes, I see what you mean. But you're my *wife*."

"Yes," said Mrs. Funston. She rose gracefully and smoothed her skirts. "I am a general's wife. Cora is a colonel's wife... Mary is a first sergeant's wife. We can all board a train, harness a cart, drive a car, run on foot if we have to. But for now, we have our place, and it's here." She turned and smiled shakily at Lang. "Willard. I haven't offered you tea; please forgive me. I'll be right back."

She strode into the hallway. Lang and Funston sat in silence for a few moments.

"I sometimes forget," said Funston slowly, "how fortunate I am. Lang, if you marry, don't settle for just anyone."

Lang rose. "Yes, sir. If I may–"

Funston pointed a finger. "You're not going anywhere until you've had your tea, son. Now sit down."

Chapter Nine

January, 1912, Dallas, Texas

"I don't know whether to call this a conspiracy, or just a whole lot of initiative in one place," said Oscar Colquitt as he sat down.

Lang smiled. This was hardly the place for skulking: the drawing room of the Governor's private home in Dallas, with a fire crackling in the hearth to ease a chilly afternoon. He shed his uniform coat to join the other three men in chairs around the fireplace.

"I'd favor the latter," said General Funston, clearly not liking the first term. He looked over to Lieutenant-General William Wright. "Look, Bill, we may as well face it: what we're going to do is not conducive to one's career. Any or all of us may be cashiered afterward. And you are one of the few lieutenant-generals we have with extensive fighting experience against the Martians. So it's not just a matter of your own ambition; if the repercussions of this mean that you do not gain an army command one day – possibly mine – then we all lose out. Are you quite sure?"

Wright knuckled his big hands together. "Yes, General, I am. Whatever you're proposing, I'll be part of it."

"Then we're agreed," said Colquitt with finality. Lang noted wryly that no one had asked him, but he could always claim he was just following orders...

Funston settled back. "Bill, you've already noticed we have been transferring quite a few tank battalions to III Corps over the past two months. You're getting the best men, too. And the train shipments of artillery and shells from out east went right on to you, not VIII Corps. Almost all of them."

"How did you manage *that*, sir?" asked Wright. "General Dickerson must have been furious."

Colquitt grinned. "General Wright, I used to be the railroad commissioner of this state. I still know quite a few people. I'm sure there were a few puzzled clerks when the trains went by that they'd been expecting, but there's been no real stink raised as yet."

"However, I do not expect any more forces, weapons, or fungible goods to be made available from back east for a long time," said Funston. "And that's the nub of it. The Martians have a great advantage logistically: whatever technology allows them to do it, they can simply build war machines continuously, directly within their military bases – and we know they breed rapidly as well. They will become stronger with each passing month, and at some point, they will inevitably attack... and roll right over us."

"But if we attack them now..." said Colquitt.

"Yes. We will have our best chance. Bill, I want you to plan and carry out an attack on the Martian base they've set up near Santa Fe. Your objective is to destroy it."

Wright flicked his gaze over to the governor, who nodded agreement. He looked back to Funston. "Uh... yes, sir."

"I know this might seem like a wild gamble, Bill, but I've had men scouting the place for over a year. They can look right down into it from the mountains. They say that periodically a swarm of tripods leave the place and head east, but no significant number come back. This fortress is clearly building tripods for their main force facing our Mississippi line, but the Martians consider it a rear area. I'm betting that it isn't strongly garrisoned, and a sudden attack could catch them unprepared."

"If you say so, sir," said Wright.

"How are your men at night fighting?"

"We've improved. The starshells help, and if we can get infantry close enough with those stovepipe launchers, they know to aim for the eye. But it's still not much good for the regular artillery batteries. Their effective range is at least halved. And the tanks have a bad habit of driving into obstacles they would have seen in daylight. I have men with flashlights leading them like cows."

"I think," said Funston, "that if we choose the time and place of battle, we can force a day action. I suggest moving up forces at night and attacking at dawn after a short preparatory bombardment. Infantry won't stand much of a chance in the open against one of their bases, but if they dig in well, perhaps the tanks can fall back if hard-pressed and draw the Martians across the entrenchments where the stovepipes are."

Wright looked thoughtful. "Might work, sir. And once a few of their machines are knocked out that way, they might get more cautious about just punching through our lines. But, sir... if we attack in a few weeks' time, we'll have eleven hours of daylight at most. If the initial assault does not breach the base, they're bound to counterattack at nightfall."

"Then we'll fall back and bleed them as best we can, and attack again the next morning with fresh units... and the next, if we have to. If we can't crack at least *one* of their bases – get back the initiative somehow – then we have all but lost!" Funston was growing flushed; he caught his breath and turned. "Sorry, Governor, but the logic is inescapable."

Lang knew how badly the general's failure to take the fortress at Gallup in 1908 still gnawed at him. *Still, he's right. If we do nothing but defend, we lose.*

"I agree," said Colquitt. "But perhaps we can give the boys a better chance when the days get a mite longer? If they can do it in one go, it would mean a lot... It would mean fewer casualties, yes?"

"They would be better trained by, say, April," admitted Wright.

Funston pondered a few moments. "Yes. But no later. It is imperative that we strike first."

"Yes, sir." Wright couldn't be said to look enthusiastic, but he did seem determined.

Colquitt frowned. "General Funston, your point about the relative strengths of men and Martians is well taken. I wish that I could offer imported arms from France, as we've discussed in the past... but although I've forwarded your requests verbatim to the French government, and spoken to Ambassador Jusserand repeatedly, I've seen no results."

Funston nodded impassively; Lang shifted in his chair. That was a bad blow to their planning. About the only thing that could hurt a tripod was an artillery piece; one wrapped in tank armor would be ideal, but even horse-drawn artillery counted for a lot.

"Why is that?" asked Funston in a controlled tone.

"My opinion is that isolationist elements within the French government are stalling the arms sales. We've certainly seen no progress in several months. But there may be an alternative. It is apparent to me from the negotiations that there is more than one political faction vying for power in France. The government is mostly in the hands of what they term 'republicans' – supporters of the recent French Republic – but many of the high military officers are monarchists – Royalists – who favor a return of power entirely to the throne, regaining old French glory and rallying the populace to this great..." He cleared his throat. "Pardon, I'm not making a speech here! But I believe much of their foreign policy depends on who will benefit at home from it. Some admirals and generals may welcome an opportunity to fight a victorious battle against the Martians, despite what their political masters would wish."

"Interesting, Governor. But that's of little use if they are overridden by Paris before they can proceed," said Funston.

Colquitt smiled. "Texan pride isn't so different from French pride, General. I can see them going along if 'the honor of the nation' is at stake. Especially if very little else is. If we lose, it isn't as though a French colony will be overrun by the Martians."

"So we could still obtain French guns, provided that Frenchmen fire them," said Funston.

"Perhaps. The Mexican federal army seems able to stand on its own feet today without direct French help. The French may have strength to spare now. I take it you've no objection to them sending any aid or force we can get?"

"None at all, Governor." Funston managed a smile. "It would not be the first time, after all."

"Hah! That's very true. I'll see to it, then." Colquitt looked at Lang. "Oh, Captain. I do hope that Senator Hudspeth's fine automobile is being treated well and giving of good service?"

"Oh, yes, Governor." Lang swallowed. "Two new coats of paint already. We're keeping her in prime shape. General Wright, have you received any allocation of requisitioned automobiles?" *Help me out here, General.*

"Not that I know of," said Wright in puzzlement. "But I can ask my staff to check and reply to you."

"Thank you, sir."

Colquitt looked at Lang, then shrugged and rose to his feet. "Then I think we have made our intentions clear to one another, gentlemen. Thank you for being my guests this evening. If–" He turned to the footsteps from the interior hallway. "Alice! Why didn't you come in earlier?"

"I didn't wish to interrupt your work, gentlemen." All three officers stood up as Alice Colquitt entered the drawing room and graced them all with her smile. "But if you are finished – Oscar, I need an immediate answer... I have a telephone call in to San Antonio with the Daughters. *Did* the House approve a budget for household supplies in the 'White Star' program today?"

"They did," said Colquitt with obvious pride. "Nine thousand dollars' worth.

And it was a pleasure seeing some of 'em do it, too. Call me 'Beer-Barrel Governor', will they?"

"Get me their names," said Mrs. Colquitt flatly. "I'll speak with their wives... or have them spoken to." She blossomed again in a smile. "I'm sorry, I must dash – musn't tie up the nation's telephone lines. Good afternoon, gentlemen!"

Colquitt looked fondly after her. "Alice is very involved in our chapter of the Daughters of the Confederacy. They're working on a program to have single households take in refugee families – they can place a white star in the window and get some help with taking care of them. It will help show who is doing their patriotic duty to help their fellow Americans. Of course, it will also show who is not."

Lang was suddenly glad he'd signed up and was safe from such attention. "That sounds like a wonderful idea, Governor."

"Do you like it? It was hers. Good afternoon, gentlemen... and good hunting."

March, 1912, Lampazos, Mexico

Ronald Gorman limped slowly, as a tired refugee might be expected to. It was not entirely an act; the Master's machine had dropped him off five miles south of the town of Lampazos, and a late afternoon squall had soaked him. His stolen finery had been traded for the plain coat of a prosperous *ranchero*, and his wet boots squeaked as he walked. The brightly braided scarf around his neck stayed there by necessity.

The town's outskirts passed in an hour, and he reached a tavern at an intersection by the dinner hour. After a year in the Masters' service, it was surreal to bang a coin on the counter and order a drink and a meal. As expected, he attracted glances, and before long a townsman approached.

"Any news from the south?"

"Not good," said Gorman. "It was quiet for a long time, and I thought I could make one more season of grazing for the herd, but then I saw one of those *máquinas* cross my land and I thought, why die for a few more pesos? I will go back to America. You are all brave to stay here, my friend."

"Not really. ASARCO has been holding our pay for a year. They know we won't leave until we get paid."

"There is a mine here, yes? Train yards? They must have defenses."

The townsman shrugged. "A few old guns, some security guards to man them – if they're awake. No one expects a real attack. They would have come by now if they wanted to."

"I am sure you are right," said Gorman, smiling but thinking of the sixty tripods massed twenty miles south, waiting. He kept the smile in place as he lied further. "I may look up someone I met a couple of years ago; I think he lives here now. He was an engineer with the Texas-Mexican Railway, he said he would be working here for some time."

"Mendez? Juan Mendez? He lives on Hidalgo, the third house."

"Juan Mendez, yes," said Gorman. "The very man. Many thanks, my friend." He tossed back his drink, left another coin, and departed.

Via Hidalgo was a prosperous street; the homes further north near the smelter would be less so, of course. A skilled worker was always treated better. Gorman knocked at the third house, a modest adobe dwelling. A stocky man answered the door.

"Good evening, Señor Mendez. May I come in?"

"What do you want?" growled Mendez. He rubbed at one sleep-red eye. "I'm not on shift for hours."

"Matters have changed," said Gorman, easing the revolver from his coat. "Please, back inside. Do have a seat. Señor Mendez, do you live alone?"

Mendez dropped into a chair in the quietly furnished parlor. "Yes. I've no family. What do you want?"

"Not to harm you, I assure you. If you had a family, I would make sure they were safe as well. Any close friends, perhaps?"

"I live in this town four days a month. Now, what—"

"Then that makes things simple," said Gorman. He unwrapped his scarf left-handed and settled into a chair himself. "As I said, you are safe with me. In fact, this is now the only safe place in this entire town." He pressed the square detent on the massive metal pendant secured around his neck and leaned back to wait.

"Do you have happen to have any cigars? I haven't smoked one in a very long time."

Mendez had excellent taste in tobacco; Gorman smoked three of them while they waited. After a few attempts, Mendez gave up asking and sat dully. It was perhaps eight o'clock when the noise began outside: shouts, driving vehicles, then the faint unmistakable sound of heat rays.

"What is it?" begged Mendez. "What's happening?"

"Your new employers have arrived. Now, stay close to me and you will be quite safe. I work for them too."

"You mean the Martians? That's impossible!"

"I am hoping every other human north of here thinks so as well... We will be traveling a long time. Do you need to bring anything?"

"I don't know. Where..."

"Splendid, a man who travels light. Then let us see who else has been recruited." Gorman rose, tipped over one of the kerosene lamps on the sideboard, and tossed his cigar butt into the pool. He ushered Mendez out as the flames flickered up. The sky glowed red as Lampazos burned; it seemed wrong to leave this one house aside. The Masters did enjoy combustion so.

Mendez yelped and stumbled back. "It's all right," said Gorman, putting a comforting arm about his shoulders and glancing up at the looming metal machine, red-licked by the fires. And, indeed, the tripod seemed to crouch protectively above them, scanning its heat ray about for any threats. "These beings have need of you. They will not harm you. Unless you disobey, of course. You will see presently what that means."

They walked in the tripod's lee for a mile to an open square where perhaps fifty people had been gathered – herded, like the cattle they were. Machines hulked on all sides. A few had the cargo baskets fitted which could carry humans – perhaps ten living, or twenty dead.

There was no need to fill them all tonight. "Everyone!" shouted Gorman. He dangled his revolver at his side. "We are looking for skilled workers. Who has worked on the trains or in the mines?"

"Don't tell him anything!" shouted an older man. "Can't you see, he's working for those horrors!"

"Quite so. Well, I have no way to compel you to speak. So who is *not* skilled?" He pointed to a woman crouched at the edge of the group. "You! Have you ever worked on a train crew?"

"Of course not," said the woman. She dragged a shawl tighter around her shoulders.

"Thank you for your honesty, *chica*." Gorman shot her in the chest. As she fell, he turned and walked a pace closer to the group. Mendez stumbled along beside him. "I am not a cruel man! If you cannot work for the Masters, you will feed them. The process is an ugly one. I can make it a quick one... Mendez, here, has already joined us. Why not join him?"

"Mendez, you dog!" spat a man. "You'll be damned if you do this!"

Gorman fired again. "Another honest soul. Why, this is an honest town! I have an engineer. Anyone else who can help him, walk to me!"

After a pause, two men shuffled forward to join him. Others jeered at them while a few wept. It was always a difficult time when the Masters applied their will.

"Please drag those three bodies over to us," directed Gorman. He gave Mendez a shove.

"What do you mean, three–"

He shot a portly man who might have been the town's mayor. Three corpses that size should suffice for a week's rations for the Masters. More would become... unpleasant after a time. There would be further opportunities.

"Bring them over here." Once the recruits had dragged the bodies close, Gorman tapped the detent on his pendant.

Heat rays sawed out from the machines, annihilating the remaining group with scarcely time for screams. At point-blank range, there was nothing really left of them. Another machine stooped, sliding manipulators under one of the corpses Gorman had shot. It lifted and flipped the body neatly into its cargo basket.

Mendez doubled over, retching. Gorman patted him on the back. "You'll grow accustomed to this. Now, which is the best engine in the train yards?"

"The..." Mendez coughed and wiped his mouth. "The Pacific on the western siding. That's my engine."

"And we will need some of the freight cars the mine uses."

"Those are twenty-ton hopper cars..." The breeze shifted and brought a scent of burned meat. Mendez retched again.

"Let us take twenty to be sure. And a first-class passenger car... perhaps a private one?" Mendez blinked up at him. "Well, why not?"

"You can't shift that many cars with a handful of men!" protested Mendez.

"Two of these machines can pick them up and set them down as needed, my friend. You are part of something marvelous, now."

The corpses had been loaded; now a machine gathered its manipulators under Mendez and picked him off the ground, while another seized Gorman. Mendez began screaming as they were borne swiftly toward the train yards through billowing clouds of smoke. It took him quite a while to calm down.

Cycle 597,845.1, Prey transport system, River 3-12

Taldarnilis' fighting machine crouched in its lowest loading position within one of the prey's transport cars, half-hidden behind the metal sidewalls. Outside it, the night landscape moved steadily past, illuminated only by a crescent of this world's satellite. The gentle clunks of the prey's transport machine were transmitted faintly into its cabin. The sensation was peculiar. Vantarsilas would probably be intrigued by it...

There was always a possibility that Vantarsilas had agreed to this expedition in order to dispose of those it felt threatened by – the most innovative members of the group. Taldarnilis thought it unlikely, but it was a risk; small compared to others involved.

One of those risks was the likelihood that the prey had taken steps to reduce their ineffectiveness at night. It was still worthwhile to time attacks for low illumination, but additional surprise was a useful factor. Thus, nine of Group 31's fighting machines had arranged themselves onto components of the prey transport they had procured for the final approach to a likely defensive position. Two other cars were loaded with drones, although they would not be needed as yet. The rest of the expedition's fighting machines followed a quel behind, concentrated tightly. Already the terrain was opening out as they approached the large watercourse that marked the northern limit of their group's territory. As the rod system curved gradually to the left, Taldarnilis could see – past the cloud of combustion products emitted by the propulsion machine – a spindly, raised construction that carried the rods high over the watercourse. It did not look strong enough for this world's gravity, but presumably it had been used before.

Beyond that was a minor habitation center. Taldarnilis studied the near side of that and the rising ground leading up from the watercourse. Small, isolated fortifications were visible, but nothing like what other groups had reported encountering. Attack did not seem to be expected here.

They proceeded across the construction and approached the far side. Small lights winked, a few prey moved about, and narrow sticks deployed across the rod system's path. Taldarnilis ignored that; firing at it could risk hitting the propulsion unit. Instead, it opened fire at the nearest ground fortification.

Immediately other heat rays opened up in turn. Firing to both sides, they raked the defensive positions, some of which did not even protect the prey inside them from such lateral attacks. Secondary explosions burst out as the heat rays found projectile-throwers. Those targets were quickly left behind without any returning fire, and Taldarnilis scanned ahead for new ones. Behind, the following fifty machines crossed the watercourse and clambered up the northern bank, taking occasional shots of their own.

The stealthy approach had done its work; the prey's defenses had fallen without a single loss of the attackers.

"All machines resume normal locomotion," Taldarnilis ordered and raised its own machine gingerly to half-height. It reached a limb out over the transport car's side and drove it downward, transferring the machine's weight outboard in one step and swinging the other limbs clear. A moment later, it was striding normally beside the car. It scanned behind; a few of the other machines had not disembarked so cleanly, but all were now moving ahead on their own.

"Advance one telequel ahead of propulsion unit, engage targets of opportunity." They fanned out northeastward, firing occasionally. Although individual machines were thrifty with energy, there were enough firing that the illumination level quickly rose from structures undergoing combustion. Prey scuttled in the light, most fleeing eastward.

"Arctilantar, detach your group to invest this area. Remember, if that watercourse construction is destroyed, our return path will be interrupted. You have full authority to carry out disruptive attacks up to four telequel from this point."

"Acknowledged, Expedition Leader." The nine machines dedicated to that task dropped behind and set about reducing the habitation center to a more defensible state.

Targets soon ceased to appear. The landscape here was more open, but no structures were visible. "Machines with detection apparatus, advance on lead element and commence search for energetic elements."

The empty terrain nagged at Taldarnilis. It had expected a larger prey population in this area. While anything that suggested this area was a neglected one was good, they had consumed the prey already obtained for nutrition. Returning to the riverside habitation center would take time, and they might be vulnerable to interception once the prey grew organized again. They would grow hungry in the several tendays to come. There were already so many demands on their limited capacities...

Ahead and to the south, it noted low structures, many laid out in rows. Lesser habitations? On impulse it strode closer. A few prey were visible around the small structures; more spilled into view as it watched.

"Groups Three and Four, rendezvous my position. Prey-creatures are available for harvest."

March, 1912, Fort Sam Houston, Texas

Daylight filtered in through the windows of the Situation Room that Lang had set up the previous month in a dining hall. The reports that he'd filtered in turn over the past four hours were just as wan and shifting.

It was clear enough that the 3rd Texas Volunteer Division based at Laredo had been overrun. Telephone and telegraph reports had flooded in during the predawn hours, ranging from terse to panicked to bizarre; claims of fifty tripods, or a hundred, or two hundred; most admitting to barely a shot fired by the defenses; a few claiming a downed machine but without details as to its location. As telephones jangled and clerks ran in and out of the Situation Room, more information trickled in.

General Funston had dismissed the largest reports. "That's panic talking. A night battle always seems worse than it is. So, perhaps a hundred tripods. That's a considerable force – much more than they'd have needed just to take Laredo."

"The 608th Tank Battalion tried to probe into the area an hour ago," said Lang. "They lost six tanks before withdrawing. The Martians are definitely still in Laredo, but we don't have a good estimate yet of their strength."

"I doubt they've halted there," said Funston grimly. "Find out where they're going!"

In the next hour, more reports arrived, as well as Governor Colquitt, who'd been driven two hundred miles from his home in Dallas after receiving the first call in the early hours. Lang admired his nerve, although losing the governor to a broken neck in a car crash wouldn't have helped matters in the least.

Haggard and unshaven, as they all were, Colquitt studied the map table. "What are our losses so far, General?"

"I'm afraid elements of the 3rd Volunteers and the 608th sustained heavy casualties at the town. Units stationed further up and down river have been able to withdraw without much loss, although a few have attacked without orders, and at least one infantry battalion was wiped out doing so."

"I suppose it's not good military sense, but I can't blame them," said Colquitt. "Not in the least... Civilians?"

"The town is nearly destroyed already, but several hundred survivors managed to flee. We're estimating four hundred dead there."

"There is a refugee camp just east of the town, isn't there?" asked Colquitt. "Another thousand people there at least."

"The Martians have definitely raided it, although we're not sure why – there were lots of people in Laredo for... for their purposes. Some survivors from the camp have contacted the 3rd Division, and they say it was more of a scattering than a slaughter..." Funston seemed to brace himself. "Governor, we simply couldn't stop them. I'll admit to concentrating our forces heavily toward Santa Fe and the northern line in general. There was so little activity to the south in Mexico, we didn't expect –"

"That's enough of that," said Colquitt sharply. "Our planned offensive there made perfect sense and you couldn't have known they'd strike here first. But now that they've taken Laredo, what are they doing there? Or are they advancing further? They could hit San Antonio by this afternoon! Or Houston by tomorrow."

"It's unlikely they're rolling north up the Rio Grande; we'd have heard from the 7th Division by now."

"And nothing from the Guard or Rangers in Brownsville either," said Colquitt. "I don't see them being content with just Laredo, General."

A clerk gestured at Lang; he ducked aside and took the telegraph paper from him. "Just in from the train station at Hebbronville, General. MARTIAN TRIPODS ADVANCING STOP ESTIMATE THIRTY STRONG STOP MOVING DUE EAST STOP TRAIN MOVING WITH THEM STOP ESTIMATE NOW FORTY... the message ended there, sir."

"I can guess why," said Colquitt. "That was a brave man."

Funston checked the map. "Due east indeed. Corpus Christi next, then... or Houston. We've *got* to get more depth!"

Lang shook off the oddity of a train accompanying a Martian invasion; the operator must have mistaken a train fleeing *from* the attack. "Sir, I can contact the next station on that line, see if they have spotted the Martians yet. That'll give us more information on the speed of their advance."

"Good. Do it. Governor, we may need to evacuate the cities and towns in their path. But... I need to move military units *into* those cities. That must be the priority for the railways. I know it's a difficult choice for you..."

"There are plans in place for that. We've requisitioned a good deal of motor transport, and there's a passenger liner moored at Corpus Christi that can take most of the town's civilians in one trip – just as well the army built those riverine docks bigger than anyone thought they'd need. Do what you need to do to fight, General; you will have my full support."

"IX Corps has the entire southern line, and there's some units training at Fort

Worth. Those can move south to protect Houston. We can start shifting forces from El Paso to San Antonio on the Southern Pacific line... But it's risky, Governor. If the Martians catch those troop trains en route..."

Colquitt managed a smile. "Sounds like you need some scouting units out ahead of them, General. I believe the LRSC is based in El Paso as well? And of course, the Rangers are at your disposal... indeed, all of Texas is."

They fell to their tasks. As Lang worked furiously to plan the movement of two full divisions' worth of troops and vehicles, something nagged at him. By midmorning, he broke off to question the telegraph clerks, and then sought out Funston.

"Sir, we've had two messages in the past hour from Realitos, the next station east along the Texas-Mexican railroad. No sign of Martians."

Funston frowned. "Odd. Have they slowed to regroup?"

"But sir, that's barely ten miles further east! They must have either stopped or gone due north. No reports from Freer to the north, though. I think they've halted somewhere around Hebbronville."

"Why in hell would they do that?" said Funston. His face fell. "Good God. They're going to build one of their bases there! This is just the beginning of their invasion... and if we can't stop it, they'll spread through all of Texas."

Cycle 597,845.1, Prey transport system, River 3-12

"We have reached a peak energetic signature zone, Group Commander," reported Raqtinoctil.

"Acknowledged," replied Taldarnilis. "All groups, concentrate on my position and commence deployment to construct the mine and holdfast."

The simplicity of that order belied how complex the task was. First, the prey transport machine was halted; the machines of the Race converged on it and removed key assemblies from some of its cars. Raqtinoctil, in charge of the mine construction, made a brief survey of the area and chose a nearby site for the digging and catalyzing machinery to be assembled. Once the critical units had been moved, the few haulers available spread out – although to a smaller perimeter than a conventional, permanent holdfast would require – and used their manipulators to begin pushing a berm into place that would encircle the whole operation. It was imperative that the prey not grasp what was being done here for as long as possible; there were too many vulnerable areas to defend to the degree Taldarnilis would prefer – to say nothing of Group Leader Vantarsilas, who would undoubtedly be in contact soon.

By nightfall, Taldarnilis considered the operation well under way. Raqtinoctil – whom it had left undisturbed to work – reported back that the ground was indeed sedimentary rock in thin layers, far more practicable to dig than the volcanic rock encountered previously. "I do have a concern, however."

"Communicate it."

"Every member of the Race at this site will be pushed to its limit due to the pressure of time. There will be no attention to spare to watch the goodprey or the prey stored for nutrition. I have noted there is no provision in the plan for confinement cells in the holdfast."

"Correct. The prey transport machine will remain at the west perimeter. It has been realigned to be able to proceed westward as soon as the cars have been filled with compound 92-12. All prey will simply remain within the transport machine's cars."

"Commander, it concerns me that we make all effort to keep the prey outside of this... minefast... while allowing others to be within it. That is an undefinable threat."

"Perhaps," agreed Taldarnilis, "but all members of the Race are to remain within their fighting machines other than to obtain nutrients. The goodprey have no access to any weapon that can penetrate the compartment of one. This is no conventional holdfast, Raqtinoctil."

"I am aware of that," said Raqtinoctil dryly. "Is the commander then certain that the goodprey have not obtained any other weapons while being allowed to salvage freely in two different habitation centers during the journey?"

"No, the commander is not. However, it is a small risk compared to others we must take. Other groups across this world have also made use of goodprey with no difficulties to date. I do not believe the prey, or even the goodprey, have any intellectual capacity or drive beyond mere survival, avarice, and avoidance of unpleasant stimuli – certainly nothing on the scale of the Race."

March, 1912, Martian Base, Texas

Ronald Gorman, having completed his day's work for the Masters, wandered the length of his small kingdom: four rail passenger cars attached to the locomotive that had faithfully brought them from Mexico to a spot a few miles east of Hebbronville, Texas. Hot and stuffy, perhaps; and yes, anyone who set foot outside would be burned down unless they carried a pendant to protect them; but *his!*

There had been a certain glee in watching the American border guards at Laredo fleeing from his onrushing train. *Why, hello there boys, I've come back! And I've brought friends!* And all without help from that pestilent U.S. ambassador. Clearly, Providence had intervened. It had become more clear as time passed that Dr. Ronald T. Gorman, LL, was slated for great things. He'd always known it, of course, but there had been... difficulties. But now all those had been cleared away in the great sweep of interplanetary history unfolding.

The fourth car's door was guarded by two of his men who stood on the connecting platform. "Good evening, Garcia," said Gorman. He smiled at the irony; Garcia was a cattle thief, and this was a cattle car. "What did the Masters deliver upon us? I'm curious."

Garcia spat. "Some peasants. It's a great joke that they fled all this way, just to be caught up for food anyway... Would you like to visit?"

"Certainly."

Garcia unlocked the door and opened it cautiously, fingering the revolver in his belt. But the humans ranged in the car were no threat. They'd strung a chain the length of the car and attached the lot of them at intervals. Stripes of sunset light through the planked walls painted them, shifting as a few moved. The hay strewn in the car was still sweet; that wouldn't last. Nor would they. *History unfolding.*

He wandered down the line; peasants, yes, dirty and terrified. A townsman in a rumpled suit called out to him; he swatted an outstretched hand away without looking. Garcia clubbed others into silence. They'd need water, of course. If the Masters did not provide it in a day or two, he'd have to ask de Gama to communicate the need to them... Further down the line, a woman turned to look at him; dressed in white as some others were, but unstained, pure. He halted, blinked. "Extraordinary. Who are you?"

"Don't speak to her!" cried the townsman. "I'm the man you need! I know the Flores brothers. I can be of great help!"

"I have no need of socialist agitators," said Gorman without turning. "Everything is as it should be here."

"The Flores brothers are anarcho-syndicalists," said the woman in a withering tone. "Like Targas there. You should at least know who you are killing."

Gorman smiled. "Are you a politician?"

"A schoolteacher."

"Oh, goodness!" Gorman lifted a hand. "Miss! May I ask a question?"

She turned her head away.

"Now that you have met the Masters, do you suppose that anything human beings do will matter from now on?"

Her face worked in profile; then she flicked her gaze back to him. "Yes. In fact I think it matters more than at any time before in history."

History. He gazed intently upon her. Such intelligence, such courage... "No, I believe that I misspoke... *almost* as it should be here."

A king must have a queen.

The men had more base appetites than his; there was no time to lose. "Garcia! Bring this one forward."

They left the cattle car behind for the more amenable third-class car which housed his men: five besides Garcia, most slouched on the seats and berths. Eyes followed them, but no one spoke out. Gorman opened the connecting door to the next car and gestured the woman forward. As she stepped through, he said quietly, "Anyone who touches this one is next to feed the Masters."

Shrugs and nods answered. Of course they were sated now, after the Lampazos raid. That might change in time.

The next car held only two men: de Gama, dressed at last in decent if shabby clothing, and the engineer Mendez, who glanced over dully. Boxes of supplies crammed most of the space ahead of them; they threaded past them. Gorman noted that the woman looked carefully about her as she walked. This queen would need watching... She stopped dead in the next car's doorway.

"Well, go on," said Gorman. He placed a hand on her shoulder and guided her in; she shook it off. "What do you think? It belonged to a vice-president of ASARCO, I believe. My men and I liberated it from the town of Lampazos."

She turned, studying the brass-gilt lamps, lace curtains, red velvet upholstery. "It reminds me more of a brothel," she said in English.

"You've noticed my accent, then." Gorman switched to the same language. "I hail from Tennessee, originally. Studied mineralogy and law, but I preferred working on my own, really. Mining, exploration... There are – were – great opportunities in Mexico for men such as myself. I suppose in a way there still are..."

"*Opportunities!* Murder, enslavement... It's impossible to believe that men like you are working for... *those.*"

"Oh, not really." Gorman settled into a banquette and reached down a cigar.

"Why, this very train is a metaphor for our human society. You do see it, don't you? The lowest class, doomed to suffer and feed those above it – the middle or professional class, desperate not to slip back into poverty – and then those of us who are fortunate enough to serve directly. The Masters – the Martians – they exist outside of the system entirely, of course. And they are destroying it." He sparked a match, puffed the cigar alight. "Who knows what they'll replace it with..."

"But they'll destroy you as well! Like everyone else!"

"Given time, yes. But it will take a very long time. The United States is a very big country. And the world is even bigger. I will be needed for years to come. You could be, too, Miss...?"

She huffed out a breath. "Idar. You don't need to know anything else."

"I am Dr. Ronald Gorman, Miss Idar. And we have a great deal to talk about."

March, 1912, San Antonio, Texas

"Where in the hell have you been?" demanded Adjutant-General Hutchings.

Emmet Smith drew a long breath. "Well, sir, I was in Laredo for most of December; then I got myself attached to Company D in El Paso while they found time to get involved with illegal alcohol sales and smuggling there. By February I was back in Laredo–"

"I meant in the past *week*," snapped Hutchings. "All Rangers were supposed to have reported back to the camps nearest them. There's still three unaccounted for." He paced two steps behind the desk and wheeled like a caged animal. His Guard uniform now sported the two stars of a major-general.

"I can account for Ranger Stanford; he's dead."

"What? *How?*"

"Heat ray. He was in Laredo when the Martians came through. Tried to get the civilians out in some kind of order, find some cover for them to follow. He got caught out in the open at the wrong time."

Hutchings settled into his chair. "Ah. I see. We knew there'd be casualties..." He picked up a pen and drew a careful line through a ledger. "My clerk will see to it. Poor fellow. Say, how do you know what happened?"

"I was there too. Luckier than Stanford. He was a good man, sir."

"Yes. Well, you do look rather dirty. Best get cleaned up; it doesn't send a good message to the populace."

"There was a burning building involved at one point. Sir, what's our situation here?"

Hutchings shuffled out a map. "That's why I sent for you. The Rangers have been shuttling back and forth around the rail lines, keeping watch for any raiding tripods, along with that motor touring club – the LRSC. But the Martians haven't made any further attacks at all. Other than holding Laredo, they've settled themselves somewhere near Hebbronville, and we don't have a clue as to why they're there – or what they're doing. You're to take two men and drive to near the Seven Sisters camp, say here," he pointed with a manicured finger, "and obtain horses, then scout that area properly over the coming weeks. I want to be able to tell His Excellency about anything and everything that's there."

Emmet rubbed his jaw. "Aren't scouting reports going to the army now? The 28th Cavalry is still active north of Laredo, I know that for a fact. They helped us get those people out. Maybe we could work along with them."

Hutchings shook his head vigorously. "No, no – you'll report to *me*, Smith. The Texas National Guard is up to division strength now, and I'll be leading it in this campaign against the invasion. The Rangers and the Guard are staying independent."

"I thought the Guard was activated as a federal force by now. Aren't you part of Second Army?"

"And put Texas men under Washington's command? No, we are *not*. His Excellency had a long talk with General Funston and laid down the law – *our* law. We're our own men in this fight – the 1st Texas *Home* Guard Division."

"Ah. I see." Emmet suspected privately that Funston had little interest in being saddled with thousands more men with little equipment – led by a freshly promoted general with no experience. If they could handle routine support tasks on their own, though, that would free up regular army units with the firepower to face the Martians to be concentrated into a striking force under Funston. Like many things, it was probably a political compromise. But if scouting information was being hoarded, that wasn't good...

Hutchings waved at an eastern part of the map. "Second Army's IX Corps is mainly deploying around Alice. Of course they have a great deal more tanks and artillery than we do – Washington's given them everything – and they can be expected to do the brunt of the heavy fighting. But our men know this country far better than some fellows from back East. If we can get vital information first, we might not have to be sidelined – we might even lead the attack!"

Dear God, I sure hope not. But I have my job... "I understand, sir. We'll leave first thing tomorrow."

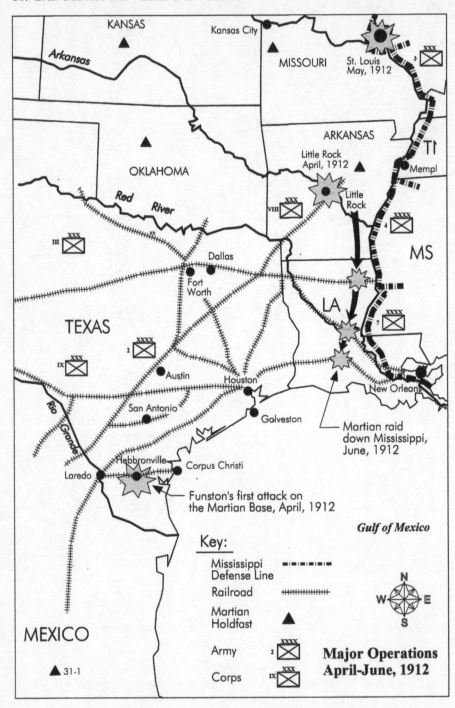

KANSAS

Kansas City

Arkansas

MISSOURI

St. Louis
May, 1912

XXX
3

ARKANSAS

TN

OKLAHOMA

Little Rock
April, 1912

Mempl

Red   River

VIII
XXX

Little
Rock

XXXX
4

III
XXX

Dallas

MS

Fort
Worth

TEXAS

LA

XXXX
2

XXXX
7

IX
XXX

Austin

Houston

New Orleans

San Antonio

Galveston

Martian raid
down Mississippi,
June, 1912

Rio   Grande

Hebbronville

Corpus Christi

Laredo

Funston's first attack on
the Martian Base, April, 1912

Gulf of Mexico

Key:

Mississippi
Defense Line

Railroad

N
W   E
S

Martian
Holdfast

Army

2
XXXX

**Major Operations
April-June, 1912**

MEXICO

31-1

Corps

IX
XXX

Chapter Ten

April, 1912, Veracruz, Mexico

Another argument had erupted among the transplanted government of Mexico.

Henri Gamelin settled back in his gilt chair and waited with the patience he'd learned by now. Admiral Faverau, who spoke no Spanish, had been spared attending these planning sessions and was glad to delegate it to him.

The Municipal Palace, once the seat of governance for the province of Veracruz as well as the city, had been repurposed as a national chamber – to the ruffled-feather fury of the governor of Veracruz, displaced into an administrative office blocks away. Twenty-two men now occupied its largest conference room. Most had some importance or other, but Henri had learned whose bluster to ignore... and which quiet figure held real power.

One of those quieter men now uncharacteristically banged an inkpot on the table. "That's enough! The appropriations will proceed unmodified. There are sufficient funds to pay the soldiers of both corps at 1909 levels." General Victoriano Huerta pushed aside the inkpot and glared about him with his pale eyes. "They will be content with that. I am content with my pay, am I not? It has not changed either. Any man who is willing to fight and die for his country in such a time of great peril cannot quibble about money! Let us proceed."

With grudging approval, the appropriations were passed. While many divisions were still evident, the electrifying news three weeks previously of a Martian invasion of the southern United States had at least imparted some energy. General Huerta appeared to channel it himself as he looked about him. "I now invite General Mangin to speak."

Charles Mangin shoved back his chair and rose. "I can now announce that, with the approval and oversight of the governments of both Mexico and France, a joint military expedition is to be prepared." His Spanish was surprisingly good; he'd been known to pick up languages quickly, although Henri suspected that most of the speech was by rote. "It will consist of IV Corps of the reconstituted Mexican army, supported by some of our own forces. I plan to take the 22nd Division from the II Corps and the 112th and 118th striking vehicle battalions from the XI Corps, plus some artillery and support units. Embarking at Veracruz, it will proceed to Corpus Christi in the United States for offloading. Its orders are to carry out a joint attack on the Martian presence within the state of Texas."

Many faces showed surprise. A few did not; one was Colonel Angeles, who smiled thinly. Henri knew that he'd brought his fresh artillery batteries to a high degree of efficiency and hadn't been looking forward to sending them into a Hell of urban streetfighting. An open battle would be more favorable.

"We anticipate two months' time to prepare the force and assemble it at Veracruz, and another month to ready it in Texas."

The head of the *federales* police force jumped to his feet. "I would ask the general, if this force *is* nearly ready, why do we not attack and retake Mexico City?" A ripple of agreement followed.

Huerta lifted a hand before Mangin could reply. "An army is of no use until it has been blooded. This assault will allow us to build strengths and find weaknesses. We have already been repulsed once from Mexico City, and we cannot afford to fight and lose there again. The effect on national morale would be disastrous. But this new Martian outpost will be weak as yet – it will make a fine practice target. And the Americans will be attacking as well; we need only do our part."

"If I may add to the general's fine logic?" said Ambassador Creel. Huerta nodded to him. "France has given us invaluable support and a secure base here in Veracruz. But America – specifically, the state of Texas – has kept us from starvation with their beef shipments. It is true that the United States is a nation of tremendous military strength, but that strength is concentrated in their eastern seaboard, and Texas is sorely pressed. France is willing to offer assistance in defeating this invasion, and Mexico is honor-bound to do likewise. With our army victorious, we can then advance southward back into our own country and present the Martians with a threat of their own, while restoring proper governance to provinces which have known only anarchy and violence for three long years!"

Many nodded approval at that. Henri had doubts about the logistics involved in sweeping an army hundreds of miles through a devastated province, but certainly a defeat of the Martians north of the border would have a great impact on them in the south as well...

"By moving along sea lanes, we will avoid the logistical demands of the difficult terrain in Nuevo Leon and be secure from Martian attacks. Admiral Favereau assures me that French and American warships will guard both ports as they are used. It may seem like a great distance, but modern technology can accomplish remarkable things.

"We will earn American gratitude. And by accomplishing this, Mexico will take her place among the leading nations of the world in defending it against these invaders!"

Henri suppressed a smile of his own. Creel meant that the current – and weakened – government of Mexico would take that place, conferring legitimacy that it badly needed.

The murmured approval that Creel basked in fell silent a moment later; he turned, then quickly sat down. At the table's far end, President Diaz rose slowly to his feet. "It may seem strange to some of you that we should travel so far to fight the Martians. It does not seem so to me. This is an opportunity to carry out a pan-American strike against the creatures that attack us all, and we will not shirk it. As my senior general said, the army needs to be blooded. I trust him to do so in a manner which will reflect to our honor, and inspire his men to liberate *all* of Mexico from the Martians, and bring it under proper order. Give him all assistance that you may. Thank you all." He turned and shuffled from the table, passing through the door to what Henri assumed were his private chambers. Creel and Huerta quickly followed; the rest began to disperse.

Mangin took Henri aside as the men milled about. "Gamelin, tell me something," he said quietly. "If Paris were in the hands of the Martians, and you had even a fragment of an army, would you do anything else but take it back?"

Henri shook his head. "It would be impossible not to try."

"I am not sure I believe their reasons. Or not entirely. You've told me there are fighters in Mexico City not affiliated with this government..."

"They are in open rebellion against it, I believe."

"Just so. I wish to know more about them. If I am to fight alongside these Mexicans, I want to know what their objectives are – and I do not think they are telling me all of them. How soon can you get away?"

"Within the week, General."

"Then do so." Mangin nodded in what might have been approval and turned away.

April, 1912, IX Corps HQ, Alice, Texas

General Funston hopped down from the delivery truck he'd commandeered at the train stop. "Drop the boxes and trunks around the side," he ordered the driver.

Lang climbed down more carefully, one arm wrapped around a satchel bursting with paperwork he didn't trust to others. Moving a full general's location was no easy task; moving one in a tearing hurry...

Alice's town hall had been converted into a temporary headquarters for IX Corps by the simple expedient of adding tents on all sides of the building. Driveways, garages, and stables lined the sides further away to accommodate vehicles and horses; telegraph wires were neatly bundled along poles; men flowed in and out.

Funston had noticed Lang taking this in. "Neat work, isn't it? Jim Wade's a hell of an administrator. This is not going to be easy... Well, let's get it over with." He strode toward the nearest entrance; Lang followed.

They found Lieutenant-General James Wade in the main building, seated at a long table. Rows of desks to each side of the room were occupied by junior officers and clerks, but Wade's area was clear except for a map of Texas.

Wade looked startled to see them. "General Funston!" he said. He shoved back his chair and rose, leaning on one hand until he was upright. He was nearly bald, with a scrim of white hair and mustache. "I'd had no word you were coming–"

"It's not an inspection tour, General." Funston forced a smile. "May we speak privately?"

"Of course." Wade gestured. "Please clear the room, everyone."

The clerks filed out briskly, a few glancing back. Funston snagged a chair and sat at the main table; Lang did the same. Wade settled back into his own seat. Lang knew he'd been brought out of retirement after the mandatory age of sixty-four was waived, as one of the very small number of officers with experience as a lieutenant-general. He'd fought with the Buffalo Soldiers; he'd fought in the Spanish-American War...

He'd fought in the Civil War.

"General Wade, I am taking over command of IX Corps around Hebbronville. I want to attack that base by the end of this month. I'm going to need your help, and your deputy's as well – what I mean to say is, this is not intended to relieve you of command of the corps. I am simply going to take control of this particular operation."

Wade's mouth worked. "General... if..."

Funston plowed on. "I would appreciate if you could call your divisional generals in for me to meet with. I have some specific tactical recommendations for them. Also, my staff will need to coordinate with yours on railroad scheduling – there are at least three more tank battalions being transferred in by rail the day after tomorrow. I know it's short notice, Jim, but I'm confident that you have fully prepared the corps."

"Oh," said Wade dully. "Oh, yes. Although we were expecting five weeks more training time. And with the news about that offer from the French and Mexican governments, well – another three or four divisions would add much to our strength for the assault."

"We don't have five weeks. And those... phantom divisions, they might take months to get here and be no good when they did! No, Jim, we'll fight with what we have right now. I understand that the 3rd Volunteer took losses; they aren't suited for a heavy assault in any case, so they can hold around Laredo. But I need to get the other four divisions into an assault formation immediately and concentrate them upon Hebbronville. We're going to destroy that base before it gets any stronger!"

Wade sat stiffly upright in his chair; he looked terribly old in that moment. "General, if you wish my resignation, I will tender it at once–"

"Hellfire, Jim! I don't!"

"Perhaps we do need a more energetic presence. I remember you in the Philippines, when you captured the President with those Filipino scouts. Inspiring, yes, inspiring, and not even a regular army man. New blood..." He sighed. "I'm a cavalryman, General; always have been. I'm proud of what I've done, but when there are creatures from another world invading America, one can understand that things have changed a very great deal from my time."

"Of course I don't want your resignation. You can stay on in IX Corps to..." Funston trailed off at Wade's expression.

"General, the weapons have changed, but men have not. You know quite well that will not work."

"Yes. Yes, I suppose so." Funston clasped his hands. "General Wade, I relieve you of command of IX Corps in order to personally direct this assault. My staff will do their best to find you a billet back at Washington, and I will be recommending you for promotion to full general."

That was a meaningless sop when there were few positions available at that rank, and Wade – the sixty-nine year old Wade – knew that. "Thank you, General. I am turning over command of IX Corps to you, effective immediately. I wish you the very best of luck."

He rose stiffly; the other two did as well and returned his salute. He walked slowly from the room.

"I'm afraid I did not handle that well," muttered Funston.

I'm afraid you made an enemy, thought Lang; then he lifted the satchel to the tabletop and snapped open the clasps. There was a great deal of work to be done.

April, 1912, Duval County, Texas

Ronald Gorman nudged his sleeping subordinate with the toe of his boot. "Saberhagen, wake up! Where is de Gama?"

"How would I know?" mumbled the blond-haired man. He turned over in the improvised cot. The rail car held half a dozen of them, most strewn with filthy blankets. This was a long way down from Gorman's private car, and de Gama was not in either, nor the third between them.

Gorman cursed. He had no idea where the mad priest had gone; anywhere outside these rail cars meant death if a Master saw him. And de Gama was irreplaceable. He walked quickly back through both lesser cars to his own. Queen Idar was reading a book from the extensive library; she ignored his entrance pointedly. That would change in time...

Beside the car's vestibule, a large case of matte-grey metal was mounted to the wall. Gorman unlocked and slid open the panel, took down one of the heavy pendants within, draped it around his neck. It clasped itself together and contracted like a snake eating its own tail, shrinking, until it settled around his throat with a finger's gap remaining. As always, he felt the irrational dread that it might simply not stop until it decapitated him. There was little of the Masters that was ordinary.

Thus protected, he opened the car's door and stepped out onto the tiny platform, scanning the surroundings. The high berm raised by the Masters blocked most of the flat horizon. Only a small gap through which the rail line passed gave a further view. Bright sunlight beat down; a warm day, but de Gama was unlikely to die of heat or thirst out there. Well, heat, perhaps – just a little more quickly than the sun could inflict.

Gorman jumped down from the platform and headed toward the spring a quarter-mile distant that was their only water source. As he drew near, he checked the water level. Still trickling, and reasonably clean... but if it were to dry up, he doubted the Masters would trouble to find another source. He had his own supply hidden, but even that would only last a week or two at most.

No sign of de Gama. Gorman shouted for him a few times to be sure and then walked south. As he approached the train again, a machine appeared above one of the hopper cars, clutching a large container in its limbs. It inverted the container to spill a load of yellowish ore into the car with a pounding rumble that seemed to shake the ground. Pale dust drifted downwind in clouds, then settled.

Whatever it was that the Masters had begun digging out of the ground here, they had filled nearly two of the cars with it in the past few days.

Despite his pendant, Gorman waited until the machine had left his sight before he climbed between two of the cars to the other side. The machine was striding quickly southward, back to the main center of activity within the berm, where other, larger machines burrowed into the ground. Slag heaps grew larger every day; the pale dust billowed. A hive of activity, power, industry. If de Gama had strayed into there, he would be crushed like an insect.

There was one other activity the Masters undertook from time to time; Gorman walked in that direction. The ground rose slightly and crumpled into age-worn, dusty runnels with clumps of scrub fighting to colonize between them. Next to one of these bushes, a man was digging a hole; several objects lay on the ground nearby.

Gorman sighed and walked on, coming up to within a few feet, then stopped. "Enrique. Leave this be. It doesn't *matter*."

The priest turned, lowering his shovel. His arms were painfully thin; he'd barely made an impression on the ground, although he panted with effort. His dark eyes were pits of infinite depth, infinite madness.

"Enrique, please. It is dangerous for you to be out here. Come back."

"No," gasped de Gama. "They have become the flesh of the Masters. Nourished them. There should be tombs – great, hallowed barrows for them. Why do they come here to do this? There must be a reason. The ground, then, the ground – it is sacred. They belong within it."

Gorman wrinkled his nose at the five leathery skeletons. So little flesh had remained after consumption that even the local scavengers had scarcely bothered with them. "I don't know why the Masters feed at this place. I cannot guess at their thinking."

"Perhaps it reminds them of their desert world. I have seen... glimpses. Dried and furrowed..." de Gama gazed over the corpses. "Dried and furrowed, yes. Help me, Gorman. They belong in the ground."

"This is nonsense. Come." Gorman took de Gama's arm; the priest tore it away with sudden strength.

"They belong in the ground!"

If the task was not completed, de Gama would undoubtedly risk his life again to do so. Gorman sighed. "Very well, my friend. Give me the shovel." He took over de Gama's work; the dry soil dug easily and sifted loosely whenever he slung a spadeful over his shoulder, but chopping the scrub roots took time.

"Your queen is very beautiful," said de Gama from where he crouched.

"You had better be a *real* priest around her," grunted Gorman.

"Not the body, the soul. So fortunate to live in this time. To be cleansed, like all of us."

"But not in any hurry. No more than I am in." Gorman straightened. "Is this deep enough?"

The priest cocked his head. "They'll be safe. What the angels have not consumed will be risen by God. Inter them. Thank you, Gorman."

Gorman climbed from the grave, hooked a boot under one of the corpses, and rolled it into the cavity. "You are my priest and my friend. How could I do any less?"

He began to regret his generosity once the sun and work had wrung a sweat from him, but it did not take long to finish the mass grave. He wondered if de Gama would say anything over the scuffed dirt, but the priest merely began to walk back toward the train, unspeaking. Gorman hefted the shovel and caught up to him.

"So you have seen their world? How do they rule it? Are there machines like these everywhere?"

"What I have seen, you cannot grasp." de Gama smiled sadly toward him. For a moment, he seemed quite sane. "No more than I could have when I was a student. They have made me into... into an intermediary, and nothing can ever be the same. Is it not wonderful?"

With de Gama so calm – spent – an idea occurred to Gorman. "Enrique, my priest. Would you wait upon my queen?"

"It would be my pleasure."

They returned to the train without incident; Gorman stowed the shovel away. He splashed water over his face from the trough and combed his hair. A monarch should not appear to have performed physical labor, after all. Even de Gama straightened his torn shirt; then they entered the private car.

"Good afternoon, my queen. Have you met our priest formally? Enrique de Gama. He speaks with the Masters and tells us their will."

Idar closed and laid aside her book – as she had not done for him – and studied de Gama. "I have seen him before. I fear whatever they do has driven him mad."

"Only a little." Gorman sat and gestured de Gama to do the same. "The Pope calls it the 'Martian Heresy'. They told us when I was still in that jail in Torreon, as though it were important. Pious fools. Then when the Masters came and the jail began to burn, the guards released us – not knowing we would serve them one day. Now the Pope thinks we are all heretics and we will burn in any case! But what does he know? He has never spoken with one of them as Enrique has."

"At least this man has an excuse for what he does."

"Serving the greatest creatures of God's creation?" asked Gorman.

"Murdering those the 'greatest' only came here to destroy."

Gorman shrugged. "I take no pleasure in it. But the Masters must feed, and better upon them than upon you and I."

"There were older ways, once," offered de Gama. His gaze cut toward and away from the woman like the beat of a bird's wing. "There were so few of us left at Zacatecas. There would soon have been no one... to see the light. We brought sacrifices to them instead – sacred bulls. Golden calfs. They served well enough."

Her face lit. "Then there *is* another way!"

Gorman gestured about. "There are no animals here."

"Not here. But close by. I know this country, Dr. Gorman. If those creatures truly allow you to act for them..."

He scowled. "They know my worth! Not like some!"

"Then take the other way."

He looked quizzically at de Gama. "There is plenty of time," said the priest. "For all to be brought to the light. Your queen is humane, Gorman. It would please her to do so."

Gorman turned, leaned forward. "Would it?"

She looked down, then abruptly back to him. "Is that what you wish to hear? Yes. It would please me."

"Then I shall seek their will in the matter," said de Gama.

"That has a cost, you know," said Gorman. "Communing with the Masters. If he does so, he will be madder still the next time that you see him."

It was fascinating to see the play of expression on her face for a moment – the balancing of de Gama's suffering against the lives of strangers. There could be levers here. He often forgot how little others meant to him in comparison to most people.

"Then pay it," she said flatly. "If you truly are my priest as you say."

de Gama bowed. "At once."

"However," put in Gorman, "on a practical note, we are not equipped to round up cattle. That is not a safe activity without horses."

"Could you manage to round up sheep?"

"Sheep? Here?"

"Millions. Many died off in the drought of 1894, but they are still an industry in this part of Texas."

"Really?" said Gorman. "I dare say there is a great deal that I do not know about Texas. I shall require a native guide. I trust you have walking shoes?"

Chapter Eleven

April, 1912, Mexico City, Mexico

Lieutenant Henri Gamelin halted along with the small group of Mexican fighters in the shade of a building's corner. While two of them carefully peered around it in both directions down the wide street, he unobtrusively unhooked his canteen and drank from it. The webbing belt he replaced it onto had been borrowed from a French infantryman; his naval uniform was not designed for inland expeditions. It was already thickly coated with pale dust after their ten-mile march into the southern sector of Mexico City. So was his throat; but he'd kept up well enough.

The outskirts had seemed almost normal, although deserted. Here in the city proper, though, the stench of smoke was everywhere, and every gaping window seemed to have a fan of soot above it. Many buildings had collapsed into the streets in heaps of bricks, burnt timbers, and debris. Here and there lay human or equine skeletons. Mexico City had been in the hands of the Martians for two and a half years.

Many unpaved areas had been colonized by an unfamiliar weed, a sort of raggedly woven mat, deep red in color. He'd heard that it had come with the Martians. Perhaps it was like tobacco or cotton – something a conqueror cultivated – but it seemed too haphazard for that. But as with anything to do with the Martians, trying to guess why they did it was bound to be as fruitless as the weed itself.

Manuel Palafox exchanged a few quiet words with the two scouts, then rejoined Henri. "All seems clear. We go underground from here on, not to give away their position."

One of his men – a giant of a fellow – levered up a sewer grating and grandly waved the others in while holding it up one-handed. Henri followed them, clutching the bricks at the opening's edge and dropping into the dim tunnel. The grating clashed into place a moment later. Once his eyes adjusted, he could follow along easily enough from one patch of light to another, stepping over the worst of the muck on the tunnel's stone floor. It didn't seem that bad; but of course, this was not a living city any more. Two rainy seasons had scoured the effluvia of half a million citizens. He walked on the city's dry bones.

A mile's slow progress ended at a wooden ladder. They clambered up to an arched brick gallery, still below ground at this point. This had been swept clean; light filtered down from barred openings onto several wooden doors laid on trestles. Henri was surprised to note a radio set and its chemical cells arranged on one – a German Telefunken. Nearby, maps and documents were laid out neatly along several more of the

107

salvaged doors. Several men surrounded them, conferring. All wore the same stained, off-white caminos and pants that Henri's group did, with a few wrapped puttees. It was obvious by the way all the men looked at the one figure in their midst who the man was that Henri had come to see.

Emiliano Zapata dropped a sheaf of papers onto the table, turned, and came up to Henri, offering a hand. Henri shook it.

"Welcome!" Zapata stood a little taller than Henri's height with a powerful build – and grasp. His face was seamed and weathered from a life outdoors; the brown eyes were very hard. He waved to the group. "Everyone! The French Navy has sent us an emissary. He is here to see what we do. Let's not disappoint him. Who will show him our ways?" Zapata's accent was unfamiliar to Henri; the mutters behind him even less so. He caught slang he didn't recognize. *Catrin?* It probably wasn't flattering.

"Come, now. Casta! How about you?"

"I could show him our navy," said the short, grizzled man he addressed, "but it's all run aground. Very strange."

"Bah. *Jefe* Casta is joking with you, Señor Gamelin. He will be delighted to take you along on a patrol to the power plant zone. It will be good exercise for him, and I have not heard much from there in too long."

"Are these all your chiefs, then?" asked Henri.

"All but three out in the eastern district. Some of this city belongs to the *diablos*, some belongs to us, and much is disputed. Few looters bother with what is left any more. It is us and them."

"But the federal army must have regained some territory when they attacked."

A few men chuckled grimly at that; one spat. "The *federales* made a brave show, it's true. Especially General Diaz, the president's favored nephew, with his gallant charge up the Zocalo plaza. How strange that he was not supported by any other troops at that critical moment. But, I am a simple farmer... We did manage to retrieve some of their artillery pieces that were not melted. They are useful, although we have only handfuls of shells. Perhaps you can arrange for more to be sent to us?"

"That's why I am here," agreed Henri. "But there is much I need to study. Lines of supply. How open the streets are – or how blocked. And – forgive me – who might follow the example of the *federales*, and choose not to support one another."

That earned him some glares, but Zapata nodded equably. "Of course. The city, the people, all are to be open to you. It is horrible, what has happened here, but there has been a certain... purifying, as well."

"I don't understand."

"Everything that can burn, has burned. Nothing remains but stone. And so it is with my men – all those who are afraid have left, and the ones who remain I can trust absolutely." He gestured. "Casta will show you. And, Manuel, can you go as well?" Palafox nodded. "Casta, when is your next patrol?"

"Now," said the chief.

Henri held his eye, conscious of his own fatigue but refusing to admit it. He had remembered what *catrin* meant – 'dandy'. "Let us waste no time, then," he said.

"Excellent! Try not to let him die, Casta." Zapata waved them on.

They formed up in an adjoining chamber: Casta, Palafox, and six men, one of them being the huge man who'd opened the grating; he slung a sledgehammer in a rope loop over his back that must have weighed forty pounds. "Mouse-holing," explained Palafox. "We go through walls when doors are not wise."

Two others picked up rifles of a kind Henri had not seen in years: beautifully engraved double-barreled guns, with shells the size of saltshakers. Elephant guns. "Pretty, eh?" offered one man, holding it for him to look over. "Four-bore. A rich man's toy from a *haciendo* in the uplands. The armor is thinner on the tops of the *diablos*. Sometimes, these can pierce it from a rooftop."

"Sometimes," agreed the other gunman. "The good part is, the recoil throws you back to enjoy your headache in safety!"

Others gathered bundles of dynamite and detonators, and one picked up an infantry rifle; then the patrol headed out, going back through the sewer tunnel but turning in a different direction, then another. Henri was quickly lost. When they emerged again to street level, the midday sun threw so little shadow that he couldn't orient; but the street grid was obvious, and the patrol headed down a side lane, picking their way over rubble when necessary and stopping at breaks in cover to look and listen.

"The *diablos* have no use for this city," said Palafox as they walked. "But they loot it. The power plant was stripped last year for its metals. Then the cables leading from it, streetcar wires, tracks. Sometimes they pick up automobiles and carry them off. They must come further south all the time." He tapped the side of his mouth. "If they want my fillings, they must come get them."

"Can you predict where they go, then? Ambush them?"

"At first, yes. They grew wiser. Now they may leave a car lying in an intersection for months, but strip wire a mile away, and they do not use a route too often. There have been more of them lately – and some of our patrols have not come back. We send reports of what activity we see, if they may be useful. You may get to see a show, Señor Gamelin, but we have learned to be very patient."

Henri ducked under a beam, trying to ignore the skeleton curled tightly into a gap beside it as casually as Palafox did. "Do you send reports on that German radio?"

Palafox smiled. "Yours is not the only arrangement we are making. But the Germans are tight-fisted. I hope your nation will be more–"

Ahead, a scout pulled sharply back from a corner. Palafox's smiled vanished. "Stay close, my friend." The group converged; Casta waved them into the adjoining building through a ground-floor window frame.

"You are lucky, Lieutenant," he said to Henri. "We may be able to show you something interesting. But you must be very quiet, and do exactly as any one of us says to do. Understood?"

"Yes, *jefe*."

"Come along." They moved slowly through what proved to be the lobby of a hotel, avoiding anything in the strewn debris that might make noise when trod upon, and proceeded up the wide, gilded staircase. Keeping low and well back from the shattered windows, they crept to the end of the mezzanine. Despite Zapata's grim claim, at least this building had not been consumed by fire.

Behind a marble-topped bar, a hole had been battered through the wall. Three layers of brick showed as Henri ducked through it.

The next building was a warehouse; here, only a few small windows opened onto the street. Casta beckoned silently to Henri and pointed. Henri edged up, careful not to expose his movement. He found his heart was hammering, but he moved steadily enough...

In the street, a Martian tripod stood, braced squarely on all three limbs. It was pulling down overhead wires with its tentacles; the creak and snap seemed too loud in a city that was otherwise eerily silent. Henri was nearly level with the bulbous central section, and he studied the joints in the metal surfaces closely. At Tampico, the tripod that wrecked his ship had been a terrifying blur in the darkness; now he looked for weak points.

He watched it work for a few moments longer; then when the others began to move along the floor, he backed away and caught up with them.

"You've brought us luck," whispered Palafox. "We have an ambush site close by. Just stay close."

They climbed through a hole chopped in the floor and down a ladder nailed to the warehouse's wall, and another into the basement. A service tunnel crossed under the street; Henri groped through the dusty blackness and emerged through another improvised exit into what he recognized as a department store. Up a flight of stairs again. Along another floor –

"Here is some of our work," said Casta with obvious pride. He gestured at the 'mousehole'. Henri approached and peered through it.

This structure had been a dry-goods store in its day, but with a storage level on the second floor. Only a few tiny windows and an open loading door gave light. Parts of the second floor had been cut away and many crates dumped below. An antique field gun rested on the remaining timbers, tucked hard against the wall. Hawsers dangled to it from purchases at several points in the roof trusses.

"I said we had no navy," murmured Casta. "But this building is like an old man-of-war. It has a broadside."

Henri climbed through the mousehole and approached the gun. Its muzzle was bowsed up tight against the wall, facing a small... well, gunport... for it to fire through.

"There are other openings there, and there." Casta pointed. "If they approach along any lane, and we have time, we can shift the gun."

The gun was painted a warm pale grey with varnished wooden wheels. "That is a Mondragón 75mm piece," marveled Henri. "It weighs over a ton with that carriage. How did you...?"

Casta punched the big sledgehammer-man beside him in the arm. "Enrico carried it up there. Didn't you?" The man beamed; then Casta clicked his fingers and the men burst to activity. Some loaded and manned the gun, others laid out dynamite bombs, the gunmen checked their weapons.

Henri stayed clear by Palafox. "Shouldn't they go topside?"

"This roof is too exposed. They might get a shot from the windows, though."

Once everyone was in place, time seemed to get terribly slow. Men watched carefully at the small windows; Casta was poised at the gun's lanyard. From outside, the whine and clunk of the moving tripod grew closer...

A clattering sounded from the rooftop. Palafox looked up in surprise. "What –" Roof tiles banged loose and fell to the street outside. The noise progressed along the roof. Men spun, looking upward.

A mechanical nightmare swung itself into the building through the loading door.

It stopped, framed in the doorway – a much smaller version of a tripod, a gleaming metal ovoid, a central red eye; some of its metal limbs clutched at the roof edge and others were planted on the floor. Men and machine seemed to stare at one another for an instant.

Then it fired a heat ray and one of the gunmen vanished in a flare of incinerating light.

Others broke from their trance and ducked for cover. Casta was grappling with another man about to throw his dynamite bomb. The machine did not fire again; instead it shifted forward in a fluid scrabble of its limbs and struck out with some of them like steel whips, smashing men aside left and right. The second gunman collided with a post; his weapon tumbled below to the ground floor.

Henri shook himself from his terror and threw himself to the floor, clutching at the jagged wood edges of one of the openings. He levered his body over the edge and dropped heavily to the ground floor, sprawling and twisting upright. Screams and an ordinary rifle shot came from above. Henri spotted the dropped elephant gun nearby, dashed to it, and picked it up. He crouched low and banged the weapon's butt onto the floor, peered upward at the mayhem unfolding above, aimed the barrels at the moving gleam of metal as best he could, and pulled both triggers.

The black-powder explosion nearly knocked him over despite his bracing the gun. Smoke blinded him. Thuds and crashes from above; the machine's central mass fell through the smoke cloud to crash onto the ground floor, smashing crates to splinters, limbs flailing. Henri was sledged aside by one. He rolled over, gasping in pain, and began to crawl away, coughing.

A steel whip coiled about his leg and dragged him back along the floor.

Henri had lost all capacity for thought. His hand clutched a broken plank; he twisted as the machine pulled him close to it and flailed at the metallic carapace with his improvised club. The wood banged harmlessly off the alien metal. The enormous red eye glared emptily at him; another limb grappled his chest and began to squeeze, crushing the breath from him. The world dimmed to a dying red glow.

More gunshots sounded, then two heavy blasts. Something swung in a blur beside him; a clank, and the limb crushing him went slack. Henri dragged in a breath; his vision cleared. Enrico stepped over him, bringing around the sledgehammer in a swinging arc. He shouted *"Viva Zapata!"* and smashed it into the red eye. As he drew back, Henri glimpsed Casta snapping the elephant gun closed. He stepped onto the machine's back and fired downward once, twice, ignoring the brutal recoil that staggered him.

Enrico hammered a few more times at what was now a wreck, then stumbled back, gasping. The eye's red glow faded. Others pulled the limp metal serpent away from Henri and dragged him upright. He swayed on his feet, his left leg spasming. It didn't seem broken, but his chest blazed with spikes of pain.

"Back to the south door!" cried Casta. He threw the gun to the man beside him and grabbed a bomb from another, holding it in his left hand. His right arm dangled at his side, but he waved on his men with the dynamite bundle.

The tripod in the street fired its far more powerful heat ray into the building, fanning it about and dissolving the interior with its shriek. The upper levels burst into flame instantly. The men scrambled through the door to the laneway. Henri gasped a breath of clean air after the sudden inferno of the store's interior and stumbled; one

111

of the men grabbed his arm and pulled him along. Casta turned and flung his bomb back inside, then sprinted after them. Before they'd reached the opposite building, the crash of its explosion punched a cloud of smoke out of the doorway. Other crashes immediately followed, then the roar of the collapsing building. Henri thought he heard the 75mm go off, but it was difficult to tell. He could still barely breathe, let alone run, but he kept up as they fled into a portico and through the building toward the next mousehole.

Casta came up and wrapped his good arm under Henri's other side. Ahead, Enrico was carrying another man, limp as a sack.

"What was that machine?" gasped Henri.

"I have never seen anything like it. This is bad, very bad. It can get inside buildings as we can... I think it was watching us before we set up our ambush. We must get back to report this to Zapata." His scowl cleared for a moment. "You did well, *catrin*. That was a *dandy* shot! But try to keep up. I am not supposed to let you die."

Chapter Twelve

April, 1912, West of Hebbronville, Texas

Emmet Smith reined in his horse to allow the others to catch up. The morning sun struck green and gold highlights along the wide horizon. The scent of mesquite was everywhere; decades of stock overgrazing had killed the rolling grasslands of much of South Texas in favor of tough scrub brush and the blocky-grained trees that supplied so many fences and structures.

He'd seen none of the scorched areas he'd expected during their patrols from the camp south of Seven Sisters, other than a few old wildfire remnants; even crossing over the railway line further to the south hadn't revealed any evidence of Martian destruction. Two tripod sightings in the past week; both times they'd easily slipped away with no pursuit. For invaders, these Martians sure kept to themselves. IX Corps was brewing up an attack from the eastward side, he'd heard, but it was eerily quiet in these parts.

Ranger Hicks pulled up next to him. As he'd bragged, he was an excellent rider. He also kept a good lookout. The other, Clell Blackwell, had six months' experience and was learning well; he'd taken to the camp chores with a will. Emmet was just as pleased that the hot-headed Tomlinson had been posted back to San Antonio.

Hicks swigged from his canteen. "Gettin' familiar with this country. I never had much to do out here before. Mostly Laredo and Piedras Negras; once the Sisters wells dried up, the boomtowns did too."

"I don't think there was ever much to do out here. Sort of a whistlestop without the whistle." Emmet turned to Blackwell. "Let's keep going southeast for a while. There's a couple of small ranches about five miles from here; sheep and goats. They've been evacuated, but seems like Martians like buildings – sure like burning 'em, anyhow – and around here even a shack amounts to a building."

They followed tracks and laneways through the scrub for most of the morning at an easy but steady pace, keeping a sharp eye out; but it wasn't until they'd passed by the second ranch's outbuildings that Blackwell called out.

"There's people there! A mile due east. They're waving at us."

"I see 'em." Emmet lifted his binoculars. "Ah, six civilians. Let's go check 'em out. Don't quit looking around for any Martians, though."

He veered off the track and began picking a route through the scrub. At half a mile, they crossed a low rise and he got a better look; there were indeed six men on foot, but another figure lay on the ground. One seemed to be tending to her.

"Hurry up, fellas." He spurred his horse into a gallop; the others joined him. The nag was no racehorse, but she rode well enough. At the next fence, Emmet signaled with his knees a few feet out and the horse gathered herself and leaped, clearing it easily, landing in a spurt of soil and a rocking, living slide, driving on ahead. For a moment, it was just like 1903; *this* was why he'd joined, a wide open space with an unknown situation to find out and prevail over. In a few minutes, they reached the small group, pulled up, and swung out of their saddles.

"Thank God you're here!" called out the crouching man in English; a southern American accent. The rest gathered around; Spanish, poorly dressed, haggard. They had a hard look about them. "We've made it this far, but then she collapsed. I don't know what to do for her!"

"Let me see." Emmet hunkered down beside them. "Did – I'll be damned!"

The woman was Jovita Idar.

His first thought was heatstroke, but her forehead felt neither dry nor clammy. Lifting an eyelid showed a normal pupil shrinking.

"What's wrong with her, Emmet?" asked Hicks.

"I don't know." He saw it then; a fresh bruise darkening along her jawline. He glanced over to the stranger, turning slightly to let his coat slip open over his hip. "Now, friend, you better–"

A pistol cocked just behind his head. "No one move," said the American. "You will all take your pistols out slowly and drop them on–"

Blackwell shouted something on Emmet's left. Emmet made a choice and grabbed for his weapon; a grunting movement behind him, and the landscape exploded into blackness.

April, 1912, West of Martian Base, Texas

Ronald Gorman straightened slowly. He surveyed the outcome of his scheme: one Ranger shot twice in the chest; one frozen, livid, at gunpoint; one clubbed unconscious. As he watched, the shot Ranger bubbled blood from his mouth and died.

"You son of a bitch," said the standing Ranger. "You are gonna be at the hurtin' end of the biggest manhunt we've ever seen."

"No, we are not. It's not men who are doing the hunting any more." He switched to Spanish. "Garcia, collect their weapons." As his man moved cautiously to obey, Gorman looked over the Rangers' horses. Nothing special, but they would make sheepherding a little easier... and could be consumed themselves, if the sheep were insufficient. So could the Rangers, for that matter. Every new body was one more between him and the Masters' needs...

Garcia rejoined him, hefting a new automatic pistol with delight. "Look what the dead one had! It's mine by right – I did for him!"

"You fool," Gorman said tiredly. "Do you think this is the only patrol? And the others cannot spot buzzards? Then they find a dead Ranger with bullets in him that no Martian ever fired. If they ever figure out what we are, we'll be shot on sight."

Garcia looked away and scratched his neck. "We could bury him."

"Did you bring a shovel? I should make you do it, Garcia, with your bare hands! But just lasso the corpse to your saddle and drag it. He won't mind the ride... " He looked down to Idar as she mumbled something. "I will carry my queen. I must apologize to her

114

for such brutality – it was a foul blow – but I hoped it would save lives in the short term. I suppose it still will; that dead Ranger goes first." In English he called out, "You! Carry your sleepy friend until he wakes up. We're marching east, but it's only a few miles."

The balding Ranger glanced up from where he crouched beside the unconscious one. "What? That's straight toward the Martians! Are you nuts? Once they spot us on foot–"

"Oh, I am quite sane." Gorman loosened his scarf. "This pendant is their work, and it will admit us to their dwelling. There are marvels there. Come, this is your great chance to see them up close. Very close."

The group proceeded back along with their reluctant guests; Gorman rode last, with Queen Idar draped across his saddle. Two miles from the mine, a Master's tripod loomed up, sauntering across the landscape from the north. It looked them over, then continued on its patrol. Gorman noted that while the two Rangers did not quail at the sight of it, they did seem... uncomfortable. The taller one had woken fairly quickly, considering how hard Gorman had struck him.

His queen awoke too at that point. His apology was not accepted – decidedly not; she jumped down from horseback and stamped along beside him. As they passed through the cut in the berm which admitted the rail tracks, Gorman realized he would need to make better amends. The answer came to him in a flash. Once their new guests had been made secure, he instructed his men to water the horses – one must care for one's stock – and repaired to his private car to join her. In the companionway, he paused to obtain a gift before he entered.

"I trust you're better? Again, my sincere apologies."

Idar was perched on the settee, holding a wet cloth to her jaw. She did not look around. "Did you know those men were there?"

"No, to be quite honest. I did not think anyone foolish enough to come so close to a Masters' nest. You seemed quite interested in them, I may say."

"I'm tired of all your ugly faces; these were new."

"Hm. Perhaps. Of course, they cannot be allowed to leave. But we did obtain several sheep. I'm more a man of high finance and scientific knowledge than a stockman, but judging by the size of them, all of your associates have gained several weeks of existence by your cooperation."

"I'm not cooperating with you! Or those *things!*"

"Of course you are. And for the best of reasons." Gorman moved closer. "As with all things, it goes in steps. Those scum out there adapted very quickly – but they are nothing. A person of worth takes time. I spent a *long* time in that jail, and longer at Zacatecas... But I have realized that confining you here in this car is unjust and unhealthy. A queen should be free to roam her domain, as I am. Please, look." He held out a pendant – twin to the one he still wore – in both hands, as though presiding at a coronation.

She turned and recoiled. "Like *you* wear? I'll have none of it!"

"Please, I insist. A monarch must have a crown, after all."

"I would simply bolt from here!"

"Then a Master would track you down, at my priest's bidding, and bring you back to me in the gentlest of embraces... Oh, the hell with this." Gorman feinted left, and lunged. He pinned her to the settee with his weight and wrestled the pendant past her flailing hands to her neck with infinite care, ignoring her blows. The physical proximity, the contact, and scent, were... intriguing, and hinted at future possibilities. Then the pendant clasped itself into an unbreakable band, and he released her and stepped back. Both them were breathing hard, he noted. Steps, steps...

She clawed at the object. "Take this cursed thing off me!"

"But it's your color." Indeed, the pewter gray did complement her black hair. He'd remembered his manners again.

"Just – just get out of here."

"I would never abandon you in distress. But I shall give you room to recover." Gorman moved off to the car's far end, studied the view outside while she wept, and smoked a cigar.

After a time, she calmed herself and was once again his regal queen, smoothing stray hairs into place. She rose and walked back to stand before him, bearing the pendant with dignity and grace, as he'd known she would.

"You were right. I have met those Rangers before. And I have a certain debt to repay them. It has to do with a newspaper in Laredo."

Gorman bowed. "I am all attention."

April, 1912, East of Hebbronville, Texas

Emmet's headache began to fade soon after they'd arrived within the fortified wall, but his fury stayed. Partly at himself for being so easily fooled – seeing Jovita Idar had thrown him for a complete loop – but also at the bastards who had them captive.

The car they were brought to was a dilapidated passenger car, half-filled with boxes. Two other men kept to themselves, barely able to look at the Rangers. They didn't seem part of the gang that ran this place, but they obviously obeyed them and were ashamed of it. One babbled nonsense from time to time. But at least those two were free; Hicks and Emmet were cuffed to a long chain that ran across the car's aisle from the rear door. Someone had thought this out; it allowed a couple of guards to unlock one end of that chain and take them outside to relieve themselves without much chance of overpowering anybody or bolting more than a couple of yards.

"You're lucky," said one guard who wandered in after an hour. "The cattle over in that car? They lie in their own filth. But Señor Gorman wants you under better guard. And some of us won't go in there. We have standards!"

Once they'd had a chance to watch the coming and going of the gang members, and with that glimpse outside of the fortified dirt wall, Emmet and Hicks began quietly talking.

"Collaborators," spat Hicks. "I can't believe it. Wouldn't we have heard about this by now? These bastards can't be the first ones!"

"I don't know about that," mused Smith. "A government or army wouldn't want word getting out that the Martians don't just kill or eat everyone outright; if people thought they could surrender, they'd not fight as hard. Anyone who found *this* going on would likely just kill 'em all on the spot and swear his men to secrecy."

"That'd suit me fine."

"Hicks, we don't know how much time we've got. They fed us, but I don't want to think much about why. If we can get out of here and get a fast look around, it'll be the best scouting any Ranger's ever done... if we can survive to get back. Get to thinking

116

on that."

"Okay." Hicks looked worried, but steady. Blackwell might have grown into that sort of a Ranger, if he'd been given time. Another reason to loathe these men; but Emmet wouldn't let it get in the way of clear thought.

The car's front door opened; another gang member entered along with Miss Idar. Emmet waited, watching as they approached–

"Damn!" cried Hicks. "What's she doing with one of those things?"

"Hm?" Emmet twisted to look at him.

Hicks pointed with his chin. "That necklace thing! Their leader has one. It talks to the Martians or somethin'. He was braggin' about it. Look, you don't think she..."

The guard looked on with obvious amusement as Idar walked up to them.

"Where the hell did you get that?" blurted Emmet. "You didn't... couldn't..." He couldn't finish. She leaned in with a fierce glare.

"*Callarte la pinche boca!* These men speak no English, they think I am haranguing you. Know this. Gorman says these creatures are digging ore out of the ground. They need it for some vital reason, you *rinche* bastard! They came all this way for it! There are ten other people captive here, in the next car. They will all die! You will too! But there are a few weeks before the creatures grow hungry again."

Emmet realized what she was doing. He had no difficulty in feigning an enraged expression. He snarled back, "You damn bitch, I'm listening!"

She stamped her foot. "We have no chance to escape from inside this fort! But once the train is filled with ore, it will leave for Mexico. You must be ready then. I can protect us from the creatures in their machines with this pendant – you must deal with these traitor men. Devise a way to free yourselves, but wait for my signal. Wait, you swine! *Rinche cabron!* We have to get past Laredo and over the river. *Do you understand?*"

"Damn right!"

"Stinkin' cow!" chipped in Hicks.

"And don't be such a fool next time!" She spun and stalked off; the guard fell in beside her, chuckling.

"I continue to be impressed by that woman," said Emmet truthfully. "Well, we better not get lazy, but until you or I come up with a better plan, let's go with hers."

Chapter Thirteen

Cycle 597,845.1, Minefast 31.01, South Texas

Taldarnilis settled itself both mentally and physically within the compartment of its fighting machine. The past tendays were the longest duration it had spent in the machine, with only brief breaks to obtain nutrients and expel waste. Rather than a sense of confinement, it had grown to feel one with the machine, appreciating every extent of its agility and power.

It would need all that skill and determination very shortly. The imminent threat was daunting. Yet the decision was not its alone. It opened a communication channel to make contact with Group 31's holdfast and requested an audience.

Group Leader Vantarsilas replied almost immediately. "Greetings, Taldarnilis. It is not yet time for your regular report. Has the situation changed?"

"Yes, Group Leader. Raqtinoctil has obtained imagery from the mapping satellite. It made a pass over this region six days ago." Taldarnilis added the image to their communication.

"But that data is apportioned by clan status. We are not eligible for it yet. How did it obtain..." Vantarsilas' transmission stopped as it absorbed the image.

"Raqtinoctil was able to simulate Level Four access temporarily. It developed this skill some time ago, but it insists that it only be used when there is great–"

"Taldarnilis! There is a considerable prey force assembling to attack you!"

"That is our conclusion as well," said Taldarnilis dryly. "The lack of activity on the prey's part despite our proximity indicated much preparation, and this imaging confirms it in approximate detail."

"You are seriously outnumbered. You must withdraw immediately with as much of the equipment as you can bring. They have reacted much faster than you predicted!"

"May I remind the group leader that we have not completed our mission yet," said Taldarnilis, ignoring the implied criticism. "The amount of compound 92-12 extracted is only enough to power the holdfast for less than half a cycle. If we are driven out now, Group 31 will almost certainly fail."

"But if the prey destroy your mine, we fail as well and with greater losses."

"We do not intend to allow that. I request authorization to carry out an immediate attack on this assembled force within the next day, and disrupt it before it may fully attack us."

The group leader was silent for a considerable time. Finally, it said with some hesitation, "This level... this level of risk was never anticipated."

"It was never necessary before. Yet I submit that it is now."

The group leader hesitated. And hesitated...

April 1912, IX Corps HQ, Alice, Texas

Willard Lang surveyed the command center. General Wade's staff had done good work before his dismissal; the telephone and telegraph desks were ranked along one wall, clerks' stations to the other side, and the large map table was illuminated by electric lamps hung from the ceiling – necessary, as it was three o'clock in the morning.

The attack on the Martian base was about to begin. Lang felt as charged as the glowing filaments in the bulbs above him.

General Funston accepted a mug of coffee from a clerk and joined him by the table. He'd slept for the previous two hours; Lang too had a veteran's knack for resting when he could, but he was amazed that Funston had managed that. Out there in the darkness, fifteen miles west, four divisions were moving up to their jumping-off lines, 'uncommon stiff and slow' as per Kipling's poem. The 83rd, 80th, and 49th divisions were regular army; the 7th Volunteer mostly Texans. Cronkhite's 80th was a veteran of the battle of Albuquerque, and with its losses long since made up, was the prime striking force. Funston had assigned most of the corps tank battalions to Cronkhite; Lang had begun calling it the 'tank division'.

All the formations were concentrated far tighter than they would have been in defense so that the highly mobile Martians couldn't strike at any isolated unit. The Martian base, from the glimpses they'd gotten of its defensive wall, was only about a mile across. That seemed smaller than ones they'd encountered before. It also made things crowded for multiple divisions to advance, to say the least – like hitting a nail with a sledgehammer. Brigadier General Dougherty of the 7th had nearly demanded the honor of leading the assault; Funston had obliged by giving him the right wing. The 49th had the left. Once they'd engaged the Martian defenders, the 80th would move up and strike.

The Martian defenders. Lang liked that phrase. He'd been around Funston long enough to have picked up some of his aggressiveness. It was about time *they* were the attackers!

The 83rd was in reserve, ready to make up losses and press on where the defenders had stopped the assault. There were going to be losses; everyone knew that.

"They're moving beyond the telephone connections, sir. The last calls are just coming in." Major Otto Prendergast had worked with Funston for three years; his easy manner overlaid a cool professionalism. Lang had learned a great deal from him.

Funston smiled wryly. "I find myself wishing that I'd spent less time badgering Leonard for guns and more time asking for radios. And aircraft."

"Perhaps aircraft with radios?" said Prendergast.

"Put heat rays on 'em while you're at it." Funston sipped his coffee. "Still, Cronkhite's well able to judge when to advance. More so than I am back here. All the comforts of home. I remember swimming the Bagbag River in the Philippines and picking the leeches off afterward. I certainly could have used a mug of coffee back then..." He swung abruptly as one of the clerks put down a telephone and nudged two of the wooden blocks forward on the map.

"Twenty miles more to the base," muttered Lang. He felt as tense as if he were driving a tank through the darkness himself. Of course the rail line ran much closer to the Martian base than that, but a single line could never be a railhead for four divisions. Even the hastily laid sidings immediately to the west of Alice couldn't support a fraction of the logistics load. They'd been more or less dumped onto the landscape in endless ranks of tents and vehicle and gun parks, and must advance from there on their own by road and the flatter areas of the countryside. Organizing who went where had been a colossal job.

And then there was the question of distance... Too close, and the Martians could attack a division's rear areas in a quick sally – they'd seen *that* before. Too far, and the steam tanks would run out of coal or water or break down before they even got into the fight. But there'd been no spoiling attacks or probes by the Martians, so moving up at night still made sense. It was going to be a terribly long day when the sun rose...

"There's a lot of reports of collisions and accidents coming in," warned Prendergast.

"Good," said Funston. "Otto, if there weren't any, they'd be spread too thin. It is acceptable."

Unlike other Martian bases, this one didn't seem to have any defensive towers. That meant that if they could push through the mobile forces, they could get artillery observers up onto that defensive wall and shell whatever was inside. Both lead divisions had objectives to get their six-inch howitzers to within three miles of the wall by midday. With the 80th backing them up, at least one ought to do it.

An hour dragged by; the blocks were pushed closer. By dawn they'd be poised to strike. Lang chafed his hands eagerly. *It's working!* Maybe, just maybe, the Martians had become so used to dominating the regions around their bases that they hadn't anticipated a rapid assault on this scale.

Just after four o'clock, a flurry of activity among the telephone clerks drew Lang's attention. One turned, looking pale. "Sir! *Sir!*"

"What's happening?" muttered Prendergast.

Cycle 597,845.1, Minefast 31.01, South Texas

Taldarnilis loped through the darkness in its fighting machine, its stride adjusted to accommodate the awkward weight of the eradicator tube it held in its manipulators. Eight other machines followed close behind, each also bearing one of the dust-projecting weapons. Twenty telequel's distance from the minefast, the first prey forces appeared in its vision – small vehicles, quadrupeds, individual prey-creatures themselves. None of the Race engaged them; instead, they avoided them and continued on. Inevitably, though, some caught sight of them and reacted. Projectile-throwers stuttered flashes across the landscape. After a short interval, spluttering flares arced into the sky, casting enough light even for the prey's feeble vision. Larger flashes opened up in turn.

"Make for those flashes," ordered Taldarnilis. It designated the location on its command screen; a large force of projectile-throwers. "Group One, attack that area on wide beam."

The lead machines began panning their heat rays in short sweeps across the flashes. The fire lessened noticeably, confirming the theory that the prey's optical instruments concentrated all wavelengths of radiation. While the heat rays were ineffective at this range against metal or wood, the prey's eyes were far more vulnerable...

Other fire was increasing. One of Group Two's machines staggered from a hit. They had only moments before risking being overwhelmed.

"Fire eradicators in sequence!" ordered Taldarnilis. It launched its own first. Invisible in the darkness, the cloud of toxic dust spread along its path. Others launched in turn, laying a nearly continuous strip. With the wind behind them, the dust drifted gradually toward the main enemy force.

A machine in Group Four twisted under multiple hits and collapsed. The others pressed on; there was no time to retrieve its pilot. Since they had no spare machines, the logic was implacable in any case. As if in response, though, the surviving machines in Group Four opened concentrated fire, targeting the projectile-throwers that had brought down their comrade. Explosions ripped out as they found their marks, but there were too many of the prey to stand and fight them for long, and there were more advancing. Instead, they spun about and retreated, gaining distance on the main body and seeking out the forward elements which they had bypassed earlier – a contest with favorable odds. The fire slackened as they moved out of the prey's limited night range; Taldarnilis noted with satisfaction that some of those projectiles had landed among the prey's own forces.

"Destroy their forward elements," ordered Taldarnilis.

April, 1912, IX Corps HQ, Alice, Texas

"The 7th has come under fire from tripods," reported Prendergast. He was filtering four telephone and three telegraph channels single-handed, reading slips as fast as they were handed over. At the map table, red counters were placed in front of the right-hand block. "They're estimating twenty."

"They didn't sit still for us after all," muttered Funston. "But once we can start engaging them, we can wear them down. Still, that's not nearly their full strength yet."

"Heavy losses in the 314th Artillery. And the 7th's lead elements report being cut off and attacked from behind."

Funston paced from the map. "That works both ways. If the main body can come up and act as the hammer..." He laid a hand on a telegraphist's shoulder. "Send a message to be forwarded by motor courier. Message begins. General Dougherty is to advance his main body at best speed and deploy to attack. End." The key began hammering; Funston turned away. "No reports from the 49th yet?"

"Only routine," said Prendergast. "And the 7th is reporting a lot more vehicle accidents... Oh, my God." He snatched up the slip he'd been reading. "Sir, there's reports of that black dust. Men in the 7th are marching and driving right into it! They must have sprayed that entire area!"

Funston whirled to the telegraphist. "Send another message, quickly!"

Cycle 597,845.1, Minefast 31.01, South Texas

Taldarnilis' force made short work of the isolated prey force, pouncing on each small group and breaking up larger ones, although another machine was lost when two of the prey's short-range accelerated projectiles flashed out from close range and struck it. Those were new – and dangerous, if even a few prey brought them within range. Soon the dark landscape was speckled with burning vehicles and equipment. The fire from behind them slackened as the dust did its work – or perhaps as well, the prey realized they attacked their own forces. They seemed easily discouraged by that...

"Commander, Group Six reports that the southern prey force is continuing to advance beyond the northern one," said Raqtinoctil.

Taldarnilis consulted its command screen. Group Six was swinging around that force, preparing to strike it from the south side. Combined with their own attack, it should be as two tendrils piercing a brain. But the danger was growing by the moment...

"Group Six, attack! Groups Two and Four, attack!"

April, 1912, IX Corps HQ, Alice, Texas

At dawn, the sporadic rumbles of gunfire that had drifted toward them during the night from the west intensified.

"They still own the night," said Funston grimly, "but we hit harder in the daytime. Now it will be decided."

The rumbling ebbed and surged. It sounded like the roaring of some huge, savage beast. And it was, thought Lang. It was the bellow of IX Corps tearing into the Martians. It seemed to galvanize the entire command team despite most not having slept at all during the night.

"They've come up with a new wrinkle," said Prendergast. "Our scouts reported dozens of odd-looking small fortifications scattered along our line of advance. Like short sections of a defensive wall, but they seemed useless. Well, the Martian tripods are crouching behind them and using them for cover. Harder to get a crippling hit on them with artillery that way. Two or three of them hide behind each one, so when we try to outflank them, they have only to deal with whoever approaches on each side. Then when it gets too hot for 'em, they fall back to the next one."

"As long as we're pushing them back, that's what matters. They'll have to make a stand before we reach the base perimeter wall." Funston studied the map table. Although the blocks were closer to the Martian base, the night had not gone well. The dust attack had seriously disrupted the 7th's advance, both by inflicting casualties on men and horses, and by forcing the use of respirators, which made marching and driving more difficult. While the 7th was slowed, the 49th had continued on, opening its right flank... and had been attacked in a pincer movement which broke up its advance in turn. While the losses were not high, the expected movement overnight hadn't materialized. Both lead divisions still had fifteen miles to cover to reach their objectives, and the Martian defenders were putting up strong resistance. The guns' thunder continued.

"General, I have a preliminary casualty report," said one of the clerks just after nine o'clock.

"Let's hear it."

"For both the 7th and 49th, eleven hundred killed or missing, four hundred wounded. The other divisions combined have a hundred wounded and forty dead, mostly from accidents."

Funston nodded without speaking. The clerk turned away, looking pale. That

123

number approached the death toll from the battle of Previtt, and the day was only beginning.

"We've got confirmed reports of five Martian tripods knocked out, including one during the night actions," said Lang, grateful that Prendergast had given him the good news to pass along. "None of the power cell explosions so far." He glanced reflexively at the one vacant desk along the wall: the government's Bureau of Investigation agent who'd manned it – their assigned 'man in gray' – had left early that morning to oversee the salvage of any Martian equipment.

"Some artillery units report ammunition shortages," said Prendergast. "Particularly in the 7th."

Lang had studied the mathematics of that. A battery loaded with a hundred shells per gun could fight a sustained engagement with the Martians, but one heat ray into a limber, and the explosion might knock out half its guns... or all of them. When defending, they could bury their ammunition deep, but in attack, they needed to keep moving up. Like the steam tanks' crews, the gunners accepted their limited combat lifespans and carried fewer shells. Each division needed to keep ammunition carts and limbers moving forward; but the 7th was hampered by the still-lethal area contaminated with black dust. Too many of the supply vehicles were still horse-drawn, and there was no practical way to protect an entire animal against the dust. Lang had driven a horse team on his farm before they graduated to a tractor; he tried not to think of the ugly picture when black dust met horseflesh.

"How much do we have left at the railhead depots?" asked Funston.

"About three thousand for the smaller calibers, a thousand for the 4.7s, and nine hundred for the six-inch. At the rate we're currently using it, and assuming that artillery losses continue proportionally as well..." Lang juggled sheets of paper to find his calculations from an hour ago. "Ah... we have two days' worth."

"Good God." Funston wheeled on him. "What are they shooting at? Thin air? Those are supposed to be trained gunners!"

"The tripods are fast-moving targets, sir. And the men... well, they're eager. They want to hit back." *As I would. As I did.*

"I can understand *that*... Well, send out a general order to conserve ammunition and get closer before opening fire. Move up as much ammunition as possible to the division dumps so we can reduce the time to supply it forward – use the rail line. And get in touch with Second Army HQ and have them start sending us more of all shell calibers from the other corps by rail. We can't run out just as they get the base in their sights!"

"No, sir! I'll get right on it." Lang scrambled to issue both directives. By eleven o'clock, he was able to report that seven boxcars of shells were moving up the rail line and a large number of trucks as well. The 7th's surgeon-in-chief was screaming at him that the line was needed for sending wounded back, but Lang had his priorities; and may God have mercy on his soul... Surely the divisional hospitals could handle it for now. As with most battles with Martians, there were far more dead than wounded, and there were other ways to transport them if needs be. He tried not to think of a burned man jouncing cross-country aboard a truck or wagon. The shells *had* to go up.

By one o'clock it was a hot, cloudless day. The gunfire was growing difficult to hear inside the command center as the guns moved forward, slowly, slowly. Funston made the clerks pause to take a meal. Lang grabbed a plate of beans himself, and more coffee. This day seemed endless; the clocks crawled. Still, they moved faster than the blocks on the map...

"Has Cronkhite moved up yet?" asked Funston for the fourth time.

Lang checked. "No, sir. Not before two o'clock, at least."

"Tell him to advance. It will be tough getting his tanks forward through all that muddle, but he can't wait any longer."

"Yes, sir." The order went out; this was the big push. At least thirty tripods were confirmed to be fighting the 7th and 49th by now, darting in to strike, dodging, inflicting losses – but being pushed steadily back. The Martians had committed most of their strength now – assuming they had no more than the forty spotted previously – and IX Corps had them pinned against their base. They couldn't run away and find a weaker human opponent. There would be no sudden pounce by a large force from a vulnerable direction. The tanks had the opportunity to grind them down.

Lang remembered his time in tanks: the glaring daylight through a viewslit, the sweltering heat of the firebox, endless lurch and jolt and buffet. "Go and get 'em, 80th," he muttered, not caring if anyone heard.

Cycle 597,845.1, Minefast 31.01, South Texas

"Group Four has lost another machine," reported Raqtinoctil.

"Acknowledged." Taldarnilis took a moment to withdraw its machine several quel to the west into comparative safety, then paused to study its command screens. Group Three was disengaging; the others were regrouping to prepare for the next advance by the prey force. Three had just reported that the prey were deploying armored vehicles in large numbers – a more dangerous threat than any so far.

The expedition had lost eleven machines now in this battle. They had been pushed back beyond the defensive mounds – nearly halfway to the minefast berm. There was no question that the prey were willing to accept large losses in order to reach there. Had Vantarsilas been right after all?

Yet if the prey *were* so determined...

It checked the exterior temperature readout: high, even for this world. The goodprey often failed at sustained tasks in temperatures at this range. Perhaps, although they had expended their supply of eradicator dust, the threat of more would be a factor. "Group Six, advance with the eradictor tubes. Perform a rapid movement across *here*," it touched the screen with a tendril, "as though you were dispensing the material."

April, 1912, IX Corps HQ, Alice, Texas

"Anything from Cronkhite yet?"

"Nothing, sir – oh, wait." Prendergast accepted a slip from a telegraph clerk. "Reports of Martians scattering more of that damned black dust. Scouts are warning the rest to avoid that area. He's having to divert the 315th and 327th tank battalions around it."

"Never mind that. Tell him to send them through it. They have respirators – and the tanks will keep most of it out. If the Martians don't want us strong there, there's a reason. We *must* hit them hard everywhere, give them no breathing space!"

125

"Yes, sir." Prendergast moved to the clerk's desk.

Funston glanced at Lang. "I know, Willard. It'll be tough on the crews, and we might lose some."

"It's not just that, sir. If they can drive through it before engaging and vent the vehicles, they'll give a good account of themselves. But fighting a tank wearing respirators in this heat... Those devils know exactly when to use this on us. At night or in hot weather."

"I know. It's on my head."

Cycle 597,845.1, Minefast 31.01, South Texas

Engagements had begun with the prey armored vehicles across a large front. Taldarnilis felt a cross-clan kinship with the other Threeborn as it observed the deft maneuvering of their machines under such an onslaught. Groups drew together smoothly on its display, concentrated their fire on a few vehicles, and withdrew as more of the prey trundled slowly toward them in response. But each time, they gave ground; and the armored vehicles' advance, though slow, was inexorable. And it seemed that each time, another machine was lost.

As the prey advanced through the zone where Taldarnilis had ordered a simulated eradication, it tracked their motion with great attention. Indeed, the two large groups there were slowing relative to others. The prey had chosen to pass through the zone, and its use of clumsy protective measures – indicated by this lessened efficiency – could be factored into the exterior temperature. It estimated probabilities, and decided.

"Groups Three, Four, and Two, advance at the center. Concentrate at this position. Apply wide beam rays to the vehicles there as a preliminary measure, then attack them at close range."

April, 1912, IX Corps HQ, Alice, Texas

At four o'clock in the afternoon, Funston ordered Lang outside for a break. He blinked in the brilliant sunshine, sat on an overturned shipping box, and closed his eyes. A hot day for April – he couldn't help but think of what the tank crews were enduring. His own former outfit, the 304th, had been rebuilt from almost nothing after its losses at Albuquerque; but it was in VIII Corps, far away from this fighting. This wouldn't be the only Martian offensive, though. They'd be bound to fight at some point.

Lang seriously considered asking for a transfer back. It was strange to issue orders, hear reports, and try to form the 'big picture'. At least in a tank, you could see what you were shooting at...

The distant guns had become sporadic. Some of the smaller Mk I tank cannon were barely audible at this range. He listened for the deeper boom of the howitzers, but he heard none. He sighed, levered himself to his feet, and walked back inside the building.

He knew immediately from Funston's expression that something was wrong. "Sir, what is it?"

"Cronkhite's had heavy losses in the center of the advance. Some of the crews are collapsing from the heat. The Martians are cutting them down like grain. How could they *know* that would happen? They're not human!"

"Maybe they just got lucky."

"General," said Prendergast hesitantly, "if we disengaged the 80th until dusk, it would cool off."

"No, Otto – a night battle's no better for us. Signal the 83rd to move up. We're committing the reserve."

Cycle 597,845.1, Minefast 31.01, South Texas

"Commander, we are suffering very high losses," signaled Arctilantar. "I propose we carry out the interdiction early. If –" Its communication broke off for a moment. "If we wait until darkness, it may be too late."

Taldarnilis checked its display for the updated total and clenched involuntarily at the controls. *Eighteen* machines lost. Almost half their force at the minefast. "I understand. Quernit! How much data have you collated from the drone pickups?"

This was their last measure. While the fighting berms scattered across the prey's line of advance had proved useful to shelter their fighting machines, their other purpose was to simply be heaps of dirt on the landscape that the prey would not suspect. Buried under several of them were drones, three per mound, with only vision pickups showing. The prey force had proceeded past them, continuing their advance, while the drones waited and watched. Four had been destroyed unknowingly by the prey's projectiles, but twenty-three were online.

There was a brief pause while Quernit, one of the three combatants remaining at the minefast, prepared its report. "I have identified eleven prime targets so far within view, Commander. Six unprepared assemblies of the projectile-throwers and five large collections of their projectiles, all two telequel or more behind the current zone of fighting." Its tone was calm, unlike the members of the Race engaged in furious combat. "Do you wish me to activate the drones?"

"Not yet. But –" Taldarnilis spotted two armored vehicles emerging from the smoke of a burning one. It targeted the nearer and fired on maximum intensity until the vehicle erupted in flame, then danced aside while its heat ray cooled. The second fired a projectile that clipped the armor of Taldarnilis' machine and staggered it. It circled further to one side where the weapon would not bear, checked the ray temperature, and fired, destroying the vehicle before it could pivot. But there were nine more close behind that one. It gave ground rapidly, dodging more projectiles. The machine's energy reserves were drawing down; even if it avoided destruction, another tenthday of combat would exhaust it, and they had no reactor to replenish energy from – even if they would have time to. "But stand by. Commander to Group Two! Withdraw one telequel! Prepare for drone interdiction!"

Acknowledgments flooded in, some relieved in tone. Even the Race could not fight indefinitely without exhaustion, mental more than physical. The fighting continued; the remaining defenders fell back; the prey, unrelenting, pressed onward. *Who indeed is the prey now?* thought Taldarnilis; then it chided itself. One side in this battle must break, and it would not be the Race that did so. "Group Two, are you clear and able to operate the drones?"

"Yes, Commander." Group Two was the sole unit that had not suffered a loss as yet; three members could easily control the available drones.

"Groups Three, Four, and One, attack across the entire area of contact. Do not retreat until the enemy force does. Group Two, carry out the interdiction!"

Across the battlefield, well behind the advancing prey forces, twenty-three drones burst forth from their concealing dirt mounds. Taldarnilis echoed the image from two of them on its screens. Lurching and skittering, the viewpoints sped across the ground, passing the surprised prey, seeking out their planned targets. In moments, an assembly of the projectile-throwers appeared on one screen, ranked in unprepared rows. The drone passed down them, firing its small heat ray at their mechanisms without pausing to observe the results. Small prey weapons began firing toward it, but it made a difficult target of its own. As it swung around the end of the row, two of the projectile transports appeared ahead. It fired at one without effect for a moment; then the view jolted crazily, flipped over and over, and stopped. The drone lurched upright, then limped in another direction, still operational, although the sidebars indicated minor damage from the explosion.

Taldarnilis checked the other screen. That drone was approaching a large group of prey and vehicles, including one of the rod transport cars. At the sight of heaped projectiles, Taldarnilis involuntarily gave a cry; although it did not hear, Quernit also saw the opportunity. The drone opened fire, closing, ignoring the spatter of small projectiles striking it. Its heat ray played upon the piled objects, but their metal casings refused to melt quickly enough. The drone collapsed to the ground as its limbs were disabled; part of the vision pickup went gray; still it fired. There was no sign of any effect—

The pickup went dead.

April, 1912, IX Corps HQ, Alice, Texas

The floor of the building trembled; Lang looked startled at Prendergast. Then they heard it: a jolting rumble that lasted for several seconds.

"My God, that's an ammo dump!" said Prendergast. "But they're nowhere near the fighting..." He ran to the telegraph desk. Other explosions sounded in turn, lesser, but still far more than artillery fire.

"What are those devils doing?" said Funston. Lang joined him as he ran outside. To the west, several columns of smoke towered over the lesser clouds that the battlefield had been shrouded in since that morning. They returned indoors silently.

In a few minutes, he had his answer as a shaken Prendergast summarized several reports. "The 83rd was moving up through the supply area when they were attacked by small versions of the tripods. We've had reports of fifty, but I think those are exaggerated – maybe thirty. The ones that weren't knocked out have fled. They went after artillery parks and ammo dumps. Serious losses near those – probably several hundred. I'm afraid the ammunition shortage for the engaged divisions is now critical."

"But where did they come from?" demanded Funston. "That whole area was taken by the 49th and 7th hours ago! No one reported anything like this. They can't have been invisible!" He blinked. "Could they?"

"I wouldn't think so. They'd have used that on larger machines, surely... Sir, those shells were meant for the line artillery. They'll be using up their basic loads by now."

"Then send more up!"

"That will take several more hours. It will be nightfall by then."

Beside Prendergast, another aide stepped forward. "General, there are fresh Martian attacks reported on both the 7th and 49th division fronts. Two of the 7th's leading tank battalions have been destroyed, and the Martians are advancing into the gap."

"Well, why aren't the infantry picking them off with those stovepipe rockets?! They've claimed enough knocked out already! They ought to be cutting them down!"

"I believe most of the stovepipes have been expended, sir. There were quite a few tripods reported destroyed, but it seems the Martians have brought up fresh tripods to replace those. They may be committing a reserve."

"Damn it! How many more do they have in there? Did they slip more tripods in during some past night?" Funston was flushed and trembling with a familiar rage.

"Sir..." Prendergast hesitated as Funston wheeled on him like a wolf at bay. "The 7th and 49th are cut to ribbons. The 83rd can move up, but they won't get near the base before dark. The 80th can still advance, but their center has been taken out of the fight as well. And if their tanks do get to the base fortification, they won't be able to fire over it or climb it."

"I know that, damn it! We have to get the howitzers up to there!"

"Reports are coming in that some of the howitzers have been disabled by that surprise attack, and the shells still have to be brought up from the rear. Sir..."

Lang saw a telegraphist twist round in his chair; he went over and took the slip. He read it, swallowed a sudden, bitter taste, and rejoined Funston.

"General... Elements of the 7th are retreating. They're falling back through the 80th and not stopping. General Halverston sends that the 49th is unable to advance beyond current positions."

Prendergast added, "General Cronkhite signals that he is willing to advance, but he only has two intact tank battalions left and about half the 315th. He estimates twenty-five tripods remaining in action. He says he may be able to reach the base wall, but he will have to expend the whole division to do so. He requests–"

Funston chopped a hand at Prendergast. "Enough." He walked to the map table and leaned on it. No one in the room spoke for several minutes; the telegraphs chattered; the distant guns boomed.

General Funston straightened from the map and turned. His face was pale and set. "Otto. Pull them out. Tell Cronkhite to hold his positions to cover the 49th and 7th as they withdraw to the railhead. The 83rd will take over and dig in. Then Cronkhite can fall back into their positions and emplace his tanks defensively. We are *not* giving up ground that we've won so far."

The room sprang to activity. Funston shuffled over to Lang.

"I won't throw men away," he said quietly. "But we've hurt them. We'll reinforce, evacuate the wounded, bring in more ammunition... and keep fighting. We'll have to create a sort of siege, I suppose." He grimaced; Lang too recalled the siege at Gallup and how *that* turned out. "Dig in and move up, mile by mile... But if those cursed small machines can appear so quickly, we may need the 1st Texas Home Guard after all."

Lang nodded. "Every depot, every railhead, headquarters... they'll all have to be protected."

"We were so damned *close*."

Chapter Fourteen

Cycle 597,845.1, Minefast 31.01, South Texas

Taldarnilis surveyed the final reports and data from the previous day's battle. Nineteen fighting machines destroyed, sixteen pilots lost. Twenty-two drones expended. The damage they had inflicted upon the prey forces was impressive, and perhaps the Conclave would consider it all a useful service to the Race; but fresh prey would soon be approaching. There were millions of them within this region and only twenty remaining within the minefast. The odds had not improved.

One damaged machine had crawled back over the course of the entire night. Unfortunately, the occupant died shortly afterward, but at least the machine's power cells could be salvaged. A few other wrecked machines' cells had been scavenged as well, but the prey occupied the majority of the battlefield and no more of the Race could be risked doing so.

There was no time to lose. Taldarnilis made contact with the main holdfast.

"These losses are very high," said Group Leader Vantarsilas once Taldarnilis had summarized the data. "Very high. This expedition should never have occurred."

"There were no alternatives, Group Leader."

"No, I suppose not. This wretched planet is against us at every tendril's tip. Still, you have prevailed in the battle? The mine is safe?"

"We have merely gained time. I propose to use it by advancing the first transport of compound 92-12 to two days from now. The transport cars are partially filled, and the return trip can bring fresh power cells–"

"You would drain more resources from the holdfast, Taldarnilis?"

"Nearly all the machines that had closely engaged the prey are down to one-seventh charge. The supply of spare cells here has been used. We must take advantage of this opportunity while the prey are recovering their strength. Additionally, the next engagement will take place closer to the minefast. I request the transfer of eight defense towers from Holdfast 31.1."

"That is – that is – Those are needed here!"

"There is no known significant prey force within three hundred telequel of Holdfast 31.1, Group Leader. If we can hold the mine against attack for another five tendays, we can finish our work. Even merely sighting the towers may deter the prey until they have made additional preparations – which will take them still more time."

"But without a holdfast reactor, the towers have no energy supply."

"They can be fitted with power cells. Their expected period of function in a battle will be short in any case."

"And they will be retrieved afterward?"

Taldarnilis chose its terms with care. "There should be several still functional even after a close engagement. They will not be wasted... Group Leader, has the Conclave issued any statement regarding our presence in this region?"

"Several," said Vantarsilas glumly. "They are ill pleased by it. But as you pointed out, they have little action left to discipline us with. I believe we are being regarded as a rogue clan and not included in central planning efforts."

"If you were to provide my report to them, it may help. I believe that for our numbers, we have inflicted a major defeat on the prey in this region. We know they have few forces along River 3-12 capable of facing us in another battle of this scale. It is probable that they will draw other forces here that currently face Group 32. That may be of interest."

"Indeed, indeed. This is a terrible gamble, Taldarnilis."

"I believe that one does not conquer a planet without risk."

"Was one not sufficient for us? I wonder... But I will consider detaching the defensive towers. Proceed with your transport of the energetic compound. Group Leader out."

Taldarnilis began planning immediately. Fresh defenses must be prepared. The goodprey must prepare the rod-transport unit for use. The single mind-adjusted goodprey would need to be instructed... It began issuing orders.

April, 1912, IX Corps HQ, Alice, Texas

"Captain Lang?" asked the man in the gray suit.

"Yeah, that's me." Lang laid down his pen. The ledgers and order books piled across his desk nearly smothered it; the process of rebuilding two wrecked divisions was a massive one. And he'd barely started...

"Daniel Mulder, Bureau of Investigation. We've got a special train moving back from the railhead, but there's too much other traffic blocking us. I need you to get things moving."

Lang cocked his head. "I'm a pretty small man to be picking up locomotives."

"You have General Funston's personal authority, don't you?"

"For carrying out General Funston's orders, yes. And he figures that our trains carrying wounded or ammunition are also *special.*"

"This is federal business, Captain. Very important. We have three boxcars of Martian salvage to get back to Washington so the eggheads there can pick it apart. You wouldn't want to interfere with the war effort, now would you?"

"Well, now. That's different." Lang fiddled with his ledgers as he got up, not wanting the Fed to see the gleam in his eye. "Lay on, Macduff."

"It's Mulder." The man led him outside to a Model T Ford; they mounted up and spluttered their way through the crowded base. Mulder was taciturn; that suited Lang, who was thinking furiously. He'd need help. He kept scanning the troops and vehicles around him as they drove; tanks, ARVs, trucks of all sizes, and *there*, a tan-painted touring car—

"Hold up here!"

Mulder braked. "What's up?"

"I need to talk to my... railroad adjutant clerk. He's over there. Just wait a minute..." Lang jumped out and trotted over to the Peerless. Eddie was stretched out in the back seat, snoring loudly enough to be heard over the throng.

"Sleeping on duty!" yelled Lang. Eddie convulsed upright. "That's two weeks in the stockade, Private!"

"Oh, jeez. Good to see you, Cap."

"You too, Eddie." They shook hands; Eddie climbed out, unfolding his lanky height. "Look, Funston wants us to grab some of that Martian power cell wire. That guy in the Ford? No, *don't* look around. He's trying to move a trainload of it out of here. If I can keep him busy, can you get into one of the cars and, um..."

"Steal some? Sure, Cap. What does it look like?"

"Damn it. I don't know. Like a spool of barb wire?"

Someone coughed to Lang's right. "Excuse me, gentlemen, but I believe it will appear as a column of gold-colored, very fine wire, about five feet high. If they have removed the outer casing."

Lang turned. "Burnham! Where did you come from?"

"Yeah, he does that," said Eddie fondly. "Mr. Burnham's been sticking with the LRSC for a while now."

"It really is the most interesting place to be," said Frederick Burnham. The skin on his face burned by the Martian heat rays had darkened into a deep tan; he seemed indecently cheerful. "And it seems it's about to get more so."

"Look," said Lang, "I don't want—"

"Oh, I don't mind if it's... unofficial. Mr. Painewick can tell you that I'm no stickler for dotting i's and crossing t's."

Lang glanced at Eddie, who nodded. "Okay. Follow me to wherever that agent is driving, and take it from there."

He rejoined Mulder. "He'll get right on it. Let's go." They proceeded two miles to the southwestern train sidings. Cars were backed in row upon row, overlapped, seemingly blocking out the landscape. A locomotive puffed slowly past; haggard soldiers looked out from windows with dull expressions that Lang knew well enough. Two days wasn't near enough time to recover from a battle like that. Sometimes two years wasn't... The train halted in a chuff of steam, leaving a gap that was quickly filled by another.

It looked like a hopeless jam; but Lang knew the priorities, and the switchmen did too. The two other Feds standing flat-footed on guard beside their special train, though, probably didn't. He noted that the boxcar doors were padlocked – that was bad. Still, not insurmountable. A glance to the north showed the Peerless parked and empty.

"Right," said Lang. "I'll go see the yard manager and get this train moving."

He led Mulder to the nearby shack, told him to wait, and trotted up the stairs to the wide-windowed office. From this height, the cars seemed to stretch on for miles. The manager waddled sideways in his chair and peered at him over tiny glasses. "Yeah? Oh, hello, Captain."

"Hi, Mick. Can you keep that train, there, can you keep it here for a couple hours?"

"Uh... sure. But I'll have to hold those two troop trains as well."

Lang frowned. "Medical trains?"

133

"Nah, just a bunch of bored soldiers."

"That's fine, then. They'd be just as bored somewhere else. Which units?"

Mick flopped open a ledger and ran his finger down the lines. "That one's the 7th... that one's the 49th. Says here I'm supposed to keep 'em separated. You know anything about that?"

"It could cause a damn riot, that's what I was told..." Lang blinked and resisted the urge to grin. "No, that's ridiculous. We're all on the same side, after all. If you put them both alongside that special train, it'll be just what I need."

"Well, whatever you say, then."

"Thanks, Mick." Lang clapped his shoulder and rejoined the agent.

"Well?" snapped Mulder.

"He's working on it. But there's been a breakdown in the switchyard, might take an hour or two to resolve that."

Mulder cursed. "Let's get back. Too many folk around here for my liking."

They settled in beside the salvage train. Lang tried to engage all three agents in conversation; it was like talking to lampposts. They kept walking around to check the cars. He needed a distraction, and this was all taking up valuable time... After a while, soldiers began dismounting from the nearest troop train and wandering. Lang wondered where their officers were.

As some drew near, he recognized the 7th Division patches. There weren't many officers left from that.

A private wandered up to the boxcar, glanced curiously in through a gap in the boards. "Well, that sure looks shiny. What have you fellas got in there?"

"Just step away from the train, soldier." Mulder was a tall man; he towered over the scruffy private as he moved between him and the car.

The man looked him up and down. "Nice suit, but I don't see no general's stars. You got no right -"

Mulder shoved him back. "Just move on, now."

"Hey!" called out another man. "Who d'you think you are?" He stepped up next to his companion.

"Listen, all of you!" shouted Mulder. "We are federal agents. This train is the property of the federal government, and we are transporting salvage. Do *not* interfere or you will be in violation of the War Measures Act!"

"You mean you stole that Martian junk from Hebbronville?"

"Salvaged! Now, beat it!" All three agents had gathered on this side of the cars. More soldiers drifted up; it was becoming a small crowd.

"Do you nice government men have any idea how many of us just died? That stuff doesn't belong to you! It belongs to us, to Texas!"

"Yeah! *Yeah!*" A number of cries went up at that. "Washington's taking everything. They got no *right!*"

"Well, the 7th got no right either," shouted a man from Lang's left. He and others had walked over from the second troop train; they were from the 49th. "Not when you ran away like that!"

"*Who said that?*"

"Everybody's sayin' it!" The two groups converged; men began shoving one another; in moments, the first punch was thrown. The Feds tried to intervene. One was decked immediately.

Another agent pulled a pistol. "Stop this! Stop it now!"

This is getting out of hand. Lang spun and sprinted to the Peerless. He climbed up and flipped off the traveling lock from the loaded cal fifty, racked the bolt. He checked around for a backstop; a pile of railway ties looked fine; he swung the weapon around. Shooting into the air around here might have consequences.

The brawl was becoming nasty. In another moment, the MPs would get here—

A pistol shot cracked out. Men spilled back, opening a gap; a soldier was down, although he was only gripping his arm. *Enough.*

Lang fired four rounds into the ties. The terrific BAM BAM BAM BAM swung every head, stopped every cocked fist.

"You're all a shame to General Funston!" he bellowed. "The 7th did all they could and then some! The 49th fought like lunatics! And what the hell d'you want with some Martian junk anyway? Get back to your trains! *Now!*"

Men slumped, stepped back, let go of collars. The three Feds shuffled back to their boxcar, still with pistols drawn. Two men helped the shot soldier stand up; it didn't look bad, but this was going to be an ugly incident. Lang waited until the groups had split apart, grumbling, then stowed the machine gun and hopped down. The MPs appeared – at last – and urged the men back to their trains; some took the wounded man off for attention.

The Feds looked shaken when Lang rejoined them. He fixed them with an icy stare, and a tone to match. "Who fired?"

"That'll be in our report. It's not your concern."

"You *idiots*. You shot one of our men. It damn well *is*." But they refused to say anything further. He kept them on that side as long as he could, but soon they remembered their jobs and redeployed on guard. Lang made two more trips to the yard manager's office, but eventually the train *did* have to move. The feds swung aboard with ill grace and departed along with it.

Lang walked back to the Peerless; it was empty. A nightjar called from behind a stack of hay bales. He got in, started the car, and backed it up to the bales. "You know, Burnham," he called out, "there are no nightjars in this part of Texas."

"Really? Oh, dear." Between the three of them, they hefted the cylinder into the car. Burnham and Eddie got in.

"Any trouble?" asked Lang.

"It was only a Yale lock. No difficulty." Burnham looked smug. "That was a marvelous diversion, Captain."

"I could have done without some of it." Lang looked over the cylinder; it was indeed wrapped in fine gold wire, but it seemed... skewed. "Fellas, there's something wrong with this."

"Cap, it was the only one without a casing. The others weighed twice as much."

"I believe that only a discharged coil can be safely exposed like this," said Burnham. "They had started taking it apart, presumably. I assumed that you might not have the equipment to open a charged coil safely. Did I misjudge?"

Lang glanced after the departing train. "It doesn't matter now. Let's get this covered with a tarp and get it started on the way to Dallas."

When Lang returned to the headquarters, he found General Funston slumped at his desk. Funston jerked awake when Lang cleared his throat; he'd been dozing. None of them were getting a lot of sleep. "Where the devil were you?"

"Sorry, sir. I found an opportunity to obtain some of that Martian wire."

"Hmph. Very well." Funston rose and beckoned Lang to the main map table. He noticed that the clerks were gone. Privacy?

"It will take many weeks to rebuild these two divisions properly," said Funston. "And time is of the essence. Those Martians will be building up their strength every day – I don't know how long it takes them to create their manufacturing system, but I don't suppose it's any less potent than their weapons.

"Given that, I have decided to shift some of our forces south temporarily from the Arkansas River line where there's the least chance of an attack. The 78th and the 5th Texas are mostly infantry, but we'll need a lot more men. There have been so many lost already..." He looked away from the map into a far distance. "But they won't have died for nothing. They will *not*. That base will be crushed."

Lang checked. "So, from the 78th Division and the 5th Texas... how many of their attached tanks and artillery are coming with them, sir?"

"All of them."

"All... very good, sir."

"It's too far to shift Bill Wright's reinforcements back here – too long. But we'll have to take some of his munition stocks. More artillery will need more shells to feed them."

Lang made notes. "That won't leave much around Little Rock and points east, sir."

"I don't–" Funston paused. "I understand your concern, Lang. But we cannot be strong everywhere. And there are plenty of Federal forces–" Lang blinked at the term from a man who was in Federal uniform – "positioned in fortifications near there. They can surely handle anything that the Martians might throw at them, especially given how much warning time they ought to have. Do you know they have *aircraft* now?"

"Yes, sir. We sure could use some of those."

"I'm telling you, they have written us off like a banker's bad investment... Get on the train scheduling right away. Today if you can."

"The easiest route is to go via Dallas..."

Funston lifted a hand. "I'd prefer to keep the trains out of the bigger cities. They might be noticed... Stage them through Shreveport instead, or perhaps the Houston & Texas Central line. And try to make it look like routine movement. I've been given a pretty free hand so far, but Leonard Wood might start looking over my shoulder. He's got his own concerns; we do not need to worry him with this. And in a month, once that base is destroyed, they'll be back on the Arkansas River, and with some fighting experience to boot."

"Yes, sir."

April, 1912, Houston Rocket Center, Texas

"That wire is downright useless!" said Major Palmer. He downshifted angrily into second gear and swerved left at the 'intersection' of two dusty tracks outside of the rocket center's main building. The official direction signs pointing to RANGE – 1 MI. and BUNKER – 500 YD had been augmented by a hand-painted one reading MARS – 35,430,153 MI.

Willard Lang sighed. "Look, sir, I know it was a damaged coil–"

"It's a Gordian knot, is what it is! Something – or some fool – tugged on just the wrong place, and now every loop seems to be linked into every other one! Corporal Stimson is fascinated by it – he says he can publish a paper on the topology – but I have three clerks working to extract the wire, and it's taken them days just to get a couple thousand yards pulled out and spooled. Then that Woods inventor showed up and took all of it."

"He did have authorization from the general," pointed out Lang.

"Sure, or I'd never have let him... Lang, this is crazy. Back east, they've got Edison and Tesla and labs full of workers to exploit the Martian technology. We've got one sickly Negro. How can we expect to get anywhere?"

"I guess he's not telling you much."

"Nope! Just to set up for a test firing today. That's why I called you. I want another witness when he falls flat on his face." Palmer braked hard at the range border and shut off the car's engine. Several other cars and trucks were parked alongside. Lang climbed out and began walking toward the firing trench.

He noted that on the launching frames, a rocket lay horizontally on a firing rail. A few yards to one side, a table and several chairs were protected by sandbags; a sort of radio console rested on it, wired up to a couple of car batteries. Two men sat at the table; one was Granville Woods.

Palmer pushed past Lang. "Corporal Stimson, what are you doing here?"

"I have been requisitioned," said the narrow-shouldered, freckled corporal in a Louisiana accent. "Mister Woods needs an operator for the test."

Woods nodded to Lang. "Afternoon, Cap'n."

"Hello, Mr. Woods. I see you've modified one of the stock four-inch rockets there."

"Yes. It's guided now."

"*Guided?*" Lang gaped at the rocket. True, it now sported an extra pair of horizontal fins at the midsection – or were they wings? "But surely there's no room in there for that sort of gear. Radios, and motors, and, and... Unless you sacrificed something else? Not the warhead..."

"No, I only added two solenoids to move the sheering vanes. Every'hing else is *there*." Woods gestured shakily toward the console. It was only then that Lang noticed the small telescope on a swivel... and the two very fine wires attached to contact posts.

Corporal Stimson patted the console fondly. "Yeah, sure is something when you get hold of Martian wire. No transmission losses, even over a mile of it; there's just no resistance at all that we can even detect. Big ol' lead-acid batteries, valves, they all stay here, driving the solenoids on the rocket. I just have to tell it to go up, down, left, or right with those knobs."

"Cooter's my right and lef' hand man," said Woods.

"Been practicing by sliding a model down a wire cable and steering it. I have gotten moderately good at it." To one side, Major Palmer shook his head in disgust. "Care to join us?"

137

"Don't mind if I do," Lang said and took one of the extra chairs. He peered downrange; nearly a mile distant, someone had dragged a small shack into place that was roughly the size of a Martian tripod. It looked awfully small from here. "How fast can you set all this gear up, Corporal?"

"Oh, maybe fifteen minutes to unload it all off the car and connect everything."

Lang blinked, glanced at the parked Ford, then back to the table. "Could you leave it *on* a car?"

"I guess. If it could take the launch rail. Like those Wichita Six-Shooters we've been making."

"I thought those had eight rails?"

"Too crowded. We cut it down to six. And besides, who ever heard of an eight-shooter?"

"Can we just get this over with?" said Palmer.

Stimson looked at Woods, who nodded. "Whenever you're ready, Cooter. Major, it's your call."

"Fire in the hole," said Palmer with ill grace.

Stimson tapped the firing key; the four-inch rocket roared off its launch rail in a terrific blast of dust and a haze of smoke. They hunched under the blast for a moment; Stimson stayed in that pose, peering through his telescope. His fingers twiddled gently at two knobs on the console – particularly the right one. "She's wantin' to sink..."

"Motor'sh out. Nose her up."

Lang could see the dot of the rocket's tail jinking over the landscape. He counted by habit; seven, eight, nine –

The shack disappeared in an explosion; the boom reached them moments later.

"Holy cow," said Stimson. "I hit that thing. I really *hit* it!" Beside him, Grantville Woods smiled without speaking.

"It appears you did," said Palmer in a tone of distaste. "As to whether that's repeatable in the field, well..."

"We'll need more trials," said Lang. "Under field conditions, too. And I'm *really* interested in vehicle mounting these... Impressive work, Mr. Woods. And, Major, thank you for including me in this. I know that General Funston will be excited to hear about this, and Major Plainview over with the LRSC... well, excited doesn't cover it; he might just fall flat on his face."

An overnight train got Lang to Fort Sam Houston by midmorning. Funston was at his house again; Lang couldn't blame him for being sick of the office. Things were moving maddeningly slowly for reinforcing IX Corps – as *he* knew in grim detail. Although there were some disturbing telegrams about a Martian attack on Little Rock that looked to be on a scale beyond anything a single corps could handle... He accepted the inevitable tea.

"The bottleneck is definitely that wire," he said after carefully describing the test. "It's incredible stuff, all right – thin as thread, strong as steel, and they were able to push a control current through a mile of it, just as Woods said. But what we have is hopelessly tangled. Stimson said it was driving men mad to tease it out, and we'll need hundreds of miles of it to build any significant number of these weapons."

"Is this about the project that I officially haven't heard of?" said Mrs. Funston, adding sugar to her own cup.

"Just so. If we can't get enough of that wire untangled, we're stuck. And Washington's being of no help at all."

"As usual," grumbled Funston.

"You said the wire is as fine as thread?" mused Mrs. Funston. "Let me think a minute." She wandered to the desk, took pen and paper, scribbled a while. After discarding a couple of sheets, she held one out to Lang.

"What do you think of this?"

Help Wanted – Female
Seamstresses over 18, reliable, discreet, to unwind and spool valuable thread for minimum of six weeks. Location Dallas. Room and board provision, pay one dollar per day clear. Also experienced Rollers, Laceworkers, and Bunchmakers. Inquire at Blough's Mftg. Co, Ross & Haskell Sts.

"Er... why Dallas? And why... Blough's?"

"They have spinning and folding frames. Mrs. Colquitt and I have been patrons. Mainly, no one will notice a lot of girls going in and out of there."

"Right," breathed Lang. "We can clear out the shop floor, chop the wire up into chunks—"

"*Cut it?*" snapped Funston.

"Well, we only need pieces a mile long. If we get forty seamstresses, we make forty pieces, and each takes one on."

"At a dollar a day, you'll get hundreds if you want," said Eda.

"If there's one thing I've learned running Second Army, it's when to delegate," said Funston. "Why don't you get Mrs. Colquitt to talk to the governor, dear, and take it from there?"

Chapter Fifteen

April, 1912, Martian Base, Texas

The sharp rapping at the train car's window woke Ronald Gorman. Disoriented, he flung his arms over his head against the expected blows of a jailer's club; then he realized where he was. This was not the Torreon cell shared with four other living men and the ghost of his foolish business partner. This was a luxurious rail car, and the jailers were outside, and not human. *It wasn't really murder anyway! He would have ruined it all. Those men in power, they all did much worse in their time...*

The metal tentacle tapped again, signaling that the Masters had some new need. Gorman groped for his coat, pulled it on, scrambled into the next car, and shook de Gama awake. "Come, priest. You are needed."

"What time is it?" muttered de Gama, scrubbing at his eyes.

"Before dawn. You know they do not sleep. It must be urgent, though. Come." They climbed down from the car's ladder. A sliver of moon, still up, glinted from the metal bulk standing over them. It shifted, scanning the area, then folded its legs and sank to the ground in a peculiar motion like a goat lying down. They walked around the curve of the hull, past the huge, glowing red disk of its eye. At the side, a hatch slid open. A dim red glow silhouetted the flaccid shape of a Master within. It crawled – oozed – its way free of the machine's confines and gestured with its tendrils. de Gama hesitated; then before Gorman could shove him forward, he shambled toward it of his own accord, bowing his head to the waiting grasp. This time, he did not cry out as the Master sent him its will. Was it from being woken so recently? Practice? After a few minutes, he staggered back; the Master struggled its way back inside; the machine closed itself, rose, and turned away to other purposes.

Gorman caught de Gama in mid-stumble, held him while he steadied on his feet, and wiped the drool from his chin with a shirttail. "Well?"

"We must go. Go back. Home – their home. Mexico, my home."

"Not mine," grumbled Gorman. "Why now? The cars are not all filled yet. Is it because of that battle we heard? *Did they lose?*"

"The dark forces strove brutally against the angels, but did not defeat them. Still, they must regird their host, gather more of their eldritch swords. Towers of light. It will be beautiful here, Gorman. But our lesser host must remain here – the sacrifices. And the empty ore cars. They take nothing back that is not of use."

"We'll have to unhook those cars. Then the Masters can shift them," mused Gorman. "Wait. How long will we be gone?"

141

"How long does it take to reach Heaven and fall back?"

"Damn it, enough of your nonsense! How *long!*" But de Gama merely stared into the night. Gorman cursed, hustled him back to the car ladder, and pushed him ahead. Inside, he found and lit a lantern. de Gama's eyes glittered in the warm light; then he closed them and settled back in a seat.

Gorman walked through the second car, giving a careful glance to the huddled forms of the two Ranger prisoners. They'd given no trouble so far, but the thought of leaving them at the mine unsupervised was not appealing. This car would come along, then. He ducked through into the next, hammered a fist on the doorframe. "Wake up! Wake up, you slugs!"

When the blinking, yawning men had focused on him, he began issuing orders. "The train is leaving here. The cattle car and the three empty ore cars need to be uncoupled. The Masters will lift them out of the way. But three of you will stay to guard and fetch water for our livestock – human and sheep – while the rest of us are gone."

"Why do we care?" muttered a sleepy Garcia.

"Because if they die from thirst, and the Masters grow hungry, then we are next! Or perhaps you'd prefer rustling more sheep from the middle of a battlefield? There is an entire army encamped out there! Now, Vicario, come with me. We'll get you a pendant so that you may move about when I am away. Mendez and his lackeys will work the engine, of course. Garcia to guard the prisoners."

He turned back toward his private car, lifted the lantern, and blinked in surprise as Queen Idar appeared in the companionway. "My queen! Did we wake you?"

"A stone could not have slept through *that*. What is happening?"

"The Masters have new orders. Our train is to travel back to their base and bring reinforcements. When–" He trailed off as he saw that she was holding the gun belt he'd taken from one of the Rangers. The big Colt dangled in its holster.

"Do not do anything rash, my dear. Boys, stay calm." Two of his men were armed, but they were *behind* him. Not a good place to be... But she merely smiled, stepped to him, and lifted the belt.

"You shouldn't leave this lying about, Doctor. You woke in something of a hurry, I gather?"

"Ah. Quite. Ah..." He passed the lantern to Vicario, swung the belt about his hips, and fastened it. "Why, thank you."

"Let's get underway." She preceded them into the next car, half-turned, and began to add, "When we—" She stumbled over one of the Rangers and fell. "Ouch! You clumsy brute!"

"What the–" blurted the Ranger muzzily in English.

"Keep out of the way!" She shoved at him angrily and pushed herself back to her feet even as Gorman offered a kindly hand. "Ah, thank you, Doctor, but I'm fine. Let us be about it."

They followed her forward toward the private car that perhaps was becoming hers as well as his. He aimed a kick at the Ranger as he passed. "Keep away from her!"

April, 1912, Hebbronville, Texas

Emmet took the kick on a hunched shoulder; it still hurt. They'd endured worse.

Once the gang members had passed forward, he opened his clenched hand. Nestled inside was the tiny screwdriver that Jovita Idar had just passed to him. It was meant for the receiver screws of a Winchester and had come from a fold of the scout belt that Gorman had stolen.

It would also make a damn fine picklock against the crude darbies that held him and Hicks to their chain.

"What's on?" asked Hicks quietly.

"Miss Idar just gave us a gift. I'm going to start working on getting us loose; you keep watch."

Darkness was no hindrance to lock picking. As Emmet worked, Hicks said, "Didn't she say to wait until we get over the Grande?"

"They seem awful busy right now. Maybe I can get a look at this Martian base first and slip back." But he was still tinkering when dawn broke. They could smell smoke from the locomotive now. Twice the car jostled; were those damn machines slinging rail cars around like toys? He got one cuff open, jammed it with a scrap of cloth, and left it on his wrist for show while he worked on the second one. "This is harder than I thought. If things get rushed, can you tear out that end of the chain in the wall? It's just wooden planks there."

Hicks braced and pulled. "Yeah, I think so."

"Okay, that leaves one padlock at the other end. Looks crude. Might have to just get that open instead, if it's not too awkward for you."

"I can do a lot of damage swinging twenty pounds of chain," said Hicks grimly. "Don't worry about it, Emmet."

The train jolted and began to move, slowly picking up speed – they were pulling a heavy load. They passed out through the berm wall; the horizon seen through the windows opened up. Several tripods paced alongside, guarding.

"No sign of any opposition," said Hicks. "I guess all our fellas are still concentrated at Alice."

"If they spread out, the Martians'll chop them up... Hah!" The second cuff clicked open. He rigged it like the first, then eyed the padlock. That looked like quick work, but he'd have to be loose to get over to it, and if someone walked in...

Several men did just that, clattering through the car toward the front of the train. He counted four without appearing to. And no signal yet from Miss Idar. Once he freed Hicks, they'd be committed – and obviously so. He'd give her until they were past Laredo.

That took a couple of hours, during which they were ignored. The train worked up to a respectable speed; several tripods ran alongside. Their strange gait always reminded Emmet of just how alien they truly were. But what was going on up there in the lead cars? Ugly possibilities occupied his thinking. He couldn't figure out the way 'Doctor' Gorman treated Idar; it seemed fantastical. The rest were just crooks who'd found a new boss, but he was a real piece of work. Maybe he'd gone crazy. His 'priest' – de Gama? – sure had.

Finally, they passed through Laredo. Emmet had known it would be bad, but the only buildings visible were charred skeletons. Nothing had been spared – except the rail bridge. The Martians needed that.

"Bastards," muttered Hicks.

"Yep. Came all this way from another planet just to kill and destroy. I just don't get it."

"Maybe no man ever will. Emmet..."

"Yeah, I know. Can't wait any longer." He slipped the darbies, moved to the padlock, and began tinkering with it. "Won't be but a minute–"

The forward door opened; a gang member walked in. Emmet recognized the man; Gorman had called him Garcia.

The man actually came halfway down the aisle before he reacted to what Emmet was doing; then he cried out in surprise and fumbled for his pistol. Emmet was already lunging in two galloping steps. He grabbed Garcia's forearm and slammed it against a seat rail; the pistol skittered onto the floor. Garcia punched him with his other hand; they grappled, rolling onto the aisle. Garcia kicked loose, leaving Emmet sprawled. Emmet didn't look for the pistol; a gunshot would ruin things. Instead he just went after Garcia again, but he tangled with the seat legs. The gang member spun and bolted toward the forward door. In an instant he'd be shouting–

A tearing crack sounded as Hicks tore the chain out of the wall. He stumbled back a couple of steps, twisted, and slung the loose chain like a lariat. It caught Garcia around the neck and jerked him clean off his feet; he landed heavily. Emmet pounced onto him, grabbed the links, twisted them tight. Garcia flailed and clawed at him; Hicks threw his weight onto the chain's other end, dragging both other men a foot down the aisle with his unbreakable, cuffed grip. Presently nature took its course. Emmet stayed put for a moment to be sure, then rose, gasping.

Miss Idar was standing at the forward doorway. She looked pale but composed. "Uh – sorry you had to see that."

"I have seen worse." She lugged a bucket of water down the aisle to them. "He was supposed to be guarding me while I brought you this. It's no matter."

Emmet scooped up the pistol, a small Browning automatic. "Hey," said Hicks. "That was Blackwell's piece."

"Yeah." Emmet didn't bother kicking Garcia's corpse. He returned to working on the padlock; in a minute it clicked open. "Hicks, are you sure..?"

"Hell, it worked like a charm the first time." Hicks coiled the chain and held it easily.

"All right then. First, let's slake. Might not be more for a while." They guzzled the water in moments between them. "Now let's see about those other folks."

Emmet went first with the automatic. The next car was empty; he moved carefully down the aisle, checking into sheltered spots. "All right, they could have a guard on the prisoners in the cattle car. There's a lot of penetration with this caliber; I don't want to shoot one of them after it goes through the guard! Miss Idar, can you take a look first? He won't be surprised to see you."

She went on tiptoe at the door's small window. "Oh... Oh, no. It's *gone*."

Emmet slid over beside her and looked. The next car... was an open hopper car, heaped with yellowish dirt. More and more of those marched back until they ended. There were no other passenger or cattle cars. Nuevo Laredo was fading in the background.

"They must have left it behind," he said. "I know they were shifting cars around... I'm sorry, Miss Idar. We can't help them."

144

"We should bail soon, unless you figure to fight all the rest with one peashooter," said Hicks. "If that pendant really gets us past those tripods, it'll only be a couple days' hike to Zapata or some other place along the Grande."

Idar looked crushed. "But they were counting on me. I promised them..."

"You told Targas?" said Emmet incredulously.

"Well, not *him*. But two others. They can be trusted, I think... I must stay and try again. You go back and report."

"No, you have to come with us," said Emmet. "Otherwise those tripods'll fry us. Besides, you're the only one who knows anything about the layout of that base. That could be vital."

"Then they'll have no one! I won't leave them!"

"Trip back's getting longer," said Hicks.

Something else occurred to Emmet; it tipped the balance in his mind. "Miss Idar. If I give you my word that I will go back with you to that mine and help them, will you come with us now? We can use your pendant to get back in, and we'll be a lot better armed than we are now. I'd say it was a good chance. Besides, that sidearm and scout belt are Ranger property, and I want 'em back."

Hicks blinked, swallowed, and added, "I'll go too. Got a score to settle."

She said nothing for a few moments while the train axles clunked rhythmically. "Very well. There should be enough livestock to feed those creatures for a few weeks. I don't know how Gorman will react to this, but his priest seems to have *some* decency left. They may be spared long enough to go back."

"I'll watch out for an upgrade." Emmet opened a window and cautiously peered ahead. After a few minutes, they began approaching some foothills. "Okay, get ready."

They assembled at the car's companionway; when the train slowed, each in turn gauged the drop and leaped, sprawling in the dust. The ore cars rumbled past as they picked themselves up and regrouped. "Everyone okay?"

Two acknowledgments; Emmet turned east. "Let's duck into that—"

A tripod loomed up, striding fluidly beside the train. Emmet stared up at it for a long, freezing moment; then it continued onward, its strange metal feet stamping into the ground beside the tracks.

"Whoo," said Hicks. "Think it saw us?"

"I don't know. That's another thing." Emmet reached out and tapped a finger on Idar's pendant. "Is there a lock on that thing that can be opened, when you don't need it?"

"No. It is... *their* work. Only the machine in Gorman's car can open it."

"You can't have that thing on you for the rest of your damn life!" said Hicks. "I mean, if it's like their power cells, you try to cut it off and it'll... And those Washington boys, they'll treat you like some experiment."

"We'll need to think on this," said Emmet. "But for now, let's get back to the Grande. It's not high right now, should be plenty of crossing points."

They set out quickly, not trusting the tripod to not swing back. Once they had hiked a couple of miles from the rail line, and there was no sign of any pursuit, Emmet called a halt under the cover of some bushes. He was worried about the period of confinement; they would all get tired faster than usual. He spent the time picking open Hicks' cuffs; he was getting quicker at it.

145

"How'd you know that screwdriver was something you'd find in the belt, anyway?" asked Hicks.

Idar smiled. "I interviewed a Texas Ranger last year, when I was still working as a journalist." Emmet expected to catch a glare at that, but she merely continued. "He was very forthcoming. He gave me more detail than I could possibly use – or so I thought."

"Hatchet job?" asked Emmet. "Not that I'm complaining right now..."

"No, I wanted his outlook and I included it. It wasn't that sort of piece. It also wasn't what *he* thought, which was the equivalent of buying me a drink at a bar. I had to stick a hatpin in him to convince him of that."

"Who was that?" asked Emmet with some disapproval.

"George Stanford. He was with Company D at Laredo."

"Ah." He busied himself with his work. People were complicated.

"I could look him up, if you like," offered Hicks.

"Just leave it. Okay, we're done. That chafe's bleeding, better wrap it." Emmet kicked a hole in the dirt and buried the chain. "Let's go."

They set out cross-country, following game trails where they could. It grew hot, but not enough to lay up and walk at night; they needed to get back quickly. The easiest route turned out to be northeast, so they angled further away from the rail line as they went. By late afternoon, they crossed a ridgeline and could see the greener valley of the Rio Grande lying eastward; there'd be water soon, no reason not to push on.

Upslope on the trail ahead, a man in a scuffed white uniform stepped out of cover, holding a rifle. "Show us your hands, my friends!" he called out in Spanish.

Emmet glanced behind. Four more riflemen back there... He mentally kicked himself for walking across a ridgeline. It was the most direct route, and the Martians and their collaborators were long gone... No matter. They halted and waited for the soldiers to gather about. He said as the first man approached, "We're just peaceful travelers." He noted sergeant's stripes. Regular army? That was better than bandits, although no guarantee. But the uniforms didn't look right.

"There is no peace in Nuevo Leon province. You appear to be coming from there." As the sergeant spoke, others pointed and nudged one another. He frowned in turn. "*Chica*, what is *that*?"

Idar placed both palms on the pendant as though to hide it. "Jewelry! Are you robbers, then?"

"We are not. But I've never seen anything like that. It looks like the machines the *diablos* use. We know they have traveled on that rail line. If you are somehow working for them..."

"You have no idea!" snapped Hicks. "Just leave her be."

"Easy, Hicks. Look, Sergeant...?"

"Rodriguez."

"Sergeant Rodriguez, I'm Emmet Smith, this is Randy Hicks and Jovita Idar. The Martians captured us and put that thing on her. We'd take it off in a heartbeat if we could, but we can't – no one can. We managed to get away when they took us into Mexico on a train this morning. We need to get somewhere to report to the authorities about that. You're fighting the Martians too, right? Can you help us?"

"There were six of those walking machines," said Rodriguez without answering. "We know how... effective they are. And yet you escaped."

Emmet thought fast. "We waited until they left a gap, and we were lucky."

"Hmm." Rodriguez slung his rifle. "Can they find that thing from a distance?"

"We don't think so. Otherwise they'd have tracked us down this morning."

"Very well. This is more complicated than a sergeant's pay will allow for. Can all of you ride?"

Emmet and Hicks looked at Idar. She said, "Well enough."

"Then you will all come along with us. We have spare horses."

"Look, it'd be simpler if we just kept on east until–"

"No. Whatever is going on here, it is a matter for the general to decide." Rodriguez whistled; other men came over the hill crest leading a train of horses. Two had machine guns slung aboard. This was a scout troop, then? Assembled, there were sixteen men. At least the horses looked in prime condition... Emmet wondered aloud, "Which general is this far in the north?"

"General Villa." The sergeant swung into his saddle and gestured for them to do the same.

May, 1912, Cuernavaca, Mexico

Henri Gamelin took a long time to awaken. Once his eyes opened properly, the ceiling overhead attracted his attention with its crazy pattern of cracks, and he wondered at them for a while. He lay in a comfortable bed; everything was quiet. His breathing seemed normal, but his right side ached with every inhalation.

A scratching noise from the left, when he turned to look, proved to be a pale, roly-poly fellow scribbling in a notebook as he sat at a desk. When Henri cleared his throat, the man jerked upright. "Oh – hello, Mr. Gamelin! Glad to see you awake. Let me tell Mrs. King that you're up." He scrambled out of his chair and trotted from the room – a simple bedroom, pleasantly furnished, bright but with paint peeling from the window trim.

The man reappeared in moments with a glass of water, which he handed gently to Henri after helping him sit up. Henri drank the glass in one gulp and cleared his throat again. "What day is this?" He spoke in English as the man had.

"Tuesday, May 3rd. You're at the Hotel Bella Vista – well, not the real one, that's been destroyed by the Martians. Mrs. King set up her business here in this house, still in Cuernavaca. It's not very big, but there's not many customers now. Actually, I think you're the first. Did you know President Diaz stayed here once when he was recovering his health, just like you? Well, not here, there. I met him there. I'm sure he remembers me to this day; we spoke about finance and politics, man to man; he's very approachable. Oh, we haven't been introduced – I'm Hubert Hall. I'm in finance and real estate, mostly."

Henri tried to digest this and managed, "I am pleased to meet you. Where are my... companions?"

"The *zapatistas*? They all went back north to fight. Gallant men. Zapata's an extraordinary fellow, isn't he? I told the State Department in my most recent communique, he's the one to watch, you'll all see. By the way, who is Pham Binh? You were asking for him. Or her. Chinese?"

"Vietnamese. Someone... I once knew." Henri's fatigued state left him wide open to a rush of sadness; he pushed it away. What was done, was done.

147

"Listen, you seem like a man of the world. Can I interest you in a remarkable opportunity?"

Henri rubbed his eyes. "I don't—"

"I call it the Liberating Army Co-operative Colony. I've arranged for a very large area of land – sixty-four *thousand* acres! – to be made available to my investors once the Martians are defeated and Zapata has won his revolution. And you can have a parcel of this verdant, valuable land for only 180,000 pesos! Payable in monthly installments – as a military man, you can divest part of your pay – I have connections with France. The money finances his revolution, and everyone wins! Now, you might well ask, what legal conturbations might arise? Yes, I see you've thought of that already! It's quite simple, I have—"

Henri glanced away gratefully as a small but very upright woman eased a tray in through the doorway. "Hubert," she said in an upper-class English accent, "thank you ever so much for watching over Mr. Gamelin. I believe we ought to leave him to eat his breakfast in peace."

"Why, of course. Mr. Gamelin, may I present Mrs. Rosa King, owner and operator of this establishment. I am sure you feel as I do, that women carry civilization with them wherever they go."

Mrs. King smiled. "Hubert is my best and only customer, and a great help. Dear fellow, perhaps you could assist Conception with drawing some more water?"

"Of course." Hall bowed to Henri and Mrs. King in turn, then strode purposefully out.

"There's a few fresh eggs from the chickens," said Mrs. King, setting the tray on the bed. "I've taken the liberty of soft-boiling them..."

Henri restrained his urge to snatch up the eggs and eat them whole, and instead tapped with a spoon at the shell. The air of unreality was overwhelming. "Er, that man... does he *really*..."

"Hubert is not a bad fellow, but I'm afraid most of his schemes are imaginary ones. He's been with me here for six months. I think he just needs to feel a little more important in the world than he really is. We all have our ways of... adjusting... to what is happening in it." She glanced about the shabby but clean room with a sad smile. "I still run my Bella Vista. My husband founded it; I took it over after his death; generals and revolutions have not dissuaded me. Why should some strange creatures do so?"

"Ah." Henri finished the last egg in two bites. "So this... Co-operative Colony is a fantasy, then."

"Oh, no. That one is quite real. He just doesn't have many investors yet..." She laid a cool palm on his forehead. "You seem a great deal better today. They said you'd been hurt in some kind of battle in the city."

"But that was only a scuffle!"

She took Hall's former chair. "I'm afraid you were in quite serious condition. You'd collapsed on the way south from Mexico City, you were feverish – really, Mr. Gamelin, marching that distance with three broken ribs and a contused leg? You must take better care of yourself. Your fellows recognized the danger and brought you here. One man carried you up here as though you were a child."

Henri chilled at the recollection of that same man facing a monstrous killing machine, of flames and gunshots...

"Oh, I'm sorry," said Mrs. King, mistaking his reaction. "I didn't mean to insult you, Mr. Gamelin."

"Eh?" He brightened at once. "Of course not, madam! Not only am I a Frenchman, I am a Gascon. Size does not matter. It is *elan* that wins the day!"

May, 1912, Coahuila Province, Mexico

General Francisco Villa leaned back in his camp chair. "Well. That is an interesting story."

"It's the truth, sir," said Emmet Smith.

"Hm." Villa was a solidly built man in his forties – much like the soldiers he commanded, who looked to be heads of households rather than youngsters – with a shrewd, weathered face. His uniform was the same as his men's. "The difficulty is that I don't believe it. No one has ever escaped from the Martians' hands, and the only survivors that have been found were in much, *much* worse shape than you people. There is something that you are not telling me."

Emmet considered what little he knew of the general. "Can you ask your men to give us privacy?"

Villa studied him a moment, then waved a hand. Sergeant Rodriguez and two of Villa's aides got up from their positions seated on the ground and moved off. Emmet, Idar, and Hicks remained in their seats. Emmet did not mistake the courtesy of those chairs for cooperation... not yet.

"There are humans working with the Martians now. Probably have been for some time. These ones are a mix of Americans and Mexicans. Put simply, they do the Martians' dirty work, and their own lives are spared. It's an ugly thing, but it's real."

Villa considered this. "There have been wild rumors, but never anything credible... And do they wear those strange objects?"

"Some of them. Their leader, well, he took a fancy to Miss Idar and gave her one. We used that to help us escape."

"So you say."

"I know it looks bad. That's why we don't share it with people unless we have to. General, I sure can't tell you what to do, but I would implore you not to give out this information."

"You're right about that part," said Villa neutrally. "Mr. Smith, there is no state of hostilities between our countries, and while America has not seen fit to recognize President Madero as yet, that's nothing I would blame you for. Normally I would treat you as guests. But your appearance in Nuevo Leon is suspicious, and you admit there are humans collaborating with Martians. Perhaps that object is gathering information right now." He pointed at the pendant.

"You don't look worried," said Hicks.

"I have been fighting for Madero in this revolution for over two years now. Anywhere I go, there are always two escape routes... and if the Martians have grown complacent, perhaps we could show them a welcome they do not expect."

"I worked for President Madero myself once," ventured Emmet. "I'd be happy to talk to him about what we've seen. Mostly, though, I need to report back about what the Martians are doing in Texas."

"And what is that?"

"Now just a minute..." began Hicks. Emmet waved him silent.

"That could be a fair exchange, General. We share what we know with you, and you get us back over the Grande so we can do our jobs."

"This is not an exchange. It is an order."

"With all due respect, General... I don't take orders from you." Emmet noted that Villa's hand had begun to tremble. "Now, if you can contact my boss, the adjutant-general of Texas, and he says to do it... then yes. Or your President, as a token of friendship. Otherwise, if you won't help us, we'll walk back home on our own feet."

"Do you think I won't shoot you if I choose?" snapped Villa. "Impudent *rinche* snake... Madero is a week's ride from here! I have no time for such an excursion!"

Emmet blinked. "Only a week? Isn't he in Chihuahua City?"

"No! Sabinas."

Along the rail line to Eagle Pass... interesting. And they'll have a telephone line there as well... "General, I apologize for my tone. But this matter of human collaborators is important to relations between our countries, and it could really blow up if it gets out. Take us to see the President, and I'm certain he'll know what to do."

"Or I could bury the tale right here," said Villa coldly.

Emmet shrugged. "There'll be others. But I think we can negotiate with the President to keep it limited to those who need to know."

"You are speaking very far above your station, sir. What are you? A couple of *rinche* on the wrong side of the border, and *you* –" he glared at Idar. "I have seen your kind before. One of those noble, well-connected families that cared nothing if a line moved on a map. Call a place Texas, or Mexico – you always do well. Where I came from, a man must work to prove himself! When I was starving, I turned bandit. When a judge sent me into the army instead of hanging me, I learned everything I could about fighting – and saw everything there is of corruption. To be an officer in *that?* I deserted instead, and took my revenge on the men who harmed my family, my town, my people. I lived by my wits until Madero's men approached me to fight for him in the north. Not for loot or glory, but for a revolution! Where a man like me can serve a man like him. That is what Madero strives to make of Mexico. And you would *negotiate* with him?"

"Well, if he's the man you say, he oughtn't to hold our lowly style against us," said Hicks.

"These *renegados* are scum," said Idar. "But they have leaders too. If another faction, another movement forms around them, you will have new enemies, General. With all the power of the Martians, and all the cunning of humans. This *must* be stopped. We can aid you, but only if you listen. Will you?"

Villa stared at her, still furious, then rose to his feet. "Sergeant Rodriguez!"

May, 1912, Veracruz, Mexico

"Gamelin! Get in here." General Charles Mangin waved Henri into his office. He shut the door on the babble of clerks outside. "Sit down. I have read your report. You had quite a little holiday in Mexico City, didn't you?"

"You might say that, General." Henri winced as he eased into the chair. Certain movements still set his ribs on fire.

"Perhaps the Navy does know how to fight after all." He thought he detected a grudging respect in Mangin's manner. "You seem to think Zapata's men do as well."

"Yes, General. But with these new, small machines, the Martians are pressing them badly. They need our help."

"The only thing worse than streetfighting in one's own city, my boy..."

Henri nodded. "Is streetfighting in someone else's."

Mangin clasped his hands on his desk. "Gamelin, when one fights Martians, whatever you do, you lose a lot of men. This is understood by now. If a battle is won, well, at least they die for something. But to lose a lot of men taking a city block, then yielding it the next day, then taking it back the next... No. This corps was sent here on the understanding back home that we would not suffer large casualties. Grinding it up in Mexico City – for goals that have nothing to do with France's objectives – is not supportable."

"I would think the goal of defeating the Martians is also France's." Henri realized as he spoke that he'd not have dared to say that a month ago.

"Certainly – but not in someone else's country!"

"We are sending men to the United States to fight them there."

"That is different. The assault on the Martian base there is certain to succeed, and the Americans will take the brunt of the casualties... Gamelin, I do not blame you for admiring this Zapata. I too salute him. But to give him my men, well, that is a different thing. To put it bluntly, they are mine to spend, not his."

"Well, what about heavier weapons, then? Or shells for their guns?"

"Tanks or artillery would be wasted on untrained men. Gamelin, your report is acknowledged, so if–"

"What about *stovepipes?*"

Mangin blinked at the English word. "How did you hear about that rumor?"

"Colonel Angeles told me last month, sir. It is no rumor. The Americans have a sort of master rocketeer, Goddard, who created them. They would be ideal weapons in a city fight! And they require little training to use, merely courage."

"But they are not ours to send to anyone."

Henri thought quickly. "General, if you attach me to the Mexican expeditionary force, I can liaise with Colonel Angeles. I know he has contacts with American businessmen in El Paso – that is, in Texas. Provide us with funds, and we can buy the rockets from the Americans in Texas on behalf of Zapata's force, and bring them in via Veracruz by ship."

"Interesting," mused Mangin, "but I doubt the Texans would give up a new and scarce weapon for any amount of money. That they have plenty of, eh?"

Merde. What did Felipe say about – Ah. "But they have no aircraft, General."

"None? Really? But we are not going to ship them aircraft. We have none here!"

"We could send them the plans for, say, the Deperdussin monoplane instead. I believe they could manufacture engines and most of the components themselves; perhaps we sell them instruments. That ought to be worth a few hundred rockets, eh?"

"Plans for a military aircraft?" spluttered Mangin.

Henri shrugged. "It is already obsolete, is it not? But airworthy. It would never become a threat to France; by the time they are building them, we will have much better ones."

151

"Gamelin, you make my head ache with your schemes. Very well, I'll send you to America and let them deal with you. I suspect you will fit right in!"

May, 1912, Sabinas, Northern Mexico

After five days of hard riding, Emmet Smith, his companions, and their Mexican escort pulled in to the small town of Sabinas on a stifling afternoon – a tiny cluster of buildings around a train station. The Mexican International Railroad ran from the central city of Torreon northeast to Piedras Negras, a town across the Rio Grande from Eagle Pass. During their approach, Emmet had observed a train puffing its way north, so presumably the Martians hadn't interrupted this line. They were nearly home... if nothing went wrong.

Sore and tired as they were, they were given no time to rest. "Madero's safety is more important than mine," said General Villa, who sat easily in his straight-legged saddle, unruffled by nearly a week in the field. "Before you can see him, you must pass by his bodyguard, Castillo. Do not be insulted if he frisks you. Indeed, he may not pass you at all."

Emmet was too tired to argue; he twitched the reins as directed and proceeded at a walk to a livery at the edge of the town. If nothing else, they'd get these horses looked after; they were fine beasts. Dismounting hurt worse than he remembered in years; Hicks and Idar looked similarly worn. One of Villa's *soldaderas* had given her a shawl to conceal the pendant.

"Here," he muttered to the stableboy. "Can you see if there is—"

"*Emmet!*" shouted a familiar voice to his left.

In an instant, his hand was being pumped and his back clapped much harder than a small, white-haired man could be expected to do. Maximo Castillo grinned in delight. "What the devil are you doing here? I haven't seen you in years!"

"Hello, Maximo. Good to see you again." He turned to a glowering Villa. "We go back a ways – when I worked for the Thiel Detective Agency, President Madero was our client."

"Well, at last, something I can believe." But Villa did appear to relax. "Come along, then. The President's offices are not fancy, but at least they are close by."

Indeed, they were the next building over. The stable had been swept clean, and tables and chairs brought in, but nothing could disguise it. Men milled about, some in uniform, most in town suits. One short, well-dressed man approached at Castillo's wave.

"Hello, Mr. President." Emmet was no flatterer, but it seemed wise to leave the 'provisional' aspect of the title aside.

"Mr. Smith! I remember you. I hope I see you well?"

"We're a bit tired and worn, sir, but we're still walking. I have a tale that I promised the general I'd share with you, but first, if I could impose on you for a favor?"

"Certainly. Please, sit, you do look exhausted." Madero ushered him to a chair and joined him.

"May one of us use your telephone to call the United States? We need to report on the activity of the Martians who have invaded Texas. It's vital."

"Yes. Ricardo!" Madero waved at one of the clerks. "Please see to their needs for any telephone connections... So, what has happened?"

"You already know the Martians went across the border at Laredo, I'm sure. They stopped about fifty miles east and set up one of their bases. We've tried to drive them out – there was one hell of a battle – but last I saw, they were still in operation. But from what we... saw, it doesn't seem like their other bases. They've built it right on the Texas-Mexican rail line, and they've sent at least one train back loaded with some sort of ore or mineral. Many tons of it. We don't know yet what they intend to use it for, but it must be important."

"Yes, General Villa has reported to me about this activity as well. May he join us?"

"Sure." While Madero beckoned to Villa, Emmet turned aside. "Hicks, why don't you call it in. You did well back there. Get some credit for it. Ah, might be best not to mention about – those people. Can't anyone else on a telephone line hear what you're saying?"

"You're asking *me*?"

"Well, let's just assume so. Go on, Hicks. You've earned it."

"Thanks. I guess." Hicks walked over to the desk, spoke with the clerk for a few moments, then picked up the receiver as gingerly as though he were gripping a rattlesnake.

Villa joined them. "Mr. Smith, it seems you are vouched for. My apologies for shouting at you."

"That's all right, General. Words can be fixed a lot easier than bullets can... So how far south does that train go from the Martian base? Could you attack it if it comes back?"

"Attack it? Hardly. They send dozens of machines along with it... There is a Martian stronghold at Monterrey. While it is not wise to get too close to that, we have seen one train traveling northward from nearby. No group of humans could have done that and lived, so it must be their work."

"Is that why you're here on this line, Mr. President, and not the Torreon hub?"

"Yes. Torreon was destroyed two years ago, and they have torn up much of the track anywhere near Monterrey. We replace it when we can, but it is hardly a reliable route – or a safe one! I have been in contact with some prominent Americans and hope to set up a meeting this summer in Eagle Pass. Do you know Sherburne Hopkins?"

"That Washington lawyer? Saw him in Laredo a few times. He sure gets around." At the telephone, Hicks was saying loudly, "No, the *Adjutant*-General. Adjutant."

"He is working to obtain belligerent status for our revolutionary movement." Emmet reflected that another man would have said *my* and not *our*. "That could change matters greatly."

Villa nodded. "It would allow the legal purchase of weapons that could give us a chance against the Martians, or even to move our troops along the Rio Grande via American railways. But there are also Americans who support Diaz, who support General Reyes, even General Huerta... It is always a changing situation."

"Sir, I did telephone as soon as I could," said Hicks in English. After a few moments, he began describing their journey.

"America's tried to stay neutral about your revolution," said Emmet. "Not perfectly, I'll admit... We can't afford to be neutral about the Martians. No one can. Particularly in Texas."

Madero said, "Mr. Smith, it has always seemed to me that the Martians changed everything when they landed, and yet they changed nothing. 'President' Diaz has no moral authority to govern any longer, ever since he canceled the election. He is propped up by military men like Huerta, and by nations like France. Still, if I genuinely thought he could rally all of Mexico behind him, I would step aside." Madero appeared to be perfectly sincere. "But instead, he is destroying it. His army will not fight. His generals vie amongst themselves to seize power after his fall. Mine – Villa, Orozco, even Garibaldi – they are united by our movement. Men have come here from all over the world – not for me, but for what I am trying to do. One of my aides, Sommerfeld, is German! Garibaldi could have followed his father into politics in Italy, but he too chose to come here! To me, the choice seems very clear. But America is as riven by factions as Mexico, it seems. Perhaps now that you are attacked on two fronts, those factions will seem less important?"

"I would not bet on that," said Villa. "Still, any ally is better than none. Smith, are you suggesting that your state, or the U.S. Army, might send forces to assist us? There are some serious legal issues around that."

"General, lawyers don't seem to have helped you much so far. Maybe it's time to try something different."

"I trusted your judgment with the Thiel Agency," said Madero. "What do you have in mind?"

"No, sir," said Hicks heavily, "we didn't get our belts and rifles back yet. Yes, sir, I'm aware of how much they cost."

Emmet glanced at Hicks, and the telephone, and thought. "Mr. President, it might take me a little while, but... I think I could get you Governor Colquitt on the telephone directly. We've been finding lately in Texas that we need to do things ourselves without waiting around for Washington. If he were to agree to meet you, wouldn't that boost your credit in general?"

"Perhaps it would," said Madero. "Although I would understand if he were angry that we could not prevent the Martians from attacking your country – his state – from the south."

"We have fought hard!" snapped Villa. "Even after the *federales* abandoned the north. It is not our fault the *diablos* have such powerful weapons. The Americans could not stop them either!"

"I don't think he's much of a man for laying blame, sir. We need to work with what we have in front of us."

"Then let us try," said Madero. "We must never stop trying."

May, 1912, Eagle Pass, Texas

Emmet Smith paced along the portico of the Grande Hotel. The crowd outside in the wide, dusty street was getting larger by the minute. They looked cheerful enough; half the town had turned out, curious to see what was happening, and a throng of Mexican citizens had crossed over the Rio Grande bridge to add to the numbers. It looked like a local election, although the supply of Mexicans would have been even larger for that.

He paused next to Castillo, who had come out to admire the crowd. "Who hung up all this bunting, Maximo?"

"Madero's brother, Hipolito, likes that sort of thing." Castillo craned his neck to study the paired Mexican and American flags. "Madero was never one for it."

"I wonder what the Martian flag looks like."

Castillo shook his head. "You were always thinking of the strangest things. We are looking for bad men and bombs, not Martians."

"'Course, nowadays it's not impossible that a tripod might pop up in that street."

"If it does..." Castillo shrugged. "It is not our responsibility. You read too many books, Emmet. Our sort of job is more simple."

"I wish it was," muttered Emmet. He had no idea how he was going to explain to the adjutant-general that he and Hicks needed to take a short vacation to raid a Martian base. Period of detached duty? Didn't a Special Ranger get to do that anyway?

"I count eighteen windows that a man could shoot from opposite this building," said Castillo crisply. "That is where your attention must be."

"Nineteen."

"What?"

"Roof hatch on the Biggs general store. I walked up there an hour ago."

"That's more like it," said Castillo. "Is that revolver suitable?"

Emmet drummed his fingers on the pistol butt. "I miss my old Colt, but this'll do. Thanks, Maximo." The small Browning had gone with Jovita Idar – over her protests. Villa's army included an auxiliary force of *soldaderas*, women who were more than camp followers, but not quite regular soldiers. She'd fit in well already, and a helpful woman had donated a deeply conservative dress that covered the Martian pendant. Still, rumors could travel. Someone might get the idea that it was priceless and not realize that it couldn't be safely removed. For all of Villa's hot temper, his men were *very* disciplined, and she was safer surrounded by them than in Eagle Pass.

Would Governor Colquitt and President Madero be? That was partly up to Emmet and Maximo...

Several motor cars appeared at the end of the street. Emmet forgot about anything but watching for threats.

The town's mayor bustled out onto the portico. "Everything's ready!" he bubbled. An old adversary of Colquitt's, he was likely hoping this visit would get him into better graces. As he stepped aside, General Villa led Madero out to join them. Villa had brought only a handful of soldiers along and was not armed himself; but Emmet figured the legalities of this visit were getting more complicated by the hour.

The motorcars pulled up at the hotel. Emmet recognized another Ranger beside Colquitt in the first car. Henry Hutchings sat in the second one.

A local photographer was jockeying for a closer spot; Emmet glared at him and he gave ground. Whatever tiny paper he worked for, he was getting a scoop today. As Colquitt climbed up the stairs, the others shifted aside and Madero offered his hand. Colquitt shook it, smiling, as the flash powder chuffed. He spoke a few words to Madero, then turned to Emmet, the smile tightening. "We'll talk later," he hissed, and waved to the crowd; some whooped and cheered. Madero waved likewise; then the two leaders walked into the hotel entrance.

Hutchings trotted up the stairs in turn and grabbed Emmet's elbow. "Smith! What the hell are you doing?"

"Sir?"

"Flags! Photographers! Mexicans! This was supposed to be a quiet *tete-a-tete!*"

"I'm more concerned with protection than decorations."

"Maybe you don't care what the rest of the United States thinks, but the 1st Texas Division sure does! Washington will go mad! Damn it, I *told* him to set it up at Fort Duncan..." Hutchings stamped off.

Castillo rejoined Emmet at the entrance. "It should be easier from here. But watch the hallways." He threw a quizzical glance back to the crowd. "Your countrymen seem to like him."

"Someone who's fighting the Martians in defiance of a central government that abandoned him? I think they can understand that."

Colquitt and Madero remained closeted in their room for the better part of an hour. When they emerged, they seemed cordial; Colquitt shook hands again, watched him set off toward his own room, and beckoned Emmet aside.

"I don't like having my hand forced, Smith. Some quiet meeting *that* was!"

"That wasn't my intention, Governor. I apologize. Did Madero speak to you about that Martian base in –"

"Yes, yes. Martians riding trains, though? I wonder if his English is really as good as he thinks... But that's all a sideshow next to the invasion of Texas. We've done some good work there."

Emmet blinked. "Sir, it may be that the only reason the Martians are *in* Texas is because of what they're moving south on that railroad. That stuff they dug up."

"Oh, come, now. There's far better mines in northern Mexico than in Texas, they wouldn't need to invade us for that! Just ask Hammond or Pierce. They're after our whole state, and they *will not* get it! However, General Funston did ask me to look into being able to maneuver military forces south of the Grande, in case we need to pursue the Martians south once we've driven them back over the border. I think we've worked out a compromise that will allow that."

"How?"

"We're going to recognize Madero as a belligerent in the Mexican civil war. That allows any American citizen to supply his forces with arms, and in turn, he can legally admit our army into Mexico if needs be."

"Governor," said Emmet with great patience, "that's a federal decision. The State Department must –"

"Damn it, man! My state is being overrun by Martians! Do you think I care if Washington approves or not – overturns it – ignores it? They can argue about it for months if they like, but they've got their own problems to address. Little Rock's been attacked, and there's a big fight going on up north, maybe the biggest yet. It might take years for them to pay attention to this! If Funston's happy with this arrangement, then I am." He glanced over. "Henry, I may tell you, is *not* happy. I leave you in his tender care. But I do think today has turned out well." He turned away as Hutchings walked up.

"Smith."

"Yes, sir." Emmet studied the wallpaper above Hutching's left shoulder; intertwined hollyhocks.

"While you were getting yourself captured, there was a *real* war going on around Hebbronville. Did you scout anything useful to that? Perhaps the number of tripods the

Martians have at their base?"

"We saw... three, sir."

"*We* saw forty. Not very useful, that information. Trains and prisoners and Mexican rebels? Even less so. I've got men in the field watching that base properly now; the 1st Texas has its own scouting elements. We know exactly where those Martians are and if they make any move. Since that Villa bandit was crying for aid, we figure to send the LRSC motor club south to help him out and scout our pursuit routes – we'll need them once we've beaten those Martians hollow – and any Rangers with nothing to do can always join in."

"Won't be many volunteering for *that*," said Emmet in his best Brer Rabbit imitation. "Going into Mexican territory with a bunch of rebels? We're not real popular there."

"No, we aren't," said Hutchings. He smiled; not a nice smile. "Smith, you're a *special* Ranger. You'll be perfect for it. Find yourself one of those tin lizzies, get in, and stay in."

Emmet took a chance. "Sir, you can't send me alone!"

"No, no; quite right. I talked to someone on the telephone last week – Bicks? Hicks?"

"Hicks, sir."

"That's what I said. He's already this close, may as well go with you. Keep all this nonsense about Martians digging mines where it belongs – out of the state. You're dismissed." He hurried off after Colquitt.

Emmet set off to look for Castillo. He slapped the borrowed revolver as he strode; maybe he could get the old Colt back after all.

May, 1912, IX Corps HQ, Alice, Texas

"Lang," said Otto Prendergast, "another telegraph's come in. Little Rock has–"

"Just give it to me." Lang held out a hand without making the effort to get up from his desk. Major Prendergast passed him the flimsy. He scanned it with sick anticipation. VIII CORPS FULL RETREAT TOWARD MISSISSIPPI STOP LITTLE ROCK LOST STOP... He tossed it onto a growing stack. "First Kansas City, now this. The Martians are going to split the country in two along an east-west axis at this rate."

"The fighting around St. Louis is nothing short of stupendous," said Prendergast. "If the Martians move south to try and get around there..."

"They won't. Not that far from a base – they won't wish to risk being cut off."

"We may be risking the same. Blast it, Lang, we should send those divisions back north now. We have allies joining us, after all."

Lang flicked a glance at the map table, which still showed the markers for Second Army's northern line. It was an illusion. Both the 78th and 5th Texas divisions were mere husks at this point, with almost all their fighting elements moved south to prepare for the second attack on Hebbronville. It was a dreadful risk... but if they could break the siege with an all-out assault, it would be over in days at most, and those forces – or what remained of them – would be heading back north the next day. The trains were staged and ready.

However, the mythical French-Mexican expeditionary force had confounded

157

Lang's opinion – the opinions of most of Funston's staff – by actually arriving yesterday. While Corpus Christi's improvised port facilities had been immediately overwhelmed by the division-scale traffic, things were being sorted out, and genuine guns and vehicles were coming ashore. Whether they were manned by genuine soldiers was another matter; but it would be sheer folly to ignore them.

"The general is going to attack with the greatest force that he can gather. Otto, when has an attack failed from too much strength?"

"Attacks have failed from too little speed. And from divided command... The Mexican and French divisions are going to be under the command of their own general officers. They got all puffed up when Funston wanted to command them directly. He had to agree to treat them as 'cooperative equals'."

"And the governor approves of this too?"

"Reluctantly," said Prendergast. "He's met with the expedition leaders, Huerta and General Anquetil, and thought they meant business. I'm looking forward to meeting them myself when they get here. But that will be another three weeks at least. Another week to form them up and get them wired in to HQ – if we even can... Who knows what will happen up north in that time?"

"That isn't our responsibility. We've got our own work to do."

"I know," said Prendergast worriedly. "But will the Martians leave us out of that fight while we do it?"

June, 1912, Allende, Northern Mexico

The train halted in a cloud of steam and the groan of worn-out machinery. From his seat in the single passenger car, Emmet Smith peered out the window. About three hundred Mexican mounted infantry were drawn up in neat lines along the platform and surrounding scrub. At first glance, they looked worn but efficient. There were a couple of small artillery pieces and their caissons, also horse-drawn. Oddly, each one carried half a dozen spare wheels – and not much else.

"Everyone out!" shouted Major Palmer at the head of the car's aisle. "Shirts in, hats level – we're meeting Villa's boys, so look sharp!"

"Glad I shaved," Emmet said to Hicks. Both men gathered up their rifles and packs from the luggage racks and joined the other men disembarking; almost all of those were part of the Long Range Scouting Company and seemed to Emmet to pride themselves on not carrying one object on their person – it was all stowed in the vehicles carried on the train's flatcars.

"Fall in over here!" shouted Palmer, who seemed to think that providing the unit's munitions made him their commander. "Make a better job of it than those bastards! Line it up!"

Hicks and Emmet bustled into formation with the rest. Palmer stalked down the line, prodding men into better alignment. He stopped at Emmet. "Who the hell are you?"

Major Plainview, the LRSC commander, intervened before Emmet could reply. "These are Texas Rangers detached from their company, Major. They'll be scouting for us."

"Rangers? Quite a reputation you've all got. Scares off crooks and rustlers. Think

158

it'll scare off a Martian?"

"Don't know, Major," said Emmet evenly. "The last one I ran into, it just looked away and kept on walking, so maybe it does work."

"Bullshit! Just because–"

"Major, the general's coming." Plainview steered him aside.

"Pretty noisy fellow, for an egghead with a couple'a clusters," muttered Hicks.

"Shh."

General Villa rode down the short line of men. "Welcome, allies!" he called out in English. "This is a peculiar arrangement among us! Now, I decide where we go, and when we fight, but I will not tell you how to fight. I ask only that when you see something I cannot, you tell me about it!" He wheeled the horse with slow precision. "Now, you have heard that I am strict with my men! It is true! But I will not make threats to you. Your officers are responsible for your conduct on the battlefield, and off it. I know you have already fought well. I look forward to fighting with you!

"As to those *diablos*, the Mar-*ti*-ans... I do not know how they came to this world. I cannot send them home! *But I can send them to Hell!*"

Cheers erupted from Villa's troops; although many must not have understood the words, they obviously knew the tone. To Emmet's surprise, many of the Americans joined in.

Villa wheeled away. "Major, start loading the troops!" he called out in Spanish.

A string of more boxcars that had been waiting at the Allende station – a tiny spot fifty miles southwest of Eagle Pass – had already hooked on to the LRSC's train. The mounted troops streamed toward them in neat rows.

"Is someone going to tell that nitwit that he's not got enough cars to hold that many men and horses?" grumbled Palmer.

"There don't seem to be enough," agreed Plainview doubtfully. He watched with the rest of them as the troops dismounted at the car doors, carefully led the horses up the loading ramps and inside – then began scrambling up the ladders on the car sides.

"Oh, hell. He's not serious..."

As they watched, the soldiers loaded the horses into the cars and packed themselves onto the rooftops, with no more protection from the elements than their broad-brimmed hats. The artillery was loaded in more conventional fashion onto an open car. For all the crudity of the arrangement, it ran like clockwork, and in a shockingly short time, the battalion was embarked; the last men hefted the ramps up into the boxcars and slid shut the doors... all but one.

Villa, who had sat his horse the whole time, approached last of all. He spurred the horse and galloped it toward the open boxcar door, then leaped it clean into the car.

"The son-of-a-bitch can ride, I'll give him that," muttered Plainview. He caught Palmer's nod. "All right! Back aboard, we're moving out!"

In a few more hours, they arrived at Sabinas, which at least boasted a proper station. Here, the unloading took much longer, as the LRSC cars and trucks had to be carefully driven down ramps. The men seemed practiced at it, though. The trucks intrigued Emmet: heavy construction flatbeds fitted with futuristic-looking rockets on railings. There were four of the trucks, and they looked like they could hit pretty hard. Once, at least.

Most of the men not driving assembled near the command officers. "Alright, everyone!" shouted Plainview. "Who speaks Spanish? Put up your hand." He scanned the group. There were a number of gaps; he grinned wryly at Emmet.

"Okay. You, Hicks, is it? You go with Four-Six." At Hicks' blink, he added, "That's the command truck for Fourth Platoon – Major Palmer, over there. He's going to be observing how the rockets make out. Smith, you're with car One-One."

"Great," muttered Hicks, but he hefted his pack and moved off. Emmet trudged through the bustle of led horses and chugging vehicles, looking for a car marked 1-1, and found it; an expensive-looking touring car, heavily modified. A driver was sleeping in his seat, hat tipped over his eyes; two more men were speaking together in back.

"Oh, hello," said one as Emmet walked up. "You must be the Texas Ranger."

"I am," allowed Emmet. "How'd you know? Emmet Smith, by the way."

"Frederick Burnham; this is Cooter Stimson; and our driver is Edward Painewick. Pleased to meet you. Oh, it's the way you carry that military pack; not used to it. More at home on a horse, I would say. I'm the same, although I'm delighted by these motor cars."

"Just drop it in here," offered Stimson. He showed Emmet a cargo box strapped to the car's side; then they mounted up.

"Mr. Painewick," called out Burnham. The driver yawned, stretched, and turned. "This is Texas Ranger Smith."

"I haven't done anything!" blurted Painewick.

"I rather doubt that," said Emmet, "but you can relax, son. I'm here to scout, not enforce the law."

"That's a relief. Those Martians are enough to worry about." Painewick twisted around and started the car. Some other vehicles began to move off; he waited his turn.

"You fellows been with this unit for long?" asked Emmet.

"Since it started, pretty much," said Painewick over his shoulder. "Mr. Burnham, he joined us six months back, and Cooter just in April. Cooter built those rockets on the trucks over there."

"Not all of 'em," muttered the young man. "Just the prototypes. Major Palmer – he's the head of the rocket program up in Houston – he said I ought to come see how they flew in action, up real nice and close in one of these here cars. I don't think he likes me much... But we think we can fit one onto a car like this. Sometime. Meanwhile, I can work on my paper about that Martian wire." He tapped the notebook that bulged a shirt pocket. The car rolled off, accelerating and turning smoother than any vehicle Emmet had ever ridden in – certainly *much* smoother than he drove himself.

They drove the rest of the day, a slow meander along trails that had once been carter's tracks in the days before the railroads, when cotton moved in single bales across half of northern Nuevo Leon and Chihuahua by mule power. At dusk, the vehicles bivouacked; the risk of running into Martians was too high in the dark, and the horses needed to be kept rested. "If they pursue us," warned Villa, "a weak horse will fall behind."

Three days of this steady travel brought them a few miles west of the rail line near Saleme Botello, a tiny village along the route. By the time the two groups had set up camp, several scout riders had trickled in. They reported to General Villa; he called on Major Plainview; and Emmet, who had been watching all this with interest, was summoned along with Hicks to the order group at dusk. The air was cooling rapidly; the campfire set in a low swale gave welcome warmth and painted their weathered, determined faces in strokes of red.

"The *diablos'* train was seen traveling south again four days ago," announced Villa. "It has not returned yet, so it will pass north in the next few days. We shall prepare a reception for it."

Emmet lifted a hand. "Do we know it's returning? Maybe they're done whatever they wanted to do."

"My men only saw six tripods. How many do you think they lost in that battle?"

"Oh, I see, General. Not enough to only have six left!"

"Just so. Now, my men will pull up some of the rail line. We have done it before, but those machines can pick them up like matchsticks, so it only creates a slight delay. We must strike quickly when the time comes. As in my favorite sport, there will be *picadores* and *matadores*. Major Plainview, if you will please attend..."

June, 1912, Northern Mexico

Ronald Gorman glowered out of the locomotive's right-side window. The rising sun glowered back at him. The valley they were trundling through was a glorious, golden sight, spring flowers in scattered bloom, harsh but beautiful. He cared nothing for it. The sooner that reddish weed brought by the Masters spread over all this place, the better. He could see it in every creekbed and wash. They did not mark their territory in any way that Gorman knew of, but the plant did for them...

He flicked a glance to Mendez, slumped at his engineer's station. The man's wide face was dull, resigned. Only the harshest threats or blows could now move him to action. Gorman had seen a few men go that way over the past year; he'd found one in a bunk with the back of his head blown off by a stolen revolver. It had been difficult to clean up.

These trips were becoming bothersome. At the main fortress of the Masters, his months-long absence was leaving an opening for an ambitious man, and one had begun to make himself noticed. Of course, without de Gama to interpolate with the Masters, this upstart was hampered; but there was also the leadership of a very hard group of men to consider and how it might erode. If the next return to Monterrey was not the final one, it would be necessary to arrange this man's death.

And de Gama himself had become uncooperative at times. Whether his madness was waning or getting worse, he no longer always accepted Gorman's will. He'd refused to inform the Masters about the theft of a pendant – and the abdication of a queen. "She will come back to us," he'd insisted when Gorman pressed him. As flattering as Gorman might find that, he considered it unlikely. There had not been time to convince her of how much better her life would have been at his side. And perhaps the men she'd escaped with had swayed her. Often women would align themselves with whichever man seemed strongest at the time...

The train began to round a curve about a foothill. Gorman was looking idly ahead when he suddenly jerked in shock; part of the track a half mile ahead was missing. "Mendez! Stop us, *now!*"

The engineer groped for a lever and pulled it; brakes shrieked. With the train lightly loaded, it slowed rapidly. They halted with a jolt; two of the Masters' machines continued on ahead.

"Back us up!" snapped Gorman. "We're in danger here." He grinned wryly. "That is, the Masters' train is in danger here... Take us back half a mile or so. There may be artillery aimed at that spot."

When they had halted again and the locomotive was secured, he cuffed Mendez lightly. "Up and out, man. A little fresh air and activity will do you good."

"What is it?" muttered Mendez.

"Some of those Mexican pests in uniform, I suppose. They have meddled with our track. Get the tools and spikes and go make repairs once the Masters have replaced the rails."

Mendez shuffled to obey. Gorman climbed down from the train with him to share his pendant's protection – the Masters could be jumpy – and another man joined them. A Master's machine, looming tall, swiveled to peer down at them. Gorman lifted up the tools, mutely hoping the creature inside would understand. It turned and stalked off toward the blockage, so presumably, yes. "Off with you. Try not to let any of them step on you, now!"

June, 1912, Northern Mexico

Emmet studied the halted train through binoculars. He lay on a ridgeline a mile and a half west of the track; scrub concealed his outline, and he was careful not to let the lenses flash back the morning sun. Once he was certain what was happening, he edged backward to join the others around car 1-1, positioned along with other LRSC vehicles behind the ridge.

"They're awfully careful," he said. "They've moved the train back out of range. Two of the tripods are working on the track, the rest are guarding the train."

Burnham glanced over at the Wichita Six-Shooter parked fifty yards south. The crew had closed the metal windshield; it was ready to fire, the launch rails cranked to the correct elevation for a mile and a half range. "Why do you suppose Major Plainview hasn't ordered the attack yet?"

"I don't know. Maybe he's waiting for Villa to open fire." Emmet winced. "Unless Villa's waiting for *him*..."

"I think they have worked it out in a bit more detail than that," said Burnham.

"What are we attacking, anyway?" asked Cooter. When the others turned to him, he shrugged. "I mean, is it the train or the Martians? We don't have enough rockets to even try to hit both."

"Major Plainview told that truck crew to 'go for the tripods' last night, so unless that's changed, I presume they are aiming their rockets at the broken stretch of track."

Emmet noted that Burnham had a way of overhearing things. He felt torn about attacking the train directly; if it was carrying more livestock to feed the Martians at their base, it might buy the people there more time... But it *was* an enemy asset.

"Come *on*," urged Painewick.

As though he'd triggered something, a red flare spluttered into the sky.

"Cover your ears," warned Burnham. They scarcely had time to do so before a roaring blast scorched across them, sounding oddly musical. Another followed immediately, then another... Six rockets thundered and moaned over the ridge, arcing downrange. Emmet scrambled up to look; no need for stealth now. He was in time to

162

glimpse a turbid pillar of dirt erupt near the rail line, the last of that salvo. Another truck's rockets were already roaring out; more volleyed into the target area, converging like the smoky spokes of a wheel. He saw one rocket's trail veer wildly off, wasted; but twenty-three rockets struck there in less than thirty seconds.

"We got one!" he howled. Hazy in the drifting smoke and dust, a machine lay on its side, unmoving. Another staggered away from the impact zone, clearly disabled. Three more machines started west toward them.

Emmet sprinted back to the car; to the south, the Six-Shooter was already in gear and grinding down the ridge slope toward its escape route – their job was to see to it that it escaped. Emmet swung aboard. Painewick promptly drove them back *up* toward the ridgeline. Burnham manned the machine gun; young Cooter hunched in his seat as the car jolted him, scribbling in his notebook.

Painewick swung them parallel to the ridgeline and just short of it. After a moment, Burnham opened fire; the hammering shots were louder than any gun Emmet had ever heard. He continued to shoot for perhaps a minute, pausing to check his aim... or estimate how close the machines were getting as they climbed toward the stinging insect above them. Abruptly he flinched, released the gun, and dropped back into his seat. "Mr. Painewick–"

The driver didn't let him get out the second syllable before he had spurted the car into motion, slewing left and down the ridgeline, but not following the Six-Shooter; they had their own route to take. Racing southwest, they jolted and jarred along a dry wash that climbed and turned around another foothill, swinging around the worn rock with only moments to spare.

Painewick braked them in a skid of dust next to the artillery piece that Villa's men manned. It peeked over the hill in a good spot of cover. Nearby, six other guns seemed to keep watch... but the only things real about them were the wooden wheels. The rest were canvas bags, painted black and filled with soil.

In the moment of quiet, Emmet could hear other machine guns firing in the distance. "Did you hit one, Burnham?"

"A few times," said the civilian. His face was turning beet red; a heat ray had brushed him and inflicted a nasty burn, even at over a mile. "Now it's up to these fellows." He looked over to where Villa's gunners manned their piece with silent intent: a four-man crew.

Emmet stood up to get a line of sight over the wash's peak. A tripod stalked toward them over the far ridgeline. He ducked back as it opened up with its heat ray, but it had mistaken one of the decoy guns for its target. To his surprise, an explosion thudded.

"What was that?"

"Probably some dynamite tucked under the wheels," said Burnham. "That ought to divert them further."

A second decoy exploded to the north. Moments later, the artillery piece fired, recoiled, and slammed back into position. Emmet sneaked a look as the team reloaded it. The tripod hadn't been hit.

Another explosion. "They'll figure this out any moment..."

"Be ready, Mr. Painewick," said Burnham intently. The car's engine revved as though it had heard him and not its driver.

The gun fired, recoiled, and the crew busied to load it. Emmet stayed low, estimating the tripod's speed. They needed to go *now*...

The instant that the crew finished loading, the gun's captain – a fat man with a red sash – shoved two of them away from the gun. "Get in the car, all of you!" he shouted. After a moment's hesitation, they and a third man dashed the few feet to the tourer and climbed aboard. Emmet locked eyes with the gun captain for a moment; the man gave a wistful smile and turned back to the breech.

The scrub along the rocks burst into flame as the heat ray screamed out. The gun captain groped for the lanyard; his clothes were burning.

"Go!" yelled Burnham. They tore into motion, lurching around the foothill, accelerating toward a gap in the rocks scouted early that morning. Behind, the gun blasted out one more round. The car shot through the gap and jolted into another wash, heading for their escape route. There was nothing to do now but run.

June, 1912, Northern Mexico

Gorman stared at Mendez. The engineer seemed unhurt – the blood on his face and arms wasn't his – but he'd dragged the limp body of the other man back the entire two hundred yards they'd started toward the broken track, to drop it at Gorman's feet.

"Why did you do that?" he asked. "The Masters are already fed."

"I don't know," said Mendez. He wiped at his face. "I suppose we'll need another man now. To help me."

To the west, Gorman could hear the rasp of the Masters' weapons, and gunfire. They would drive off their tormentors soon enough. But even half a mile away, that barrage had been shocking. New weapons. Didn't people understand when they were beaten?

"They killed him," added Mendez stupidly. "Alberto. Our own kind – humans."

"That troubles you?"

"They should have killed me."

"Just find the tools and I'll send another man with you." Gorman studied him for a moment. He would need to be watched.

June, 1912, Coahuila Province, Mexico

Emmet Smith didn't want to be the skeleton at the feast. But while everyone else – Mexican and American – seemed jubilant over a victory that had claimed at least one Martian tripod, he kept thinking about the fifty or sixty of them still holding their grip on Texas. And a certain promise he'd made. In hindsight, it seemed awfully rash, even irresponsible; but he'd made it.

Burnham and Painewick too seemed less excited as they drove up to the encampment of Villa's battalion at dusk, but they'd been in battles before and likely felt that it was winning the war that mattered. Once they'd dropped off young Cooter, Emmet broached an idea. "Could you fellows help me look someone up among the auxiliaries, the *soldaderas*? Her name's Jovita Idar, she's an American."

"They don't seem like an approachable group, from what I've seen," said Burnham. "Well, apart from a few who seem... professional company."

"That's not it," said Emmet. "She was at that Martian base when we broke out."

"Oh. Now, that could be interesting. Mr. Painewick, shall we swing around the north side of the camp and pay our respects? A nice car always gets one noticed."

"Sure," said Painewick. He lit the car's headlights in the evening twilight and drove slowly over the rough ground, watching for people – sometimes swerving around one. Around the campfires, men were shouting and singing. There was already a lengthy ballad about Villa; this raid would probably add a new stanza. He heard, "*The machines walked primly / clutching the skirts of their train / Then we asked them to dance...*"

They stopped at a knot of female figures, many in the same rough uniforms as Villa's men. Although the initial reaction was as flat as Burnham had predicted, the mention of Idar's name changed that, and they were waved on toward one of the fires. Painewick parked the car; they dismounted and walked toward the glow. Faces turned, hands pointed –

"*Emmet!*" shouted one small figure. She jumped up from beside the fire and ran several steps, then slowed abruptly and walked up to them. "I was – They said the LRSC had lost a car to the Martians, but no one seemed to know – that is–" She stopped and took a breath. "I was concerned."

"The communication between the units isn't the best at times," admitted Emmet. "That was car Three-One – a couple of good men gone, I'm afraid. May we join you?"

"Yes. Of course. Have you eaten?"

"Not very well."

"They're roasting a pig."

"Top-notch." Emmet gestured at his companions. "Enough for them too? They did most of the work in that fight, not me."

Idar smiled, teeth flashing in the gloom. "If they brought you back in good health, they are welcome." All of them found spots on the ground near the fire; plates were circulating heaped with food. Emmet snagged one and tore in.

"Ranger Smith mentions that you've seen Martians up close," said Burnham. He was eating in careful bites, unlike Painewick and Emmet, who were making the best of food far better than what the LRSC cooks dispensed.

Idar cooled slightly. "Yes, and it was most unpleasant. I really don't like to talk about that."

"Of course; I'm sorry. It's just that part of my work is finding out all that I can about them. The idea of getting inside one of those bases is... intriguing."

Emmet set down a gnawed rib. "Burnham, what *is* your line of work, exactly?"

"Much like yours, really. I... *scout*. The more difficult, the more... exacting the task, the more I enjoy it. And, sometimes, I carry out a small action in the right place and time, and it seems to make a difference. I'm no man for murder, but if one has a choice between a battle that kills a thousand and a single, careful shot that wins the day, surely it's the right thing to do? Perhaps not the honorable thing, but... Given the scale of *this* conflict, though, it's hard to see that happening."

"Maybe not," said Emmet thoughtfully. "Burnham, I figure to get inside that Martian base. Ranger Hicks and I, we... well, we think we have a way to sneak in past the tripods."

"Holy cow," said Painewick.

"That is... very difficult," said Burnham with keen interest. "Darkness is no cover, for one. And there are no ordinary humans to slip among, as would be in a human society."

"There are. I've seen them. Not prisoners... trusties. Roaming freely."

Burnham blinked. "You've – humans that *work for the Martians?*"

"Yes. Killed one of 'em; wouldn't mind adding a few to that. And there's prisoners in there, too – innocents kept to be used for food. I doubt they have much more than a few weeks left. IX Corps is working up a full-scale assault, but even if it doesn't kill them, it could be too late."

"Well. What did you have in mind?"

"Those human trusties, they wear gadgets that tell the Martian tripods they're allies." Emmet glanced at Idar before he said anything further; she hesitated, then nodded. She twisted away from others' view and unfastened the top button of her dress' high neck.

"What do they look like?"

"Like this, Mr. Burnham," she said, parting the cloth. Metal gleamed in the hollow of her throat.

"Extraordinary!" Burnham bent close to peer at it, then abruptly realized the circumstances and recoiled. "Er... terribly sorry. I didn't..."

"If we told the Bureau's agents about this," said Emmet, "I don't think it would go well. You see, there's no way to get that thing off her. They'd haul her off to Washington like... like a laboratory specimen." He hadn't realized until he said it how much that troubled him.

"Every necklace has a clasp," said Painewick.

"Not this one," said Idar. Her face contorted. "It is *their* work, like a living creature. Horrible, like all else they do. There is a machine that takes it off, and nothing else can."

"Quite the shine. Is it gold?"

Burnham chuckled. "Mr. Painewick, that alloy is probably worth far more than gold."

"It's the first Martian thing I've seen that was... portable." The gleam in Painewick's eye was brighter than the pendant's.

"If you're thinking of traveling back into Texas," said Burnham, "the quickest way is by car. But you would need an excellent driver."

Painewick grimaced at him. "No need to butter me up, Mr. Burnham. If you can swing it, I'm in. But I want you to provide me one of those gewgaws afterward, fair and square. It's only stealing if an enlisted man does it."

Emmet opened his mouth; Burnham gestured subtly. Instead, Emmet said, "Well, thanks. Be glad to have you. But I don't think Major Plainview is going to just give us one of his fighting cars. And he'd sure notice if one went missing."

"Two cars, ideally," said Burnham. "One to tow the other if it breaks down. Let me see what I can do, Mr. Smith. There are... favors owed. Forgive me if I'm not more specific."

"No need," said Emmet. He glanced up; people nearby were turning their heads southward, and several rose to their feet, murmuring. A solidly built figure shifted past them, turning to speak and gesture as he went. He picked up a plate of food, bowed thanks, and moved toward their group.

"Good evening, General," said Emmet. As a civilian, even one who'd fought under Villa's command, he did not salute, but he noticed few others had either as Villa settled to the ground, placing his plate carefully in his lap. There was little spit and polish in this army.

"Good evening. And it was a good day! I am grateful to you, Mr. Smith. The rockets brought by your compatriots have proven very useful. I hope we will see more of them."

"I do too, General. I've heard that sometimes it takes the loss of a regiment to take down a tripod in open fighting. That's a cruel rate of exchange; this attack turned out much better."

"It is only the little war – the *guerilla*. I would rather lead the entire Division del Norte against a Martian horde – or General Huerta's dogs! But it helps the morale of my army and my people to strike a blow, and the *diablos* will need to send many of their machines after me if they wish to keep using this route. That may weaken them in Texas as well."

Emmet thought that not many men would be this sanguine with a bunch of Martian tripods hunting them. "General, I may need to go back to Texas soon myself. But I wouldn't want you to think that I was sliding out on you – or anyone else who might go along with me. Do I have your permission? I can promise you that it's to fight the same bunch of Martians that you just did."

Villa nodded. "I have always held that any man who fights for me can leave at his own will – unless it is during a battle. Then it is desertion. So you have nothing to worry about from me, Smith. It is your own officers who may present the problem. But I leave that to you." Villa had finished eating as he spoke; he rose, handed the plate to a man next to him, and sauntered off through the camp.

June, 1912, IX Corps HQ, Alice, Texas

Lang looked up from his desk, blinked, and rose to his feet. "Governor! What brings you here?"

"Not a favorable errand," said Oscar Colquitt. He pulled off his hat and knocked it against his leg; road dust puffed away. His suit was filthy. "Not at all, Captain. I need to see General Funston immediately."

"He's in conference with Major Prendergast. They are planning–"

"*Immediately*, Captain. I have driven here from Austin and I will not be kept waiting."

"I... I understand, sir. Just a moment." Lang walked into the back corridor and knocked at the left door.

"Away with you!" called Prendergast.

"Sorry, Otto. General, it's the governor, and he needs to see you immediately."

After a moment, the door opened and Funston stepped out. "I see," he said in a flat tone. "You'd better dismiss the clerks, Willard. I think I know what this is about."

Lang nodded. "I too, sir." He trotted back to the main area and yelled, "Everyone out! Clear the room!"

Colquitt pointed at Lang as he walked after the scurrying clerks. "Not you, Lang. You were present at our first meeting, and you'll stay for this." Prendergast shot him a worried look as he left; they'd known this was coming.

Funston settled into a chair. He'd known too, of course. "Yes, Governor?"

"Leonard Wood's office has informed me that the Martians have taken Little Rock and have advanced nearly to Memphis. Were you aware of this, General?"

"Yes."

"The Martian forces are advancing rapidly down the Mississippi's western bank. They have cut off our rail connections with all eastern and northern states. Second Army divisions that were meant to protect those areas... have not. They appear to be absent altogether. General, I demand an explanation."

"I have already explained my plan of attack, Governor. It is to drive out the Martians in this state as soon as feasible, and it is proceeding."

"Did you move those units that Wood's office was asking about – redeploy them against Hebbronville?"

"Elements of the 78th and 5th Texas divisions..." offered Lang. Colquitt looked at him; he shut up.

"Yes. As Second Army's commander, that is my responsibility, and I am carrying it out. Once the Martians are defeated here, those divisions will be shifted north again. By July, at the latest."

"But you must shift them now!"

"Order, counterorder, disorder," recited Funston. "One does not turn a division around on a dime, Governor. General Wood has access to far more resources than we do here. He is closer to the situation, and he knows his work. He'll deal with that incursion. We must deal with ours."

"I cannot believe this. Those are our fellow Americans in the path of those – those *things!* You have shirked your responsibilities, sir!"

Funston flushed darkly. "Hold your tongue! I have never shirked a duty in my life!"

Colquitt paced away a few steps, and turned. "Very well, I misspoke. But I take grave exception to your judgment in this matter. The rail connection is vital. Even if the Martian forces are repelled quickly, they may well have destroyed so much track that it will take months to repair. And if they realize how thinly defended – how wide open – Texas is from the north, we'll have *two* incursions. And the French have supplied us no weapons or assistance as yet. There's no guarantee they ever will. To make an enemy of the United States Chief of Staff..."

"I have no hostility toward Leonard Wood. He's a good man. But just as he understood that Texas is a salient which he could not fully defend, he will have to understand that this incursion is for the armies of the eastern states to handle. They have sixty divisions, Governor! They have hordes of tanks, they are building giant landships! What good would two puny divisions do, even if they were available in time and good order? At least here, they can smash a Martian base. The news of *that* is bound to help morale all over the United States. In these military matters, you, you must..." Funston strove visibly for calm. "Governor, in these matters, you must leave all judgment to me. We agreed once that Washington was defensive-minded; well, then, this is their hour. They must defend. We must attack!"

"But at what cost, sir?"

"At any cost. This is war to the death, Governor. If I were to send those divisions back now... we might lose. And they would win nothing for it. We are committed, and I accept full responsibility for that. Second Army's task is to destroy that base, and we *will* carry it out."

"Hudspeth will have a field day with this," muttered Colquitt. "General, I don't think you grasp the political aspect of your actions. The *impact* of those actions."

"Are you concerned about your political enemies, Governor?"

"More about my allies. There are some that are all but calling for secession. They'll blame Washington for the loss of the rail connection, and I can hardly hold up your leadership as a counter-example, now can I? *It's all right, boys, we did it ourselves...* Fuel to the fire."

"A victory will shut up the naysayers. It always does."

Colquitt carefully picked up his hat from the desk and brushed it. "I hope so. Good day to you, General." He walked to the front door, paused, and turned. "The Martians may have crossed the Arkansas, General, but I fear we have crossed the Rubicon."

The door thumped shut behind him. Neither Lang nor Funston spoke for nearly a minute. Then the general levered himself to his feet. "Lang... the governor is right. We have... I have... crossed a sort of threshold." He raised his voice. "*Otto!* Get everyone back to work, then join us in the conference room!"

Lang followed the general to the back room, noting how his usual bouncing stride had become a shuffle. Once Prendergast had chivved the clerks back to place and joined them, though, Funston revived to his usual energy.

"We do need a genuine victory. I am confident that we have sufficient force assembled to assault the base at Hebbronville. And the French and Mexican units that have joined us seem like they can fight. General Huerta is very touchy, but he seems to know his trade – still, we have enough artillery of our own to supply, so once he's fired off what he has brought with him, I don't much care what he does. I've assigned a liaison to the French armored unit, ah, Captain, ah..."

Prendergast did not need to flip open the ledger before him. "George Patton, sir."

"Yes. They're far more mobile, so if that radio they left out there actually works, we may be able to coordinate a pursuit of some kind. But all that is not to be of much use if the Martians choose to retreat and outpace us. I want that base, but I also want them to pay the kind of price we've been paying. But I dare not split off part of IX Corps to encircle the base and invite defeat in detail."

"And without that, those tripods can retreat in a dozen directions and break through our lines where they please," agreed Lang.

"That's what we thought until this morning," said Prendergast.

"What?"

"We've received intelligence that the real purpose of the Martian base is to dig up and extract a mineral, and they have been using a stolen freight train to ship it back to their main base in Mexico."

Lang recalled the bizarre telegram report of a train with the Martian invasion. "Who's the source? The 3rd Volunteer Division?"

"No, they've been kept well outside of Laredo since March. The report came from some Texas Rangers." Prendergast grinned at Lang's bewilderment. "They'd reported from Mexico by telephone to the Adjutant-General, but Hutchings seems to have ignored it. I heard rumors via the LRSC last week, so I telephoned back and eventually got hold of them. All the details match, Willard. That's why they stopped so quickly once they got into Texas; they'd found whatever they wanted and got to digging. They could have rolled over San Antonio or Houston easily enough if they'd wanted to."

"When was the last train?"

"About six weeks ago."

Lang shook his head. "All that for – But, hang on. If they're still digging–"

"They're not done."

"And that is the key," put in Funston. "I don't know what they'll do when we attack, but if they do retreat, they'll surely want to bring back another trainload. And the only route to do so is through Laredo. The Martian force will head right down that rail line."

"Then that's why they secured the town to begin with. Not a supply line... a getaway plan."

"Yes. And that is why you are going to take it back."

"Sir?"

"I'm not leaving IX Corps headquarters until that base is taken or destroyed. Certainly not now. If the governor tries to pull out those divisions..." Funston flicked his hand angrily. "But the 3rd Volunteer is simply not up to the task of blocking the entire Martian force long enough for us to catch them. Harlan Slater's a brave man, but his division's been frittered away in small attacks. I understand their need to hit back, but if I send him more forces, I can't trust him to use them in the right way, at the right time. I'm sending you, Willard. I trust you to know when to fight... or to hold your fire to the last moment. I haven't forgotten your last stand at Albuquerque, you know." Funston smiled wanly. "Maybe I haven't forgiven... You'll have my full authority behind you. Take Laredo back from them, and hold. I'll drive them into you. If there are too many of them... don't throw away your men. Hurt them as best you can as they pass through. But if there's any real chance, you *must* stop them."

"Right," said Lang absently. "Sir. I could blow the bridge as well–"

"No!" said Prendergast. "That's the only thing keeping them on that path. Don't even scratch it."

"So I'll hold it hostage, then, and they must come and pay the toll." *Carson. Billings. Jed Gillray. I said you wouldn't come cheap.* Lang felt cold and clear; the accumulated fatigue of weeks of work seemed to drop away. "Very good. What do I have, and how do I get it there?"

"We're still working on that," said Funston. "It's too far to drive tanks even if we could pass near Hebbronville, and the Martians control the other rail lines near Laredo. But the LRSC is being recalled from Mexico, and they've proven these rocket trucks do work. And they've fought alongside Madero's generals. We have a new batch of rockets and trucks available now – it's too open country here and they'd be wiped out in an assault, but in an ambush, they can have a good chance. We're going to send them well around the Martians, down into Mexico, and you can slip them back across at Laredo and surprise the Martian garrison there."

"By 'batch', the general means eighty-two trucks," said Prendergast. "Fully loaded."

Lang digested this. "Sir, there isn't enough logistics support in Nuevo Leon for anything much beyond cavalry. One battle, and we'll be done."

"I know. That is why you must drive out the Martian presence in Laredo – I won't say retake the town, as there's little of it left. But push them back long enough to bring in trains from El Paso, and you will be able to reinforce the defenses with fresh rockets, fuel, and ammunition."

"How many more munitions are staging through there?"

"Two hundred and twenty of the four-inch rockets, and forty-three guided versions," said Prendergast.

"Forty– Where did you get that much wire? Did you get more than forty girls working after all?"

"They've got one hundred and seventeen there in Dallas. They're pulling out miles of it a day, working three shifts. Glenda – the supervisor – she says she has to force them to take breaks."

"They're that good at sewing?"

"About half the ones that stick have a relative or boyfriend in IX Corps."

"And it won't hurt to put you as far away from James Wade's attention as possible," added Funston. "He's heading up a Congressional committee looking into officers who haven't performed to their expectations, and he'll be looking very closely here. I'm sure he remembers you from his... superannuation."

"Can I go too?" said Prendergast.

"You'll survive anything, Otto."

"Other than my hurt feelings, yes." Prendergast turned to Lang. "Come on, Willard, we'll get you on your way to getting across the hawse of Martians instead of politicians."

Cycle 597,845.2, Minefast 31.01, South Texas

"Define *nearly completed*," said Group Leader Vantarsilas.

Taldarnilis regarded the communication screen impassively. "The third movement of the prey transport system will commence in approximately ten days, according to Raqtinoctil's estimate. It is nearly loaded with compound 92-12, but every day allows more to be loaded for the final passage."

"But that also increases the risk. You were attacked while returning to the minefast, so the prey are aware of our use of their transport system."

"The prey do not coordinate as we do. The group of them that bombarded us to the southwest during our passage, in all likelihood, are not part of the much larger force besieging us from the east."

"How can you be certain?"

"I cannot. However, if the large group did know, they would surely have encircled the minefast to cut off our passage. Instead, they fear our concentrating on a small part of their force, and so keep it in a single location. I have found that prey may be manipulated by a mere threat as readily as by applied force."

"Your newfound knowledge is sure to be of vast use," said Vantarsilas, "if you survive to return with it. The Conclave, though, seems to not grasp your value. Your claim of navigational error has been denied, and Group 31 has been proscribed for violating Group 32's territory. Without an elder to speak for us –"

"Pardon, Group Leader, but if you inquire again, I believe you will find that our operation is taking place to the south of the large watercourse, not the north. It is actually in our own territory."

"Nonsense! Taldarnilis, are you—"

"The accusation was based on flawed imaging from the satellite – an error in processing. Arctilantar has... corrected it. We no longer have access to its data flow, but no one can now be certain exactly what occurred, or more importantly, where. Our own fighting machines' logs indicate we are well to the south of the watercourse. Each group may claim what they wish, but in any case, Group 32 has its attention fully upon their offensive to the east. Territorial quibbles must wait until a future time."

"Taldarnilis, we have very little of that remaining!"

"Have the initial loads of 92-12 been processed successfully into energetic fuel?"

Vantarsilas blinked. "Yes. The holdfast reactor has been fully refueled, and stocks prepared to last two local cycles."

"That is gratifying, even if we do not survive. With a successful third transport, though, Group 31 will have enough fuel to last more than three cycles. And a great deal can occur in that much time, Group Leader."

"More has occurred than you know."

Taldarnilis suppressed its reaction. "I request clarification, Group Leader."

"The Conclave has announced that this world is no longer to receive emigrants of the Race. Instead, its resources will be exploited and transported back to the Homeworld, to support civilization there in its true and highest form." Vantarsilas seemed wistful as it spoke.

"But... we were to build a new civilization here! For all the Race to thrive within!" Taldarnilis' mind whirled. "The technical and resource cost of moving materials between planets will consume almost all that we create. We will require a hundredfold more resources to support a member of the Race living on the Homeworld, compared to here. Can they really mean to... *lay waste* this rich, rich world?"

"It appears so." Vantarsilas drew itself up. "At the moment, what matters is that you need not trouble to safely process the wastes from the mine in the normal fashion any longer. Abandon whatever is not to be used."

"But that is... irresponsible! It may be Group 32's territory, but no clan should treat its surroundings in such—"

"No. Leave the minefast the instant the maximum amount of 92-12 is extracted. This world is no longer to be colonized, Taldarnilis. It is to be consumed."

July, 1912, East of Alice, Texas

"You and I both look ahead to the future, I sense," said General Victoriano Huerta.

"Yes, General," said Lieutenant Henri Gamelin, rather than nodding. Huerta's cataracts made it difficult to gesture to him in a conversation. He would never drive an automobile; the staff car that Henri rode in was being driven by a Mexican Army major. Another staff officer rode in the front seat, leaving the two of them to share the back. Luxurious and powerful, the American touring car did not keep out a speck of the road dust with its top down, but the view of the military convoy was impressive: lines of trucks, ranks of cavalry, trundling towed artillery. With the rail lines from Corpus Christi overloaded by three divisions' worth of traffic from the combined expedition, the road received the overflow, and Huerta had chosen to pace his soldiers here – and he had invited Henri.

"Once these Martian invaders within Texas are defeated, our work will not end, will it?"

"I do have further work in America," said Henri in a neutral tone. "I have heard that you will press on into northern Mexico."

"Yes. But that mission will not be one of war or extermination – rather one of peace. I will exhaust all means of resolving this... sorrowful situation, in order to cure these social wounds." Huerta paused as the car swerved past a slower vehicle; they had passed many such during the morning's drive. "Not the unsheathed sword of the avenger, but the extended hand, the desire to bring together all good citizens. Our country has been divided for too long in the face of this Martian horror."

"You have seen much of that, I understand."

"Indeed! My very homeland, Monterrey, was obliterated by one of their strongholds. I had just retired, you know – laid down my sword for a peaceful career."

"Something more constructive?"

"You might say that. I became a paving engineer." Huerta waved over the side of the car. "This road is terrible. But it must serve... So did I, again, after the Martians attacked and our country went mad with revolution. My wife came with me to Mexico City and within a year had to flee from there as well. France has been fortunate to avoid such a fate."

"There are some Frenchmen who think they are immune," said Henri. "I do not, and so I will go wherever the fight is. Better than to wait until it comes to me."

"Well said. And here, just ahead, are many more just like you!" Huerta gestured. Perhaps he could not see the details of the vehicles they were coming up on, but the hulking mass of them – and the distinct rumble of their wheels – were unmistakable. The 118th Striking Vehicle Battalion comprised more than forty vehicles; each one was slung between six huge wheels, well armored – against heat rays, at least – and fitted with a rotating turret holding a 90mm gun. The metal discs that would shield their tires in combat were stowed on the decks for travel.

"I lust after these," said Huerta cheerfully. "Tanks break down so quickly, but these can travel a hundred miles or more and arrive ready to fight! That could give a Martian a real surprise, eh?"

Or a revolutionary column, thought Henri; but he said nothing. Huerta was a difficult man to read. His reputation was not pleasant, but then, neither was Mangin's. It was true that these vehicles were deployed outside of France not only because of their limited mobility in wet conditions as opposed to the North African desert, but their usefulness in maintaining order within colonies. Plentiful oil in Mexico had become part of that; the 118th would never go thirsty as long as Tampico stayed out of Martian hands. But what did Huerta really think of France's meddling in his country?

The major in the front seat twisted to look behind them. "General! The column has halted!"

"What is it?" Huerta peered back as well. A large gap had opened up.

"Some sort of accident..."

"Well, then, go back and see what it is!" The car swung into a tight turn. Huerta glanced wistfully toward the wheeled tanks; then they drove back until Mexican vehicles appeared and pulled up. Two trucks had collided, spilling cargo – and soldiers. Figures clustered around one truck's back wheels.

"I don't see any damage to the vehicles... It looks as though they're waiting for something," said the major.

"There is no time to wait," said Huerta. He climbed out of the car and strode to the truck's side. For a few moments, he gestured and shouted; then he spun on his heel and walked back to the staff car.

"Drive on!"

They swung about; Henri glimpsed the trucks edging apart and getting under way. "What was wrong, General?"

"Some fool soldier fell under the wheels," grumbled Huerta. "They didn't want to move the vehicles until a surgeon arrived – as though he could do anything useful. There is no time to waste."

"Is he still alive?" asked Henri.

"It does not matter now." Huerta craned his neck to look ahead for the wheeled tanks as the staff car accelerated.

The general said little more as they traveled for another two hours; perhaps he'd realized his friendly affectation would no longer work or simply couldn't think of anything but the marvelous wheeled tanks he could not have. At one point, the column slowed to pass through a small settlement, vehicles crowded closely along the narrow street, and the inhabitants clustered about in handfuls to cheer this advancing army. Their faces changed when they saw the French and Mexican flags fluttering over the tanks and cars – some looked astonished – but when Henri turned to look behind, the cheers had resumed. *Yes, we are strangers, but we are here to fight your enemies, and we travel toward the sound of the guns.*

After another hour, they arrived at the combined staging area. Once Huerta's car had forced itself through the mass of vehicles thronging the town of Alice and reached the headquarters building for IX Corps, he bade a quick goodbye to Henri, dismounted, and strode to the building's side entrance. Henri glanced over as he got down; another man in civilian clothes was greeting the general. They turned and went inside.

Henri shrugged and waved farewell to the staff major, then walked into the HQ. It was bustling with activity like a disturbed hive. Dozens of clerks seemed to be playing musical chairs with the stools at the telegraph stations along one wall. He looked about for General Funston, head of IX Corps, but did not see any such rank. All seemed to dash about intently, and short of tripping one and sitting on him, Henri could get nowhere.

Another figure detached from the military mob and moved to meet him. "Now tell me, what kind of uniform is that?"

Henri managed to smile. He'd gotten used to this. "*Marine Nationale*. Lieutenant Henri Gamelin, on detached duty from the 12th Division in Veracruz – I am a naval liaison for them."

"Long way from here! I'm Bill Mitchell, colonel of not much at all." They shook hands. "Do you happen to have an appointment with the general?"

"General Funston? I was hoping perhaps you did." Henri noted that Mitchell's uniform, while not standing out as much as his own, was not standard for the American army either. Something odd about the collar...

"Not by a long shot! The last time we spoke, he told me, 'You should have come to me six months ago, Mitchell. I *know* where the damn Martians are now!'" The colonel grinned wryly. "Everyone tells me it's not the right time. But they're wrong."

"Time for what?"

"Aircraft. Not the toys they have now, but something bigger, more advanced. The sort of heavy bomber that can hit the enemy hard, move faster than a tripod can, concentrate on a base in hours instead of months."

"I cannot argue with that. Are you with IX Corps?"

"Not really." Mitchell scowled. "They kicked me out of Washington when I became a nuisance and sent me out here. Then I was assigned to the 1st Texas Guard Division – that's what we call the National Guard, they sort of play at being soldiers on weekends. You can imagine how many aircraft *they* have. I even tried hiring a private pilot to fly reconnaissance, but the poor fellow crashed on me. Hutchings – Brigadier-General Hutchings, in charge of the 1st Guard – he says aircraft are playthings. Well, perhaps he's right, but that's all we have right now! He thinks that if it cannot wear a Stetson, it can't scout. But by God, with this big offensive about to kick off, I could show them a real bit of scouting. And perhaps that's all I need to get people to *listen*."

"It can be difficult when you do not have anything to show them."

"Well, not *yet*. They've written me off in Washington, but I've been speaking to manufacturers here in Texas that could build aircraft – well, most of an aircraft – if they only had the budget to get started! And they like things big in Texas, so it could be my natural habitat. Even if they can only build a handful of bombers, perhaps Washington will follow suit. But it's been very difficult thus far."

Henri considered this. "Do you have *any* aircraft available right now?"

"A couple of Curtiss trainers. Two-seater deathtraps, but if you're careful, you can get some range out of them. But, trust me, once the shooting starts, no one bothers to pick up a little bit of paper with a report written on it."

"Ah. Regarding that, Colonel... The 118th *bataillon frappant véhicule* is joining this assault. Four of their – tanks – are equipped with spark radios. I believe they have one or two spares, which could be placed in..."

Mitchell guided him into a corner. "You think they could fit in an aircraft?"

"Just so."

"Well, it's not a bomb load, but it's a start! Show these Texans they're wrong about air reconnaissance, and they might listen about air power. It's infuriating, Gamelin. Why is there so much... inertia... when we're fighting for our very existence?"

"I understand, Colonel. I too have a project that is difficult to persuade people to recognize. Perhaps if we..." Henri spotted General Huerta entering the main area with the civilian beside him; they stopped to talk with a major, who seemed quite deferential to a mere civilian in the midst of this frenetic activity.

Mitchell followed his gaze. "Well, well. Sherburne Hopkins. I've crossed paths with him in Washington a few times. He's what we term the 'fixer' type – a political operative. While I was getting a cold shoulder, he got virtually everything he wanted... Now, Lieutenant Gamelin, we don't have a lot of time. The offensive starts in a few days. Are you prepared to really *do* something?"

"I am. I can introduce you to Colonel Estienne at once."

"Marvelous." Mitchell grinned. "It'll be revolutionary! And our revolutions always go better with a bit of French help."

July, 1912, Hidalgo, Northern Mexico

"Careful with that!" shouted Willard Lang. The two privates flinched but managed to control the swing of the wooden crate they had slung between them as they stepped across the road. "Set it down easy."

"They're not really that delicate," said the corporal accompanying them – Cooter Stimson, that was his name. "Sure, the valve set is, but the rockets just have solenoids in 'em."

"And a warhead with the kick of a five-inch shell. Let's stick with careful." Lang directed the shifting of the crate toward a growing pile. Fifteen miles northwest of Laredo, the village of Hidalgo on the Mexican side was going to be the LRSC's staging area. A couple of boxcars' worth of munitions and supplies had been laboriously ferried across the Grande. Neither Lang nor Funston was willing to risk the entire output of Texas' production within an hour's stroll for a Martian tripod. *One thing at a time. First catch your rabbit...*

Outriders from the LRSC had arrived two hours previously from the south and were directing the rest of the unit to its encampment – and it seemed they'd brought friends. White-uniformed Mexican soldiers were riding alongside the LRSC cars and mounted soldiers with casual ease. Lang wasn't sure about that, but he had more rockets than men at the moment.

More vehicles of the LRSC drew up as the unloading finished. A couple of figures disembarked from one and approached him.

Lang chivvied away the soldiers and saluted, recognizing the second man by description. "Major. Good day, General. I'm Captain Willard Lang, and I speak for General Funston." He wasn't absolutely sure that this Villa character was truly a general, but he'd heard the man had a temper.

Daniel Plainview returned the salute; General Villa did not, but he inclined his head and said, "I admire General Funston as a fighting soldier, Captain. I am sure he has sent his best. You could say that I am simply a man looking for a good fight. Perhaps you can assist me."

"I'd be happy to... I have something for you, Major." Lang fished in his shirt pocket, pulled out an envelope. He passed it to Plainview, who tore it open and froze.

"There's eighty-two Wichita rocket trucks parked back along this road," said Lang. "General Funston and I figure they'll need a full colonel to organize them."

Plainvew stared down at the silver eagles. "I... well, I'll be damned."

"Congratulations," said Villa. "On your promotion, not your spiritual condition."

Lang watched Plainview closely as he pinned on the eagles; his face was tight and closed as he absorbed the change, but his hands didn't shake. "Alright," he said bluntly. "You didn't drag me here just to give me presents, Lang. What does General Funston want?"

"We are going to attack Laredo, drive out the Martian garrison there, and secure the north railhead so that fresh rockets can be shipped in. Then we dig in, and we hold. The general will drive the Martians out of Hebbronville and straight into us; the Martians need that bridge to move their ore train south into Mexico. We'll stop them. Or at least try to."

Plainview considered it for a moment. "The new trucks are fully loaded?"

"Yes."

"Four hundred ninety-two rockets. That's a helluva punch, but I don't have trained crews to launch a quarter of that. Unless you supplied those?"

Lang shook his head. "The drive from Dallas to here was all the experience they've got."

"Then we'll have to create a cadre. Bulk out each platoon to company strength, team up the inexperienced men with my crews. On a two-mile frontage I can't put all the trucks up on the line anyway..."

"Pull back the empty trucks, swap the firing crew to a fresh truck, move it up, reload the empty one. We'll need muscle for the reloading and guards with small arms in case any of those damned spiders are around. General, I have no idea of the legalities once we cross back into Texas, and frankly, I don't care. Will your men take orders from Maj– Colonel Plainview and his officers?"

Villa nodded. "They will fight with you. And I can provide drivers as well." Lang glanced at him, surprised; he shrugged. "It is a revolutionary army. I have men from farms who have never sat in a motor car. I have townsmen who can drive them. A few, at least."

"There's also a new weapon that your crews haven't even seen yet, Colonel." Lang gestured at the growing stack of crates. "They'll go on the cars, not on the big trucks."

"What are they?" said Villa.

"Rockets. Much like the ones you have used already, but these can be steered to a target."

Villa's weathered face crinkled into a broad smile. "How interesting. What is their range?"

"There's a mile of wire, so not much more than that."

"Wire?"

"Look," snapped Plainview, "my scout cars aren't to be used for transporting rockets."

"Ah, not *transport*," said Cooter. "Shoot."

Plainview leaned around Lang. "What did you say, Corporal?"

"We intend to mount a launch rail on each car, ah, sir," said Cooter. "And a spare rocket. We're calling it the Coyote."

"Pop off two rockets? What good's that when you need twenty for a hit? Lang, who is this pipsqueak? I know his face..."

"My name is Cooter Stimson, and I work for the smartest man in Texas. Sir. Once they launch, the operator will guide the rocket to hit its target. One rocket... one hit." Plainview swiveled to look at Lang, who nodded. "Yes, sir. I've seen it tested."

"Tested," said Villa. "So no one has used this weapon in a fight yet."

"No, General."

"Well, if you can mount them on a car, it's a damn sight better than a cal fifty," said Plainview. "We can shift those onto some of the trucks. Get on it, Corporal."

"Uh, sir?"

"Excuse me. *Sergeant*. Grab a uniform jacket from Philbin over there for the stripes and get what you need."

"Yessir." Cooter dashed away.

Plainview watched him absently. "*Coyote*. Eggheads, I'm telling you... Open ground east of Laredo. Too flat to risk the trucks on. That doesn't give us much depth for a defense."

"Perhaps we can use a distraction," said Villa. "Give them something else to shoot at during a critical moment. And certainly if they want that train to reach Monterrey, then I do not want to allow that."

"Just remember," said Lang, "our goal is to sucker in the Martians and trap them between us and General Funston. We can't destroy the ore train—or the bridge—too soon, or the Martians will just slip off in any direction they want. I have to assume the Martians will slip in a spider or two to check the bridge. They could spot any explosives we rig and they're smart enough to abandon the effort. And if I tell off a few rocket trucks or scout cars to hit that train, it could mean one less tripod knocked out."

"Of course, Captain, I understand. My men will be very busy as well. But perhaps we can add something... new."

Plainview grinned. "I'm guessing you have a trick up your sleeve, General."

"Oh, yes. I propose to send a picked group back southward to the town of Cameron, along the rail line the *diablos* use. There are train yards there, and my scouts have reported a locomotive. They will bring it up to just south of the Rio Grande and prepare it. We call it the *máquina loca*... We will need a large amount of dynamite."

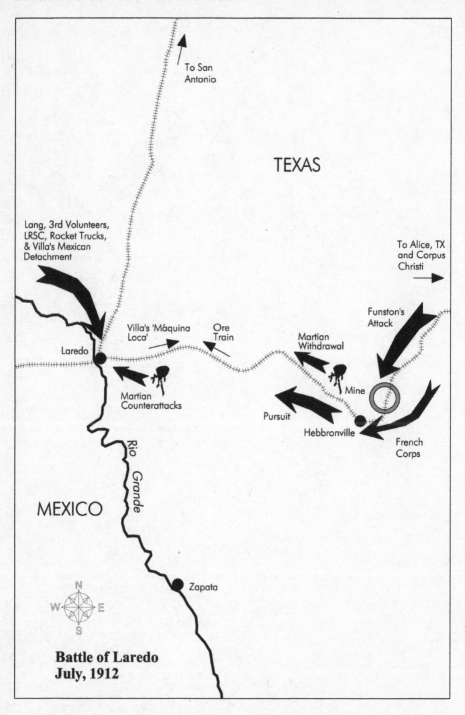

TEXAS

To San
Antonio

Lang, 3rd Volunteers,
LRSC, Rocket Trucks,
& Villa's Mexican
Detachment

To Alice, TX
and Corpus
Christi

Villa's 'Máquina
Loca'

Ore
Train

Funston's
Attack

Martian
Withdrawal

Laredo

Mine

Martian
Counterattacks

Pursuit

Hebbronville

French
Corps

Rio Grande

MEXICO

Zapata

N
W   E
S

**Battle of Laredo
July, 1912**

"We can ship *that* in once we've taken Laredo." Plainview glanced at Lang, who was nonplussed. "It means 'crazy machine'."

Chapter Sixteen

July, 1912, West of Hebbronville, Texas

Emmet Smith held up a palm; even in the gathering dusk, Painewick noticed and stopped the crowded car. "This is as far as you go, Eddie." Emmet knew this patch of country well enough. He'd been tricked and captured only a couple miles further east.

"Yeah. About that..."

Burnham looked up from the pack he was fastening. "Mr. Painewick, the car is simply too conspicuous. Our only hope is that the Martians are preoccupied with their own situation and assume us to be a working party of trusties. Such would hardly be driving."

"And you can't exactly cover us," put in Hicks.

Painewick glanced over to the car's empty pintle mount. "Shouldn't'a pulled her teeth like that."

"Horse-trading was the only way to get through the 3rd's picket line and refuel." Emmet grinned momentarily, remembering a young lieutenant's glee as he patted the massive weapon, still warm from Burnham's demonstration firing. He'd drained two car's gas tanks to fill the Peerless... "Come on, let's get unloaded."

"But what if some of 'em can't walk out?"

"How many could you fit in and still outrun a tripod if you had to?" Emmet dumped his own pack to the ground and followed it out, hefting the Winchester rifle he'd obtained.

"I've been considering that question," said Burnham. "I think if the captives prove to be too weak to hike out, we can smuggle them in one of the train cars loaded with ore – provided the Martians oblige us by leaving within a few days. Sometimes the best way to escape is to sit tight while they search everywhere else... But that can't be predicted. We may need to improvise."

Jovita Idar stepped down from the rear seat. "*May* need to? Dealing with alien monsters, madmen, and deluded criminals? Nothing can be predicted. But thank you, Mr. Painewick. You've gotten us this far." She smiled impishly and patted her pendant. "I'll make certain this gets to you... once I am rid of it."

Burnham checked through the vehicle. "Well, that's the lot. We'll see you soon." He shook hands with Painewick, who muttered something and mounted up. The Peerless spluttered into life, swung into a bumping turn around the track, and headed west into what seemed an empty landscape.

In a few moments, it became awfully quiet.

"Let's get some rest," said Emmet a bit too loudly. "We'll head out two hours before dawn. It's easy going."

"Least I won't be carryin' you this time," said Hicks. They got settled about; a fire would be too dangerous, but it was going to be a warm night. Tomorrow would be hot; a lot of their packs' weight was extra water.

"A great deal will change in the next while," said Idar as they watched the sun's last light fade in a riot of colors. "There will be a tremendous battle to drive these Martians out. Entire armies are converging here... We seem like mosquitoes, next to that. A tiny jab against enemies who may never even feel it."

"Tilting at windmills, are we?" said Emmet.

She looked over. "I didn't know you read."

"Cervantes? He's an old favorite. 'Fortune is arranging matters for us better than we could have for ourselves – for look there, where thirty or more monstrous giants present themselves, all of whom I mean to engage in battle'."

"'For this is righteous warfare, and it is God's good service to sweep so evil a breed from the face of the earth'." She chuckled. "For a governor's lackey, you do surprise, Emmet."

"I'm cut to the quick." Emmet couldn't feel good about what awaited; but he felt better.

Burnham tossed aside a handful of grass stalks he'd been braiding. "You're quite right, Miss Idar. The scale of these things... Who has the biggest armies, the best weapons, who can build more of them? Napoleon said that God was on the side of the bigger battalions, but his whole army couldn't scratch a single tripod. Well, I can't build an army's worth of weaponry, but by God I can try and find out what secrets they've got! So, once your captives are freed, I hope you won't mind if I act independently for a time."

"Not at all. Your help's been invaluable, even if I don't know what it is you do."

Hicks laughed. "None of us 'r exactly in our regular jobs anyhow. I guess I'm still with the LRSC, but I bet that General Hutchings won't see it that way if I get back in the way of his big ol' war."

"Shouldn't have gotten out of the car," said Emmet.

"Cars, machine guns... Rangers are gettin' awful military nowadays. You start carryin' that kind of metal, you get the itch to use it."

"Like Tomlinson? Yeah. I always felt there was a peaceable way to settle almost anything, if you just keep your nerve and look for it. Not many will stand up against a man who's got right on his side and keeps coming. But that's people, not Martians. No way to get through to them I can imagine, but for killing 'em."

"You found a peaceable way to take away *my* job," said Idar. "Some day, I would like it back."

"Some day." Emmet nodded in the gloom. "Well, we need to get there first. Try to get some sleep. We'll need to be inside that base by first light."

July, 1912, South of Laredo, Texas

182

Lang wasn't exactly surprised when the brigadier-general commanding the 3rd Volunteer Division arrived on horseback.

The LRSC itself was practically running on fumes; ever since they'd halted six miles southwest of Laredo to prepare for their attack, Colonel Plainview had men trotting about with gas cans, trying to even out the shortest-supplied vehicles. The 3rd was likely even worse off. Why waste gasoline on routine movements?

Although when Brigadier-General Slater joined Lang and Plainview at the temporary command center – tarpaulins stretched between three trucks, maps on trestle tables – he didn't look as though he was doing anything routine. Slater was tall and lean, with a face whittled by strain and fatigue. He swung out of the saddle and ducked under a tarp. "You're Lang?"

"That's right, General. Here on behalf of General Funston."

They studied one another for a moment. Lang didn't expect much of a welcome, but he did speak with Funston's voice, and if Slater tried to get in his way...

Instead, Slater offered a hand; Lang shook it. "Heard you fellas have some serious rocketry on these trucks. I guess you're meaning to attack the Martians here with them?"

"That's right, sir. This is Colonel Plainview, commanding the Long Range Scouting Company – which is more of a brigade by now."

"Well, I don't like how General Funston's left things hanging out here, but if you fellas can hit 'em with those, I'll see what I can do. Which isn't much. We've got nothing hardly left that'll even hurt 'em. They burned Laredo, killed half my boys, and wrecked near all my tanks – Funston won't spare us a damn lug wrench to fix 'em – and they just sit there, sauntering around the ruins like lords of it all..." Lang recognized that sort of anger in men at being beaten by the Martians, but here it was incandescent.

"How far out do they patrol, General?"

Slater got back to business. "No more than three miles up and down the riverside, maybe four miles east. Just one or two of 'em, but the rest can come in a few minutes to back them up."

"The same distance at night?"

Slater rubbed his jaw. "Uh, I suppose so. We don't get too close at night; they can surprise you awful fast. They see just as well as in daytime."

"Yes. General, IX Corps will be attacking the main Martian base at Hebbronville tomorrow morning..."

"Yeah. They told us, for what that's worth."

Plainview nodded. "The LRSC will retake Laredo and attempt to hold it as a blocking position."

"Well, seeing as General Funston didn't see fit to assign all these new weapons to the 3rd, I can't do much but wave as you go by. Best of luck, though."

"Sir, these rockets can't just be worked into an existing unit without–"

"I'm sure the general knows that, Daniel." Lang turned from Plainview's startled expression to face Slater again. "Sir, do you have any telephones? And how much wire for them?"

"I got maybe three in the regimental HQs. They're wired into the line running to Piedras Negras; the Martians tore down all the lines at Laredo, they know about them. Couple miles' worth for each. What are you thinking, Captain?"

Lang glanced at Plainview, who looked intrigued. "Well, sir, we could attack this afternoon, but we've only got a few hours' daylight, and the Martians will have all night to react to us – when they fight best. My intention is rather to infiltrate scouts late tonight and into the early morning, locate as many tripods as possible, then move up the rocket trucks into range and use telephone links and runners to relay the target positions. We'll attack just before dawn, engage the survivors independently, then once we've destroyed or driven them out, we can move in our supply trains."

"Ever tried to hit a tripod in the dark?" asked Slater.

"The rockets are fired in mass launches, sir. It's not a precise task like aiming a tank cannon."

Plainview shifted. "Are you sure about this? Men don't function well in those early hours. Just driving a truck over rough ground is problematic."

"Yes, it will be slow going. We'll have to tiptoe up..."

"Look, now," snapped Slater. "Funston can send you whiz kids through here if he wants, but I'm telling you, sparring with a few tripods in Mexico and runnin' away isn't the same as fighting them in a stand-up match to take ground. Fancy ideas and tactics won't get you far. This is the real war, Captain, and we've been fighting it since March. If you have some clever scheme, you can damn well carry it out on your own."

Lang drew breath to announce his authority – and paused. He could order any man in this encampment to do his bidding, even Slater. He could send them out while he stayed here with the maps and reports and requisitioned telephones.

But he couldn't. "General, I was not clear. I will be leading one of the scouting parties myself."

"Will you, now." Slater studied him. "Know the ground around here much?"

"No, sir, I just know the rockets. I'll need someone from the 3rd to guide me. In fact, we could use guides for all the scouting parties."

"You're either damned cocky, Captain, or you know what you're doing." Slater looked closely at Lang, as though he could see which it was.

"I had a Mark II at Albuquerque, General. I've seen the real war too. When a tank meets a tripod, it's ugly. When a tripod meets a sheaf of rockets... I like those odds better. And I'm willing to take risks to get there."

"Alright," said Slater slowly. "The 209th Infantry has been patrolling outside Laredo since April. I think I can find you a few men who know the ground. Let's talk some, Captain..."

By midnight, Lang's plan was underway. The scout parties were only two or three men each; Lang didn't want riflemen making noise who would only give away the infiltration attempt if they fired. He warned them not to hurry, then assigned them a route on the map toward likely positions. They all knew about the small spiders that the Martians used. There weren't a large number of them known to be at Laredo, but they did have some sort of mechanical eyes and they were bound to be in use for sneaky patrolling.

Nearby, a dozen mechanics from the LRSC were working on some of the scout cars by lantern light, attaching a single rocket rail aimed forward to each car. It looked risky to Lang compared to the bigger Wichita trucks with their protected cabs. The car's crew would bail before launching, but there was sure going to be some scorched upholstery; and even with the cal fifty removed, the cars would wallow under the extra

184

weight until one rocket was gone...

He'd supervised the organization and departure of six scout parties when Slater's man showed up.

"You're Captain Lang?" The soldier was a solid, weathered man in a worn uniform; he gave a sloppy salute. "Private Jenkins, reporting for scout duty." West Texas accent.

"Yep. Where are you from?" Lang passed over the map; Jenkins studied it.

"Amarillo. You?"

"Wichita Falls."

Jenkins grinned up at him. "Figures they'd send an Easterner. Sir. Well, I'll take the wire spool, I guess."

"No, I want you unencumbered, Private." Lang hefted the last wire reel one-handed – just barely. "We'll get as far as we can until this runs out, set up the phone in cover, and keep going."

He regretted the decision as soon as they'd left the forward post and begun climbing slowly toward the east bank. The reel wasn't that heavy, but it was terribly clumsy to walk in a crouch and unwind it, and his hands were cramping after a hundred yards. He refused to order Jenkins to take over, although the bigger man would have an easier task of it. His dad had diagnosed a bad case of Little Guy Syndrome for Lang years ago; it seemed to be progressing.

Low scrub and brush began to give way to larger trees as they worked their way eastward and up out of the river floodplain. A half moon threw enough light to walk now that they'd left the lantern light behind, and Lang's eyes had adjusted. At least the reel was getting lighter; and after half a mile, it ran out.

Jenkins, who hadn't spoken since they started out, doubled back when Lang halted. They settled the telephone amongst some bushes, scuffed dirt over the wire for a ways, and set out again. Jenkins was heading toward a small forested hill that loomed as a slightly darker edge to the horizon, another half-mile east. He moved slowly, looking where he stepped and scanning around, gliding from cover to cover when possible. Lang mimicked his every step.

Near the top of the hill, they stepped into an abrupt depression, then another a few yards onward. The irregular shapes were difficult to make out in the moonlight; with a cold realization, Lang recognized a tripod's footprints. They were crossing a patrol route –

Jenkins tapped his arm and dropped into one of the prints. Lang shifted left hastily and found another, managed to squirm fairly deep despite the hole's taper. He waited without asking. After a few moments' silence, he heard a scuffing rustle of foliage and a sort of liquid purr unlike anything he'd ever heard in his life.

One of the Martian spiders was crossing below the hilltop, perhaps twenty feet away.

Lang stayed frozen in his footprint, which felt about an inch deep right then. A flicker of red light showed through the grass stalks at the top of the ground, swept away, and the noises faded off.

They stayed that way for almost five minutes, until Lang's leg was cramping under him; but he did not shift until Jenkins very slowly rose up and looked around. Then he rolled off his leg and hunched upright, ignoring the spasms. They crawled the rest of the way up the hill and slid between two trees.

Somehow, Lang had been expecting Laredo to be illuminated. It was utterly dark; what outlines of buildings he could make out against the sky were irregular, like crumbled black bone. *Gone.* He slid out his binoculars and set to a careful search across the field of view. Jenkins was keeping his own watch for that spider; Lang's skin crawled at the thought that it was still creeping about somewhere nearby, but he studied every bit of ground with great care.

There. Two glinting curves, nothing of human manufacture, nestled in a swale another half mile east. They did not move as he watched; Lang resumed his search, but after fifteen more minutes he decided those were the only targets in his view. Hopefully, others were noting their own.

He tapped Jenkins' leg, backed away over the hilltop, and rose to study the ground back along the way they'd covered. Assuming those stationary tripods didn't move – a necessary risk – there were at least two good firing positions in rocket range and hull-down from them.

They crept back downhill without incident, set up the telephone, and cranked it. Lang picked up the receiver; his hand was shaking. He forced it to stillness and began issuing orders.

It was four o'clock by Lang's watch when the first Wichita truck grunted its slow lurching way up the slope. Two more followed close behind. He made his way downhill to meet the figure walking ahead of them as a guide; it proved to be a lieutenant from the 3rd who didn't look old enough to shave yet. The moon was setting and Lang could barely make out that the lead truck was one from the Mexico expedition rather than the new batch. He waved it over to the launch spot and stepped aside as it halted. An awkward-looking pintle mount was welded on the passenger-side cab door; Lang recognized the bearded corporal at the cal fifty from the LRSC, but the driver was a Mexican soldier in their off-white uniform. "How come you're not driving, Steadley?"

"Not enough of us to do everything," grumbled the corporal. "Sir, I got a spare tripod for this. Where do you want it?"

"Upslope, where you can cover everyone." *Except you.*

"Sir, how'm I gonna see to shoot if I got to?"

Lang grinned tightly. "One good thing, the 3rd has some starshells. They're going to put them up at five o'clock to start things off, and then keep them going until they run out." He walked over to the other trucks which were just getting into their proper firing positions. The crews were already cranking the launch rails into place and checking inclinometers. A scout crouched over a lantern-lit map, passing his information to the launch sergeant who worked out the coordinates and calculated the firing angle and azimuth. A couple of trucks began backing and nudging to get lined up. The whole process worried Lang; it seemed even slower than a conventional artillery battery preparing for indirect fire. *We've got to speed this up somehow.*

Lang went back upslope to the phone, managed to get a connection with Plainview, and confirmed that all the trucks were in place. Two had gotten bogged near the river, but there were enough of them to fill every spot with plenty left over. Once fired, the empty trucks could be reloaded later in the day... if they survived.

He realized he hadn't seen Jenkins for some time, but guessed where the scout might be. If so, they both had the same wish. Half an hour to firing time, and Lang had nothing left to carry out. He made his careful way uphill to the crest and crawled between the trees to find Jenkins there, watching the two motionless tripods.

The fellow didn't talk much; that suited Lang, Nervous chatter would have prolonged an already ghastly wait. Nothing moved or sounded. The moon was down by now, and only starlight glittered over a black landscape...

Artillery fire rumbled to the south. Lang swallowed a sour taste of tension; then the starshell burst into hard blue-white light overhead. A thundering roar behind them, and a gout of fire that threw a shadow into the grass ahead of him, shifting as the rockets trails tore out, rippling overhead, burning out within a few moments, leaving him almost blinded.

Reacting instantly, the Martian tripods rose up on their legs, lurching into motion; but eighteen rockets scythed downward and landed in a series of strikes that sounded as one continuous hammering explosion. Lang closed his eyes to block the flares. When the sounds ceased, he looked again. Other rocket trails drew blazing arcs all over the landscape as laggards fired. Burning brush illuminated a cratered area across their own impact zone. Wreckage lay there. He threw the glasses to his eyes and scanned it; nothing moved, and the sheer amount of it must add to two tripods' worth.

Jubilant, he nudged Jenkins and twisted to head back downslope just as the spider burst out of the nearby darkness and scuttled toward the trucks.

Jenkins aimed his rifle and fired a shot; it may have hit, but it also warned the crews downslope – and Steadley. The LRSC man opened up with the fifty at the furtive shape; other shots flickered and hammered from the trucks.

Grass burst afire in a sweeping arc that reached upslope. Lang and Jenkins flattened; the fifty's fire stopped. Lang looked again. The spider was moving erratically, some of its legs damaged, but it fired its small heat ray at the remaining machine gun on another truck until that too stopped firing. *They know!* Jenkins cracked out another shot; other rifles joined his, but the spider was almost on top of the trucks now.

The LRSC truck's engine roared and it jerked forward, swinging into a turn. The burning grass near the spider illuminated it more than the waning starshell did. It spun and fired at the truck, but the vehicle's rumbling acceleration closed the distance in moments. Gouting flame and steam from front bumper to hood, it rolled over the spider, jumbled and bounced on the rough ground, stopped... and reversed, rolling back down the hillside and crunching over the spider again before grinding to a halt as the radiator exploded. The cab was engulfed in flame by now; men ran to the vehicle. Others stood and snapped shots into what looked like a stepped-on cockroach.

Lang stumbled over to Steadley's gun position. Even in the dimness, one glance told him the man was a charred corpse. The gun might be salvageable. He made his way downhill, told off two men to go check the weapon, and slouched over to the burning truck. Three men were slapping at the driver's smoldering clothing, but the high-pitched laughter coming from under their blows sounded lively enough. And peculiar... Lang came closer.

The driver rolled upright and spat rapid Spanish, scrubbing with one hand at the burned hair falling over her forehead. Lang recoiled in surprise. It was one of Villa's *soldaderas.* "What's she saying?" he asked.

An LRSC sergeant with a better command of the language said, "Her brother told her it was too dangerous to learn to drive in Chihuahua City."

"All right," yelled Lang. "Leave this truck, it's a bonfire and a damn fine target! Get back downhill *now!* You've got two tripods to your credit!"

A few men cheered as they mounted up; the ones carrying back the cal fifty didn't. Lang swung onto a turning truck, clung on as it bounced downslope, and jumped off as it passed the telephone station. He'd been enough of a spectator this morning. Still, he wondered as he cranked the phone: *how did that spider know the machine guns were its chief threat if there was no Martian inside?*

Plainview had a report for Lang within minutes. "We've hit 'em hard, Captain! One or two tripods are still fighting, but we're driving them back."

"They're retreating?"

"Yeah! They sure don't like the rockets. It's been a long time since I saw a tripod run away!" Plainview sounded jubilant even over the terrible connection.

"There's a lot to do yet, Colonel."

"I know. The 3rd is moving infantry up into the western edge of Laredo. I've got men out scouting routes to shift the bulk of our trucks and, ah, Coyotes into the town by daylight."

"Casualties?"

"Not too bad. Five trucks gone for sure. One of the scouting parties, I think. I don't know about the 3rd, but we pasted most of those tripods before they got a shot off."

Lang braced a hand on the phone case, legs suddenly weak. He hadn't slept in a day and a half or eaten in ten hours. It would get harder yet... "That's good! That's good. But they'll be back soon enough, Colonel. We've *got* to be ready for them. The 3rd can deploy well to the north and south along the river to warn us if the Martians try and flank around very far, but they can't possibly hold east of the town. That's all up to us. I'm going to hang up now and contact the supply trains to move in, then I'll get up to the railyard and supervise that – you deploy your brigade as best you see fit." He paused. "I think the 3rd can rustle up a couple of field kitchens, so try and get all the men fed. It's going to be a very long day, Colonel."

Chapter Seventeen

Cycle 597,845.2, Minefast 31.01, South Texas

Arctilantar's priority signal had summarized an unexpected attack that had destroyed at least six fighting machines at the river crossing – and then the signal had stopped. A significant time passed before Taldarnilis' repeated efforts could contact Arctilantar again. Its thoughts were becoming... less organized. At last the link was reestablished.

"Report!"

"I am withdrawing eastward from the crossing area, Expedition Leader. Prey vehicles employing accelerated projectiles advanced close to the area during the night and struck at all stationary machines. The number destroyed is now confirmed at seven. These weapons strike a considerable area at once and are extremely dangerous to any machine not moving rapidly and constantly. One patrol machine counterattacked and had some success before close-range accelerated projectiles destroyed it. "

"Your action is correct. Continue to withdraw. Is the transport system bridge still intact?"

"To my knowledge."

"Are there any drone assets remaining?"

"Yes, Expedition Leader, there are four. I have withdrawn them as well, but only two telequel to the southeast."

"Good. They may be useful to confirm its status. Arctilantar, another and much larger prey attack is about to commence at the minefast."

"Will you withdraw westward?"

"Not immediately. The mine operation must be shut down and the transport unit prepared to move. We will fight a delaying action during the first part of this day. In the meantime, I am dispatching a force of twelve machines to join you and resecure the crossing area. It is leaving now at maximum speed. You are to take command of the force, probe into the habitation center, and attack only if the crossing point is still intact. Use only drones near that point in case of damage to it."

"This constrains our operational flexibility. Perhaps we may abandon the transport unit entirely?"

Taldarnilis reflected that only a Threeborn would question orders in such a manner. *Perhaps this is what Vantarsilas thinks of my own... initiative.* "This last portion of compound 92-12 represents a whole cycle of energy. It is still our first priority to return it safely to the holdfast."

"Understood, Expedition Leader."

189

July, 1912, Alice, Texas

The first light of false dawn picked out the hunkered shapes of tents and shacks, clumped on an isolated patch of open ground twenty miles south of Alice and IX Corps HQ. A motor car spluttered past, steering cautiously by the fan of light cast by its lanterns. For a moment, they picked out a frail, ungainly skeleton of wood and fabric squatting on its wheels, then it faded back into semidarkness.

Henri Gamelin walked toward the vague shape of the Curtiss biplane. The night was warm, although not as muggy as he remembered Vietnam. A dry and brittle heat, here. As a pilot had remarked, sometimes hot enough to melt and loosen the glue binding the wooden layers of a propeller.

He supposed that was one advantage of a 'pusher' aircraft like the Curtiss; if the prop flew apart, the crew would live a few moments longer before the crash...

"Good morning!" he called to the figure he glimpsed working underneath the lower of the two wings.

"Lieutenant Gamelin!" A Signals Corps captain, Robert Hines, twisted upright. "Can't mistake that accent. Come to see us off? Tom's fitting a fresh cell for the transmitter right now. Done there, Tom?"

"All hooked up, yeah." A second figure joined them. There was just enough light for Henri to make out the lieutenant's bars on his coveralls. "Say, Gamelin, is the 118th ready to move out? We can take off any time now. Still going to be swinging south as per plan?"

"Ah," said Henri, "ah, there are changes. I will update Captain Hines as we fly."

"What?"

"Colonel Estienne has instructed me that no one else is to use the transmitter. It is the property of the French Army, and is merely on loan. And I am trained in Morse code and semaphore."

"Well, that's..." The lieutenant spun on his heel, kicked at the dirt. "Goddammit!"

"Easy, Tom. There'll be other chances."

"Not to see a Martian base in Texas get flattened!" But the lieutenant dragged his gloves and hat free of his belt and thrust them at Henri. "Here. Gets cold at altitude, even in summer. Don't you *dare* let him down."

"I will not," said Henri sincerely. "But we should take off immediately. The 118th is already on the move."

Following Hines' directions, he clambered awkwardly into the wooden seat at the very front of the aircraft. It resembled a folding picnic chair... and felt about as solid. Hines settled in behind him, fitting his shoulder harness that would steer the aircraft into turns. Even the two men's careful movements made the entire aircraft wobble.

For his part, Henri had only a Morse key and a pair of heavy binoculars slung about his neck. It seemed like very little to take into the field against a Martian invader, but a pair of eyes in the right place had turned many a battle before.

Still, he could not help but compare the fragility of this aircraft with the armored bulk of the striking vehicles. The previous night, he'd conferred with Colonel Estienne at the 118th's bivouac. Once separated from the American liaison officer – an abrasive, angry captain named Patton, who at least spoke fluent French – they had shared views. Estienne, jealous of glory, insisted that the scouting be a French matter. "It is an honorable fight, Gamelin, and we will conduct ourselves with proper action and *elan*. But be wary of those who have their own agendas in this. I do not trust these Americans – their Roosevelt is making himself president for life, and I have a sense that some of his generals may intend a coup d'etat. Or at least to go their own way. And the Mexicans! Have you heard General Huerta's speeches? He may hardly pause to fight the Martians on his way to fight his rebel countrymen! We must stick to our own soldiering. Now, if only they would do so back home..."

He'd gone on to share disquieting rumors about the political situation in France – and the military outlook on it. Could the Republic truly be in danger from sheer dissatisfaction and anxiety?

"Alright, Gamelin, let's go!" Hines called out orders to the pair of mechanics who'd joined them. Along with Tom, they shoved and wrestled the half-ton aircraft clear of the tents and swung it to line up with a dirt track stretching away to the west. The day continued to brighten. Henri noticed clouds of dust rising to the north; a great many vehicles were on the move, like some vast herd in Africa.

Then the engine blasted into life behind him and the whole contraption sped down the track, shaking and jouncing until it lurched up into flight. The ground fell away below him, creating a vast void of air that his rickety seat seemed to be hurtling through without any means of support, airstream tearing around him. The horizon rocked in irregular motion as Hines struggled to keep the aircraft going in some sort of straight direction; it opened up further by the minute as the ground continued to sink and lose detail – although occasionally the aircraft's wings seemed to lose their grip and lurch it downward for a gut-clenching moment. Henri didn't know whether to be terrified or exhilarated.

Instead, he wrestled his binoculars into place against the windstream and peered north. There were others out there who needed to know what he could see – possibly to survive. Long-shadowed vehicles came into his view, moving west; he panned left until he glimpsed the Martian perimeter fortification, even many miles distant. In perhaps twenty minutes, he'd be able to see inside it. Today, he had the eyes of an eagle!

Yes, definitely exhilarated.

July, 1912, West of Martian Base, near Hebbronville

The towers loomed along the top of the high dirt wall like gallows, outlined darkly against the sunrise glow. Emmet could see four, which suggested eight or ten in total around the perimeter of the base. From Burnham's terse description, any one could obliterate all four humans in an instant. The red pinpricks of the heavily-protected weapons at their tops traversed slowly, tirelessly, scanning the landscape like cyclops' eyes.

There was no good way to move across open ground toward an industrial-sized weapon overlooking it. Walking upright would do as well as anything else; it was still too dark to risk running. The three men clustered closely about Miss Idar, rifles slung tightly to be as inconspicuous as possible. Emmet glanced over his shoulder, nodded to her; but she stared straight ahead, walking stiffly upright, scorning any instinctive crouch. He looked forward again, realizing wryly that he'd shifted as they walked to be between her and the nearest tower almost directly ahead. If it fired, that heat ray would burn through his body like a mosquito caught in a blowtorch, but some instincts were less easily controlled.

Hicks glanced nervously back toward the two Martian tripods they'd passed on their way, although they'd continued on what looked like patrol routes even after the humans had come close enough to see their own glowing markers. "Leave 'em," said Emmet tightly. "They'd have gone after us by now if they were going to. Make for that gap to the left. Walk like... like you're coming off a shift at a factory." Their path was angling in to meet the rail line, which curved slightly at this point. He'd not had time to notice when they'd left, but the perimeter walls turned inward into a sort of corridor for a short distance, shielding the interior from view. They walked straight into it.

"No gate," said Burnham. "No real control of access at all. It certainly doesn't seem like a fortress."

Hicks pointed with his chin without lifting a hand. "No need, with them two towers covering it all."

"True, but they were not there when you were inside, I believe. Ah–" Burnham gestured. "We should not creep along the wall. Workers would not."

"You're right." Emmet forced himself to stay well away from the heaped dirt and rocks that offered the illusion of cover. "But it's getting lighter. Soon those trusties'll be able to spot us."

A few minutes' walk brought them to within sight of the bulk of a locomotive at the head of a row of rail cars. In the distance beyond, moving metal shapes glinted in the first rays of sunrise, colossal, toiling at some work that raised a volcano plume of dust. "We've found our thirty giants all right... Trick is not to get stepped on. Stay close to this train." They slunk along the south side of the locomotive past the tall iron wheels. Burnham reached a hand up, touched the metal of the boiler. "It's warm," he whispered. "The firebox is banked – they're on short notice to leave."

Voices sounded from the locomotive's cab as they moved past; Spanish, tense but not alarmed. At least two in there. Unless they leaned out, they'd likely not spot the infiltrators... A coal tender was linked on the back of the cab. Next, a fancy first-class or private car; then an ordinary passenger one, all too familiar – they'd been confined in it. Hicks stumbled over a rail tie, stifled a curse; all of them were as tense as steel wire.

The following cars were low-slung hopper cars, filled with tons of that strange yellow aggregate. It had spilled around them in ten-foot splashes and coated the wheels and trucks; the Martians were probably in a hurry. "Come on," said Emmet, and they broke into a jog, kicking up spurts of the stuff as they ran. There sure were a lot of cars. Seventeen, eighteen... He pulled up ten feet short of a boxcar.

No – a cattle car.

"This is where the prisoners are kept," said Idar.

Emmet unslung the Winchester and nodded to the other two, who did the same. "No shooting unless you absolutely have to. We'll watch this car for a spell, try to figure if there's guards inside..."

"Tripod to the east," said Burnham quietly. They looked over; one was approaching, carrying a metal bin that sifted yellow dust with each undulating step.

"Under the car." They dropped to the ground, shed their packs hastily and scrunched between the wheel trucks. The tripod continued its slow, tireless motion until it passed by them and reached the hopper cars, then stopped. A tremendous rumble announced that it was dumping its load into one of the cars. After a few moments it reappeared, returning eastward.

The rumbling went on, and in a different tone. It seemed to be from the east now. Idar glanced over to him from her crouch. "Was that..."

"Yeah. Artillery fire, or tank guns. Might just be probing..."

The machine that had just dumped a load of ore – or whatever that aggregate was – discarded the container like a man dropping his cigarette butt, and accelerated to a considerable speed. As they watched, others fanned out from different locations to join it. The skittering movement across half the visible landscape reminded Emmet of a disturbed anthill – and the distant gunfire continued. "Nope. There's something big going on, all right."

"IX Corps was about to stage a combined attack," said Burnham.

"Now?" said Hicks. "They sit around for months, and now?"

"It is a useful distraction," said Burnham. "We may be able to scout further now, without any fear of encountering..."

A faint breeze stirred the dry grass stalks between the rail ties as he spoke. The day was warming already. Idar gasped, "What is that *smell?*"

Emmet glanced over; his eyes had adjusted to the gloom under the cars, and he could see dark heaps under the cattle car. He recognized the smell right enough; human waste, and worse. The smaller piles must have accumulated as they dripped through the floorboards, but the larger shape showed a desiccated hand.

"God damn *bastards*," said Hicks in a lilting tone. Closest one to the open, he wrenched himself out from under the car.

"Hicks! Wait!" Emmet squirmed into the open as well. Hicks was already rounding the car's end. Emmet ran after him, braced for a gunshot. As he swung around the car, a man tumbled down the small iron steps. Hicks jumped after him, gripping his rifle by the barrel. He swung it in a high arc that connected with the man's head and laid him out flat. Hicks continued to strike at the sprawled figure until a piece of wood flew loose; he threw aside the rifle with a curse, dropped to his knees, and began punching with a fist. No one shouted at him to stop. After several more blows, Hicks staggered upright. He stooped and picked up the Winchester, shaking his head at the broken stock.

"Done?" said Emmet calmly.

"Yeah." Hicks gulped air.

"Put him with his... work." They each took an arm and dragged the corpse to where they could roll it under the car. "Now let's see to these people."

They kicked open the car door and entered behind pointed sidearms, but there was no guard waiting inside. The stench nearly doubled him over. Eleven people were ranged about the car. Some blinked in the doorway's bright illumination; others lay inert in filthy straw. A long chain connected them all.

Emmet had seen poverty and squalor enough growing up, and a Ranger got to see worse; violence, abuse, or a drunk who'd strangled on his own vomit. This was much worse. He wasn't even seeing any injuries. The traitors hadn't bothered to abuse their captives. What would be the point? They were just... meat.

"This is inhuman," rasped Idar. A couple of the captives shrank back from the figures standing over them; she moved forward instinctively, speaking gently but rapidly in Spanish and English.

"Oh, it's human doing, all right. No Martians got in here... Burnham, keep an eye over Miss Idar, will you? Folks can panic." He motioned to Hicks. "Let's go get all our packs inside. Armed men're scaring 'em right now."

Outside, they drew clean air in lungfuls. Hicks was silent as they gathered all four packs and lugged them around the car's corner. "Randy," said Emmet carefully. "I don't disagree with what you did... but next time, we may need a few alive. For information."

"Will they hang, afterward?"

"I'm sure of it."

"Then I'm fine with that. I want to ask one of 'em how they... I'm fine with that." Emmet took a deep, pointless breath and they ducked back into the car, passing the packs inward. He rummaged through his own pack and produced the cold chisel and hammer they'd expected to need. He and Hicks got to work breaking the chain. Idar seized two of the many canteens they'd brought and pushed past them, ignoring the filth. "Those two first," she said crisply. Triage, of course... Emmet worked steadily. In a few minutes they'd loosed and organized the five worst cases, easing them carefully into at least a cleaner space.

"There's a tripod out there," warned Burnham. He'd kept a lookout. Not a man easily distracted...

"Plenty of work in here," said Emmet. He struck loose another darby and winced at the bloody sores under it edged by a tattered suit sleeve. He recognized Señor Targas' face under a coating of dirt and worse. Emmet felt no petty validation of Targas' foolishness. In this horror, he was just another human reduced to far less than that.

Targas' eyes fluttered; he coughed and stirred, locked eyes with Emmet. "Please, get us out of here."

Emmet gently detached a clawed hand from his arm. "Ah, we can't do that yet. But we'll stay with you. No one's leaving until all of you are, once that thing out there moves off." He repeated the last sentence in English for others' benefit.

"There may be difficulty with that," said Burnham from his post.

Emmet joined him and peered out through the gap. The Martian tripod was stalking closer, heading toward the locomotive.

Cycle 597,845.2, Minefast 31.01, South Texas

Taldarnilis paced its machine along the length of the transport vehicles, checking the quantity of 92-12 that had been loaded. Two of the vehicles still offered unused volume... but all processed compound had already been loaded. Another day's output must be balanced against the risk of being overwhelmed by the coming assault. "Report, Group Three Leader."

"Prey vehicles and projectile-throwers are converging from northeast through southeast directions. Confirmed as a full attack. Group Two has engaged and is pulling back. One machine lost."

"Larger than the previous attack?"

"Additional numbers deploying to both south and north flanks. Estimated forty percent larger fighting capacity overall. With the individual prey screening the major fighting units, it is difficult to move drones close enough to confirm accurately."

And we are half the mobile strength we were then... Taldarnilis made its decision. "We will proceed with the withdrawal from the minefast at once. Delay and disrupt the prey's assault. Adjust the operational plan as necessary to deal with more powerful attacking units. Abandon the digging and catalyzing machines in place." It was unlikely that the prey would learn anything useful from studying them, but to be certain, a few long bursts from the defense towers would see to it that there was nothing intact. The minefast constructor machines had already been transferred back to Holdfast 31.1. With the added strength of this assault, there was little time or effort to spare.

It shifted communication links. "Raqtinoctil, report to the prey transport. I require contact with the adjusted prey-creature."

"Commander, my present location is sixteen telequel east of there. It will require—"

"Disregard." Taldarnilis mentally acknowledged its own error. Raqtinoctil should have been stationed much closer to the task that only it performed. The stored memories of the Race that Taldarnilis carried contained very few errors, but the new environment of this world seemed to be a positive incubator for them... "I will perform the contact myself. Other than making physical contact tendril-to-calvarium, what information can you offer?"

"None, Commander."

Taldarnilis paused. "Clarify."

"There is nothing which can be explained. One simply must perform it."

"Very well. Continue to deploy defensively eastward, but risk as few machines as possible. Rely on the drones wherever feasible and expend them as needed."

"Yes, Commander."

Taldarnilis halted beside the propulsion vehicle and tapped at its viewport with a fine manipulator. After a short time, one of the prey-creatures emerged, propelled by a push from another's upper limbs. While Taldarnilis did not possess Raqtinoctil's familiarity with the goodprey, it did recognize the shape and coloration of this creature; it was indeed the correct one.

The other goodprey were armed and sometimes unpredictable; emerging from the fighting machine carried risk. Yet time was pressing. Taldarnilis scooped up the creature, strode barely half a telequel southward, and set it down again. The creature waited passively, its lower limbs folded on the ground, as Taldarnilis lowered its machine and unsealed the egress port. Squirming out of the machine's confines – for the first time in tendays – it fought the world's gravity with all the strength of its major limbs and lurched forward. Tentatively, it settled tendrils onto the creature's rigid braincase, ignoring the peculiar obstacle of thousands of follicular spikes. The prey's anatomy was bizarre... But there was indeed a consciousness of sorts. Fascinating.

Attempting to meld, as one would within the Race, gave no result. The other was a blur of impulses, urges, deep limbic drives that drowned out any rational thought processes. Some of them Taldarnilis had no concept to fit to. It mentally groped for alternatives to engage with the chaotic impulses it sensed; then it realized that cooperation was not the answer. The prey's consciousness must be controlled and shaped into a coherent form instead. Taldarnilis carefully imposed structure, aligning the hot, clashing impulses to its own far colder thoughts – or to a small fraction of its own. To overwhelm and annihilate this tiny brain would be to lose a useful asset.

Once some semblance of structure was obtained, Taldarnilis impressed its wishes. *All is ready. Go. Go quickly. Holdfast. Home.*

July, 1912, Martian Base near Hebbronville, Texas

"What's it *doing?*" hissed Emmet.

Burham held his binoculars against the car's planked walls where a gap offered vision. "It is touching the trusty with its appendages. It... appears to be interacting in some way."

"That how they get orders?" said Hicks. All three men were peering out now. Idar seemed to prefer not to.

"It certainly isn't killing him. They do *that* very quickly." Burnham set down the binoculars and lifted his Winchester without glancing down.

"Burnham..."

"Four hundred yards, I make it." The scout eased the rifle up to the opening, keeping all but the muzzle inside as he settled it and looked down the sights. "The first shot may not hit... but it's almost helpless in the open, Mr. Smith. I believe I can score a hit before it can crawl back inside that machine."

"And if that hit don't drop it, it burns us all down," snapped Hicks.

"It might turn the tide of this battle," breathed Burnham. He stared, unblinking; his forefinger slipped inside the trigger guard.

"No," said Emmet.

"I believe we spoke of my acting independently."

"After we get these people out. Our lives are ours to risk – not theirs. Hold your fire, Burnham."

After a moment, the scout lowered the rifle. "Very well. In any case, we have missed our opportunity. It is going back inside its tripod."

The tripod rose and headed off eastward as they watched. After a few minutes, the lone man staggered back to the train. Emmet turned to the others. "Well, now. Might be we can set an ambush, if those trusties make their way back here... But that'd still tip our hand in time."

"I need another canteen," called out Idar.

"Yeah. Sorry." Emmet dug one out of his pack and stepped over to where she was carefully administering water to a survivor. He handed it to her and studied the man. "Friend, can you walk?"

The man mumbled something. Jovita steadied his head and trickled water into his mouth. He wasn't even strong enough to try to grab the canteen. Emmet snorted in frustration. "Damn it, they can't walk ten yards!"

"Food and water will give them some strength in time," said Burnham. "If we can protect them for a day, they may be able to walk out at night."

"I figured one or two injured, but... You take care of your cattle even if you don't give a damn about 'em!" fumed Emmet.

"That's another indication they mean to leave shortly. They've neglected their food supply. Ah..." Burnham glanced outward again. "I believe you can deal with any threat from the trusties, Mr. Smith. Since we have a few hours at least, I intend to scout at least part of this base."

"Goin' for some glory?" said Hicks sourly.

"If you like."

"If you get spotted, it'll alert them."

Burnham quirked a smile. "I won't be spotted."

"Look, IX Corps is bound to take this base anyhow on their second go. They'll find whatever's here."

"Possibly after it's been wrecked by shelling. There could be something vital out there, something that... makes a difference. Something that's *needed*."

Jovita Idar placed a hand on his arm. "Mr. Burnham. Look at these people. You are needed here, we all are."

Burnham's eyes flicked around the misery of the cattle car. Haggard faces looked back at him. "I suppose so. There is glory, and then there is service. I shall stay."

July, 1912, Martian Base near Hebbronville, Texas

Ronald Gorman helped de Gama haltingly climb the locomotive's metal steps. "You have done a great service, my friend. What does it instruct?"

"This one was different," mumbled de Gama. "Another angel, a different light. Oh, to see all of them..."

"What does it instruct?" repeated Gorman patiently. The priest seemed even more shaken than usual by his contact with a Master.

"Home. Holdfast. Quickly, go. Go. All is ready." de Gama settled onto a bench in the cab.

"And none too soon! That is artillery fire, and it is getting closer. *Mendez!* Stoke the firebox. We must leave as soon as steam is fully up." The engineer shuffled to obey. "Now, do the Masters wish their food to be brought on this journey?"

"I do not know. Angels think of greater things. They have succeeded in winning their sustenance from the soil. The dark forces mean to overwhelm them, but their claws will close upon empty air instead."

"Back to their fortress in Monterrey, then," mused Gorman. "Well, I for one am not risking my neck outside to unhook a car when some stray shell lands. Spivey can remain back there, and they can rot. What else did you see that has you so perturbed, priest?"

"Glimpses of another's glimpses. Palimpsests, erased and redrawn from mind to mind. Figures walking, weapons tracking. An angel's sword lifted, saw the familiar, and was stayed. It is our queen, Gorman. She has come back, as I prophesied."

Gorman digested this. "You are certain?"

"Yes."

The certainty of a madman... Still. "If she has, she would have brought friends – just as I did returning to America. I will certainly *not* walk out into their guns... But I expect I know her reasoning. She is tired of her crown."

"Abdication?"

"Precisely. We shall be well prepared."

Chapter Eighteen

July, 1912, Laredo, Texas

Lang was trying to be in three places at once. It wasn't working very well.

He'd supervised the dawn arrival and unloading of their supply train at the surviving railyard to the north of Laredo. Unlike other cities that the Martians had occupied for a length of time, they hadn't troubled to loot any materials, and the only signs of them that far out of the town were the queer triangular tracks of their patrol machines.

Then he'd caught a ride on one of the supply trucks back into town – or what was left of the town. Laredo's buildings were generally low enough that they'd not collapsed into the streets after being gutted, and a few had survived more-or-less intact. The LRSC had established a command post in one, a burnt-out general store at the eastern verge. Lang figured he'd be of best use there, while Plainview took his one-rocket scout cars – Coyotes – further east. They at least had a better chance of hitting and running in the open.

At least there was plenty of light slanting in through the shattered windows and the portion of the roof that gaped open. The shop's counters were intact, so they'd set up telephones and maps across them. Debris was piled into a corner – charred boards, glass, and bricks. A cash register lay skewed on top like a cherry on a sundae. *Whatever works.* But the line of sight through the windows didn't show much past the opposite building. Lang sent four men with Private Jenkins to find the town's fire hall and salvage a ladder so that he could access the roof.

They returned in half an hour carrying a ladder, but looking pale. "Spiders must've got in there, sir," blurted out one of the men. "When the Martians took the town. The firemen, they were all still in their coats, but they..."

"They're dead," said Jenkins. "Where d'you want the ladder, sir?"

"That corner."

While the other men set it up, Jenkins spoke quietly to Lang. "Sir, maybe take him up top. I think he's better off outside for a while."

Lang beckoned the shaken man, clambered up the ladder, and stepped carefully onto the damaged flat roof. It did offer a decent view to the south and east over open, flat country, and Lang took some time to study the area through binoculars. He could see several Coyotes set up in their positions two miles east, and three groups of rocket trucks along the edge of town. There were a lot more further back west covering the routes toward the bridge. A fair bit of firepower, but once the rockets were gone, they'd have nothing...

When he climbed back down, he noticed Jenkins eating from an open tin can. "What are you doing?"

"I guess you'd call it scavenging, sir. Tinned peaches. Not bad." Jenkins speared one with a hunting knife and offered it. "Try one?"

Lang was suddenly aware of his hunger. "I'll pay the owner afterward – if we can still find him. Or this store." He wolfed the peach and settled on the dirty floor as Jenkins hacked open another tin.

General Villa joined Lang an hour after sunup. "My men are ready. At least every rocket truck will have one or two machine guns and some infantry protecting it, if the enemy send in their *pequeños diablos*. And my men to the south have prepared the surprise I spoke to you about."

"The explosive train? That could help. IX Corps is attacking the main base right now, so we can expect the Martians to try and push into here within a few hours." He showed Villa the map. They'd be coming right at the bridge, but from which route? And he didn't dare place rockets where they might land near it. The Martians could fight right up to the edge of their precious bridge without much risk of damaging it, but Lang's weapons were far less precise. *We're like two desperadoes fistfighting over a bottle of nitroglycerin. And speaking of explosives...*

"What do you think the Martians will do when we send out that train?"

Villa sighed. "You have been fighting them nearly as long as I have. We have used this trick once before. They are very intelligent – and a *máquina loca* is a memorable thing. They will see the threat quickly enough and destroy it. But where? If they destroy it somewhere outside of Laredo, it will delay them while they repair the tracks. If they have pushed into this town by that point, they might even fire on it as it crosses the bridge, and wreck *that* – but that is unlikely. Either way, it will do some damage. Now, the *best* outcome would be for it to collide with their southbound ore train, if it does not run out of steam first. That would be spectacular! But we cannot control that."

"Well, General, Colonel Plainview thinks we just might, if the Martians do show up with that train."

"Indeed. My men are ready too. If the Martians concentrate fire upon the *máquina loca*, we will all have a free hand. If they are busy fighting us, the *loca* may get through. Either way, we will make use of this distraction."

"But I expect we won't be the only ones." Lang had noted men of the 3rd Volunteer Division trickling past in the street since daybreak. Without orders or announcements – certainly without his control – they still seemed to know something was about to happen, and they all seemed to be headed east.

Now, a rising grumble in the street heralded the grim bulk of a steam tank trundling past with the markings of the 608th Tank Battalion. Two other tanks followed closely after; infantry marched alongside. "General, do you know where those tanks are going?"

"Well, toward the enemy, I would say. Perhaps *he* can tell you more." Villa pointed at the officer walking past the store's windows. He turned in abruptly, heels crunching on debris.

"Oh, damn. That's General Slater..."

Slater strode up. "Where's Plainview?"

"He's getting the last rockets loaded, sir. Just south of town."

"Well, when is he attacking? We need to coordinate!"

"Attacking?" Lang stared at him. *What have you got to attack with? Ten working tanks?* "General, my orders are to hold *here*, at Laredo. We're *defending.* Our best place to stop them is in the town itself. It's true we're deploying our scout cars to the east, but they're only a skirmish line at best, to buy some time. Is the 608th going to push further east?"

"Yeah. Them and a bunch of other units. It's our own ground. It's our own land. If there's a chance now, we're going to drive back the Martians as far east of the town as we can get, and not let one tripod set foot in it ever again. That's all we can do, Captain. If somebody drops, someone else grabs the machinery, but *nobody stops.*"

"But it's wide open out there. General Slater, you've got to order them to wait!"

Harlan Slater looked at him with empty eyes. "Captain, my family lived in Laredo. I don't know how to order them to wait." He turned and walked out of the command post, rejoining the stream of men marching east.

The scouts sighted oncoming tripods half an hour later, instead of the few hours' grace that Lang had hoped for. The good aspect was that IX Corps was still hotly engaged with the base, so this must be only a detachment; the bad was that the LRSC wasn't fully prepared, and the 3rd scattered well to the east of Laredo. General Villa summoned a horse and rode off to his own men's command; a few minutes later, an LRSC scout spluttered into town in a civilian coupe to pass Plainview's detailed report. "A baker's dozen of 'em coming straight in from the east," said the scout. "Every Coyote we have is up front, and they already hit 'em once. I think we got four, maybe five, then they pulled back for a spell."

Lang cursed; he'd hoped for more results from the surprise of the new weapon. At least half the guided rockets must have missed or not scored a fatal hit. The Martians had the rising sun behind them; that didn't help. He'd known of that, but there wasn't anything to be done. *If Funston could move the sun's path, he would.*

"The colonel, he figures the Martians were expecting us to throw more rocket salvoes at 'em, so they stayed split up and kept moving around as they advanced. Didn't stop the guided rockets. Anyway, we're falling back to the second line of positions."

"What?" Lang rounded on him. "Why'd you give up that ground if they weren't coming on?"

"Don't know, sir. I guess we was just following the plan."

Which is changing by the minute... Lang looked at the useless telephones. With the LRSC vehicles shifting so quickly, there was no practical way to string wire any further forward even if he had time. "Alright. Drive me back up to the firing line, wherever you think Colonel Plainview may be."

They rattled out of town and emerged onto an open landscape. Pillars of black smoke rose up well to the east; a few moving vehicles raised dust clouds. Otherwise, the day was clear and warm. Once they'd traveled a mile, he had no difficulty sighting a half-dozen tripods approaching from the east, three or four miles distant.

The driver halted. "I think the colonel's just up here. But there's no road crossing over to that one."

Lang eyed the mild slope rising to the south. "Never mind! Just get back to the command post in case Villa goes there. Tell him to wait for me!"

He hopped out of the car and set off. An attempt at the quarter-mile uphill run left him gasping and reduced to a limping trot. *Come on, damn it. Staff officer living...* although even as a line tanker, he'd not been much for running. But the LRSC car the scout had pointed out was still there, pulled back into low ground for reloading. The car was Two-Six; he recognized Cooter Stimson and Colonel Plainview. They were wrestling a guided four-inch rocket onto the Coyote's launch rail. Lang managed to sprint the last few steps, jumped up, and lent a hand. The massive piece of ordnance wavered, steadied, and clunked onto the rail.

"Get it wired up!" yelled the colonel. He stepped up onto the car's hood and glared around at the chaos of the battlefield. Lang joined him, having no idea what was needed to prepare the rocket. The hood's paint was scorched and smoldering in places, windshield shattered. The cars weren't *meant* for getting inside a mile range without terrain to take cover behind, for getting into this kind of slugging match.

Neither were human bodies. "Where's your driver?" he asked.

"Heat ray brushed him." Plainview pointed to the figure huddled a few feet away in a swale of ground. "He didn't duck. Once we've fired the second round, we'll get him to the 3rd's aid station."

"Why did you fall back, Colonel?"

"Because, Captain, I don't have enough cars to have half of them fire and the rest wait to cover them while they reload. Slater's men *could* have, but he's gone mad and tried to attack eastward. Those smoke signals over there are what's left of his tanks. Still, he bought us some time..." He lifted binoculars and panned the horizon. "Yeah, about what I thought. The remaining tripods have massed together and they're working around to the south of us."

"You can't let them get past out of range—"

"That's what I have company COs for," snapped Plainview without looking away. "There. Two-One and Two-Two just pulled into firing positions. They're loaded and ready. There's also nineteen trucks in south Laredo pre-aimed at beaten zones, and I think these tripods'll cross at least two of the zones on that course."

He lowered the binoculars and glanced at Lang. "Can you drive?"

"Not very well. But I can pull her up to the fire step, if that's what you need."

"Good enough." He took another look around as fresh rocket trails tore across the landscape. "Dammit, the rest are already reloaded! *Stimson!*"

"Almost done, sir!" The freshly-promoted sergeant was fumbling with the last wire connections.

"If you miss with this one, Sergeant..."

Lang realized why Stimson looked shaken – not that he needed any particular reason right now. Both he and Plainview ducked as a heat ray snarled nearby. He exchanged a look with the colonel, remembering a young tank loader named Billings, just as green and hesitant, who'd never had a chance to grow any older.

After a moment, Plainview jerked a nod. He dropped down to the car's open floor beside the sergeant – the Louisiana mathematician with a sergeant's rank. "Look, Stimson. Soldiers miss shots. But we've only got one of these left, and I want it to connect with one of those tripods over there. Just do what you know how to do. And *get that shot.* Because otherwise, I will personally kick you out of this outfit."

Stimson blinked at him. "Out? Sir? You mean I'm *in?*"

"Damn right you are. Palmer can go piss up a tentacle; I'm getting you transferred."

"Yes, *sir!* Ready to launch, sir!"

"Remember, Stimson. Those tripods are dangerous machines, but inside every one of them, there's a flabby sack of shit – and *that's* what you're aiming at. *Lang!* Move her up!"

Lang settled into the driver's seat. He started, shifted, and edged the vehicle up the slope until Plainview yelled "*Halt!* Stimson, rig for launch!"

Lang switched off and helped Cooter lug the battery and console out of the car and up a few more steps to where they had a view of the battlefield. At least one more tank was burning now, and some of the already-wrecked buildings at the south edge of town were freshly aflame.

A heat ray sawed close by. He flattened next to Cooter; Plainview crouched to one knee and rasped, "Target, tripod two o'clock, one thousand yards."

"I see it," breathed Cooter. He adjusted his small telescope.

"Fire when ready!"

Cooter tapped the firing key without the least hesitation. The rocket roared off the rail, blasting exhaust over them; then it steadied into level flight. Two seconds, three, four...

Plainview stood up. Lang did too, even though every fiber in his body screamed not to. Half a mile downrange, the tripod swiveled and swung its weapon around toward them – or toward the rocket flying at a level fifty feet, hunting gently under Cooter's adjustments, merging visually with its target.

A heartbeat later, it struck.

The visible explosion was mostly unburnt fuel; but the warhead punched into the tripod's hull like an assassin's blade, dead center. The machine remained motionless for a long moment while smoke and fragments billowed outward. Then the legs folded and it collapsed.

"*Hah!*" cried Plainview. "That's more like it!" They dropped down as two other tripods emerged from the smoke three-quarters of a mile off. Lang watched as another rocket trail reached out toward one; this time, the trail wandered into a corkscrew and crashed halfway.

"They're learning," said Plainview grimly. "They're shooting wild back along the rocket course and blinding the gunner. I bet in an hour they'll know to cover one another as they advance..."

The two tripods seemed to do just that, striding west untouched for a minute or two. Then a sheaf of rockets tore out from the edge of Laredo, curved over, and detonated in a rush of explosions. When the dust and smoke cleared, one tripod was down and the other retreating back to the east.

Plainview jumped up onto the car hood and looked around. "I don't see any others advancing. Lang, I think we stopped them!"

For now... "Look, Colonel, let's get your driver to the aid station. There's nothing more we can do here."

"There ought to be," grumbled Plainview. "In the future, there *will* be." But he lent a hand to carrying the equipment – and his wounded driver, another sergeant – back to the car. Lang started up and carefully reversed the vehicle into a turn. "Where to?"

"Southwest along this road. There's a sort of HQ four miles downriver. Then we'll see about getting Sergeant Stimson another rocket." Plainview barked a laugh. "Officers driving sergeants around! This army's gone mad. Maybe it needs to."

Cycle 597,845.2, West of Minefast 31.01, South Texas

Taldarnilis monitored several communication links simultaneously. The expedition's withdrawal from the minefast was beginning in good order. Losses were light, and most of the prey forces had lost contact and been left behind. A few, more mobile, groups continued to harass some trailing elements, swinging south and west of the minefast. Others closed in gradually on the minefast itself. "Raqtinoctil, is your group taking control of the defense towers?"

"Yes, Commander. We have no targets as yet, but there are prey approaching quickly now that our mobile machines have disengaged. We will engage them at optimum range."

"Very good. When –"

"Commander! Urgent report!"

"Proceed, Arctilantar."

"Our battle group's attempt to secure the bridge crossing River 3-12 has failed. Prey forces are established in the cover of the habitation center and further east. We have been able to advance two telequel since resistance began, but it is increasing rapidly and consists of varied weapon types. Eight machines lost to this point. We have insufficient force remaining to reach the bridge and secure it."

"I concur. Withdraw until our main body arrives." Taldarnilis kept the link open, even with the awareness that it ought to restrict its attention to its own surroundings. The background link traffic between Arctilantar's units surged, indicating heavy fighting. "Many fighting groups are on their way. You will not need to fight alone for long." *Why did I repeat redundant information?*

"Fire from the habitation area continue to increase in – Gantaldarjir, move your group immediately south four hundred quel, there is a heavy concentration of prey near to you! Are – Commander, there are incoming propelled projectiles similar to –"

The communication link ceased abruptly. "Arctilantar, respond."

"This is Gantaldarjir of Group One, Commander. Arctilantar's machine has been struck by projectiles. I am assuming operational command."

"Acknowledged. Arctilantar, respond." Taldarnilis checked its displays. No machines were falling behind as they proceeded westward; every one of them should be at full fighting capability. They would have far more force than needed to brush aside these obstructing prey, once arrived at the watercourse habitation.

"Arctilantar, respond."

Chapter Nineteen

July, 1912, Southwest of Hebbronville, Texas

Henri Gamelin rode the rickety aircraft like an unruly horse. They had climbed to a great height over the past hour – it seemed a great height to him, at least – and half of Texas appeared to be laid out before him as the day brightened. The Martian base, perhaps four miles north, had no secrets behind its walls any longer. Quick glances through the binoculars gave enough detail to map their activity. He avoided longer use of them for worry of the *monstres'* heat rays. Oddly, he felt no fear of being burned to death or mangled in a crash, but to be blinded... And his only usefulness at the moment was as a pair of *working* eyes.

But the battle was his main focus. A group of tripods were collecting to the southwest of the base, like wolves forming a tight pack. Henri set to his Morse key. *9 TRIPODS ADVANCING SW AT 110-340 STOP 8 KM NE YOUR POSITION STOP.*

The 118th could not reply; he had no receiver, nor could they spare weight for one. But that did not matter. As had happened several times over the past hour, soon he would see the unit's deployment shifting over the ground as Colonel Estienne, forewarned, prepared to receive the attack. Flanking companies would shift into low ground; the main group must align its frontal armor. It would be like watching a pugilist's fist draw back to deliver a blow, but over the course of many minutes, and it had worked splendidly twice already...

The clouds of dust and turbid shell bursts sometimes obscured his view as IX Corps' attack pressed on toward the fortifications, but the air at this height was clear and cold as promised. He could see another handful of the Martian tripods emerging from their base. He watched carefully to see which way they would advance; instead, they proceeded due west. In the far distance, others involved in the fighting began to drop back as well. From his vantage point far above the furious combat, a picture became clear that no one at ground level could see.

Everywhere that he looked, tripods were flowing westward. This was no redeployment; it must be a retreat.

A glance at the ground nearby showed no change in the 118th's dispositions. That was odd. And that group of tripods were not fleeing west, but continued to close on them... Henri had a chilling thought. He twisted far enough to see the small gauge on the electric cell's top. The needle was at zero.

Henri turned the other way and waved to get Hines' attention. "The transmitter does not work any longer! I need to warn them! Can you land in the field?"

205

"Maybe! Hell, we're short of fuel anyway!" Hines banked the Curtiss in a sickening lurch. The ground wheeled beneath them, then Hines got the aircraft level again.

"You got a preference where to land, Gamelin? Other than away from Martians?"

He pointed northward. "There! That group of vehicles!"

They turned again and began to descend rapidly. The 118th was traveling northwest, but slowly; they came up on the unit in a few minutes, dropping onto it. The landscape, although flat, began to look anything but smooth as they got lower. Everything seemed to happen very quickly. Hines sawed the aircraft into a couple of quick turns, perhaps aiming for a track along the ground; dry brown shrubs and soil seemed to blur past, an armored vehicle loomed up and flashed by. The wheels settled, punched at the ground, and yanked at Henri with a rattling and snapping racket; then the aircraft overturned and flung him hard sideways, hanging precariously by his death grip on the seat which was now above him.

Suddenly it was very quiet. Henri gasped a breath and fumbled at his seat belt, dropped loose awkwardly onto the ground – that lovely, solid, stable ground – and managed to twist upright. He turned to see Hines also untangling from the aircraft; flames were gushing from the engine. They scrambled away, taking a few stumbling steps. Henri tried to regain his composure; he needed to speak calmly. He looked around and spotted the larger bulk of Colonel Estienne's command vehicle approaching; their arrival had been noticed. A plume of smoke did have that effect. The aircraft's doped fabric roared into flame as they watched and was consumed in moments.

"I am so sorry, Captain Hines," said Henri. He set a hand on the pilot's shoulder. They studied the wreck of his Curtiss; the fire was dying down already. "I thought it was not a bad landing, myself. Like falling off a horse."

"Any one you walk away from, I guess." Hines sighed. "I sure hope we did some good up there. Well, one thing about a biffy when you're almost out of fuel – the bonfire's not that big. I think you can get your transmitter out now, if you want."

"Yes." Henri walked up to the wreck and beat out a stray flame with his gloved hands. He extracted the transmitter and slung it over his shoulder; the battery cell was not worth recovering.

The command vehicle pulled up nearby. As Henri walked over on shaky legs, the side hatch swung open and an American officer stuck out his head.

"Well, get in," he rasped in English. "It's a damn jamboree in here anyway, what's two more?"

Henri set his foot onto the metal step and hopped up into the hatchway. The vehicle's interior was a cramped metal cave whose white paint could not make any larger, although the custom-built, boxy hull at the rear did give more room than a regular fighting vehicle. That held a radio and space for its operator and Colonel Estienne. Henri saluted him, banging his fingers on a metal rail just above. The American squeezed back against the bulkhead to give room for the two newcomers. Hines closed the hatch and the vehicle lurched into motion. Its gasoline engine roared from the midsection, much noisier than steam, but powerful enough to accelerate the big vehicle rapidly.

"I remember you," said the officer – Patton, that was his name. He'd switched to French. He appeared to be acting as the radio operator as well as liaison. In a sense, Henri had been 'speaking' to him all morning.

"Hello, Captain. Colonel, my transmitter has failed. A group of nine tripods approaches you from the northeast."

"Very good. Captain?"

"Yeah. Green, white, green, right?" Patton reached across the compartment and took down three Very pistols from a rack. He opened the roof hatch and extended his arm up through the opening with one pistol, fired it, and exchanged it for another, then the third.

"Jules, turn northeast!" called out Estienne. The car rumbled into a turn.

"There is more, Colonel," said Henri. "I have observed Martian tripods heading westward across the entire field of battle. I believe they are carrying out a retreat."

"How many?"

"Perhaps twenty-two."

"Then there are still more fighting to defend their base. The Americans and Mexicans are pushing up from the east. Captain Patton, when do you think they could enter the base itself, now that the Martians are withdrawing at least part of their strength?"

"At least two hours," said Patton. "Our steam tanks can't move as fast as these armored cars. Mexican artillery's horse-drawn."

"I thought so. We can press closely from the southern flank, then."

Patton snorted. "I thought you were relying on all this mobility? Getting in that close, they might just jump on you from their base if you piss them off too much." For all his grating American accent, Patton had a very fluent grasp of French.

"We can withdraw to the east if we must. We can get much closer. But first, we have to see to this present attack. *Galere!* Open fire at eight hundred yards, target by company as before!"

The gunner barked acknowledgment. They continued to rumble toward the oncoming tripods – and the base further distant.

July, 1912, Martian Base near Hebbronville, Texas

Emmet had pulled out every canteen they'd brought by now. They'd tended the survivors for the better part of an hour while trading ideas on what their course of action should be. The fighting to the east intensified – as far as its distant thunder communicated. Burnham was adamant that the base would soon become too dangerous to leave the people within. "There's no cover to speak of. One stray shell and they'd be wiped out."

"We could dig a trench. When the infantry gets inside, they'll see to them. Sure can't mistake 'em for Martians!"

"It's more overhead cover they'd need, Mr. Hicks. We have no material for that. But we could sling the healthiest four or five of them under the ore cars, so that..."
He was interrupted by a gentle lurch that made two people stumble. "Aw, hell," said Emmet.

Hicks tensed. "Train's moving out. We bailing?"

Emmet locked eyes with Idar where she was tending to the sole woman among the survivors. "Can't do that, Hicks."

"Oh. Yeah."

Burnham cleared his throat in an oddly civilized interruption. "I did have an opportunity to observe the open area of the base in detail. There were no structures as have been described in other bases – only the mining operation. Even the defensive berm is incomplete. I don't think this was meant to be a full-fledged base at all. And that artillery fire is getting closer quite rapidly."

Hicks nodded. "I heard that in the big fight in April, it took Funston all day just to push up fifteen miles."

"Then – they're leaving without a real fight." Emmet looked at Burnham blankly. "Have Martians ever done that before? Just skedaddled?"

"I don't think so."

Hicks snickered. "Maybe we got 'em demoralized."

"Well, this train is nearly filled with ore," said Burnham. "Probably their mission is completed. Where does that leave ours?"

"Going west at a good clip already."

Emmet stepped in. "Along with what we came here for. Most of us. Burnham, you staying aboard?"

The scout smiled wryly. "I suppose so. You are the most interesting place, right now. Will it be the same route that we drove?"

"No, the line runs a bit north of that. Right past where the 1st Texas Division is deployed."

Hicks cursed. "They may not be tooled up to fight dozens of tripods, but they can sure-hell go after a train. All it takes is one shell."

"Then we need to get the hell off this train." Emmet turned to Idar. "But first, we need to get that damn thing off *you*."

"God, I hate it." Idar hooked her fingers through the pendant as though she could pull it loose. "Still, it has worked so far. What if we need it again to get these people out?"

"The Martians will pay little attention to this car it if becomes separated," said Burnham. "It's the ore they want."

"We can't be sure of that!" snapped Idar. "As long as I stay here, they should be safe."

"Can't be sure of that either."

"Look on the bright side," said Hicks. "We're gettin' further away from an artillery zone every minute. That's no bad thing. Whyn't we stick with that a bit longer?"

July, 1912, Southwest of Hebbronville, Texas

Henri had grown accustomed to the jolting travel of the armored car. The acrid smell of the spent shell casings rolling on the decking was another matter. Their gunner had not claimed any hits from the eight rounds fired so far; but the 118th had pushed north almost to the defensive wall surrounding the Martian base.

The gun crashed out another shot. This time, a whoop of joy followed it. "We've knocked out the nearest defense tower," called out the gunner.

"Well done!" said Colonel Etienne.

"Another message from IX Corps," said Patton. "Resistance has stopped. The Martians are falling back. Can we observe any movement west of us?"

"If only I knew! Damn these tiny peepholes! They tell me nothing." Estienne clambered over to the roof hatch, undogged it, and swung it upward. He stepped onto a bracket and thrust his head out.

"Colonel!" cried Henri.

Estienne waved a hand down at him. "Gamelin, there are dozens of them emerging now! And behind, my God, who would have – a train! So General Funston was right after –"

He screamed in agony at the same instant the driver did; a heat ray had swept over the armored car. The vehicle swerved, braked, and stopped.

Estienne banged downward in a jumble of limbs, collapsing to the deck. His hair and a sleeve were burning. The others beat out the flames, leaving him contorted into a fetal position, hands clamped over his eyes. The smell of burnt paint – and flesh – roiled through the open compartment.

"He's out of action," growled Patton. He stood up, grabbed the hatch, and swung it shut.

"Colonel, we must get you back to–"

"No!" howled Estienne through his fingers. "Do not – do not stop the attack."

Patton looked at Henri, then twisted to face forward. "Loader, take over driving! Keep us heading into the base!" The man shifted into the driver's seat as soon as the gunner dragged his crewmate out of it. He revved the engine and started them moving again.

Henri checked Estienne's condition; he had fallen unconscious. The burns to his face and arm were severe. The former driver hunched in a corner, not as severely injured, but surely just as blind. Hines tended to him as best he could. It had been his ill luck to have the vision slit line up exactly with the Martian's heat ray...

Patton was hammering out Morse at the radio. "At least IX Corps knows now. But they'll never catch a bunch of running tripods."

"Captain," said Henri, "you had better signal Major Flambeau to take over command – his vehicle has a radio too."

"Yeah, I suppose so. But I've met the man, and he wants to be the first into that base to beat Funston. The Martians aren't fighting for that base any more, so why should we when..."

"Sir," cried the driver, "there is a fortification ahead!"

"Well, drive up it, then!"

They tilted upward; the engine struggled to climb the steep slope, wheels scrabbling for traction. Then the driver braked hard and stopped at what must be the edge.

"Not sticking my damned head out," muttered Patton. He shifted to peer out of a vision slit with his good eye and cursed inventively in English. "I can hardly see a thing at this angle! But there's nothing moving."

Henri tensed, considering the risk – and opened the side hatch. He slipped out onto the rock-strewn slope and dropped to the ground.

"*Gamelin!* Get back in here!"

Henri crawled up past the armored wheel to the hill's lip. On the far side, the whole Martian base lay open to view. At other points around the perimeter wall, defense towers were firing their heat rays at their attackers, but two already destroyed. Within the enclosure, enormous pits gaped open in the ground; machinery hulked nearby, although much of it also appeared to have been destroyed despite the wall's protection. In fact, it looked... melted. *Their weapons, not ours.*

A handful of Martian tripods scuttled over the wall to the west as he watched. One swiveled as though to give a parting shot; Henri scrambled back below the lip of the berm. He slipped back into the vehicle.

"Idiot," growled Patton. "What did you see?"

"Captain, they have left!"

"Are you sure?"

"I cannot be. But they have destroyed their own facility to deny it to us! Er, *spiked their guns*, yes? Why else but to leave?"

"Then I say we don't tell Flambeau. Not yet – until we go after the last of the tripods. If we can't catch them, we can at least drive them right out of Texas."

Henri shook his head. "That is very irregular. Neither of us are in this chain of command, Captain."

"This is the only force with enough mobility to chase these bastards down. You want to waste it occupying a fortress they've already abandoned?"

"But you must notify Flambeau!" Still, Henri agreed with the American's assessment of the man. Would he give up his own desire in favor of theirs?

"The only *must* is the destruction of the enemy. And when your enemy turns and runs, Gamelin, you put a knife in his back!" Patton reached into the shelf holding the flares, drew out a binder, flipped pages. "Here it is. *General pursuit, west.* Green, green, green. Figures. Well, Gamelin – are you with me?"

It is elan that wins the day. "Yes. Let us strike!"

"Damn right!" Patton loaded the flare guns, opened the hatch, and loosed off the flares. Henri looked up at the soaring colors. *This one would make a fine Gascon.*

"Let's move out! Gamelin, can you load?"

He looked at the breech mechanism – it wasn't much different from what he was used to aboard ship – and nodded. "I... I think so."

"Fixed shell casing, it's simple. Just keep your goddamn fingers clear."

They jolted back down the slope, turned, and headed due west in pursuit of the Martian force at the head of the 118th.

July, 1912, East of Laredo, Texas

They'd knocked a gap through the train car's planking with rifle butts. Emmet leaned out through it. *"Cavalry?* Where are they?"

"Over there!" cried Burnham. He pointed northwest and offered his binoculars. Emmet took them and glassed the horizon. He glimpsed pennants, coal smoke, glints of metal in plumes of dust – a few vehicles, towed guns, and yes, cavalry; an army on the move.

The sort of army that didn't stand a chance against Martians. "That must be the 1st Texas!"

"I thought they'd gone to guarding ammo dumps and such," said Hicks.

"Not all of 'em. The A-G kept a bunch in these parts in case... oh, Hutchings, why're you doing this? You're just gonna get a whole lot of men killed..."

"They may inflict some damage," said Burnham dispassionately. "Meanwhile, the Martians seem to be taking more interest in them than in us." He pointed out the nine tripods fanning out to the north, obviously intending to keep the Texan force well away from their precious train. That left none immediately around them.

"Yeah. And it might give us a chance to make our move... Alright, keep an eye out for a culvert or something for cover." Emmet turned back to the survivors grouped – huddled – in one corner of the car. "Listen, my friends. We are looking for a safe place for you to hide out until the Martians have left the area. You have the rest of our water. Señor Burnham will stay with you until help can arrive."

He quirked a smile at Antonio Targas. "I apologize if some of them are from a government."

Something flickered in Targas' drawn face that might have been answering humor. "Perhaps I will feel strong enough to debate with them."

"I'm sorry," said another man, "but I don't think I can jump from a train." He could scarcely hold his head up, but he was clearly trying.

"You won't have to. We will uncouple this car and it will coast to a halt. But you must slip out as quickly as you can and find cover, in case the Martians approach. Most likely they will just keep going west. There is a whole army chasing them!" He scanned the group. "Anything else?"

"I suppose, well..." The man hacked a cough. "Thank you. All of you. For a handful of lives in the... midst of all this madness." Others murmured agreement.

"Ah. Right. We'd best be getting ready ourselves." Emmet turned away. "Burnham, we'll leave you our rifles; this'll be close work." He tossed his own Winchester to Hicks. "Give me a hand here."

They unbolted and rolled open the big side door. Straw whirled in the breeze as the clean air rushed through. A few of the survivors lifted faces to the sunlight. Emmet took a moment to fix the image in his memory. He might get himself shot in the next while... and even those who lived to a ripe old age sometimes had bad nights when they wondered *what good did I ever do?*

This'd do.

"Culvert coming up, a mile ahead," called out Burnham.

"Let's go, then." Idar joined him and Hicks at the front passenger door; they pushed through, crowding the tiny connecting platform. The two of them climbed up onto the adjacent ore car, freeing up room for Burnham to emerge. Impulsively, Emmet shook his hand. "The Guard'll mop up through here at some point later on today. Whatever's left of 'em. If we run into 'em further west, we'll let them know to come get your people."

"Right! Well, good hunting!" Burnham dropped down in three careful lunges to the car coupling, got a solid grip on the pin, and peered over the side, waiting.

Emmet tipped his hat to the scout, grabbed the metal of the ore car's lip, and awkwardly hoisted himself up. With Hicks and Idar flanking him, he set out along the heaped yellow granules, which had settled already to a smoother shape. A few cautious steps proved it to be surprisingly solid underfoot.

A glance back showed the cattle car dropping back as it slowed. "Good luck to 'em. Come on, let's bust that pendant loose and get out of here!"

July, 1912, Laredo, Texas

The sun was high enough now to warm the roof's surface. Lang could smell charred asphalt and old smoke as he stood on it. To the east, the sun no longer hid anything in its glare; he could easily make out the horizon filled with the glinting dots of moving – advancing – Martian tripods.

The sun couldn't warm *him*. Lang felt like ice. There were at least twenty tripods in clear sight, and hints of more moving in the far distance. They were *all* headed this way. The LRSC had redeployed ten Coyotes, but most of those only carried a single rocket. Plainview had ordered them to run for it as soon as they launched and either hit or missed their target. A mile's head start wasn't much of a margin.

He made his way down the ladder – his legs didn't seem to work smoothly – and joined General Villa in the store. "They'll be here in a quarter of an hour, General. Better get your courier ready."

"I agree." Villa ducked outside and returned in a few minutes. "It is all arranged. The *máquina loca* is standing by just north of the bridge; that will give it a good run through the town to work up speed."

"Good." Lang turned to the signals clerk at the telephones. "Get me A Company, will you?" After a couple of minutes' fussing, he offered the headset to Lang.

"Stivers here."

"Lang. They're coming straight on from the east. Do you have them in sight yet?"

"Yes, sir. I can see four of 'em look like they're swinging northward, we may get a shot at them first. The colonel, he's gone up to the firing line to – *Shit! Billy – spiders, over there!*"

"What? How many?"

"*Look out!*" Gunshots sounded over the phone line.

"Stivers! *Stivers!* Corporal, can you raise them again?"

The clerk shook his head. "Line's dead, sir."

Lang slumped against the counter and tossed the headset onto the phone. "They sent in the spiders first."

"They are afraid of our weapons," said Villa. "So they are attacking the men who aim them. It was wise to put infantry with the rocket trucks, but they may not be able to protect them all."

"Or any."

"I got C Company on the other line," said the clerk. Heavily reinforced, that company had been tasked with defending the direct eastern approach.

"Henderson! Are you there?"

"Yes, sir. Six targets. Almost in range."

"Watch out for the spiders! They're using them as sappers."

"No sign of 'em yet, sir. Ah, the tripods are splitting up, but First Platoon'll get a shot at the leading ones for –" A musical roaring overprinted his voice, sounding a few seconds later through the open windowframe of the store. "Yeah, that's it! Now if – Goddamn it!"

"Henderson?" More rocket fire sounded from the north as well as the east.

"I can see crews bailing. Those sons-of-bitches haven't fired yet! Sir, I gotta go. Maybe we can shift those trucks and still get a shot in. Then –" An explosion sounded, flatter and harsher. "Oh, shit. Third Platoon lost two trucks. Sir, they're in among us now! I'm going to try and swing one truck around."

"Alright, but – Alright." Lang hung up. More explosions were sounding almost continuously now. Most weren't outgoing rockets.

The LRSC couldn't hold them. There weren't enough experienced crews to recalculate target zones on the fly. They'd bulked up the unit too quickly, pushed the vehicles and men too hard getting back to Texas – there were limits, and they'd reached them. And the rest of the tripods were still coming on from their base, no more than a quarter-hour behind these ones...

"General, send out your crazy machine. We've got nothing else at this point."

"Very well." Villa strode to the doorway and waved. "Hermos! Ride!" In the street, a horse curveted and lunged into a gallop, spraying gravel from its hooves. Villa laughed aloud at the sight. "*Ride!*"

Now they could hear the snarl of heat rays along with the explosions. A Coyote, its launch rail empty, roared through the street outside, withdrawing west. Fleeing west. It only took a few more minutes for the telephones and runners to inform Lang that most of the LRSC was either overrun, retreating, or expended. He shouted into a phone, cursed an exhausted runner, and finally went up the ladder again and burst out onto the roof, despite the risk.

Smoke boiled from burning wreckage to the southeast – Wichita trucks. Across the street, a building gouted flame; a tripod strode behind it, firing to the south. Ruined buildings that had long since burned out on their own now broke out in fresh fires under the rays as the advance force pushed further into Laredo. More smoke rolled toward the Rio Grande valley and the rail bridge, dissipating – and *there*. A low dark shape tore through it, traveling east out of Laredo at what looked like forty miles an hour with its own black smoke streaming behind. *Maybe A Company's done it, and the rest of us as well. In four square miles of mayhem, who'll even notice a runaway locomotive? But it isn't worth it!*

Despite Lang's misgivings, at least two advancing tripods pivoted and fired on the locomotive. It began streaming grey smoke from onboard fires as well as the black plume from its stack. Death rode a dappled horse today. It was almost clear of the immediate fighting already, and there was a chance it might actually work, but – *God, yes. Let them shoot at that, not at living men.*

July, 1912, East of Laredo, Texas

Yellow powder crunched under Emmet's boots as he leaped into the next ore car.

They'd begun by climbing between the cars along the couplings, then back up to the next, but it was tedious and the sense of being exposed out here was becoming nerve-wracking. There was no reason for anyone to look through that last passenger car's door window back along the line of ore cars... but there was no reason not to. They'd be picked off like flies on a sunflower...

He turned and braced Hicks as he landed; then the two spread their arms to give a safe berth for Jovita Idar as she jumped. It was hardly safe, but nothing about this was.

They jogged along the shifting surface to reach the last remaining ore car. Emmet pointed. "Go left when we reach the Pullman platform. Stay out of sight from the window and we'll figure it from there."

They leaped, sprinted, and scrambled their way onto the tiny balcony. Emmet clung to the car's roof ladder to give enough room for the others. They took a moment to catch their breath. He could hear shouting and laughter from inside, then the crash of a bottle.

"Think they're celebrating?" said Hicks.

"Sounds like it – a lot of 'em, though. Maybe we can bypass 'em." He climbed up the ladder, peeked over the roof edge. "Okay, come on. Stay in the middle where it's flat." They clambered up and walked forward with exceeding care; the rocking of the car was amplified at this height, and the stately progress of a loaded freight still gave quite a headwind. At least there were no tripods close enough to notice beetles crawling on their biscuit.

There was no leaping from one car's roof to another – apart from the chance of skidding off, it would be too noisy. Instead they clambered down and up to bypass the next passenger car in turn.

At the forward lip of the roof, Emmet stood and studied the foremost passenger car, the fancy one. "Where's the machine that you need?"

"Just inside the vestibule, at the back end. It is... about ten feet from us." Idar's hair whipped about her face in stray strands.

"Good. We'll go in first, but if we don't run into anyone right away, we'll stick close, cover you while you work. Still got that Browning?"

"Yes."

"Well. If things go wrong – just keep one bullet for yourself. I can't stand the thought of Martians – that is– "

"No," said Idar. She eased the flat weapon from the folds of her dress and offered it to him. "This is your trade, not mine. You will use it better. And I would rather die horribly than waste a bullet that might have killed one of *them*."

"You'll do, Miss Idar. You'll do." Emmet took the piece and checked it.

She smiled. "You may call me Jovita, Emmet. After all, I won't be 'royalty' much longer."

"Amen to –"

"What the hell is that?" rasped Hicks. "Is that another goddamned train?"

Emmet looked up – and ahead. The landscape here, getting closer to Laredo, was flat and wide open, and the track ran line-straight for miles. Tripods strode up there, fighting their way into the town, wreaking havoc about them – but at the distant end of the rail line, a dot of black smoke showed, a glint of metal beneath it.

"Aw, hell, it *is*."

"Well, it sure ain't the 8:25 from Laredo! More collaborators?"

Emmet chilled. "No. Probably Villa's boys got hold of a loco. I heard about that trick. Even if they brake this train and go in reverse, it'll catch us – and if they don't, we've only got a few minutes. Quick, now!"

Idar was already climbing down and dropped to the balcony moments before the two men joined her. They crossed in turn and flattened beside the private car's door. Emmet slipped the Browning into his belt and drew his borrowed revolver. "No noise if you can help." He unlatched the door and swung it inward; they entered quickly and quietly, creeping forward into the vestibule on its soft carpeting. A partition mostly blocked off the rest of the car, with a narrow gap at one side that Emmet watched carefully. Even this utilitarian part of the car was decked out in red brocade curtains and gold trim; but it was the plain sturdy cabinet on one wall that Idar rushed to.

Emmet gestured Hicks to cover the door they'd entered through; he kept his own eyes forward. "Is it locked?" he whispered.

"It is!" She rattled the padlock. "You must shoot it off."

"Okay." He half-turned. "Hicks, you do it –"

The door's small window shattered at a gunshot; Hicks grunted and lurched into the wall. Motion caught at the edge of Emmet's vision. He snapped a shot without aiming, turned and fired twice more at the man flinching from the first quick round, hitting him solidly. Another man's arm flailed around the partition, shooting blindly. Someone was shouting, overwhelmed by the gunshots. Emmet took a careful moment to aim and clipped the man's arm; he yanked it back. Hicks fired behind him, returning fire at whoever had shot him through the door.

"Stop shooting, idiots!" yelled the same voice in Spanish. Emmet recognized it. The gunfire stopped. Cordite reeked in the car's confines.

"Hicks, how are you?" he hissed.

"I'm hit hard, Emmet." Hicks' strained voice sounded from floor level, and that told Emmet a lot. "Covering that car roof behind us. Rifleman – up there, in cover."

Idar shifted. "Let me see that."

Emmet stared over the sights of his half-empty revolver for the slightest movement. No chance to reload in this...

"My old friends!" called out Ronald Gorman. "My priest told me you were coming – we even put on a show for you in that Pullman car. I know why you are here! There is no need for this violence! My man on the roof was too eager. I can give you what you wish, Miss Idar – your abdication. And I'll even spare your life! But I must warn you, as a commoner, you will ride in that last car. Do you –"

"We don't have time for this, Gorman!" yelled Emmet. "There's another loco closing on this track, probably packed with explosives! Everyone on this train needs to bail out, *now!*"

"A clumsy lie!" answered Gorman. He spoke in Spanish as Emmet had – and for the same reason. A couple of other voices began murmuring nervously. "Mendez would have stopped us by now!"

"You sure of that? I'm sure that it's coming!"

"Or, you may keep your crown," continued Gorman. "Come back to Mexico and rule with me! I will be merciful, with you at my side."

"Maybe you should," rasped Hicks.

"I will *not*–"

The car jolted forward as a grinding screech tore out. Men staggered; Emmet fired instinctively at the figure that swayed out of cover, fired again blindly through the partition, and dropped his revolver. He drew the Browning and moved up along the wall, trading a couple of shots with the remaining men. More pistol shots sounded behind him; Hicks crowed weakly, "*Got 'im!* Dropped right in m'lap!"

"Come back, you–" shouted Gorman. Another shot cracked out. "*Coward!* He's lying!" Their locomotive's locked wheels continued to howl, grinding on the rails as the loaded ore cars' inertia drove it onward.

"He is not," said someone else. A man stepped calmly around the partition.

Emmet's finger squeezed – and stopped. It was the so-called priest, de Gama, hands spread. A ring of keys dangled from his left fingers. He took another step forward, eerily calm, as though he did not stand unarmed in the middle of a gunfight. "I know truth when I hear it. And she will never leave with her crown. She must find the light on her own, Gorman. Let her go."

"I won't!"

"She isn't yours to keep!" yelled Emmet. "Not a possession. And I want mine back! My horse, my belt–"

The screeching wheels cut off abruptly, although the train was still moving. After a moment, the car jolted everyone *rearward* – someone was trying to speed *up*.

"What t'hell are they *doin'?*" said Hicks.

"Your horse? I fed your horse to the Martians!"

"You trust this man to open that, Jovita?" Emmet figured he had all three men in the compartment placed by now. With more in the car behind, their best route out was forward – through these jaspers.

"I – yes. I do."

Emmet waved de Gama past him. "If you turn on her, I'm coming back for you." He took a couple of fast breaths, went in low around the partition.

July, 1912, Laredo, Texas

The breeze drifting in off the street was acrid with smoke. It smelled to Lang like defeat.

If the *máquina loca* had distracted the Martians, it hadn't for long. They were closing in on the rail bridge, the lure, the goal. The noise of rocket fire had dwindled as the truck racks emptied; the heat rays played on. The LRSC had hurt them badly, but they were too agile for a killing blow, and they'd cut the defenders to pieces.

Not just the LRSC, though... He turned to General Villa, who waited stolidly beside him despite the losses his own force must be taking.

"There's nothing left for you to do here, General. They'll send their spiders into the town any time now and clear it house to house. Best take whatever men you can gather and try to slip out to the south..."

Villa smiled and shook his head. "The time for that is long past, Captain. It would be desertion, by my own rule. If it is to be street fighting, my men will give a good account of themselves. And you?"

Lang wanted very badly to slip out himself. He looked around at the clerks hunched over telephones; the sole runner waiting by the doorway, still sweaty from his previous dash; Jenkins and two other privates, their rifles aimed toward the gaping windows that a spider could vault through in an eyeblink. Two of the muzzles were shaking visibly; Jenkins' wasn't. "If there's anyone still fighting and they need orders... well, even if it doesn't change anything, I don't want the last thing they do – I don't want them to call for General Funston's voice, and hear nothing."

Villa clapped him on the shoulder. "I have lost battles before. As long as you still breathe, you are not defeated."

"I shouldn't have pushed them so hard."

"Vehicles break, horses die. Men break too. But although we call the Mar-ti-ans

216

diablos, I do not truly think they are supernatural beings. They will break as well. If we cannot do it, someone else can, some other day."

"*Who?*" snarled Lang.

Villa shrugged. "Someone else."

The A Company telephone jangled. Lang jerked, then snatched up the handset before the clerk could.

"Anyone there?" said a hoarse voice.

"Stivers!" cried Lang. "What happened?"

"They got right in the HQ," said Stivers. "Hell of a fight, sir. At least six dead I can see. Lost eight trucks for sure to the tripods. They were too close together – there's two trucks damaged in explosions that I think we could fix. But, sir, that's not it. I called 'cause I can see vehicles coming up *behind* the Martians. We got anything out a few miles east of the town?"

"No! Nothing. Are they tanks?"

"Sir... I don't rightly know *what* they are."

"But they're not Martians." Lang blinked hard. "Ah, get on repairing those trucks, but stay low in case a tripod swings back." He hung up, rested his palms on the dusty counter, breathed, and looked at Villa. "Someone else just got here."

Cycle 597,845.2, Approaching River 3-12, South Texas

The imaging transmitted to Taldarnilis from the minefast showed a lost but still useful battle, as the remotely operated defense towers continued to keep the prey massed about there occupied. Another of the towers collapsed as a prey projectile scored a hit on a vital part of the structure. That left only two still functioning. But it had delayed the pursuit significantly. Machinery was easily replaced; the mounting losses from this expedition would not be.

Ahead to the west, Gantaldarjir's Group One, reinforced by additional machines, had nearly secured the habitation center. More machines flowed westward; the ones detached to defend against the mobile force to the north were rejoining as well. A persistent, more mobile prey force continued to pursue them, and would regain contact shortly. But Gantaldarjir would prevail before that. Once across River 3-12, they would leave behind any surviving prey...

"Commander! There is an incoming threat from the west along the transport system!"

Taldarnilis echoed the data in its screens. Imaging showed a propulsion vehicle similar to the one they were employing, but moving at a higher speed.

Further inquiry was logically unnecessary; Taldarnilis switched links. "All group members able to, concentrate fire on the transport vehicle approaching from the west."

Its own machine was well out of range. Indeed, no one was located in a position to fire at it effectively. Taldarnilis slowed and then halted its advance northward. In the screens, the vehicle began to leave an even larger trail of combustion products as several weapons bore on it at their extreme ranges, but none seemed able to obtain a killing concentration and disable it. If anything, it was gradually accelerating. *Of course, these vehicles are heat engines.*

"Cease fire! Move to intercept that vehicle, disrupt the rail system in its path!" But the ratios and distances on the screens already had a cold answer. While the skirmishing against the prey force interfering from the north – one slower, weaker, more primitive than any that Taldarnilis had encountered – had gone overwhelmingly in their favor, this new threat could not be stopped.

Still, it was a single vehicle, and their own transport assembly outmassed it by several times. Taldarnilis zeroed onto the collision point.

July, 1912, East of Laredo, Texas

Three enraged men confronted Emmet within the luxurious car interior. One man open-mouthed and already firing wildly; Emmet put two shots into him, dodged sideways behind a settee, saw the second man shifting halfway behind Gorman, fired again, and clipped the man's shoulder. Gorman shoved him away, lifting the Colt – but it was flipped open to load, spilling a single bullet. Emmet shot the third man once more. The Browning locked open, empty. He had no reloads; but Gorman jerked the Colt uselessly, momentarily panicked.

Emmet clubbed the Browning and charged around the settee. Gorman flung down the pistol and drew a knife from his belt – the Ranger scout belt. He cut in a vicious overhand; Emmet dodged past him and forthrightly backed away. No loose furniture in the compartment to snatch up. Captain Hughes used to say, 'A man is meat, and when meat fights steel, steel wins.' He backed further. There'd be a shovel in the coal tender – and every slash and duck moved them further away from Idar and the wounded Hicks.

His back bumped the door; he pitched the automatic at Gorman's face, spun, and yanked open the latch. He got through a split-second before the knife clanged on the doorframe. The low metal wall of the tender blocked him; he set a foot, lunged up toward the heaped coal – but the tender was nearly empty, and his hand swept through open air. He twisted, pivoting on the edge, and scrabbled a foot onto a grip bar.

A hard blow in his left calf; the foot went out from under his weight. He pitched down into the tender, landing on his right side and crunching into the low layer of coal, leg spasming as the calf pounded with pain as though the knife were still inside.

Before he could gather himself to move, Gorman appeared over the tender's wall, livid, clutching the knife overhand. "You are not welcome here," he wheezed. He braced to cross over the wall, lunged upward – and jerked to a halt.

Gorman twisted, his face a perfect study of surprise. It changed back to rage instantly. "You *bitch!*" he howled, and lunged back toward his car.

Emmet rolled up onto his good leg, grabbed the wall edge – ignoring the instinct that screamed he'd lose his fingers to a knife stroke – and managed to haul and push himself up.

Jovita Idar ducked back to the car's doorway. Gorman slashed at her – but came up considerably short. His right leg was locked straight, holding him back. Between the pant leg and shoe, Emmet glimpsed a flash of Martian alloy linked around the grip bar. Idar laughed at Gorman. If that was meant to hold his attention, it worked; he howled inarticulately, pulling at the immovable pendant.

Emmet looked around; the tender did indeed have a coal shovel. He slipped it out of the loop, wrenched around to where he could reach, and struck Gorman across the back of his head. Gorman collapsed to stillness.

Idar straightened from her crouch; Emmet saw her exposed, unhindered neck. *Free!* Behind her, de Gama shouldered into the doorway, Hicks' arm looped over his back. The Ranger's face was chalk white; blood soaked his lower shirt and trousers.

"*Jump!*" shouted Emmet. The landing might kill Hicks, but they had no choice –

"No," called back Idar. She got a grip on Hicks' other arm, steered both men to the left side of the car balcony. "*Here!*" she screamed. "*Right here!*"

The motorcar pacing the train edged up further, spraying dust and gravel as it pounded over the rail ties. *What the hell?*

He glimpsed Painewick at the wheel. The driver nudged up next to the train, matching its speed precisely despite the visible hammering the car was soaking up. Idar and de Gama lowered the wounded man until he slipped out of their grasp and spilled limply into the side seat of the Peerless tourer. Painewick sped up slightly, bringing the back seat up to the balcony stair.

Emmet shook off some of his shock and clambered back out of the tender. His calf was hurting badly; he ignored it. de Gama jumped down into the car. Idar was doing something to Gorman's inert or dead body – not that Emmet cared, but he yelled, "No time! Jump!"

She stood up, holding the scout belt. "Give me your hand!" He slipped down to land one-legged on the balcony with an involuntary gasp, steadied himself with her aid, and slid off ungracefully, letting go to thump into the waiting seat. She joined him a moment later.

The motorcar peeled away from the train, Painewick braking gradually in the uncertain traction. It drew on ahead. The oncoming locomotive was only a few hundred yards and closing. It was a smoldering shambles, jetting steam and smoke from many points; the stack had slumped to one side; there was more smoke gushing from the burning cab and tender than boiled from the damaged stack.

And someone had gotten hold of some paint and scrawled 'BIENVENIDOS A MEXICO' across the boiler's iron bow.

Painewick spotted a route and wrestled the car into a left turn. They jounced and crashed through low brush, putting distance between them and both of the titans about to collide.

July, 1912, East of Laredo, Texas

Ronald Gorman managed to focus his vision. He pushed up from the car balcony as much as his trapped leg would allow, hands shaking on the iron grating. A man stepped down onto it. Gorman peered up through the aching haze and sighed relief. But there was so little time... "Mendez! You must cut this bar and free me!"

Mendez settled himself just out of reach. He took off his cap and ran his fingers through his hair, smoothing it.

"Go up to the cab and get a hacksaw! *Now!*"

"Emilio tried to stop the train," said Mendez in a monotone. He fastened the top button of his shirt. "I hit him with a wrench and rolled him off the side. I hope he lives. He was kind to me sometimes; he seemed the best of your lot."

Gorman gaped at him for a moment. "Didn't you hear what I said? *Get me out of here!"*

"I will. We shall leave together. And I shall explain to God what you did." Mendez stared into an unknown distance. His lips moved as though praying – no, not praying. He was counting seconds.

July, 1912, East of Laredo, Texas

Painewick braked the car to a skidding halt. He turned. "I gotta see this."

Emmet turned as well. Half a mile away, the charging, burning locomotive struck the Martians' train head-on. The fronts of both locos crumpled; one boiler exploded an instant before the other. The heavier freight's chassis crushed through Villa's lighter engine, stopping its motion in a few yards but slowing sharply itself as the cars behind it started to buckle onto one another.

Then an explosion from inside Villa's locomotive blasted it apart and half of the freight loco with it.

The freight loco – or what was left of it – derailed and slammed into the ground, half-seen in the cloud of smoke, soot, and debris. The passenger cars followed it, tumbling, wooden slats flying, window glass twinkling in the air. Onrushing, the heavier ore cars pulverized them and punched them aside, then derailed in their turn. Clouds of yellow dust billowed out, spread, and began to settle.

Not a single car was left on the rails.

"Done it, by God," said Painewick with relish. Hicks would have whooped in triumph; but Hicks lay unconscious across the front passenger seat, and that dampened Emmet's own exultation. *He's a good man, don't want to lose him.*

"That dressing will not hold," said Idar. "Help me get his shirt off and tear that up... Do you know where the aid station is for the 3rd Volunteers Division?" she asked Painewick. He nodded. "Can you get us there before the Martians arrive?"

"Miss, I can leave them in my dust," said Painewick. "Half an hour, I promise." He threw the car back into gear and accelerated, finding a track and turning west onto it.

Cycle 597,845.2, West of Minefast 31.01, South Texas

Taldarnilis studied the imaging as the raised dust cleared. All of the vehicles appeared inoperative. The 92-12 compound had scattered over a large area. It would be a day's work to collect it, even assuming some of the vehicles might be salvageable, and there were three prey forces converging upon them. It opened a communications link.

"Gantaldarjir."

"Yes, Commander!"

"This expedition is terminated. Cease efforts to secure the watercourse crossing. We will no longer require its use. All groups! Withdraw immediately to the north and seek out an undefended crossing point. Continue to withdraw to the holdfast."

July, 1912, Laredo, Texas

The thunderous explosion had brought Lang and Villa clambering up to the roof, despite the risk. As they emerged, Lang thought bleakly that he'd prefer dying from a point-blank heat ray to what a man looked like after a spider got through with him... But no towering tripod was waiting there to burn them down. Lang's eye followed the rail line out to a pillar of smoke several miles east. Tripods clustered around it, looking for all Lang knew like a crowd of spectators at a road accident.

As the two men studied them, Lang became aware of the quiet in the town. Fire crackled in the building next door, but the noise of battle had stopped. A tripod slouched northward just outside the town, joining up with others that were moving off that way.

"They're leaving!" cried Lang, dizzied with relief. "Otto was right! With the train wrecked, they no longer need the bridge."

"Well," muttered Villa. He scrubbed at his face with his palms. "It seems we have not lost after all. Those gun flashes further behind the *diablos*, they are your allies approaching?"

"Yes. French tanks and Mexican artillery batteries. And the rest of IX Corps can't be far behind!" Lang wanted to dash below and inform anyone still in contact, but he just needed a moment first. His heart was hammering as though it had just started up again... *It won't be today, then. Not for me, at least. Just for plenty of others.*

"Then, Captain, let us watch a while to make sure the *diablos* are truly retreating, and discuss my own withdrawal from your country. For some friendships forged in battle last a lifetime, and some end along with their mutual enemy."

Lang looked over to Villa's shrewd expression. "Ah. You don't trust General Huerta?"

"I might trust him if I had the Division del Norte with me," said Villa wryly. "I have less than three hundred men. I will not allow them to be brought under his guns. There are many rumors about Huerta – that he is out of favor with Diaz, that he wishes to replace Diaz, that he will throw his lot in with Madero. I will preserve my force until we see what the real tale is to be. With your permission, Captain, I will assemble all my men and lead them south back into Nueovo Leon."

"Getting some distance on him?"

"Indeed. Also, I will follow the *diablos* and make sure they retreat to their stronghold. You know, Captain, I can keep watch on them there and warn you of their movements. You may not be surprised once again."

Lang smiled. "Yes, you can go, General. I would have said so anyway... but strategic warning would be very welcome."

Villa bowed. "*Vaya con Dios*, Captain Lang."

"Good hunting, sir."

July 1912, East of Laredo, Texas

They were two miles out of Laredo when Hicks recovered consciousness and began pawing at Jovita's arm. Emmet noticed from his seat at the back of the car; he'd settled there – after reloading his Colt out of the belt loops – to keep an eye on the so-called priest sitting opposite him.

Of course, it made things a bit odd that the priest had given him back the Colt in the first place. Emmet sure hadn't thought to spare time to go back and look for the piece...

221

"Hold up, Eddie!" cried Jovita. Painewick stopped the car in a cloud of dust. Emmet hunched forward over the seat. "What is it, Hicks?"

"Got some things to settle – before we rejoin an army, with all those rules, and MPs, and such." Hicks was able to speak, but barely. Emmet didn't want to think about what would happen if the man tried to stand up.

"Hicks, we need to get you to that aid station right–"

"I *know* that, I'm the one who's been shot here. I guess that makes it my call too, though, don't it?"

Emmet scratched his head. "Never really thought of it that way, but... okay. Make it fast."

"We need to do something about *him*."

de Gama was impassive in the face of English he probably didn't grasp, but Emmet had an odd feeling that the man would be the same if they were speaking Spanish. "No. Wait until they hang him. He's in custody, and that means he stays alive."

"Not what I meant," said Hicks. He wet his cracked lips. "Emmet, you saw those people in that boxcar. And those Martians aren't beat proper yet. When they go back home, back to Mexico – if they can't get trusties to work for 'em and keep stock, they'll go back to rounding folks up and eating them again. I don't want that. Those trusties make me sick – but that car was worse."

"He does have a point," said Jovita. "And de Gama, whatever he is, is no man of cruelty. I am not even sure we can judge him at all."

"Do you really think he'd go back to them? Keep them eating animals, not people?"

Hicks managed a grin. "Whyn't you ask him?"

"Huh. All right." Emmet switched to Spanish. "de Gama, or whatever you call yourself – if you were given a choice, would you return to serve the Martians?"

"Of course I would," said the priest without hesitation. "I have no purpose here otherwise. Not any longer."

"But they'd just burn you down if you walked up to one..."

"Perhaps. Or they may take me for food, and then I may have time to regain my... connection with them."

Emmet couldn't help but be fascinated. "What's that *like?*"

"Lawman, you cannot conceive it, no more than I could have once. To be a tiny part of an entity so much greater... They must be terribly old. Older than Earth, older than the Fall. Wise beyond compare. And merciless, yes. But for us to accuse them of it is as though... an ant you trod upon accused you of not following its trail like another of its kind. Their purpose is greater than that."

"Jovita, what's your take?"

"I say yes, and quickly. We have everything we came for." She lifted a handful of the Martian pendants. "I have what I wanted – freedom. We can spare him one of these. The third is spoken for... But he was a part of that."

de Gama smiled thinly. "Indeed. That Ranger said that unless I picked up that old revolver, I should be better off staying aboard. So I did."

"Doesn't it bother you that we killed your boss?"

"It was his time," said de Gama in a voice as empty as a tomb. "I do not think he was brought to the light. In the end, he saw avarice and power in the Masters, not cleansing and glory." He shrugged. "Even angels must work with the tools to hand."

"Right. Jovita, it's up to you."

Idar weighed the pendant in her fingers a moment, then passed it over the seatback to de Gama. "Take this. And some food, a canteen—"

He bowed over the object. "Not necessary. I shall find what I need on the way. Go help your friend; it is not yet his time." He slipped over the side of the car, turned, and strode off southward. And he did look like a hermit or a holy man in that moment; ragged, but illuminated from within.

"Eddie, you best not say anything about a priest to anyone," said Emmet after a pause.

"What priest?"

"Good man. Let's go."

Chapter Twenty

August, 1912, San Antonio, Texas

"*Eyes right!*" bawled a sergeant. A brass band struck up *The Star-Spangled Banner* for the fifth time that day.

Willard Lang stood among a crowd of civilians lining Chavez Boulevard ten deep, hemmed into both sidewalks to allow the wide column of troops to march past. His uniform gained him space and obvious respect, but he felt out of place. It wasn't his choice; General Funston, up on the reviewing stand along with the governor, had forbidden Lang from joining them that morning. "People will be watching, Willard, and taking note. I shouldn't be there either – but these men fought well, and lost comrades. They deserve recognition. If I do get recalled to Washington, I ought to at least leave IX Corps with a sense of accomplishment. They may need it. Perhaps it will be the only thing they have to hand, if the material losses are not made up."

The men marching past Lang – tankers from the 80th, Cronkhite's 'tank division' – certainly looked accomplished. Most of their vehicles were in too poor shape to risk trundling them down city streets, but the crews were in high spirits. The ranks were thinner than they ought to be, of course. Men were flocking to be picked as replacements. Lang wondered grimly if his own unit's heavy losses at Albuquerque had filled out as fast... But if people lost their will to fight, it would all be over.

Infantry marched by, their nearly-useless rifles sloped at shoulders, from a regiment of the 83rd Infantry Division that hadn't even been engaged. Lang couldn't begrudge them anything. If there'd been no tanks – or if all the tanks had been destroyed, and Martian tripods advancing on this city – those men would have thrown themselves into the field, fought, and died. That might still happen. It was part of Lang's job to see that it didn't.

Units from the 78th and 5th Texas divisions were conspicuously absent. The logjam of reorganizing them after the 40-mile pursuit – a couple of tanks had actually made it as far as Laredo, which had to be a distance record – was still going on. Some of the men had already gone north on troop trains, but tanks and guns were still trickling in as they were salvaged and recovered, and were being shipped out to follow them.

There was a counterattack underway at Memphis that made the fighting in Texas look like a skirmish. Lang doubted either division would make it north in any time to contribute to that, and it troubled him.

Also, anyone from the 7th Texas and 49th divisions had to be separated in the parade. They still didn't get along too well...

But there was no way he'd try telling that to the exuberant crowd around him. It was as though Sherman had suddenly turned tail and left Atlanta untouched, or the Alamo had held out. *The Martians were gone!* They'd forced their way into Texas, gotten a bloody nose, and been promptly repulsed. In four months. With French and Mexican help. Well, people were excited; they weren't thinking of little details like that.

And if they weren't aware of the cost, the next group of marchers changed that. The remaining effectives of the 608th Tank Battalion had chosen to march as a unit, and in recognition of their extraordinary effort and loss, were allocated the space they would have needed at full strength. Lang forced himself to count them as they passed.

Seventy-six men marched in an area that should have held three hundred.

General Slater wasn't among them, or among the rest of the 3rd Volunteers, or among anyone. Lang had been told he'd been killed trying to move a cal fifty. Might have been one of the ones that the LRSC turned over from the refitted cars... But it had stopped a trainload of ore. He didn't know what they wanted it for, but they'd obviously wanted it very badly. How much damage could the Martians have done with that?

The crowd grew noticeably quieter as the 608th's survivors marched by. Perhaps deliberately, a brass band followed afterward. People remembered themselves, and as the band struck up *The Yellow Rose of Texas*, they even resumed cheering.

A short distance from Lang within the crowd, men started bawling their own lyrics. "*Hurrah for Fearless Freddie, who taught Ninth Corps their drill; He sent those Martians packing, while Washington stood still!*"

Some continued singing even after the band moved out of earshot. Nearby, a couple of civilians carrying satchels and notebooks pushed past onlookers, moved up to the men still singing, and spoke to them. One turned and pointed at Lang.

They rushed at him in a body: reporters. "Captain Lang! Jeff Talbot, the *Post*. We have reports of guided rockets knocking out Martian tripods! Using their own wire! How did you manage that?"

"I can't say," Lang answered, truthfully enough. "Our heavy weapons are supplied by IX Corps."

"Aw, they don't have anything like that! I have a pal in the Washington bureau, he says they're supposed to have all that stuff locked up out east. Well, you sure showed them!"

"Please don't print that."

"What? It's a great story! 'You Won't Believe How Texan Ingenuity Showed Up Foggy Bottom's Best'!" The man ducked away, scribbling.

A group of the French wheeled tanks rumbled by just then, saving Lang further indignity as the press rushed to scrutinize them. He faded back into the crowd, shooting a worried glance toward the reviewing stand.

Jim Wade had more ammunition now than when he'd commanded IX Corps.

August, 1912, Austin, Texas

Emmet Smith knocked twice at the closed door to the governor's office. "Come in!" sounded Colquitt's voice. Emmet entered; seated in the room were Colquitt, Francisco Chapas, and another man, tall, with pomaded hair parted in the middle and a bushy mustache – an old-fashioned look, almost Victorian.

"Come in, come in. Close the door," said Colquitt genially from behind his desk. "You know Francisco, of course... This is Henry Lane Wilson, the ambassador to Mexico. Ambassador, meet Special Ranger Smith."

Wilson nodded tightly from where he sat to Colquitt's right. "Heard good things about you, Smith."

"Ambassador." Emmet walked to the chair that Colquitt gestured to. "I've done some work, yes. Had some help with it."

"Let's get that spoken to first," said Colquitt. He flipped open a wooden case on his desk; it held an automatic pistol. "That's a brand-new Model 1911. I'll be presenting it to you later this morning, when we appear before the press. You are to appear suitably honored, yet modest."

"Governor, I already have a Colt."

"Not like this, you don't. Latest and best. Do not bind the mouths of the kine, and all that. Of course, it's just a tool. It's the man we'll be honoring. And that's partly why I've asked you here. Partly." He closed the case. "How's your fellow Ranger? Hicks, wasn't it?"

"He's doing well, Governor, but he'll be a fair time healing."

"Seems I owe him and you a favor, if not an apology," said Colquitt. "Francisco, and a few other papers, are putting out the story that he was shot while stopping the theft of some Martian salvage by black marketeers. I'm afraid he won't get any credit for being inside a Martian base."

"Why is that?" asked Emmet; but he realized in the next moment.

"Because the Martians don't have guns, and he has a bullet wound."

"Ah. Right. Doesn't seem fair."

"It isn't, and I apologize – I'll tell him myself when I get the chance. I'll get Henry to promote him to a Captain. That ought to help. How's your own wound?"

Emmet slapped his leg. "Not bad. I can get around well enough, now."

"It's too bad there were no Americans in that group of prisoners. Other than – that woman. It would be better for the public."

"There were a couple in that gang of collaborators," pointed out Emmet dryly.

Chapas winced. "Do not spread *that* around."

"No, of course not. I get it. Bad for morale."

"Governor Colquitt says you are a man of discretion," said Lane Wilson. "And not a political sort. He has you in mind to assist in... an intervention. I know what's going on in Mexico, and I gather you do too. Especially when it comes to the Provisional President."

"Yeah, I've worked for Madero in the past. Met him recently, too."

"What you may not be aware of," said Lane Wilson, "is that the 'true' president, Diaz, is losing his grip on the country by the day, and there is no clear contender to replace him. The commander of the Mexican expeditionary force in Texas, General Huerta, has offered to recognize Madero as president and give him military support. The force that Huerta commands will be enough to ensure Madero's supremacy once it moves into Chihuahua. A number of American interests support this. It would stop the revolutionary fighting in northern Mexico, for one thing."

"And secure our southern flank," put in Colquitt.

"But that wouldn't address the rest of Mexico," said Emmet. "You'd need a national election to settle that."

Chapas shrugged. "The French rule in all but name in Veracruz. Whoever sits in a president's chair there does not matter. We think Madero may secede the northern Mexican states if he thinks he cannot unite the whole country, and with the Martians keeping it split in half, that may even be best. But that's up to him."

"But only if he agrees to Huerta's proposal," said Lane Wilson. "Hopkins and I are arranging a meeting in Eagle Pass two weeks from now. We want men there we can trust – and Madero can trust. I'll admit the governor here has forced our hand somewhat," he nodded to Colquitt, "but while he's broken a few rules, what he did makes sense. We *must* push the Martians back into central Mexico, then ultimately defeat them there. We cannot do that while the Mexicans fight amongst themselves."

"And I suppose you'd prefer the fighting against the Martians to take place in someone else's country."

"Yes," said Chapas bluntly. "Patriotism aside, there are far fewer people dwelling now in Nuevo Leon than in Texas. Many of them have fled here. Would you wish to see a battle spread onto another of those refugee camps just inside the border?"

"I wouldn't, no." Emmet studied Lane Wilson for a moment; the man was no dilettante, certainly. Taut and experienced. If General Huerta was willing to join with Madero, things could change drastically.

"Well, I'm in."

August, 1912, San Antonio, Texas

"This is to be your air base?" asked Henri Gamelin. He glanced around the industrial warehouse; beyond a few stacked crates, it showed no sign of military endeavor.

Colonel Mitchell laughed. "Oh, no. It's just a temporary spot to position the items your country sends us. And we're getting in six draftsmen tomorrow to begin copying those." He gestured to the rolls of drafting paper that Henri had delivered, heaped on a desk.

The third man, a weathered Texan, flipped idly through the sheets. "Doesn't look easy to build," he said.

"I can assure you, Mr. Laseter, that it is a proven design. And as least complicated as any flying today."

"Right," said the rancher king. "Well, you've delivered enough material already that it'd be discourteous to pick at what's our part to carry out."

"Yes, both artillery and armor. Given the distances you must deal with here, it is a great advantage to have wheeled fighting vehicles. I ran across a captain in Funston's army who was wild to get hold of some. He had the look of a man in love."

"Oh, him," said Mitchell. "He's another exile like myself. But I think, after this battle, we're going to get a better hearing if we stick around. More aircraft for scouting, a lot more – or for attack. Just think, we might one day fit those guided rockets to an *aircraft!* We could become the hunters for a change, call in a wolf-pack of airplanes to chase down tripods... And we can go outside the military procurement chain. The LRSC proved that well enough! Your friend Colonel Angeles knows a *lot* of businessmen around here."

"General Angeles, now. He has been promoted." Henri smiled at the recollection, but he worried about his friend. If Huerta saw him as a greater rival now... "Some of his business connections are proposing to build the aircraft instruments locally as well."

"That's a tall order for one company," said Lasater.

"He said they are planning a... consortium. They are thinking of calling it Texas Instruments."

Ed Lasater tapped the blueprints neatly together. "Okay. This is outside my purview anyway. What about the stovepipe deal? I heard from Jusserand that he was approving it, but are your navy brass going to let them go through?"

"Admiral Favereau is sending a squadron for escort. You have another beef shipment to proceed with in any case, Mr. Lasater."

"Thing is, if I ship beef to Veracruz, it might get stolen or black-marketed, but I don't worry about someone picking up a steak and beating another fellow to death with it. You start sending weapons into another country... Isn't this Zapata a rebel?"

"There is nothing left there to rebel against," said Henri. "I believe that as long as Zapata fights the Martians, the central government – whoever it may be in the next year – is content to let him do so. His men will never have a large number of stovepipes at one time, so it should not give them a major advantage if they choose to fight a human army which has many more targets than a Martian force. That would be more a matter of morale, organization, and the loyalty of the population – and if he gains all those, he may win in any case."

"I guess I won't worry about southern Mexico," said Lasater. "Our concerns are in the north, and we'd best get busy on 'em." He stuck out a hand to Henri, who took it. "I do like your style, son. Come on up to one of my ranches some time, I'll show you around. But we'll need to get you a proper hat!"

Cycle 597,845.3, Holdfast 31.2, Northern Mexico

Taldarnilis backed its machine away from the storage depot – the heap of compound 92-12 that had been deposited at the northern holdfast – to allow the heavy transport better access. The heap was diminishing by the day... "You may proceed," it signaled.

The two escorting fighting machines stood aside as the hauler settled into position and began ingesting the compound. One swiveled toward Taldarnilis' machine and sent a query signal. Taldarnilis accepted the link. "Yes?"

"Greetings, Taldarnilis."

"Group Leader!" This was entirely unexpected. "My full report will be –"

"Will be studied in due course. I wished to see the northern holdfast for myself. This will be the last transfer of energetic compound to 31.1; the rest will be needed here."

"Clarify."

"We shall build a new reactor at this holdfast to replace the one sent south in its support role. It will require fuel."

Taldarnilis blinked. "Group Leader, it was anticipated that without a reactor, this holdfast would be withdrawn."

"Was it? I do not recall specific instructions to that from the Conclave. I believe that Group 31 – what remains of Group 31 – was expected to wither passively away.

After seeing your efforts and others', Taldarnilis, I see the matter differently."

Taldarnilis mentally set aside the curious change in the group leader's outlook. "But there are no prebuilt components available to construct a reactor here."

"That is correct. I understand that Arctilantar was lost on the expedition, but perhaps young Raqtinoctil will have some ideas on the matter. Improvisations and simplifications may be possible, even to a statistically significant risk of malfunction. Recall and impress on others that with this world no longer being a colony, we have no requirement to observe the same care with it that the Homeworld demanded over millennia. For example, I no longer see any need to be concerned with waste processing into neutral elements... Do you intend to resume operations involving the goodprey?"

"That is not yet a priority beyond quadruped nutrition sources, but Raqtinoctil did report that one equipped with a tracking device has returned on its own initiative."

"How intriguing. Can we rebuild that resource to use here?"

Taldarnilis recalled the unique flavor of that prey's mind. "I believe so, Group Leader. It has proven to be a useful adaptation."

The Group Leader skittered its machine in a clumsy gesture of respect – or admonition. "Adaptation, yes! Hold nothing back, Taldarnilis! This is a new era. Other groups which have been dominant due to their successes are now encountering some sharp reversals. No attention is spared for us. Perhaps it is time we exploited that fact."

Chapter Twenty One

September, 1912, Eagle Pass, Texas

The Grande Hotel seemed an empty shell as Emmet Smith walked its hallways to check them. There were no cheering crowds this time; even most of the hotel staff had been cleared out. Ambassador Lane Wilson insisted that this agreement be private; on the train journey that morning, he'd expressed concern that General Huerta might reconsider if pressed – or bolt. "There are a great many American interests at stake here, Smith. This *must* go as planned."

Wilson had brought a plainclothes agent of his own, a sallow, taciturn man named Saunders; Emmet didn't like him. He'd have preferred Hicks by far to a stranger he'd never worked with, but Hicks would be a while yet recovering.

At least some men he knew. He turned the last corner to the meeting room door and nodded to the little man waiting there. "All clear, Maximo."

"Very well. I'll go fetch him. I'll be in the outer chamber, with that Saunders fellow."

"I'll take the interior room." Emmet walked through the small antechamber with its desk and chairs, nodded to Saunders, passed through the wide doorway, and entered the meeting room. It was high-ceilinged, paneled, and held two large oak tables and several men.

"The President will be here shortly, gentlemen," he said.

"Good," said General Huerta without quibbling over 'provisional'. He ushered his two aides – a Mexican Army major and a civilian – toward the larger table. They filed onto the far side, but remained standing as they waited.

At the smaller table, Ambassador Lane Wilson was already seated. He gestured sharply at Emmet to join him. Emmet swung around the table, drew out a chair, and sat beside Wilson where he could see the room.

In a few minutes, Madero arrived. Castillo escorted him inside, nodded once to Emmet, and withdrew, closing the big doors together behind him.

"Welcome, Mr. President," said Huerta. His aides bowed deeper than he did; Madero returned the gesture. "Please, sit, we have much to discuss. Carra has many details already worked out to show you, but of course we may resolve those as we proceed. First, there is a guarantee of–"

As the men spoke, Lane Wilson leaned over to Emmet. "Smith," he said softly. "This is no place for cowboys. Take off that gunbelt and put it on the table over here."

"Now, why would I want to do that?"

231

"Because they'll be jumpy. This *cannot* go wrong. Madero has his own bodyguard – we can't be seen as partisan. That's an order, now, Smith."

"I understand," said Emmet. He moved slowly, easily, unbuckling the scout belt – nothing any *cowboy* would be wearing, but Lane Wilson hardly knew that – and gathering it up in a bundle that he placed onto the tabletop and pushed out of easy reach. The chattering leaders and subordinates didn't react – or notice. If Wilson was right, it'd help things along.

If he was wrong – well, it might still help.

The discussion of leaders continued. Madero seemed calm, as Emmet usually found him, and Huerta showed only the intentness of a poker champion in his greatest game of all. The two aides grew increasingly tense, though. Emmet wondered how much they'd staked in this, and their plans if Huerta failed and they all returned to face an angry President Diaz...

Voices sounded from outside the doors. Lane Wilson grabbed Emmet's shoulder. "Do *not interfere*," he hissed. "This is an internal Mex–"

Three gunshots echoed through the doors in close succession, pistol and a flatter rifle shot, then a fourth. Madero pushed back from the table; Huerta's civilian aide drew a pistol.

"Not on American soil!" snapped Lane Wilson.

"Of course, my friend," said Huerta, placing a calming hand on his aide's arm. "The proprieties must be observed... Mister President," he added to Madero, "our agreement does not appear to be viable. You will accompany us to Nuevo Leon, where we can settle it properly."

"Oh," said Madero. "I had hoped – You know Diaz cannot rule in the north."

"I can," said Huerta. "In this world, only the strongest can."

"If that is so, we have no greater claim to it than the Martians have."

There was that about Madero – he was not an imposing man, but people tended to look at him. And at that moment, no one was looking at Emmet when he leaned forward and drew the Colt automatic from the small of his back. He took a careful moment to cock the unfamiliar hammer, then shot the armed aide turning toward the sound, once, then again as the man tried to bring his own weapon around. He collapsed. The major jumped up from the table, knocking over his chair and grabbing at his dress holster. Emmet fired at him, missed, and hit with his next shot; the major stumbled into Huerta and fell.

Huerta clawed free of him and looked up at Emmet with his pale eyes. Emmet placed a careful shot into the general's chest. "*Sir, get down!*" he shouted to Madero. His ears rang as everyone else's would, but Madero crouched down beside the table. No other movement.

Emmet had lost track of how many shots he'd just fired; his conscious mind still hadn't caught up to the unfolding treachery. He dropped the weapon, pushed aside the ambassador, and snatched up his holstered revolver. He slid it free just as the doors banged open and a soldier in uniform burst in, shouting something. Emmmet fired twice and felled the man.

Nothing stirred or sounded for a moment in the meeting room except swirling powder smoke and a liquid rattle from Huerta's civilian aide. Emmet spared a glance for Lane Wilson; he was white-faced and frozen, unlikely to snatch up a weapon and take action. The thought to make sure of that crossed Emmet's mind; he rejected it, and instead moved in a fast lope to the doorway, snatched a glimpse around, and entered the antechamber.

Bodies lay about the room in a tableau that resolved as a coldly rational sequence. *Saunders* – face-down with an exit wound in his back – drew on Castillo. *Castillo* – toppled over a chair, shot multiple times – fired back, but was hit again, then shot at *the second soldier* who had burst in from the hallway once Saunders began shooting. That man lay curled around a belly wound, groaning. His rifle was close by. Emmet shot him in the chest to make certain, quite dispassionately; he wasn't riled. Just careful, as Maximo Castillo had always been.

He knelt by Castillo's side and shifted the chair from under him, settled him on the floor. The fancy carpeting was soaked with blood. Castillo was breathing in shallow wheezes, but those holes weren't going to heal. He was unconscious. There wouldn't have been anything useful to say anyway. Emmet kept trying to think of a next step, of getting Madero out safely...

Did it matter if you died doing a job as best you could, or betraying someone for sheer ambition? Castillo would have said to keep at his own job, to work, to *move*. Instead, Emmet stayed put until the wheezing stopped. He knelt in a room of dead men, the old Colt heavy in his hand.

"Oh, Maximo," said a familiar voice behind him. Madero shuffled up and crouched beside Emmet. "He is gone, isn't he?"

"Yeah. We should get moving."

"I shouldn't have come here. Perhaps it was vanity. I really thought..."

"We all did. Most of us did. Well, come on."

"*Smith!*" cried Ambassador Lane Wilson. "What the *devil* have you done?"

Emmet turned, part of him hoping that Wilson had picked up a gun; but the ambassador stood open-handed, shaking visibly, in the doorway. "You knew," Emmet said.

"Well, of course! For God's sake, man, do you really think this, this *pissant* can lead a war against Martians? Huerta was our best chance! Now their strongest general is dead! All of northern Mexico is wide open, all our investments... you..."

Madero stooped and picked up the soldier's rifle, worked the bolt. "I am no pistoleer," he said. "But I suppose I can aim this. What do we do?"

"Get a car, head over that bridge."

"*Get back here!*" screamed Wilson. "You're going to jail for this! Insubordination – murder – assassination –"

"I don't work for you, Ambassador," said Emmet. His hearing was coming back; he didn't bother to shout. "I work for Texas."

He set off with the President of Mexico to steal a car.

Epilogue

October, 1912, Sabinas, Northern Mexico

Felix Sommerfeld settled into a chair within the telephone exchange and extended a hand. The telephone clerk placed an earpiece into it. Sommerfeld lifted it to his ear to hear the familiar crackle of Madero's telephone line through the wiretap.

Sommerfeld had been operating within Madero's administration for several months now and had followed him to Sabinas. Other German agents were in place at Veracruz and considered to be more important there than his own role; but he was beginning to think they had underestimated Madero. He had survived an assassination attempt; he had gathered an army...

And allies. There had been many calls like this one to a location in Austin, Texas. By now, the telephone clerk, Ricardo, was Sommerfeld's creature; his sexual tastes had provided the initial lever, and once he'd begun passing information about Madero to German intelligence, the hook had been fully set. Sommerfeld laid out his encrypted notebook and a pencil, and waited. In a few moments, a familiar voice came over the earpiece – the American policeman in a nearby room. "Hello, Hicks, is that you? How's the wound?"

"Yeah. Healing pretty well. I'm a captain, would you believe that? But what about you, Emmet?"

"I'm staying put here for now. There's a lot of heat in the States after... after Huerta."

Hicks chuckled. "You mean you fled to Mexico to escape the authorities? Ain't you usually on the other end of that story?"

"Very funny. What *are* the authorities doing?"

Hicks' voice changed. "It's secession. The governor tried to stop it when the Senate voted, but it was like waving your arms at a stampede. No one knows what that really means as yet. We're just not taking any orders from Washington any more. General Funston got cashiered, and a bunch of his officers too – but even some of the ones that weren't still joined him."

"Joined him in what?"

"They're callin' it the Texas Army. Funston's leading it. But there's Mexican soldiers joining as well, and French tanks, and... there's some kinda alliance. France, Texas, and Mexico Norte. It doesn't make much sense to me, but all they want to do is go after Martians, so I guess it's not complicated."

"Huh. Here we got General Angeles backing Madero. I hope it's not a permanent style of things... Did *I* get cashiered?"

"No. Not that I'd care, or a lot of other Rangers. You did a good job there, Emmet."

Sommerfeld noted that the Texas Rangers might become a more political force after the state's secession – of course, their frequent role of 'supervising elections' was obvious already. American democracy was a farce; an oligarchy ruled over flag-waving sheep. Rule was essential, but Sommerfeld preferred a proper aristocracy and Empire, united and orderly in the face of threats both Martian and human.

Mexico, with its oil and mineral wealth, was of great interest to the Kaiser. And once the Americans had exhausted themselves defeating their Martian foes – just as with Germany's other enemies and rivals – Mexico might prove to be their soft underbelly. But if the French had committed this far... They appeared to be pushing out the British oil interests already, with the doddering Diaz leaving to exile and new figures taking control in the south. Zapata was still fighting the Martians, and perhaps even beginning to win. And there was some bizarre land scheme in Cuernavaca that French naval officers were going mad over.

"Hicks, I need a favor. I'm stuck here for a while, looks like. Can you go to that warehouse and get that crate, and return it to our mutual friend? I think she'd like her old job back. The governor said he owes me a favor – I'm calling it in."

"Okay."

"And tell her... no, ask her. Ask her if I'll do."

Definitely political. He made another note. Ambassador Creel would still be working the American side, so he would need to be alerted. And Sommerfeld himself would need more agents in Mexico, and soon. Duquesne was erratic, but he did have a way of improvising...

"Okay, Emmet, I will. Oh, Burnham's going south too, with the LRSC. You'll have some company."

Despite his training, Sommerfeld jerked upright in his chair. There might be more than one Burnham in the American foreign force – but he felt by instinct it was Frederick Russell Burnham. An old thorn in the side of German intelligence. Duquesne – the flamboyant 'Black Panther' – had missed his chance to take care of that during the Boer War, but perhaps...

"And Senator Hudspeth keeps askin' people what happened to his damn car. You know anything about that?"

"Not a thing. Hicks, I gotta go. Can you, ah..."

"I'll keep an eye on her, Emmet, don't worry. You keep an eye on *him.*"

"I'll see you in a while, then." There was a click and the line went dead.

Sommerfeld passed the earpiece over without looking. He would need to work on Madero's brother; having Texas Rangers guarding the president of Mexico Norte was unacceptable. The man was already proving to be more dynamic than expected. If he united Mexico again as an American ally... well. There was time yet to work.

THE END

ABOUT THE AUTHORS

Jonathan Cresswell-Jones is a graphic artist living in Ontario, Canada, who has written SF and fantasy for OnSpec, Polar Borealis, and the *Ring of Fire* anthologies. This is his first collaborative novel published in the Great Martian War series.

Scott Washburn is an architectural designer by profession, an avid reader of military history as well as long time re-enactor and wargamer. He has written the first three novels in the Great Martian War series, is the author of *The Terran Consensus*, and has contributed short stories to the Beyond the Gates of Antares novels.

Look for more books from Pike & Powder – E-books, paperbacks and Limited
Edition hardcovers. The best in history, science fiction and fantasy at:

www.PikeandPowder.com & www.wingedhussarpublishing.com

twitter: @pike_powder
facebook: @PikeandPowder
For information and upcoming publications

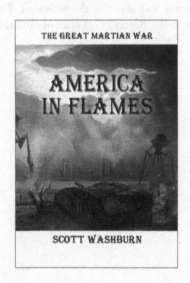